ACROSS A WILD SEA

SASHA LORD

A SIGNET ECLIPSE BOOK

SIGNET ECLIPSE
Published by New American Library, a division of
Penguin Group (USA) Inc., 375 Hudson Street,
New York, New York 10014, USA
Penguin Group (Canada), 10 Alcorn Avenue, Toronto,
Ontario M4V 3B2, Canada (a division of Pearson Penguin Canada Inc.)
Penguin Books Ltd., 80 Strand, London WC2R 0RL, England
Penguin Ireland, 25 St. Stephen's Green, Dublin 2,
Ireland (a division of Penguin Books Ltd.)
Penguin Group (Australia), 250 Camberwell Road, Camberwell, Victoria 3124,
Australia (a division of Pearson Australia Group Pty. Ltd.)
Penguin Books India Pvt. Ltd., 11 Community Centre, Panchsheel Park,
New Delhi - 110 017, India
Penguin Group (NZ), cnr Airborne and Rosedale Roads, Albany,
Auckland 1310, New Zealand (a division of Pearson New Zealand Ltd.)
Penguin Books (South Africa) (Pty.) Ltd., 24 Sturdee Avenue,
Rosebank, Johannesburg 2196, South Africa

Penguin Books Ltd., Registered Offices:
80 Strand, London WC2R 0RL, England

First published by Signet Eclipse, an imprint of New American Library,
a division of Penguin Group (USA) Inc.

First Printing, February 2005
10 9 8 7 6 5 4 3 2 1

You are, and will always be, my hero.
I love you, Matt.

Acknowledgments

Thank you to my support group: Ellen Edwards, Bob Mecoy, Jennifer McCord, my family and dear friends. Without you, none of this would ever happen.

We climb to heaven most often on the ruins of our cherished plans, finding our failures were successes.

—Amos Bronson Alcott

Prologue

The woman stumbled through the brush, tears streaming down her face. Her red hair was matted and her face was twisted with pain, yet her green eyes glowed with brilliant color. With a sob, she fell to her knees, carefully cradling the infant in her arms. She looked back, holding her breath, fearing that *he* was close behind.

He was Lothian, Laird of the Serpent Clan, and his hurtful hands had forced her more times than she could remember. He had plucked her from her parents' garden when she was only fifteen and he had kept her as one of his house playthings for three years. She was almost nothing to him, just Zarina the pretty peasant girl, but last year she had become pregnant. It was her own fault, she had been told. She was Lothian's property and should not allow the disfigurement of growing a babe to infringe upon his enjoyment. Zarina had cowered from his wrath, terrified of his anger, mutely submissive to his desires.

Yet, despite the herbs and the beatings, racing across the fields on horseback and deliberately flinging herself to the ground, the child had prospered. It had clung tenaciously to life, developing week by week, month by month, until Zarina could no longer hide the bulge in her abdomen. When Lothian had come to her with a knife in his hand to carve the baby from her, she had felt the little one move, kicking its tiny haven in furious rebellion.

It was then that she had finally disobeyed Lothian. She had grabbed the poker from the fireplace and threatened him. She would keep the child, she had cried. If he would only let her keep the child, she would do anything else he asked!

But his rage had burst and he had picked up her struggling body and tossed her down the long, winding staircase, yelling at her, threatening her, screaming at her. She could still hear his shouts even now, many months later as she hid in the woods, her former beauty dulled by hunger, filth and constant fear. Yet the child lived, thrived even. She was a strong infant, and even though her green eyes could not focus, she was the most beautiful baby ever born.

Zarina heard horses stamping through the brush, their bridles jangling in the dusk. A bright flash of sunlight streaked through the trees, then winked out as the sun sank behind the Scottish Highland mountains that towered far in the distance. The crash of nearby ocean waves mixed with the murmur of men's voices as they continued to relentlessly stalk her and the babe.

She breathed quickly, trying to quiet the sounds of her harsh lungs and pounding heart, but her fear was too great. Bounding like a rabbit flushed from its burrow, she rose and raced forward again, trying desperately to escape Lothian's men. A shout from behind her indicated that they had found her makeshift home only twenty lengths away. A spark leaped into the air behind her; then the wood and grass shelter burst into flames.

She froze, staring through the trees in horror as flames devoured the only items she had for survival. The men were laughing. She could see their faces. They were cruel, hateful. Zarina looked down at her gorgeous daughter. It was not right. She should not have to grow up in a world where merciless men could destroy everything that was lovely and beautiful.

With sudden determination, Zarina headed to the edge of the sea where a small boat lay beached. After carefully placing her daughter on the sand, she dragged the boat down to the water and pushed it past the break. Then, returning to her child, she bundled her firmly and kissed her lovingly on her forehead, her cheeks, her nose. Pulling an amulet from her neck, she wrapped it into the blankets. She hugged her baby, trembling with the force of her emotion, but the sound of the approaching men galvanized her into action. She waded to where the boat was freely drifting out with the tide and placed her daughter in a bassinet secured between the gunwales. Then, with a quick glance behind her, she shoved the boat and her daughter out to sea.

Part I

The Isle of Wild Horses

Chapter 1

Alannah stood where sea met land, her eyes closed, her face to the wind. She sensed the moisture that hung like a fragile sheet of silk upon the breeze, and the tension of the thunderclouds building to the northwest. She inhaled deeply, smelling the verdant grass as it rippled behind her and the tangy salt of the sea in front of her. Smiling, she turned and spoke to the powerful white stallion that stood with her.

"There is an early storm approaching, Claudius. Tomorrow."

The horse lifted his nose to the air and whinnied. In the field a dozen other horses lifted their heads. Then, as if connected by invisible strings, they all sprang into a gallop, racing with abandon across the flat grassland. The stallion reared, trumpeting his pride, and dashed after them.

Alannah laughed, feeling the ground tremble with their pounding hooves.

" 'Tis a lot of foolish expenditure of energy, if you ask me," grumbled an old woman who was climbing the last few steps up the coastal rocks.

"Only because you cannot run with them, Grandmother," Alannah replied. "If your legs were as long and strong, you would be racing the colts."

"Humph. I would beat them, too," Grand-mother replied.

"Indeed. I think you still could."

Grandmother smiled sadly, watching the herd skid to a stop, wheel and race back in the other direction. "Sometimes I wish you could see them, Alannah."

"I can see them. I see them with my ears and feel them in my blood. I do not need my eyes."

"Aye, I know this is true, but I am growing old and . . ."

"And?" Alannah prompted.

"And I fear for you, all alone here. Without vision."

Alannah laughed again. Tossing her auburn hair behind her, she strode down the field without fal-tering. "Grandmother, you worry for nothing. I have all I need and I will never be alone. The horses are my brothers and sisters, and you are strong and hearty. I have never known what it is to see; thus I do not miss it. Fear naught, Grand-mother. All is well."

Alannah paused as the white stallion reached her, his hide damp from his exertions. She grasped his mane and pulled herself atop his withers. Grip-ping him with her thighs, she sent him galloping again, this time speeding through the herd and scat-tering the mares in all directions.

Grandmother watched her. Alannah was a beau-tiful woman, her glorious dark hair flowing wildly down her back, alive with red highlights. Her skin was golden with sun-kissed health and her sightless eyes were emerald green, fringed by sable lashes. She was very tall for a woman, and rode with con-fidence and pride.

But Grandmother was concerned for her. Alannah feared nothing. Her willful arrogance often caused her to ignore caution, for she would not acknowledge her limitations. On this isolated island, away from civilization, she functioned well. She knew every stone, every tree and meadow, for her other senses had heightened to an almost mystical level. She could "feel" the environment as if she were an integral part of it. Yet, despite her gifts, there were still dangers that threatened to harm her. Grandmother feared that a misstep could result in a broken leg, or worse. Alannah, however, dismissed Grandmother's concerns, assured that nothing bad would happen to her.

"You are a fool, Alannah!" Grandmother yelled after her. "Life can change in an instant. All that you believe is permanent now can change with tomorrow's sunrise!"

Alannah wheeled the stallion and tilted her face into the wind. "Nothing will change," she shouted. "This island will be my home, and you will be my grandmother." She tossed her hair and flung out her arms. "Here is everything I will ever want!"

Grandmother shook her head, remembering how her own life had changed over the years. As she watched Alannah spin once again and gallop away, she thought back to thirty years ago when her lover, Gondin, had brought her to the island to save her life from those who sought to end it. Since then, her only connection to the outside world had been when Gondin came to bring her supplies once every five years.

On one of those trips, Gondin had come across a boat that capricious currents had pulled from some distant land and set adrift in the immense ocean. Inside the boat lay a crying infant. Gondin had rescued the baby and brought her to the Isle of

Wild Horses where Grandmother lived. Discovering the child's blindness, Gondin and Grandmother had decided to raise the baby on the island where she would be protected from people's harsh judgments.

The infant had been hungry and helpless, but clearly blessed with love, for her blankets had been handwoven and a small amulet bag had been hidden in one of them. Inside the bag were a few gold medallions, a key, a letter, and a necklace of exquisite emerald and gold. The letter meant nothing to Grandmother, who could not read, but she had saved it nonetheless. The necklace was beautiful, with carvings that stood for love and protection. The other items held no value on the isle, but she had put them away as well.

Raising the infant had been difficult at first. Grandmother had been without human companionship for so long, she was unsure how to care for the babe. But her arrival had been a blessing, and now Grandmother nodded with pleasure as she watched Alannah race around on the stallion. Alannah had given Grandmother a reason to live again, and the joy she had brought was immeasurable. Smiling, Grandmother walked slowly back to the cottage, lost in memories.

As night descended, Alannah and Grandmother did their evening chores with little discussion. Grandmother built a fire while Alannah cleaned and prepared vegetables she had picked from the garden. As Grandmother moved toward her chair to rest, Alannah walked briskly outside to collect water. She knew the path to the water hole, where the roots stuck up from the ground and stones made the path unsteady. She was finely tuned to the sounds of the insects as they clicked and chirped, talking to her as if she were one of them. Without hesitation, she dipped the bucket into the stream, using her fingers and the weight of the water to tell her when it was full.

She returned to the cottage and poured some water into the pot with the vegetables. With unerring accuracy she selected two dried herbs from the wall where they hung, and crumbled them into the water. Grandmother grunted approval at the selection, and pulled a blanket over her knees.

"You will need to put the sheep in the cave before the storm hits. Otherwise they will wander and perish."

"Yes, I know, Grandmother. I already fenced them in."

"What about wood? Do we have enough?"

"Yes. I took care of that."

"What about—"

"Grandmother!" Alannah cried in exasperation. "It is only a storm. We have weathered many storms and I know how to prepare. Cease this nagging and eat."

Thunder crashed overhead and the ocean roared with fury. Commodore Xanthier O'Bannon, cast-out heir to Scotland's Kirkcaldy, shouted at the elements, daring them to fight. His tormented soul matched the anger of the storm, and he stood at the helm like a devil at the gate of hell.

"Hold her, you fools! If you let her founder then all the gold will be lost and you will die poor men!"

When one sailor failed to respond, cowering against the railing, Xanthier strode over to him with an oath and lifted him by his soaked shirt.

"Do you understand? If you don't hold her, you will die! Now get your ass moving and lash that sail!"

The ship listed, caught in a trough, and the pair were flung against the railing, splintering it. Xanthier grabbed the broken edge, forcibly pulling himself back aboard, and then swung around to help the sailor, but the lad was gone, lost instantly to the frothing waves.

Cursing, Xanthier staggered back to the helm and shouted orders. The men crawled over the ship, struggling to stay aboard. A short scream from starboard was cut short as another sailor lost his life.

The commodore squinted through the sheeting rain, watching his flagship sail farther and farther from the rest of his fleet. Three other scattered ships all battled the storm. He had taken command of this ship because it was new, captured during a sea fight only two months ago, and he had yet to train the men adequately.

"God's wrath! It should not be storming yet! Not for another month at least!" he shouted. Another blast of thunder shook the ship, vibrating it from stem to stern. Lightning snaked across the sky, illuminating the rabid sea for one terrifying moment, then blinked out, casting the ship back into darkness.

"Stay to your stations! Shorten the sail! Tack right! Reef ahead!"

Xanthier grasped the ship's railing and ducked, letting the wild sea waves crash over him and across the deck. His muscles bulged with the effort to keep himself upright and on board. A shout to his left drew his gaze and he saw the first mate wash over the side and into the raging water below.

Xanthier braced himself as the ship sank into a

furrow. He gripped the mainsail rope for security and quickly gauged the pattern of the ocean waves, waiting for the right split second when the ship paused at the top of a swell and he could quickly tie himself to the mast. Another sailor skidded across the deck as the ship tilted, and his head crashed against a barrel that was lashed to the planks. Within seconds his limp body tumbled off the ship.

Xanthier's gray eyes remained cold and unfeeling. He had no liking for the men on the ship; indeed, he cared little for any human. Years ago he had lost his land, his birthright and his title. Now he raged across the sea as a marauding sea captain, commissioned by Scotland's king, liked by no one and feared by all.

The ship cracked, the force of the seething ocean far stronger than her hull. She was going to sink. Xanthier saw the realization strike the hearts of the remaining sailors. They appeared to him like children looking to a father they disliked but trusted. He stared back, giving no comfort.

"She is going down!" he shouted. "Lower a lifeboat if you dare, or swim for the isles!"

Three men dropped the wooden boat, but a blast of wind crashed it against the side of the ship. "Commodore!" cried a sailor. "I don't want to die! Help us!"

Xanthier snarled in fury, disgusted with the whimpering men. Lightning streaked across the sky and struck an island nearby, making a crack that throbbed in the air. He looked up, narrowing his gaze, and tried to see through the driving rain. In the far distance he saw the black outline of a coast, and made a rapid calculation. He had no intention of dying today.

He wiped his wet, black hair out of his face, as he focused on how to get to shore. There was too much unfinished business back home for him to die now. He had property to buy, power to gain and success to prove.

A wave crashed overhead, pushing Xanthier to his knees and drenching him in cold froth. He shook his head, ignoring the sting of the salt water, and peered at the land. On the coast a fire flickered, presumably caused by the lightning strike, and he smiled coolly. It would act as a beacon.

Holding the rope, he untied one end and inched over to the barrels, whereupon he lashed the rope to the cask. When the ship dropped suddenly he was flung backwards and he groaned in pain as his back crashed against the hatch door. He lost his breath for a moment, and struggled to draw in air before the ship listed again. Thunder crashed and Xanthier looked up, realizing that his chances of survival were slim. Anger consumed him.

"No!" he shouted into the gale. "No! I will survive! I am not done yet!"

Another flash of lightning answered him, illuminating the broken deck. All the sailors had been swept overboard. Only he remained. A great creaking signaled the ship's final resistance; then it abruptly rolled to its side.

Xanthier was flung aft, his powerful muscles defenseless. The rope that held him snapped taut, stringing him between the mast and the barrel. The mast swayed. The barrel shook. Dragging his knife from his boot, Xanthier sliced through the rope, choosing to stay with the buoyant barrel rather than the massive mast. He gripped the barrel's side and hacked at the rope that held it to the floorboards.

Suddenly water flooded the deck and the ship groaned once again, accepting defeat. The top of the mast abruptly snapped, sending splinters of wood cascading around him, pelting him with thousands of sharp pieces. Xanthier ducked, protecting his face and eyes. He stumbled, blood dripping from his face, and snarled at the elements.

"I will never give up!" he shouted. "You cannot stop me. I dare you to try!"

As if in answer, a flash of lightning snaked down from the heavens and struck the remaining mast. Instantly exploding, the mast turned into a tower of fire that blasted Xanthier, and immense heat erupted in his face, searing his skin and hair.

He howled in rage and pain, his hands gripping the right side of his face. The smell of burnt flesh mixed with the scent of burning wood. Xanthier screamed and fell to his knees. For a moment he wondered if he was in hell, if the evils of his past had found him and enwrapped him in the devil's fire. Then the ship tossed a final time and rolled, her heavy belly turning upwards like a great, dying whale.

Xanthier and the barrel were thrown from the deck and into the ocean. He plunged down, deep into the freezing depths, until the rope that bound him to the barrel halted his downward momentum and forced him to come back to the surface. Xanthier tried to swim, but the currents pulled him in every direction. Only the barrel kept him afloat, kept him knowing which direction was up and which was down. Breaking the surface, he gasped for air and looked around, seeing that the sinking ship was already many lengths away. With a groan, it twisted on its stern, then plunged down and sank into the wind-tossed ocean.

Xanthier looked for the beacon of light on land and found it. Ignoring the sting of salt in his wounds, he glared at the surging storm; he glared at the pounding waves. He would not be defeated!

Then, with supreme effort and indomitable will, he clung to the barrel and kicked, heading for salvation.

Chapter 2

By morning the squall had died, leaving the ocean a seething mess of seaweed and debris. Planks of wood were scattered along the beach, and bits of wreckage dotted the coast. Alannah swept a stick before her, checking the path for obstructions before stepping along the sand. Her senses hummed with the aftermath of the storm. The power generated by thunder and lightning was one of the few things that made her truly defenseless, for her senses became overloaded. Her hearing, touch and smell—even her extra powers of perception—became useless for a period of time.

Alannah did not like to admit her vulnerability, especially to herself. This morning, she sought to reestablish her equilibrium. Bit by bit she regained her senses, testing them and smiling when they responded to her silent requests.

Her bare toes curled in the wet gravel, and she could feel the soft silt of newly tossed ocean floor cast upon the isle's beach. With a quick intake of breath, she caught herself just before stepping on a jellyfish. She could feel the creature's life force. Carefully avoiding it, she knelt down and let her hands hover. The vibration of faint pulses spread to her fingertips.

Using a piece of bark, she scooped up the jellyfish along with some sand and carefully returned it to the sea. The warning cry of seagulls caught her attention as she straightened. Cautiously exiting the rippling waves, she followed the bird sounds. Her stick bumped against a log that had not been on the beach before. It was freshly burnt, probably struck by lightning in the storm. Touching the fallen tree, she felt the remaining heat that simmered deep within the core.

The effects of the storm were fading. Her senses were coming alive again. She stood facing the sea and absorbed her surroundings. She was connected to the island and every animal on it. This was her home, her family.

The seagulls cried again, and Alannah frowned. Something was amiss. She stepped over the log and walked slowly forward, seeking the cause of her disquiet.

Xanthier crawled up onto the beach, his body trembling with fatigue and shivering with cold, his face blazing with pain. His fingertips were blue where they were wound around the barrel's bindings and he had no sensation in his toes, but the feel of earth beneath his knees was incredible. He stared triumphantly at the sky, reveling in his success against the storm. No man, or beast, or act of God would beat him!

He uncurled his fingers and flexed them, making the blood rush through his hand once more. Then he touched his face, feeling the ravaged flesh where the burns blistered. The action was excruciatingly painful, but Xanthier did not flinch. He rose slowly to his feet and took a breath.

Taking deliberate steps, he walked up the beach, seeking shelter. He needed to tend his wounds and find food to eat. It did not occur to him to mourn his shipmates. His heart was cold. He stumbled to the ground, weak, but rose again. Weakness would not subdue him! he raged internally. Xanthier clenched his teeth and frowned. The storm had taken the lives of many. Only the strong survived. Only the strong *deserved* to survive. It was the way of the world.

Stumbling a few steps farther, he rounded a penin-sula that formed one arm of a sheltered cove. Above the cove was a cliff with a high, sheer face. Xan-thier frowned, searching for somewhere to rest. A momentary hopelessness overcame him. Why should he struggle? Why not just die? What was there to live for?

A movement up the beach made him spin around. A woman was coming toward him, her au-burn hair blowing in the gentle breeze. Her face was turned up to the sky and she waved a object in front of her like a woman swinging a basket in a manicured garden. He blinked, not certain if what he saw was real. She was like a goddess . . . so tall and slender . . . so ethereal and composed. His legs gave way and he fell to his knees. His head screamed in pain and his muscles quivered with fatigue. Black spots danced around his vision, and he tried to clear them by shaking his head. He did not want to lose sight of her. But despite his power-ful force of will, the black spots spread out, and he collapsed, unconscious.

Alannah heard a groan and she froze, her stick in midswing. A sense of foreboding overwhelmed her, and she hesitated, not sure what to do. Slow, raspy breaths came to her on the wind, breaths that did not sound like any animal she knew. They were deeper, huskier. She shook, suddenly frightened.

She heard another groan, and abruptly realized that the creature she sensed was nearby, and hurt. "Oh!" she cried as she continued forward, not allowing fear to halt her steps.

As she got closer, the sense of strength emanating from the creature made her steps falter yet again. She wrinkled her brow, confused. Then, with a deep breath, she kneeled down and stretched her fingers out. They contacted warm, supple, hairless flesh. She jerked back, stunned. She smelled the air. No scent of wet fur came to her. She trembled but was inexorably drawn back to touching the creature again.

Smooth yet hard. Muscled. She stroked down, feeling the contours of a human arm—yet an arm that was three times the size of her own, and easily five times as strong. As her fingers swept down the arm, she encountered hands that clearly proved the hurt creature was a human. Suddenly filled with both excitement and alarm, she reached out and gripped the human's shoulders, ran her hands down its slightly furred chest to the waistband of clothing that covered its legs. She brushed against a bulge and paused, intrigued, letting her fingers feel what her eyes could not see.

Xanthier woke groggily to the sensation of light touches sweeping over him. He was immediately aroused, and without thinking, he grabbed the woman and rolled his body over hers, tucking her easily underneath him. He leaned down, intent on kissing her, when a blast of pain erupted in his head.

"What?" he gasped, as the woman punched him

again and struggled to get out from under him. "Stop that!" he commanded, trying to get his bearings. The ache in his groin warred with the pounding in his temples.

"Get off!" she screamed, pummeling him with her fists. With a hearty kick, she shoved his weight off her body and scrambled to her feet. "What are you? Who are you?" she shouted.

Xanthier blinked and shook his head, then looked up at the woman towering over him, her hair disheveled, her eyes darting to and fro. "My name is Xanthier, and may I point out that you were touching me. I only accepted your blatant invitation."

Alannah was stunned to hear a human voice other than her own and Grandmother's. "What are you doing here?"

Raising his eyebrows in disbelief, he motioned to the pieces of ship's debris that littered the coastline. "Is the reason not clear?"

"Why are you here?" Alannah repeated sharply. She took a step back and leaned down, trying to locate her staff.

Xanthier watched her hands sweep the sand. He frowned again, wondering at her strange actions. "Are you simple? Can you not see that my ship lies in broken bits all around me? It sank in the storm, and the crew was lost. By the grace of my own fortitude, I am on this isle in one piece."

"You cannot stay here. Go away!" Alannah commanded.

Xanthier laughed. "I have no ship. I have been shipwrecked and stranded. I would expect a touch of courtesy. At the very least, a bowl of warm soup."

Alannah flushed. She turned away, hiding her

eyes from the stranger. For the first time in her life, she felt uncomfortable with her lack of sight. She had always known that other people roamed the seas. Grandmother had described the white sails and sloping hulls of their boats as they silently passed the island, skirting its hazardous coral reef. Alannah knew that she had come from far across the water, born to a family that had cast her out, presumably because of her blindness. Grandmother had told her how cruel people could be, how they would reject her because of her defect.

Alannah had no desire to interact with the outside world. The Isle of the Wild Horses was her life. She knew every inch of its beautiful hills and every beast that roamed its lush meadows. But this man was here. A man from across the sea. A man named Xanthier who was wounded and in need of care. If he had been a colt, she would not have hesitated to offer tender concern. It was not right of her to deny him simply because he was the wrong species.

"Xanthier," she finally said. "You appear to be injured."

"I think that is obvious," he retorted.

"There is no need to be rude," Alannah responded as she turned back to him. "I am sorry that I reacted to you as I did. I will offer you assistance until your people come for you. They *will* come for you, won't they?" she asked with sudden trepidation.

"They will come," Xanthier said grimly as he glanced out over the calm water. "They will come, or I will go after them and make them regret having left me behind."

Alannah nodded, satisfied with his answer. "Then come, follow me." She immediately walked away, leaving him to scramble to his feet unassisted. The stick she carried swung in front of her in graceful, smooth back-and-forth strokes, occasionally brushing against rocks or debris. She moved with confidence, never breaking stride.

Xanthier glared at her back, irritated by her cavalier attitude. "If you think you can dismiss me so easily," he grumbled under his breath, "think again." He followed her slowly, unable to force his tired legs to keep up with hers. When she rounded a bend and was lost to sight, he shouted after her. "Miss! Miss! Is this what you call consideration? Have care that I am just a tad tired!" He leaned against a tree, exhausted. "You probably will give me a pile of bitter leaves to eat and some milk to drink," he complained to himself, anticipating her lack of hospitality.

The thunder of hooves interrupted his thoughts. Glancing up in alarm, he beheld a herd of horses racing across the top of the cliff. In the lead was a dark brown mare, followed closely by a pristine white stallion. Trumpeting, the stallion skidded to a stop, then wheeled and reared in the air. The other horses slowed, then turned in unison, heading in the other direction. The stallion came down on all fours and stood staring down the cliff.

Suddenly, the horse leaped forward. He galloped down the cliff on a narrow path that zigzagged until ending at the beach. Without stopping, he raced out of sight around the rocks. Xanthier moved to where he could see him, amazed at his agility and strength. "Incredible," Xanthier whispered. "He is wilder than any beast I have seen in Scotland. An untamed stallion . . ." Xanthier looked the beast over, noting his heavy musculature and intelligent eyes. "You would be worth a fortune."

Alannah appeared from behind an outcropping, and the stallion wheeled to face her. He swished his tail, then lifted it high in the air as he arched his neck. She had dropped her stick, and was approaching the wild horse with steady, even strides. Xanthier watched in surprise as she reached him, gripped his rippling mane, and swung aboard with lithe grace.

Xanthier stumbled back, blinking. His mouth dropped open and he held his breath. She was so beautiful . . . they were so beautiful together. Her long legs were wrapped around the stallion's broad girth, and her proud chin was tilted at the same angle as his equine jaw. Xanthier had never seen anything so absolutely perfect. He felt his soul shudder, incapable of comprehending anything so clearly beyond his experience.

Swaying, he widened his eyes, trying to focus. Suddenly the horse seemed to be moving and the girl riding him was talking, but he could not understand her. Her voice echoed oddly, as if it was coming from underwater. He fell to his knees, fighting the sensation, the loss of control. The horse brushed against him, providing ballast. Xanthier looked up, trying to see into the sea green eyes of the woman as she tilted her head down toward him. Her eyes saw through him, not looking at him but *into* him. He tried to pull away, but his overwhelming weakness made it impossible to escape her penetrating gaze.

As black spots flickered in his vision, her voice came to him again. She seemed to frown, then reach down. Xanthier clasped her hands, eager to feel her palms. They were callused in spots, yet soft like a woman's. She was pulling him up astride the magnificent stallion. Then he lost all sensation and his world went black once again.

Alannah grimaced as Xanthier's full weight collapsed against her. "Oaf," she grunted. "You could have remained conscious until we reached the highland meadow! Now I will have to support you all the way up. If I drop you, I will leave you wherever you fall!" she warned him as she nudged the stallion back to the zigzag path. "Walk steady Claudius," she whispered to the stallion. "Walk steady . . ."

The pair managed to reach the top, and Alannah shifted to accommodate Xanthier's bulk as they headed toward the cottage. The herd of horses appeared. Several trotted up with curiosity while a few hung back, distrustful of Xanthier's foreign scent. Alannah smiled and touched the muzzles that butted against her, murmuring to the beasts. Within minutes, they reached the cottage and Alannah listened for Grandmother's breathing.

"Grandmother?" she called out. "Grandmother?"

"What?" the old woman responded irritably. "I am washing the blankets. They are musty."

"Grandmother, you must come here. I found something on the beach."

"I care naught for what shell or piece of wood you've brought now, child. Our home is cluttered enough with your treasures."

Alannah grinned. "Very well, Grandmother. If you don't want to see the man I found, I will simply dump him on the ground."

Silence greeted her glib answer, and Alannah strained to hear Grandmother's steps. When she heard nothing, Alannah spoke up again. "As I said—"

"What is that?" Grandmother interrupted, her voice unusually quiet. She stood just around the corner of the cottage, her voice carrying in the still air.

"I found a man, Grandmother. He was ship-wrecked and washed ashore. He is injured. I was not sure what to do."

"Where is he from? Why is he here? Has he come to take you away?"

Alannah heard the fear in Grandmother's voice and she instantly leapt down from the stallion and raced forward. "Grandmother! Never think that! He is only a lost sailor who accidentally found a haven on our isle. He knows nothing of us. We will nurse him to health, then send him on his way."

"I knew this day would come."

"You know nothing!" Alannah repeated. "*He* is nothing!"

Grandmother walked toward the stallion that stood patiently with his burden draped across his back. "Perhaps this was meant to be . . ."

"Ach! Grandmother. Stop trying to read any-thing into this happenstance. The man assures me that his ships will come looking for him. We only need to offer him food and shelter until then."

"What did he say about your eyes?"

Alannah ducked her head. "He does not know."

Grandmother stared at Alannah, watching the telltale flush spread across her cheeks.

"Did you find him unconscious then?"

"No, he was awake. We talked. His name is Xanthier."

"Then how could he not know?"

Alannah shrugged. "I did not let him become aware of it."

"Alannah, you should not be ashamed of your

blindness. You have been raised to be proud of who you are. You do not need eyes to see. Do not hide yourself."

"Even so," Alannah mumbled, "I would wish to keep him ignorant of my affliction."

She helped Grandmother lift him down and drag him into the cottage. "I felt his face," Alannah said. "He has a gash across his cheek that needs stitches, and terrible burns. I will get your medicines."

"Aye, he needs a careful hand, but mine are painful with bone disease after such a storm. You will have to do it, Alannah."

Alannah brushed her fingers across Xanthier's face, feeling the jagged cut, the dried blood, the burns that seared his face. She also felt the wrinkled brow, the facial muscles knotted with tension. Her own brows drew together with concern. "Sleep well, sailor," she whispered. "Sleep for awhile. 'Tis clear from the lines on your face that you have little of that luxury. I will clean you and care for you while you rest."

Then, with a nod toward the place where Grandmother was boiling water, Alannah left the cottage to collect the fresh herbs she would need.

Chapter 3

The stranger woke moaning with pain, but immediately stifled the sounds and gritted his teeth. Alannah sat in the shadows, listening to him, sensing him . . . feeling him. He was full of tension and fury, presumably because he was injured and at the mercy of her hospitality, yet he conveyed a power that she was at a loss to explain. She knew he had sat up and scanned the room, had probably located her, so she smiled in strained welcome.

"I am surprised you did not leave me on the beach to die," he said harshly.

Alannah's smile widened. "And you are not usually surprised, are you, sailor?"

"I am not a sailor. I am a commodore, leader of a hundred sailors."

"Do you not sail the sea?" Alannah asked mockingly. When he did not answer, she shrugged. "Then to me you are simply a sailor."

"And you are a peasant girl!" he shot back.

Alannah laughed. "Aye. That is the truth. Although some would say I am the princess of this island. Princess, subject and servant all in one."

Xanthier shook his head, trying hard not to groan as his temple burst into pain at the action.

"You are not saying that you are alone here, are you? Surely you are part of a village?"

"I live with Grandmother. She is the only other person here. Do you want some soup? Or would you rather some bitter leaves?"

"You heard me? How could you have heard my comments on the beach? You were far away . . ."

"Soup?" Alannah offered again as she carefully ladled some into a bowl. She knew exactly how much the ladle held and how much the bowl could contain, and easily filled it to the brim without spilling any. She turned and handed it to him, waiting until his fingers wrapped around the bowl before she let go. She reached behind her, located a spoon, and handed that to him as well.

"Where is your father? Mother? How do you communicate with the outside world?"

"As I said, it is only Grandmother and I. We have no need for anyone else."

Xanthier absorbed her answer as he looked around the cottage. There were fine blankets and simple, well-made wooden furniture. A spinning wheel took up one corner, piles of wool ready to be carded lying next to it. The bowl he was using was made from a shell, and the spoon was carved from bone. The cottage was rustic, to say the least, but it was comfortable, weatherproof and warm.

"How long have you been here?" he finally asked after taking another bite of the soup. It was rich and flavorful, made of meat, vegetables and broth.

"I have always been here," Alannah answered. Quickly changing the subject, she motioned to her own cheek. "How does it feel?"

Xanthier lifted his fingers and felt a neat row of

stitches and a moist unguent. "I will have scars," he stated.

"Yes. I believe you will. From my needle and also from those burns."

"Do you think to distract me from questioning you? I do not understand how you came to be here, alone, with only an old woman for company. How do you survive?"

Alannah rose in agitation. "If you want to benefit from our assistance, you should be more respectful of our privacy." She moved quickly toward the door, unaware of Xanthier's outstretched foot. She stumbled over it, gasping in embarrassment.

"I'm sorry . . ." Xanthier mumbled, moving his leg out of the way as Alannah regained her balance.

"No matter," she replied, and carefully made the final steps to the door. She shuddered internally, aware of how much he was affecting her. Her senses were jumbled and his energy was surging through her. Her feelings frightened her. "Finish your food," she said. "Then feel free to rest. I will not be back until morning. Grandmother will return shortly. Please, don't ask her too many questions. She is less tolerant of you than I."

Stunned, Xanthier stared after Alannah as the door swung shut behind her. No woman had ever walked away from him. Even the women who despised or feared him did not turn their backs on him. His reputation preceded him and everyone knew he was not a man to ignore.

He stared at the closed door, willing it to open, but it remained stubbornly shut. Finally accepting defeat—if only temporarily—he sank back and stared at the small flame flickering in the fireplace. Curious, he stared at the spindle on the spinning wheel, noting the simple workmanship. Alannah's clothes were unadorned but durable. Although no gentlewoman would have worn them, a peasant would have thought them fine indeed.

Xanthier heard footsteps approaching and he paused in his analysis to wait for someone's arrival. When Grandmother finally opened the door, he was struck by her sad face and weary stoop.

"Ahhh, the sailor is awake at last," she said as she shuffled in. "And Alannah left you all alone. At least she gave you some food."

"Indeed," he answered.

"How did you find her?" Grandmother asked as she swung her penetrating gaze in his direction.

"Rather rude, I would say," he replied.

"Is that all?"

"That is enough," he said, irritated.

Grandmother shrugged. "Very well. If she is rude, 'tis only because she has never spoken with anyone but myself. I think she is very brave to have rescued you. Have you thanked her?"

Xanthier raised his eyebrows. "I hardly call her actions a 'rescue.' Rather, she was bound by common decency to drag me to this cottage."

"So you did not thank her. It would seem that she is not the only rude one here." Grandmother shook her head, then sat on a chair and leaned over to ladle soup into a shell-bowl.

Xanthier glared at her, furious that she would reprimand him. "I am a commodore. I can say whatever I please," he growled.

"Do you think so?" Grandmother replied. "Have you found that caring only for yourself has made you happy?"

"I have no desire to be happy," he grumbled. "I seek greater accomplishments."

Grandmother shook her head again. "Perhaps you will learn how wrong you are," she murmured.

She ate in silence. Then, without bidding him good night, she lay down in her bed and fell asleep.

Xanthier frowned at her, confused by her words. His head hurt and his cheek throbbed. He could not verbally war with Grandmother in his state of weakness, for her words were echoing with a strange intensity and he found it hard to come up with an adequate response. He was left with no choice but to rest his eyes as well, for the small fire smoldered and the cottage was soon dark. Exhausted, he, too, fell asleep.

In the darkness, Alannah raced the white stallion twice around the island before pulling him to a breathless halt. Both she and the beast were drenched in sweat.

"I should have left him," she whispered. "I should not have helped him. Perhaps we should have hid from him. I do not like him in my home or on the isle. He and his kind deserted me, cast me out of their world. Whatever longing I have to see other people, to experience how others live, is senseless. This man is only confusing matters. This island is all I need! I do not desire anything else!"

The stallion snorted, stamping his foot in agreement. He twitched his ears back and forth, listening to her words.

Alannah rode up to the top of the cliff, then slipped off the animal's back. She opened her arms wide, absorbing the night scents. "The tides are long and deep. I can hear the waves lapping at the rocks. That means the moon is full. The air is crisp and clean, with a cool, soft wind. That means there are few clouds. With a full moon and few clouds, the night is bright and Grandmother can easily make her way to the water hole. These are things that only I know. This man is probably ignorant of all the subtle signs I can sense. He is probably so dependent upon his sight, he cannot truly see."

She sniffed, then leaned down and unerringly found a pink blossom growing in the grass. She plucked it and tucked it behind her ear. "I will avoid him until he is gone. Then I will not think about him again."

She walked down a familiar path, hearing the hoofbeats of the stallion walking behind her. Together they reached a small pool near the beach. Fresh water that bubbled up from an underground spring was responsible for the verdant meadows. It was her favorite spot on the isle. She sank to her knees, feeling the mud stain her dress. She dipped her hands into the cool water, then dashed it against her flushed cheeks. Her fingers still tingled from touching his skin this morning. She scrubbed harder, trying to erase the sensation, but his unique texture remained in her hand's memory. Finally, in exasperation, she ripped off her dress and dove into the pool, immersing her body in its refreshing embrace. But the feel of the water reminded her of the liquid strength of his arms, and she was soon more agitated than before.

In desperation, she clenched her hands and rocked, frightened by these new feelings. Despite her avowals, she could not wait to be near him again.

By morning, she had composed herself. As seagulls swooped overhead, she walked with calm purpose to the sheltered cove and felt the sand for telltale bubbles of water. Feeling a clam below the surface, she dug quickly and captured it. Smiling, she continued on her way, finding and collecting several more.

On the cliff far above her, Xanthier stood watching her progress. "How old is she?" he asked Grandmother, who was tending the garden nearby.

"About sixteen summers. More or less."

"How did she get here?" He turned and faced the older woman. "For that matter, how did you get here and why are you both here, alone, on this deserted island?"

"Why are you here?" Grandmother countered.

"I was shipwrecked. I had no choice."

"I had no choice either," Grandmother said quietly.

"Tell me what happened," Xanthier demanded, taking a step toward her. When Grandmother looked up with an arched eyebrow, he paused and took another approach. "I would like to know how two women found themselves on this island. I want to know how you survive without assistance."

"Anything is possible," she answered. "If you need something enough, and have the strength to go after it, you can achieve anything. Even living without a man to help," she added wryly.

"You are being condescending," he accused.

"Absolutely. You deserve it."

Xanthier stepped back, confused. Unsure, he turned to watch Alannah on the beach. "She is very beautiful."

"Hummm . . ."

"She is perhaps the most beautiful woman I have ever seen."

"Hummmm . . ." Grandmother replied as she drifted away, finding and picking small green leaves that burst into pungent scent when plucked from the ground.

Realizing that he had lost his audience, Xanthier scanned the cliff top and located a path that led down to the beach. Glancing back at Grandmother, he waved and set off down the pathway. Within moments he reached the sand and saw Alannah going toward a sheltered cove. He followed, drawn by her natural grace. She walked with an economy of movement that made every step seem planned. She carried a stick again, and was swinging it with seemingly careless abandon in front of her. As she went around a curve, he heard her giggle with delight.

Following more swiftly, he rounded the same curve, curious as to what had amused her.

She stood in the middle of a streambed that trickled into the ocean. Grass lined the banks, and moss made the rocks slick. Ferns and flowers grew with wild abandon. But something else made him freeze. He stood, his mouth open, his breath caught in his throat.

White butterflies swirled, dipped, swooped, filled the air . . . they fluttered with delicate magnificence. In the center stood Alannah, her auburn hair covered with white wings. Her eyes were closed and she seemed to be absorbing the butterflies . . . feeling them.

Alannah breathed in, sensing the tiny flickers of wingtips all around her. She could smell the powder that covered their soft wings; she could feel the vibrations of their bodies filling the air. Smiling, she slowly lifted her hands, spreading her fingers wide. Instantly, hundreds of the white insects landed on her shoulders and palms, drawn by the salt of her skin. She was draped in a living cloak of white, as if a cloud billowed around her.

Xanthier moved forward, drawn by her magic and she turned as if she had been aware of him all along. She lifted her palms, sending a dusting of butterflies into the air. They swirled around, milling in their world of mists and breezes, until they found Xanthier. They settled upon him, touching him, stroking him, then lifting off and dancing again.

"Stay still," Alannah whispered. "They do not recognize your scent."

Xanthier concentrated on remaining still, his eyes focused on Alannah's face.

"Can you feel them?" she asked.

"I can see them. They are everywhere," he answered softly.

"No. Close your eyes. *Feel* them . . ."

Hesitating, he glanced around.

"You are safe," she murmured. "There is no one else here. You have no enemies to watch out for. Close your eyes and feel them . . ."

He closed his eyes.

"Now," she whispered. "Now, feel their tiny feet, their sweet breath, their sighs as they float around you."

"How do you know what they feel like?" he murmured, entranced by the multitude of sensations.

"I spend time feeling. Do you?"

After a moment, he shook his head. "I guess not . . ."

"Listen to them. Can you hear the sound of their wings?"

"Yes."

Alannah smiled with appreciation. "They are

singing. They are talking to each other, signaling with the different patterns of their wing beats."

"I cannot hear that," he admitted. "You can hear more than I."

"Perhaps, if you take the time to learn, you will hear it, too."

Xanthier opened his eyes and gazed at Alannah's upturned face. He was struck again by her beauty, but more than her facial structure made her stunning. She glowed with a radiance that stemmed from her soul, and he was at a loss to explain it. The slope of her cheek was perfect and the curve of her lips was entrancing. He had an urge to kiss her, to kiss her amidst the fluttering white butterflies. For a second he leaned forward, tempted to capture her loveliness and drink it in. But he hesitated. She was pure and he was tainted. She was a virgin on this isle of wild horses, and he was a feckless and corrupt pirate of the seas.

He stepped back, suddenly disgusted with himself for thinking even for a second that she would welcome his caress. "Sometimes I do listen to the ocean," he said quietly as he gazed at the gentle waves. An eddy swirled around the base of the stream where it merged with the ocean. A line of algae stopped abruptly where the salt water began, and turned into a meadow of sea urchins and mussels. "She is my solace."

Alannah turned toward him, tilting her head to listen to the tone underneath his words. "Do you have other forms of solace?"

He laughed harshly. "No. Yes. I suppose you could say that fighting is my other source of release."

"Whom do you fight?" She took a step toward

him, causing the butterflies to lift into the air and fly crazily about her.

"Whom do I not? My brother, my father . . . England, France. It is my way of living." He turned, facing her. She was staring at him, yet seemed to be looking through him. He stared into her green eyes, noting their ethereal beauty.

She blinked and turned away. "I do not understand what you are talking about, but I can hear the pain in your voice. I am sorry you have suffered."

He laughed again. "I think you are the only person who would say such a thing to me. Your isolation has made you naive."

"Indeed. I do not understand how other men and women act. I only know Grandmother." She licked her lips, removing a droplet of salt water.

Xanthier stared at her lips. The urge to kiss her became stronger. His voice turned husky. "There are many things men and women do together that you do not know about," he whispered.

Alannah jumped, startled. She tripped on a rock and struggled to keep her balance. Once again, his nearness made her tingle, made her senses quiver.

Xanthier grabbed her arm to steady her, then pulled her toward him. "Can I show you?" he asked as he stared at her mouth.

Alannah pulled back, shaking her head in confusion. Xanthier held her for a moment, loath to let her go, but then he released her. His face closed and his eyes grew shuttered. "My apologies, Alannah."

She looked up at him, her brow knotted in consternation. She reached up, her hand searching for his face, trying to feel his abrupt change in emotion, but he jerked back to avoid her touch.

"It will not happen again," he said. "I should

not have dallied here. I have work to do. I must
set up a signal for my men, so they will be able to
locate me. Good day, Alannah.''

She nodded, his sudden coldness discomfiting
her. As he walked briskly away, she listened to his
footsteps in the sand, already familiar with his
stride. The butterflies danced above the streambed,
their fragile wings fluttering like the pulse in her
wrist.

Chapter 4

Over the next few days, she avoided him. The incident in the streambed played in her mind, and she could barely concentrate on anything else. Her already heightened senses were attuned to him, and she was well aware of him, no matter where he was on the island.

She did not understand what had happened. He had asked to show her something, yet had jerked away and apologized. These feelings were confusing and she had no experience dealing with them. Sparks of anger warred with strange yearnings, and she felt as if an internal storm was brewing. In defense, she stayed as far from him as the isle shores would allow.

As he built the signal tower during the next several days, he only caught occasional glimpses of her, and he soon realized that she was purposefully avoiding him. She did not know how to be coy, which made her skittishness all the more enticing. Alannah did not want anything from him. She was so unusual, and he was intrigued despite himself. As the days passed, he caught himself watching her in fascination.

Most of the time she played with the white stallion, riding him, walking with him or resting against him. The horses accepted her as one of the herd, barely noting her when she moved among them. The foals romped around her, rearing and nipping as if she was one of them. She rode like an athlete, her body supple and strong. The white stallion should have terrified her, but she handled him with ease using no bridle or training aid. He had never seen such a talented and relaxed woman in his life, and yet she was incredibly young and untutored. Wild. Free. Different.

But something about her movements confused him. She was so graceful, she seemed to float as she walked, yet there was something in her stride that struck him as odd. And her stick. She carried it with her almost all the time, swinging it in a steady arc, back and forth.

He felt his healing scar, noting the raised ridge that marred his face. Back home, people would see the mark as another indication of his scarred soul. He was feared and despised. Now they would dislike his looks as well.

He was disfigured and she was exquisite. She avoided him, whereas he was drawn to her. She was innocent and he was jaded. They were complete opposites.

As if sensing his attention, Alannah turned and faced the signal tower. She was down in the meadow, surrounded by tall grasses that whispered in the ocean breeze.

"It has been five days. Will his people come for him?" she said to Grandmother, who was standing nearby.

"He seems to think so. Do you want him gone so badly, Alannah?"

"Yes. I want him to leave. He disturbs my sleep."

Grandmother coughed. She rubbed her forehead, feeling the increased heat there. "I have not slept well since the night of the storm either, although I believe for different reasons."

"Are you still ill, Grandmother? I thought you were getting better."

"I was, until the chill of the north wind caught up with me."

"And here I have been avoiding the cottage! I am sorry, Grandmother. I should have attended you. Have you been drinking tea?"

"Ach, I drink a bit. I am just getting old."

"Come, let's collect some herbs from the garden and make you some tea. You should rest."

Grandmother sighed. "All right. Perhaps I will lie down." She reached out to Alannah and leaned against her shoulder, letting the younger woman guide her across the field. The white stallion lifted his head from grazing and monitored their progress, then resumed eating when the pair entered the trees.

Xanthier paused as well, noting the sudden solicitation Alannah afforded Grandmother. He frowned, worried about the two females.

Hours later he returned to the cottage with a string of fish. The signal tower was finished and all he could do now was wait. He had fashioned a fishing hook and line from materials he had salvaged from the debris that had floated ashore. Since all the debris had come from his ship, he felt entitled to use the items. He could hardly remember when he'd last spent an afternoon fishing. A faint smile lifted his lips, and he hummed in unconscious relaxation.

The music faded when he beheld Alannah's worried face upon entering the cottage. "What is wrong?" he demanded in a harsh voice.

Alannah bristled and tossed him an angry look. "Can you not see that she is sleeping? Keep your voice down." She turned her back on him in agitation.

Abashed, Xanthier closed the door and walked over to the fire pit. Placing his fish on the flat stone they used for frying, he deliberately softened his words. "Is Grandmother tired so early in the evening?"

"Yes. She is tired. Be kind, and let her sleep." Alannah lowered her head and stroked Grandmother's face, pushing the gray hair back behind her ear.

Xanthier nodded, and turned from them to prepare the fish for dinner. He was pleased that Alannah was in the cottage, for it gave him an opportunity to be near her. Without speaking, he cleaned and gutted the fish, then filleted and fried them on a small fire. When the fish was done, he placed some on a shell and brought it over to Alannah. She reached her hand out, waiting for him to place the bowl in her palm.

"My thanks," she murmured when he gave her the dinner.

"It is the least I can do," he answered. He stood still, expecting her to make eye contact, but she slid her gaze away from him and stared at the wall as she picked up pieces of fish and nibbled on them.

Raising his eyebrows, he sat in a chair and looked at her. "This is the first time in many nights that you have stayed in the cottage while I am here. You always leave within minutes of my arrival."

"Mayhap I do not like you," Alannah replied tartly.

He laughed and leaned forward. "Mayhap I make you uncomfortable." When she still did not look at him, he shook his head and leaned back. "Why don't you ever look at me?"

Alannah flushed. Tossing the bowl aside, she rose and stared toward him angrily. "I see nothing to look at!"

Xanthier rose as well, equally angry. He touched his scar and narrowed his gaze. "So my scar is so disfiguring that you cannot even look at me?" He pointed at her. "You think you are too beautiful for someone like me? Let me remind you, there is no one else here!"

Alannah gaped as she realized that he had misunderstood her response. "You are a dunce!"

"What?" He stepped forward and gripped her shoulders. "No one says that to me!"

"Well, I did! You are an idiot. And the sooner you realize it, the sooner you can get beyond it!" She pushed against him, but his grip tightened.

"Is the scar really that repulsive?" he asked with true concern. When she did not respond, he shook her. "Look at it! Is it that repulsive?"

Alannah blinked, knitting her brow in consternation. "That is what I was trying to tell you. I can't look at it, and if you weren't so self-centered, you would know why!"

Xanthier stepped back as if burned. "I already know why. You don't have to say any more. But there is more to a man than his face, Alannah, and I intend to show what you are missing. You will regret your arrogance." He grabbed her arm and tugged, pulling her to the door. "The night is warm, Alannah," he whispered seductively. "Come, join me for a walk. You like midnight walks, don't you?"

"Stop. Let go of me."

"Why? Are you afraid of me? You, the strong Alannah who strides all over this island like a queen. You are not afraid, are you? Not afraid of your reactions to a disfigured man like me?"

"Stop! You understand nothing!"

"Grandmother is sleeping soundly. She doesn't need you right now. Come." He shoved her ahead of him, then was obliged to catch her when she stumbled. "Are you suddenly nervous? Has your grace deserted you?" he said condescendingly. He opened the door and pushed her outside, then closed it firmly behind them. "All you have to do is look at me and I will stop. One look, Alannah."

Alannah pulled away and spun around. She turned her face toward him, and narrowed her eyelids.

"That is no good, little filly. You have to look at me, not just turn your gaze toward me. I want to see your green eyes focus on mine. Just do that, and I will leave you to your innocence."

Tears of helplessness sprang to her eyes, and Alannah jerked away from him. "You are the one who is blind!" she screamed. "Leave me alone!" She dashed down the path.

Xanthier stared after her for a moment, surprised that she still refused to look at him. His façade of confidence was shaken, and the need to assert his dominance over her surged forward. He ran after her, easily catching up with her. "What are you running from?" he taunted as he matched her strides.

"What are you chasing?" she gasped as she ducked into a side path and leapt over a stream she knew was there.

Xanthier missed the turn, and crashed through

the underbrush as he struggled to find her. He fell
into the stream, becoming drenched. He rose, cursing. The moon had gone behind a cloud, and the
stars were faint in the black sky. He was submerged
in darkness. "You are running because you fear
what I can make you feel. You are a young woman
and I am the only man you have seen. The emotions I evoke must—"

"You are chasing me because you have nothing!
Whatever power you have accumulated has left
you empty!"

Xanthier spun around, hearing her voice from
behind him. He jumped forward, his strong body
breaking through the underbrush with ease.

Alannah gasped, amazed at how quickly he located her in the night. She ran once again, using
her memory of the isle to guide her rapid footsteps.
Drawing her senses together, she concentrated on
feeling the magic of the night. She absorbed everything, suddenly feeling blazingly alive. Her body
vibrated, tingled, tickled as her extra sense took
over and guided her through the forest. She felt
the sea breeze and the whisper of the leaves. She
felt him coming for her.

"There you are!" Xanthier shouted, spotting her
shadowy figure. He burst out of the underbrush
and onto the path.

A rush of excitement flooded Alannah, and she
raced down the path, silently daring him to follow
deeper into the night. When she rounded a curve,
she skidded to a halt, and crept silently off into the
shelter of the trees. Reaching gingerly with her feet,
she avoided the small sticks that would snap and
reveal her location, and stretching carefully with
her arms, she plucked the low hanging branches
away from her face before they scratched her. She

strained, listening for him, but her heart was thudding so hard, she could hardly hear anything.

Xanthier padded through the woods, peering through the trees. As he approached a curve, he stopped and listened. The forest was silent. He deliberately stepped off the path and slunk around the curve, searching for her. Her constant composure drew him. She was always so perfect in her movements, her actions. It was as if she planned everything she did. He wanted to see her when she could not plan ahead, when her body took over and she became wild with emotion. Then she would look at him! He would make her!

They both located each other at the same moment. She heard his breathing and he saw her gleaming skin. Alannah leapt forward, running through the forest, but she was hampered by the numerous rocks and roots that sprang from the earth. She tempered her pace, using her senses to move quickly but safely. She trembled with excitement, feeling things that she had never felt before. He reminded her of the white stallion. He was all male . . . powerful and strong, yet he was completely human. She heard him gaining on her, and her breathing quickened.

She dashed through the last of the trees and out into the high meadow. The open space afforded her freedom, and she ran forward. Her long legs swept through the grass and her auburn hair streamed out behind her.

Xanthier ducked under a branch, then found himself at the edge of an exquisite meadow. Halfway across, Alannah was running with a speed he never knew a woman could possess. He grinned and took off after her, angling himself so that he would intercept her only feet away from the far edge of the clearing. But Alannah suddenly changed direction like a deer in flight. She sprang to the side, rapidly outdistancing him.

In an instant, Xanthier's patience ended and he leapt forward, gaining upon her in seconds. He reached out and grabbed her fluttering blouse. It snagged her for a suspended moment, then ripped and released her. Xanthier's eyes darkened with desire as she spun around and faced him, her blouse hanging loosely from one shoulder.

He halted and stared at her warily, noting that she kept her face averted. He circled her slowly as she turned in place, keeping him in front of her. The moon finally peeked out and flooded the meadow with soft blue light.

"Will you look at me?" he whispered.

Alannah smiled mysteriously, but shook her head.

"Then stop running."

"I am not running," she answered, her voice as soft as the ocean breeze.

Xanthier took one step closer, seeing her muscles tense. He froze, letting her acclimate to his presence. As she relaxed, he smiled seductively. "You amaze me," he said. "You almost got away."

"I could have if I had wanted to."

"You think so?" he answered, amused. Without warning, he sprang forward and grabbed her face between his two hands. He tilted her chin up and stared down at her. "One day, I will make you look at me."

"I doubt that," she replied as she lifted her own hands to his shoulders.

He leaned down and brushed his lips across hers, feeling her rapid breathing.

Alannah jerked back, startled at his touch.

"No," he whispered. "Don't leave me this time. I want to show you . . . I need to feel you."

Alannah stilled. His words were seductive and she was hypnotized. Such vibrations, such heat . . . she was overwhelmed, yet strangely peaceful. His presence felt right. Taking a step closer to him, she turned her face up.

Releasing his pent-up breath in relief, he gathered her in his arms and lowered his mouth to hers. He gently kissed her, smoothing his lips against hers as he held her face. He took her lower lip into his mouth, nibbled it, then kissed her once again. When she did not pull away, he dropped one hand and placed it at the small of her back, pulling her fully against him. The other he dug into the wealth of her hair and pulled her head back, exposing her throat. He explored her lips, discovering their fullness, their winsome shape and trembling responses.

Alannah sank into his arms, reveling in the new sensations. She had no desire to stop him. Instead, she wanted to feel every nuance of him, and she showed him her desire by pressing her body against his.

Xanthier thrilled at her response and his heart started beating erratically. Sliding a few inches down her body, he placed his mouth against her neck, licking and sucking this most vulnerable place. He could not believe how soft and luxurious she felt, how sweet and tender she tasted. He drifted to the other side, completely mesmerized by the silky texture of her body.

Alannah collapsed against his supporting hand as he devoured her. She clung to his shoulders, kneading them as she clutched and released his muscles.

She could feel the length of him against her, could sense the vibrations coming from him as his desire escalated.

He abruptly abandoned her throat and dipped lower, between her breasts. The hand that held her head let go, and dropped down to her blouse. With little effort, he yanked, ripping it fully from her. As the mounds of her breasts rose in the moonlight, Xanthier shook. She was so perfect, he was almost afraid to touch her. Almost. He stared at her face, fearing that she would balk, but she swayed toward him. Moaning with need, he picked her up, lifting her legs free from the earth. Her weight was slight, soft, easy to support. He slid one hand down and gently pulled one of her legs around his waist so she faced him with her breasts pointing toward his mouth.

She took a quick, indrawn breath and held on to his shoulders as she wrapped her other leg around him, clasping his waist with her thighs. Just like when she rode the stallion, she balanced her weight effortlessly and kept her upper body supple. She leaned back, letting his arm hold her.

His mouth found her tingling nipple, and he tasted the ambrosia of her virgin flesh. It puckered and tightened, thrusting forward with impudence. Xanthier tried to be gentle, but the delicious moans that were starting in Alannah's throat drove him wild, and he sucked on her firmly, drawing her deeply into his mouth. He lost control, his need for her spiraling upwards. Faintly aware that he should stop now, before things progressed, he shoved his chivalrous thoughts aside and let his emotions guide him. He gripped her back with his fingers, but swept his thumb forward to stroke the side of her breast, reveling in the swelling that could fill both his hands.

She gasped, sparkling with the sensations he elicited with his mouth and thumb. She tightened her grip on him, feeling the rippling musculature of his waist and hips. She was only peripherally aware of his switching to the other breast, then back again as he drank from her. He drank fully, immersed in her, then was abruptly desperate to rip his own clothes off and feel her.

Suddenly, they were on the ground and crushing the meadow plants and Xanthier had removed the rest of their clothes, tossing them carelessly aside. Rich aromas filled the air as the grasses cloaked the two lovers, stroking their bodies with sensitive feathers of seeds and fronds. The moon gleamed, searching through the shadows to illuminate their naked bodies that shone with passion's sweat.

"This is unbelievable," he whispered as he feverishly felt her body, sweeping his hands down her breasts to her small waist, then over her curved hips. "I need you . . ." With considerable restraint, he avoided touching her most sensitive area, not wanting to frighten her. He ran his hands up again, enjoying the beauty of her lean body. "I need this feeling. I must be with you, merge with you, become part of your purity."

He lowered his body onto hers, letting her feel his flesh against hers for the first time. But it was he who felt like a new child, for she frightened him. He trembled and stared at her face, searching for an answering need.

She felt his trembling just as she felt his firmness against her. He was dusted with hair and she raked her nails down his arms, lost in his world. "I want you, too. Show me what you know. Teach me . . ." Her voice was husky and her head tossed in the meadow grass. Her eyes were closed as she focused all her senses on him . . . his smell, his touch, his voice and heartbeat, his deep breathing. He hummed with energy and she was pulsing with him.

Peripherally, Xanthier became aware that the ground was shaking. He dragged himself away from her welcoming arms and glanced up. His lifetime of war, his timeless experiences with deceit and intrigue made him pull away from Alannah and glance around them defensively. He reached beside them for a sword, then frowned when he realized he did not have one.

"What?" Alannah whispered as she reached up for him, still floating in unfulfilled desire.

"Don't touch me," he growled as he saw shadows racing toward them. In shock, he beheld the wild horses galloping madly across the meadow, only a few lengths from where they lay. He sprang upright, dragging Alannah's unresisting body up with him, and held her tightly against him.

The mare in the lead started, sprang to the side, then whinnied in alarm as the other horses thundered past, unable to stop in time. They streamed around Xanthier and Alannah, rolling their eyes and tossing their heads. The meadow echoed with their hoofbeats until, within seconds, they were gone.

Stunned, Xanthier looked up. The white stallion stood two feet from them, his majestic neck arched in splendor. His nostrils flared. His forefoot struck the ground. Once. Twice. Then he whinnied.

Alannah slowly pulled back and tilted her head up at Xanthier. "Don't touch me?" she repeated, stunned and unbelievably vulnerable.

"I . . . I meant . . ." Xanthier struggled to explain that he did not mean to reject her but only to protect her from what he had thought was a threat. He stared at her miraculous face, at a loss for words.

Tears of hurt glistened in her eyes when he said nothing more. Shivering, she yanked out of Xanthier's hold. Dashing the moisture from her cheeks, she stumbled over to her stallion, grabbed his mane and sprang onto his back. Then, without another word between them, she and the horse leapt into a gallop, leaving Xanthier standing alone.

Chapter 5

The image of her naked body atop the white stallion galloping in a moonlit meadow haunted him. He tossed and turned, unable to sleep. His nether regions ached with desire and his soul screamed with need. He couldn't talk to her. He couldn't look at her. If he did, he would explode.

Yet, everything was about her. When he saw the horses, he thought of her. When he saw the seashells that peppered the beach, he thought of her. When he smelled the meadow grasses, he yearned to feel her again. He relived his response to her question over and over, rehearsing better answers, forming plausible words that would explain to her that he had not meant to hurt her feelings, but she gave him no chance to speak them aloud.

He went over those wonderful moments over and over in his mind, and finally, as the image crystallized, he began to realize that he was missing something. There was a truth he was not seeing—something that accounted for her uniqueness that he had yet to define. As he thought about her, he recognized that almost every time he had talked to her, it had been evening. She avoided him during the day. Until now he had assumed that her oddi-

ties were related to her seclusion. Now he began
to wonder if there was more to it.

He knew it was wrong to think of her so often.
He should forget her. She should remain un-
touched. His own history made him a blighted creature and he had no right to sully her beauty. Soon
he would be gone and she would live her days on
this gorgeous island, surrounded by wild horses and
endless sky. She did not need to know what the
world was really all about. She did not need to
learn that contests over land and riches could tear
families apart and rip countries in half. For once
in his life, he could give a gift to someone deserving. He would gift her with a lack of knowledge.
By sacrificing his own desires, he could let her live
in chaste paradise.

He rolled over, stretching uncomfortably on the
hard floor of the signal tower. "For the love of
God!" he shouted. "I need to be rescued! I know
you would not answer my prayers, for I deserve
no kindness from you, but let my men find me for
her sake!" He shifted again, and looked out over
the horizon. When he still saw no ship upon the
water, he pounded his head against the tower's
wall.

Alannah stayed with Grandmother and focused
all her energy on caring for her.

"Drink, Grandmother. You must drink!"

Grandmother pushed the cup aside and waved
listlessly. "I have had enough. Let me rest, child."

"Please, Grandmother. You are frightening me."

Grandmother looked up, staring at Alannah's ex-
pressive eyes. It was uncanny how one so blind
could show more emotion than one who could see.

"You were a beautiful baby. I remember your eyes from the very first day . . ."

"Grandmother, if you don't drink, you will weaken. You must keep liquids inside. That is what you always taught me."

"The first day I saw you, I told Gondin to take you away. I thought you might bring people here. People looking for you, and then they would find me. I was scared. But then you cried and I had to go see you. And your eyes . . . lovely green eyes. I had never seen an infant with green eyes before. You were a gift to me. You made living worthwhile."

"You are rambling, Grandmother. Perhaps you should close your eyes for a while. Rest."

"I knew right away that there was something special about you. We were meant to find each other in this world. I needed you and you needed me. But you don't need me anymore. What do you need now, little one?"

"Don't be silly. I need you very much. When you say such things, you make me anxious."

Grandmother looked around, her old eyes suddenly sharp. "Where is he? The sailor?"

"Don't worry. He stays in the tower he built, day and night. He leaves to catch fish, then goes back. He does not come near the cottage anymore." Alannah blushed, remembering the moment in the meadow when he had touched her. The feelings . . . the sensations . . . he had unleashed something in her she did not understand. Alannah bit her lip as she tried to stifle her thoughts and concentrate on Grandmother.

"You have the most incredible eyes, Alannah. Remember, you can see more with your eyes than most people can hope to see with theirs. Never forget that."

"Here, let me tuck you in. Sleep for a bit. When you wake, you will drink more tea."

Grandmother sighed and sank against the grass-filled pillow. She drifted to sleep, muttering to herself.

Alannah placed her hand on Grandmother's chest, feeling for the moment when her breathing steadied and slowed, indicating that she slept. Once assured of her comfort, Alannah went outside. She whistled, and within moments the white stallion appeared. As he butted his head against her, she pulled herself onto his back and went for a ride.

Grandmother was worrying her. The lung illness was not going away, and she did not know what more to do to help her. Alannah and the horse meandered for an hour as Alannah contemplated Grandmother's health. Eventually they returned to the cottage, and Alannah resumed her vigil.

That night the winds howled and clouds covered the night sky. Great raindrops fell with increasing force until the island became drenched in a sheeting downpour. Alannah wrapped another blanket around Grandmother and listened worriedly. She touched the dwindling wood supply, then decided to go out to collect more.

Grandmother leaned forward and coughed into her hand. Droplets of blood covered her palm and she stared at them with resignation. As more coughs racked her frail body, she took off the blankets and stood up. Black dots disturbed her vision and she swayed, but her constant shivering suddenly stopped as warmth spread through her. She smiled, seeing an old friend walking toward her.

"Where have you been? I have not seen you in

so long," Grandmother said to the apparition. When it did not answer, Grandmother opened the door and stared out. The biting wind swirled around her, but she was oblivious. Instead, she saw the rolling hills of her homeland and the welcoming flowers that graced her doorstep. Grandmother walked out into the storm, wandering in her daze. Old memories swam in her mind, and she drifted in their grip.

A pair of boys ran up to her. "Mistress Anne! Can you come? The bishop's niece is sick."

"How much did she eat this time?" Grandmother answered, shaking her head. "She is only hurting herself by gaining so much weight. It will kill her."

"No, that is not it this time. She has terrible stomach cramps. She is screaming."

"Aye, I will come. Let me get my herbs." They walked down the cobbled path, aware of the beautiful sunshine, but hurrying nonetheless. Suddenly Grandmother stopped and looked up. A dark cloud passed over the sun, and she shivered. The boys regarded her with concern.

"Come on, Mistress Anne. We must hurry."

Nodding, she followed them once again.

Inside the bishop's brother's house, the obese girl was panting, her eyes wide with fear. "Mistress!" she gasped. "My insides are being ripped apart! Augh! It comes again! The pain!"

"Leanna, relax. Perhaps it is just indigestion."

"No! This is worse. Much worse! My belly . . ."

As she meandered in her delusion, Grandmother walked forward in the drenching rain and pantomimed touching the girl's swollen abdomen. She looked up as if she was gazing at Leanna. "It moves . . . as if you were in labor. Leanna? Are you carrying a child?"

Leanna stared back at her, aghast. "I am not married, mistress. How could you ask such a thing?"

"Of course, of course," Grandmother whispered into the rain. "You could not be carrying . . . you could not have gone nine months without knowing . . ."

"Augh! Stop! Stop the pain!"

"What goes on here?" a strident voice demanded as Grandmother spun around and beheld the bishop striding in.

"Your niece has stomach pains."

"Aaaaauuuuuugh!"

"Give her some ginger to settle her stomach and be gone, Mistress Anne. I do not like you. A woman your age should be married, not fooling around with potions and the like. Leave this holy home of my brother."

"I fear it is more serious and a bit of ginger will not help. I need to examine her."

"You will be gone—"

"Help! Please help! Mistress, I cannot bear it. Father, let her do what she can! I need help, some kind of help! It hurts!"

The bishop stepped back as Leanna screamed in agony. A gush of warm liquid erupted from between her legs and soaked the chair in which she was sprawled, then formed a pool at her feet. The bishop turned white and stumbled from the room.

Grandmother rushed forward, reliving the horror of discovering that Leanna was truly having a baby that she had had no knowledge of carrying. Her heavy weight had hidden her condition from everyone, even herself. Grandmother fell to her knees in the mud, crying as she pulled forth the memory-ghost of the blue infant. It had been strangled by the cord, and despite all efforts, it had not taken even one small breath.

Then things seemed to happen quickly. Grandmother rose again, peering about her at the imaginary people who were throwing stones at her, hurling accusations of witchcraft and sorcery.

The bishop led them, his face contorted with hatred. It was terrible. . . . Terrible. She turned around, seeing the fierce anger of the town focused on her. No one admitted to having bedded Leanna, and Leanna vehemently denied sinning against the Lord. She hid in the church, screaming that the devil had taken over her insides, and only the Lord could save her. Desperate and mortified, the bishop turned his rage outward and focused it upon the healer, publicly accusing her of setting Lucifer in his daughter's belly and trying to bring him to life for wicked purposes.

Grandmother stood frozen, paralyzed by her memories. She searched her mind, trying to find the person who had saved her and set her up on this deserted isle, but the person's face was like mist. "Gondin . . ." she whispered into the rain. "You haven't been here in so long. Have you deserted me?" She reached out and suddenly found herself supported by a pair of strong arms. "Gondin!" she cried, as she collapsed in his embrace, thankful once again for his kindness.

Xanthier grabbed Grandmother, appalled to find her crying in the storm. He lifted her slight body and held her close to his chest. She was cold, yet her skin was burning with fever. He lifted one of her eyelids, and noted the dilated pupils.

"Grandmother!" he shouted over the wind. "Can you hear me? What are you doing out here? Where is Alannah?" When she did not respond, he broke into a run, heading for the cottage.

Within minutes he burst into the cozy home. He

glanced quickly around, but when it was clear that Alannah was not there he grimly set about caring for Grandmother himself. He stripped off her wet clothes and wrapped her in warm blankets. She was weak, only occasionally producing a feeble cough. She did not seem to understand what was happening around her, for she mumbled incoherently and her eyes remained closed.

Xanthier built the fire higher and made sure Grandmother was secure; then he ducked out again to find Alannah. Although he was certain she would not appreciate his concern, he did not want her out in the storm. He closed the door firmly and squinted through the rain. He shivered, then rubbed his arms to warm them. Looking at the two paths that led to the cottage, he opted to take the one that led down to the beach since he had come from the other. Leaning against the wind, he walked swiftly down the path, looking left and right for evidence of Alannah's whereabouts.

An hour later, he returned to the cottage, exhausted and freezing, predicting that she was probably cuddled up next to the warm fire. But when he entered, he found only Grandmother. She was sitting upright, the blankets wrapped around her like a shawl.

"Grandmother, are you feeling better?"

She smiled sadly and coughed. Blood covered the cloth she held to her lips. "Where is Alannah?" she whispered weakly.

"I don't know. I was looking for her but when I could not find her, I hoped she would be back here."

"She gets lost in storms. She cannot hear and she loses all sense of direction. You must find her. She is too reckless. Please find her."

Xanthier strode over to her and kneeled down. "Why, Grandmother? What is so different about her?"

"In your world only the strongest survive," Grandmother stated. "You probably have never dealt with the 'unfortunate' people who hide in the shadows of village streets."

"What do you mean, the unfortunate?"

"The crippled, the deformed . . ."

"No," he answered slowly. "I suppose I have not."

"Why? Why do you avoid them?"

Xanthier frowned. "Because the crippled are useless. They take from our resources and return nothing. They should be destroyed as infants."

Grandmother shook her head. "You will change your opinion one day. Remember, all people have something to offer, and it is only the foolish who discard those they do not understand."

Xanthier rose and stared at her. Her words were incomprehensible. She must still be delusional. "Grandmother, stay here. I will lock the door from the outside. Now I must go find Alannah."

When he found the wild horses but still saw no sign of her, he became very concerned. The white stallion was huddled with the others in a tight bunch, their combined mass protecting the small foals from the worst of the storm. Although not as bad as on the night he was shipwrecked, the storm was ferocious, and it whipped over the island, bending trees and flooding the lower flats.

She knows the island. She grew up here. She has weathered many storms. Surely my concern is misplaced. But fear drove him on, and he followed every path and scanned every meadow. Doubting she would be foolish enough to go to the shoreline, he nonetheless climbed down the treacherous rocks and fought the crashing waves to search the area where she had originally found him.

Nothing. No Alannah. He was exhausted, yet he did not consider giving up. Something was seriously wrong. She would not have left Grandmother. He paused as he fought the elements to reach the farthest point where his signal tower loomed. Alannah never came to this part of the island, for it had minimal vegetation and less wildlife. Rocks tumbled on top of each other in chaotic profusion, and Xanthier proceeded with care. One misstep could cause a broken ankle.

He was climbing over the last row of rocks and was about to enter the low shrubbery leading back into the island when a flash of white caught his eye. He turned and peered through the rain, locating the pale shimmer wedged between two boulders.

"Alannah? Alannah!" A faint cry came to him and he was galvanized into action. "What are you doing out here? Are you hurt?" He raced over the slippery rocks until he reached her huddled form. "Alannah?" he whispered when he saw her ashen face.

She reached out and touched him, her fingers rapidly tracing the lines of his face. "Xanthier?" she questioned incredulously. Rain coursed down her cheeks, melding with her tears of gratitude.

"Yes. Why are you out here? You should be inside the cottage. Come on." He held a hand out to help her rise, but she appeared to ignore his offering. He frowned and turned his back on her, suddenly angry. Without waiting for her, he retraced his steps for several feet. When she did not follow, he paused and glared at her. "Are you coming?" he shouted over the wind.

Alannah shivered. She was frightened and terribly cold. Storms made her helpless. The wind whistled around her ears, obliterating the sounds she normally relied upon for her sense of direction. As the cold bit into her fingertips and seeped into her flesh, her sense of touch became useless. Without sound, touch or sight, she was lost—lost even on her familiar island. From past experience she knew to stay still until the storm passed, but it scared her nonetheless.

"Xanthier?" she called out, groping in the darkness. "Did you leave?"

He paused and his anger faded away. He returned slowly to her, watching her carefully. When he was only a foot away, he said, "No. I have not left."

Alannah turned toward his voice, trying to pinpoint his location, but the words whipped around her and she shook her head in frustration.

Xanthier placed his hand under her elbow and helped her rise. She clung to him, her small hands clutching his arm as if she feared she would be swept away. He searched her face for the secret to why she acted so strangely. She was normally so self-sufficient and self-reliant. He was stunned by her clear need for assistance.

Alannah nodded, indicating that she was ready. Xanthier took a step, and Alannah copied his movements, placing her feet in the exact location his had vacated. Again Xanthier paused, searching her face, but Alannah simply waited for him to continue.

"Are you hurt?" he questioned.

She shook her head but leaned closer to him. She felt comforted by his strong presence in a way that she had never felt before. In the beginning, Grandmother had been the strong one. Grandmother had raised her and taught her everything she needed to know. But as the years had passed, their roles had reversed and Alannah had been the stronger of the two. She could not remember a time in the recent past when she had had the luxury of leaning—both physically and emotionally—against another human being.

Xanthier guided her carefully. Several times she stumbled, her feet sliding on the wet surfaces, but he was quick to support her. Step by step they crept over the stones until they reached safer terrain.

Assuming that she would be fine now that the rocks were behind them, he let go of her and moved ahead.

"Wait!" she cried, and Xanthier came back to her. He took off his wool shirt and wrapped it around her, calming her shivers. He ignored the cold rain as it sluiced down his bare chest, and stared at her with an unguarded expression. He ran his gaze down her form, noting the womanly curves revealed by her wet clothing. Her face was drenched with rain and her auburn hair was almost black as it curled wetly against her neck. Then, slowly, as if dreading what he would see, he looked at her eyes, noting how the brilliant green color reflected the swaying trees behind him. He shook his head, doubting himself, trying desperately to convince himself that what he was thinking could not be true.

He took her hand, enfolding it securely in his, and she moved to his side with a smile of gratitude. Warmth spread through her fingers and his pres-

ence soothed her. She felt him looking at her, and
a frisson of awareness raced through her. She lifted
her chin, not sure how to respond. When he tugged
on her hand, she stepped nearer.

He leaned close to her. "Do the storms bother
you?" he murmured in her ear.

The heat of his breath against her neck made
her tremble anew, and she haltingly nodded. "They
make me disoriented."

"Hummm," Xanthier replied. He stepped back
and stared at her. Her eyes . . . they did not gaze
back at him. She could not see him. Emotions
flashed through him—incredulity, denial, fascination, amazement. "If the storm bothers you, then I
am glad I came to find you."

"I would have been fine by morning," she said
with a flare of spirit while lightning flashed across
the sky.

"Indeed. I know you would have. Nonetheless, I
did find you, and I intend to bring you back to the
cottage tonight." He wanted to ask her about her
vision, but he couldn't. Not yet. He was confused
and needed to think about this new realization.
Alannah had intrigued him before, but now . . .
now he was utterly beguiled! She was such a combination of strength and fragility.

Unaware of Xanthier's thoughts, Alannah relented, grateful for his help. "Thank you. I am
ready to go home." He nodded and carefully led
her over the uneven ground. She followed him
trustingly, and they moved through the storm in
tandem. As thunder crashed around them, Xanthier tugged, and they broke into a run across the
meadow.

He laughed aloud, suddenly reveling in the wild
storm, the drenching rain, the electric air. He

turned and grabbed Alannah and spun her around in a circle, holding her high.

She gripped his bare shoulders. "What are you doing?" she gasped as he slowed down and held her flush against him.

He closed his eyes and tilted his face up to the sky. "I'm feeling the storm . . . I'm feeling you. Do you feel me?"

Alannah sighed. She flexed her fingers against his shoulders, kneading his muscles. She stroked her thumbs against his flesh. It was hard yet smooth, unmarred by the hair that dusted his chest. Letting him support her, she released his shoulders and stroked his arms. "Yes," she whispered as another crash of thunder vibrated around them.

He lowered her, inch by inch, until her lips were even with his. He brushed his mouth across hers and nibbled her lower lip. Then, as she opened to him, he moved away and placed a soft kiss upon her closed eyelids. "You are fascinating," he murmured. "Do you know that? You are the most intriguing woman I have ever met." He captured her earlobe and sucked on it gently, relishing the wet flesh. "I have sailed the far seas . . . I have visited many countries, yet here, on this tiny isle, I find you." He pulled away and looked at her wryly. "And you have no idea what I am talking about."

Alannah shook her head, bewildered by his mercurial moods.

He lowered her until her face was pressed against his bare chest; then he bent his head and placed a soft kiss upon her hair. "Come, Grandmother is ill and you are shivering. We must go back."

Alannah nodded, but as she followed him through the meadowlands, she knew that she was shivering from far more than cold.

Chapter 6

Grandmother lay sprawled on the floor, her face white with blotches of red staining her cheeks. She had fallen from the bed and been unable to rise. Her hand was flung out toward the dwindling fire, reaching for the warmth. Her harsh breath was audible when Xanthier and Alannah burst into the room.

Alannah dropped to her knees and stretched her hands out, touching the old woman's forehead, neck and chest. "Grandmother!" she cried.

Dread filled Xanthier as he assessed the situation. The old woman was more ill than he had thought. He doubted she would survive. He stepped around the pair and stoked the fire, then went out to bring in more wood. He was uncomfortable with the wealth of emotion on Alannah's face, yet part of him envied her ability to express herself.

He had seen his own father murdered before his eyes and his estranged wife plummet to her death. He had lost his homeland, his inheritance and his twin brother in a family feud. Yet despite the horrors he had endured, or perhaps because of them, he had never released the tight hold on his emotions. He did not know how to mourn.

He returned to find Alannah sobbing, holding Grandmother's head in her lap. She rocked, crooning softly. She still wore the wet wool shirt he had given her, and she sat in a puddle of water. He knelt down and carefully, so as not to disturb her, pulled the shirt from her shoulders. He gently disengaged one arm at a time, peeling the wet fabric from her. Then, reaching behind him, he dragged the blanket from the bed and draped it over her.

Throughout the procedure, Alannah ignored him, focusing all her attention on her beloved companion. She felt numb. She could not imagine life without Grandmother, yet she could feel her life force sliding away. "Grandmother," she moaned. "Grandmother, I need you. Please. Last year you were sick, but you got better. You can do it again."

"Where is Gondin?" Grandmother murmured.

"He is not here, Grandmother. He has not been here for many years. He told you last time that he did not think he could make the trip again."

"He would not have left us alone," Grandmother whispered, then doubled over as coughs ripped through her. "Find him . . . Find your family, my family . . ."

"Save your strength." Alannah held Grandmother upright, but her frail body was limp. Lifting her, Alannah placed her back on the bed and wrapped more blankets around her. "Don't worry about anything, Grandmother. I will take care of you. For now, just concentrate on breathing and getting well."

Grandmother opened her eyes and stared at Alannah. Then her gaze shifted to Xanthier, who stood quietly to one side. "She is going to need you." She coughed, then continued talking with strained effort. "Protect her. Protect her from those who would wish her harm. Protect her from her own impulsiveness, from her own sense of immortality. She has unique needs . . . she should have someone who will watch over her, caring for and enabling her."

Xanthier nodded and was about to answer, but Alannah interrupted him sharply. "Don't speak like that! I do not need anyone, especially not a sailor. I have the isle and the horses. I am fully capable."

"Promise me," Grandmother whispered with waning strength. "Watch over her . . ."

"Stop!" Alannah cried, but this time Xanthier stepped forward and ignored her interruption.

"I promise, Grandmother."

"There are things . . . things you should know. About her and her family . . . about me."

"If you seek to frighten me, you will fail," Xanthier replied.

"You should have more humility, Xanthier . . . I worry that you will not be right for her but I have no choice . . . I pray that someday you will know what it means to fear. When you do, you will understand what it means to love." She coughed again and her eyelids fluttered closed.

"Please, Grandmother," he urged. "Don't talk. Just rest. I will do as you ask, regardless of the consequences."

Grandmother nodded as she sank back. The short conversation had drained her, but she had elicited the promise that she wanted, and she was satisfied that Xanthier would keep his word. Gondin's image floated through her mind, and she turned to his comforting presence.

The wide green valley of her home slowly formed in her vision, and she smiled. It was beautiful. The land stretched for miles and no matter how hard she looked, she could not see the ocean. Gondin, appearing as a young man, walked up to her and handed her a sprig of yellow flowers.

Then his face melted into older lines, and his dark hair lightened with streaks of gray. A boat rocked behind him and he stood on the beach, handing her other presents. A spinning wheel, a pair of sheep, a knife . . . necessary items that made her life easier. Tears slipped down her cheeks when, with a shy smile, he produced one more item from behind his back.

"What is it?" she asked.

"A packet of seeds," he answered. "I brought you flowers, like I used to. You will have to grow them, but every time you see them, know I am thinking of you."

The ocean drifted away . . . the boat was gone. Gondin was gone. Grandmother walked amidst the flowers and tried to explain them to the blind child who tumbled along beside her. The girl nodded as if she understood, but Grandmother wasn't sure. She leaned down and captured Alannah's hand and placed it gently on a petal. When a smile spread across the child's face, Grandmother smiled in return.

Then even the girl slipped away and only flowers and sunshine filled her mind. Yellow sprigs and purple blossoms. Pink honeysuckle and white jasmine. Heather . . . daisies . . . fragrant roses . . .

Grandmother sank peacefully into the embrace of the petals, as her painful breathing ceased and her soul floated free.

Beside her, Alannah bent her head in sorrow. She felt as if her own heart had stopped beating, and the world had collapsed around her. She was lost without Grandmother, frightened, angry, guilty . . . She didn't know what to feel.

She stretched out beside Grandmother's still figure and wrapped her arms around her. Clutching her tight, Alannah tried to bring life back into Grandmother's body. She scolded her, shook her, and finally, stroked her. She kissed her weathered cheeks and held her wrinkled hands as she talked, remembering the many things they had done together. Then, as the hours lengthened and the rain calmed to a pitter-patter of tiny droplets, Alannah fell into an exhausted sleep.

When she woke, Xanthier was gone, but he had placed a long, thin stick against the doorframe for Alannah's use. Alannah held it, noting that Xanthier had not only stripped the bark from it, but had also smoothed the small knobs where little branches had been broken off. The wood was warm, and fit snugly in her hand. Alannah touched it, feeling the work that had gone into making it so perfect. She pressed it against her lips, silently thanking him.

He must know! He must know that she was blind! Sometime, somehow, he had realized the truth, and yet he had not turned from her in disgust. In fact, he had given her a token showing his concern. Within the darkness of the day, a blossom of trust bloomed in her heart and she hugged the stick close.

Then, keeping her staff nearby, she returned to Grandmother. Her body was cold. Her spirit was gone. As the sun broke out and flooded the island with sunshine, Alannah washed and dressed her. She wept as she dug a trench behind the cottage, and sobbed as she placed Grandmother's frail body

within the grave and covered her with fresh dirt.
Then, taking her new walking stick, she left the
cottage to find the horses.

She found them in the second meadow, peacefully grazing on the sparkling grasses. The white
stallion lifted his head immediately and whinnied.
Swishing his tail, he walked over to her, and placed
his muzzle on her shoulder.

"Just as I helped raise you, Grandmother raised
me. I will miss her. I am terrified to be without
her."

The stallion blew softly through his nostrils. He
stood still as she leaned against him and released
all her grief.

She rode as if she and the horse were one. They
moved in perfect harmony, her body swaying with
his as he loped through a meadow and powered up
a hillside. She melded with him, her muscles rippling with strength and her hair flowing with
beauty. She was a master rider, and her lack of
vision only deepened the bond between her and
her beast. She felt the tiny changes in his stride
that signaled a shift in direction or a leap of surprise, and, equally important, the horse felt her
commands through the intensity of their mutual
connection.

Alannah tried to run away by asking the stallion
to flee as fast as he could, but there were only so
many places to go on the island, and they soon
found themselves back where they had started.
Lonely and frightened, she stayed with her equine
companion, sleeping upon his back when he rested,
and meandering with him as he grazed. She ate and
drank little, only nibbling on wild fruits and sipping

from the streams. For days they were as one, never parting, never straying, until slowly, bit by bit, Alannah began to accept her loss.

Xanthier watched her from afar, wanting to help her but knowing from personal experience that self-reflection was the single most important step. He had his own feelings to work out. His own world of harsh reality had been jolted, for he had always assumed that only the strongest could—or should— survive. Alannah's blindness shocked him. She was a powerful woman yet she had a flaw that could not be changed, one that would forever separate her from other people.

She moved with incredible grace, and when she rode the white stallion, she was exquisite. He was drawn to her, as if by being near her he could drink from the goodness that emanated from her. She had a purity about her that was unique. As day after day passed, and no ship appeared on the horizon, Xanthier spent less time waiting for rescue, and more time yearning for Alannah's affection.

On the fifth night she came to him. He was sitting on the beach with a small campfire, roasting a rabbit. He was gazing into the flames, thinking of his past deeds, when he heard the soft swish of her stick followed by the tread of her footsteps on the sand.

"Alannah," he breathed.

She materialized slowly out of the darkness, her face illuminated by the flickering flames. The rhythmic crash of ocean waves matched the thudding in his heart as she reached him and appeared to stare at him.

"There is a seat to your left," he offered, hoping she would stay.

She hesitated, then swung her stick to the left and located the proffered stump.

As she sat down, Xanthier tested the meat. "Hungry?"

Alannah licked her lips and nodded. His eyes dropped immediately to her mouth. The plump redness glistened in the firelight. Using his dagger, he sliced a thin piece off the edge of the meat where the fat sizzled and formed a crusty, semiburnt edge. He stabbed it, then blew softly on it and held it out to her.

Alannah smelled the meat, her mouth watering, and leaned forward. She ate mostly vegetables and seafood, for hunting was not easy for her. The scent of the roasting rabbit was irresistible. While Xanthier turned his dagger and carefully, slowly slid the blade into her mouth, she opened wide and flicked her tongue out to test the meat, ensuring its safe temperature. Satisfied, she closed her teeth and pulled the succulent piece off the steel and chewed it with delight.

Xanthier's eyelids drooped and his gray eyes darkened. Without saying anything, he sliced another piece, stabbed it, and offered it again. Alannah leaned forward greedily, opening her mouth like a bird waiting to be fed. Xanthier placed his blade on top of her tongue, watching the metal reflect the glow in her eyes before she closed them and pulled the meat smoothly, fully into her mouth. A dribble of dark fluid dripped from the corner of her lips, and she rubbed it absently with her thumb. She tilted her head up at him expectantly.

He dragged his gaze from her face and roughly cut another piece, not caring that the meat he carved was now rare and cool. Alannah seemed oblivious as well, for her breathing quickened at the faint trembling in his strong hands. She slowly opened her mouth and ran her tongue briefly over her upper teeth. Xanthier offered the meat, waiting. She closed her teeth on either side of the sharp steel, and slid them down the length. As the meat fell from the blade, Xanthier pressed the flat side of it down, pushing upon her lower jaw to open it wider. Alannah poked her tongue out to touch the tip of the dagger.

Xanthier drew in a harsh breath and pulled the dagger out slightly, concerned for her safety, but she leaned closer and gently placed her tongue on top of the blade, resting upon it erotically. She curved her tongue down, arching it, and slid it delicately down the flat upper side of the steel. Droplets of saliva dotted the surface, and Alannah breathed out around it. Condensation briefly covered the metal but warmed immediately as she breathed in. Xanthier slowly withdrew the blade and touched its tip to her chin where a drip of grease still remained. He scraped her flesh gently, lifting the stain, then stroked the blade down her neck.

"I want to stay here," he whispered.

"Stay?" Alannah answered just as softly.

"I want to stay with you, on this island."

Alannah stroked his cheek, smoothing her hands over the roughened scars that marred one side of his face. "This is a small world. The horses, the ocean . . . that is all there is."

"There is you. I want to get to know you and understand you."

"My blindness . . ."

"It fascinates me. You are not limited by vision. You are in tune with the world around you. The deep ocean lives in your eyes and the sunrise is born in your auburn hair. You have shown me what it means to live and I realize that I have spent thirty years without living a day. Do you understand? I am more alive now than I have ever been!

"Every day of my life I have woken with anger in my soul and rage racing through my blood, yet you have lived without seeing and have melded with your world. I want you to teach me how to live without fighting. I want to learn from you.

"But I also want to teach you what you do not know. I want to show you what it means to be a woman. You have feelings for me . . . I can see them in the way you tremble when I am near. You sense my arousal and you respond to it. I want to awaken your body."

"Why?" Alannah whispered. "Why is this important to you?"

Xanthier laughed and leaned back. He stared up at the stars and smiled. "I am not sure, Alannah. But I know that my life depends upon it." He gazed at her, watching the way she reacted to the nuances in his tone. She seemed to pick up the differences that others missed because she did not rely on body language to filter spoken words.

Although he could not fully express it, he knew that his salvation lay within her arms. He needed to taste her purity, needed to share her strength and partake of her innate tranquility, for his own turbulent soul was dying.

"I would like you to stay," she replied. "I would like to show you my island as I know it. I would like to discover the secrets you speak of."

He grinned and moved closer to her, picking up her hand and cradling it in his own. "We have all the time in the world."

Chapter 7

The capricious winds swept the cool morning mists aside, and left the isle drenched in glorious sunshine. Although the stormy season was ending, scattered showers occasionally wet the landscape. As Alannah and Xanthier left the beach and headed for the cottage, he was amazed at how lovely the island looked. The meadows sparkled from the previous night's rain and the treetops glimmered with reflected light. Xanthier stared at the sight, transfixed. He turned toward Alannah, noting that she, too, appeared transported.

"How do you know that the morning is so beautiful?" he asked.

She smiled. "The sun beats upon my shoulders, and the clear air spreads through my chest. A tingle fills the air. I can hear the birds singing." She laughed. "How could anyone not know it is a beautiful day? Come, let me show you."

She grabbed his hand and pulled him to a halt. "Stay here," she commanded, and ducked inside the cottage. Within moments, she reappeared holding a length of cloth. She walked up to him and gently stroked his face with it. "Do you trust me?" she whispered.

Xanthier nodded, his gaze trained on her face.

"Then turn around." Alannah wound the cloth around his head, covering his eyes. "Don't tense. There is nothing here to harm you. I will be with you. I will help you. Just relax." When the blindfold was secure, she tugged him forward.

Xanthier froze, his sense of direction completely obliterated by the lack of sight. "This isn't necessary."

"Don't be frightened," she replied as she pulled him one step forward. "The path is ahead of us. It is five steps away."

Xanthier held out his other hand, making sure that he did not run into a tree. He took a hesitant step, then paused.

"Can you feel the shadow of the tree you are passing under? You are passing a tree on your right."

Xanthier nodded, amazed to realize that he did feel the temperature change. He took another step, then stumbled as he walked into a bush.

Alannah giggled. "You must go slowly until you know where you are. Have you forgotten about that bush? It has always been there. Surely you have seen it before."

Xanthier shook his head wryly. "Indeed. I remember now, but you must have a very good memory to recall where all the trees and bushes are. Still, I am not sure we need to do this . . ."

Ignoring him, Alannah captured his hand and led him to the path. "We will go through the forest. I want you to feel the island around you. Can you hear the animals and the rustling leaves? Can you smell the different kinds of trees? The various meadow grasses?"

Xanthier followed Alannah as she moved into the trees. "This is where you ran that night I followed you," he said.

"Yes. It is the path I am most familiar with. It leads to the high meadow."

"That night you were very swift. I did not know you could not see. You amaze me."

"Grandmother always told me that anything is possible."

"You were very lucky, Alannah— Augh!"

"Careful!" she cried as Xanthier tripped over an exposed root. She laughed as he grunted his displeasure. "You should slide your feet just off the ground so they can sense the changes before you trip over them."

"Wait," Xanthier said as he tilted his head. "I can hear the squirrels." He remained still, listening to the chitter-chatter of the squirrels around him as they leapt from branch to branch. He could hear the leaves shake and the occasional snap of a broken twig when they raced after each other. He smiled. "I never listened to them before."

Alannah smiled as well. She enjoyed sharing her special world with him. She could hear his breathing, and could smell the scent of his skin. His vulnerability made her bold, and she moved closer to him. Her heart began beating faster, and she wondered if he would sense her excitement. "There is more," she murmured.

A sudden charge in the air caused Xanthier to swing his head toward her, and even though he could not see her, he was instantly aroused. "Indeed? I am ready."

"No more hesitation?" she asked. She let go of his hand and stepped back, daring him to follow on his own.

The taunting in her voice was new, and Xanthier responded to her challenge. He slid his foot and took a step toward her. "I am ready, Alannah. Are you?"

She moved away on nearly silent feet. She was breathing quickly as she listened for his footsteps and she gasped when his hand brushed her cheek.

"Use caution, Alannah. If you intend to tease me, you had best be prepared for the consequences. I have only so much patience."

"Keep your blindfold on," she said, her voice shaking.

After a slight pause, Xanthier acceded. "If that is what you want."

She turned away and moved carefully down the path to the meadow. She could feel the dominance of his personality wash over her, and a fluttering feeling grew in her stomach. Ahead of her, the meadow wildflowers swayed in the breeze, and she could hear the swish of the grasses as clearly as she could sense the heat of the sun. An occasional stamp and snort indicated that the horses were grazing at the far end. She ran forward and whistled.

The swish of her legs acted as a beacon, and Xanthier followed after her. He, too, could feel the sun as he left the shelter of the trees and entered the open space, but her whistle startled him. He froze, waiting for what she planned next. When he heard an answering whinny, he knelt down and felt the ground, feeling for the vibrations of the stallion's hooves.

Within moments, the white stallion bore down upon them and Alannah turned to Xanthier. "Do you ride?"

"Yes," he replied. "I have warhorses for battle,

and other horses for travel. I have even competed in occasional races."

"Then riding is not something you do for pleasure."

"There are few things I do for pleasure, but I wouldn't mind showing you one of them."

"Well, today you will learn something new," Alannah promised.

"As will you," Xanthier replied. He could feel her inner quivering at his words, and he grinned. "Not seeing you and not seeing your responses is difficult, but I find I am understanding you better. Your heart is racing and you are anxious, despite your brave words. Am I making you nervous?"

Alannah caught her breath. "I do not get nervous."

"Of course not," Xanthier said as he laughed and reached out to touch her. When she jumped he added, "As I said, I am beginning to understand you very well."

The stallion leaned his head down and bumped Alannah, just as aware of her tension as Xanthier was. He whinnied again.

Alannah gripped his mane and, with a small, running leap, mounted. Within seconds, Xanthier joined her and wrapped one arm around her waist while gripping the horse's mane with his other hand. The stallion reared, furious at the unfamiliar weight.

Both Alannah and Xanthier clung to the stallion's back, their legs wrapping around his girth. The horse pawed the air, trumpeting his displeasure, then crashed to the ground and bounded forward. The other horses neighed as well, and the entire herd galloped after the stallion in a thundering mass.

Xanthier gripped Alannah tightly, fearing for their safety. He ducked, covering her small frame with his in case the horse ran under a tree. As he was about to tear off the blindfold and take control of the wild stallion, he felt her supple body meld with his as she turned her face into his neck.

"Feel . . ." she whispered. "Trust the stallion. Feel the beast move and the wind whip against your cheeks. Do not rely upon your sight."

With supreme self-control, he left the blindfold in place and let the horse carry them across the meadow and down to the beach. He focused on holding her body tight to his, and letting her peaceful spirit calm his. The brush of the grasses changed to the thud of the sand, and the smell of flowers and crushed foliage changed to the tang of salt water as the stallion galloped onto the beach. Stride after stride brought them over the sand, until the relaxed rhythm soothed Xanthier's concerns and he could enjoy the beauty of the ride.

He sat up slowly and lifted his face to the sky. "Yes!" he cried out, suddenly feeling what she was trying to show him. The wind merged with the tendrils of Alannah's hair, and filled his nose with the scent of her womanhood as her hair snapped around his face. The splash of the ocean spray touched him like the caressing hand of a lover. He shouted, urging the stallion faster, and the beast sprang forward.

Alannah leaned against Xanthier, reveling in his awakening. This was what she wanted to give him. She had felt his twisted anger and knew that he needed to release his tight control and trust in something. It was not just the sense of riding for pleasure, or the feeling of navigating blind; it was the freedom to believe in a safe, loving world.

They swept around the peninsula and pounded over the coastline that enclosed the sheltered cove at the southern tip. The brisk wind slowed, and radiant warmth filled the area. Xanthier released his hold on the stallion's mane and shifted his hand to Alannah's waist. He held her gently, reverently, letting his fingers brush over her abdomen and down her hips.

She took a quick breath as his hands slid under her blouse and stroked her bare flesh. She twitched, and the stallion turned, leaving the dry sand and splashing into the ocean waves. Both Alannah and Xanthier gasped, surprised at the sudden drenching, but the horse surged forward until he was chest-deep and the salt water was washing against their thighs. Slowing to a halt, the stallion stood in the water, his head high.

Xanthier slid off, dragging Alannah with him. Around them spun the smells of wet horseflesh, seawater, kelp and human arousal. Xanthier held Alannah, knowing that she was not tall enough to stand. Rhythmic waves rolled around them, and they could both hear the crash as the waves hit the coast and broke into small, white row of rippling water, followed within seconds by another and another.

"I can feel you . . ." Xanthier whispered as he pulled her close. "I want you to feel me." He nudged her blouse up, then slowly drew it over her head. Unlike any other time he had undressed a woman, he could not see her breasts. All he could do was feel them. The difference was erotic, and he hardened with powerful intensity. He guided her to her back, allowing her to float with his support. Then, leaning forward, he licked her nipple.

Alannah almost fainted. She sank against his restraining arm, submissive to his exploration. Because he had trusted her, she trusted him. His sojourn into blind vulnerability made her believe in his ability to take her into sexual surrender. He had proven his power by becoming defenseless. Now she, too, could show her strength by trusting his knowledge of this newly discovered realm.

Underneath the sting of the salt was the sweetness of her skin. His tongue became his eyes as he felt the pebbled tip and the sprinkling of goose bumps that spread over her flesh. He tasted the warmth of her and felt her fullness. He brushed his cheek over her chest, discovering her perfect, rounded curves.

The stallion whinnied as the rest of the herd caught up with them and circled around the peninsula. Deserting the humans, the stallion spun and powered out of the ocean. Reaching the sand, he paused, shook his body free of water, and dashed toward the other horses. They whinnied, welcoming him back to the herd.

Xanthier lifted Alannah and carried her out of the water and up to the soft grass just above the beach. Taking slow, deliberate steps, he felt for driftwood or rocks, avoiding them when his foot came against one. As his feet sank into the cool grass, he stopped and dipped his head down to taste her again.

"I cannot let you stop me this time," he murmured. "I have wanted you since the moment I saw you and you immediately despised me. I have to have you."

"I did not despise you. You scared me."

"Do I scare you now?"

Alannah wrapped her arms around his neck and leaned against his chest. "Yes."

Xanthier kneeled, placing her gently upon the ground. He touched her face, running his fingers over her lips and then tracing the lines on her forehead. "I will show you that you do not need to fear me. Do you trust me?"

In answer, she touched his blindfold, then stroked down to his cheeks. Softly, as if she was not sure what to do, she pulled him toward her.

He complied, leaning over her until his lips hovered over hers. He brushed her mouth, reveling in feeling her lips for the first time without any visual distraction. He concentrated completely on touch and sensation. The world funneled down to one tiny island, and one pair of lovers discovering the joy of an exquisite kiss.

He sank atop her, indulging his senses. He could feel the press of her bare breasts against his wet shirt as her mouth opened under his tutelage and he explored the wet recesses with his tongue. She responded passionately, arching into him, giving herself over to him. Together they soared, tasting the pleasure of intimacy with their lips, until Xanthier bent down and transferred his attention to her neck.

There he suckled, resting his lips against her pulse, feeling the erratic increase in her heartbeat, the flush of her inner heat surging to the surface of her skin. He nibbled lower, returning to her breasts where he captured each nipple in turn and laved and worshipped it.

Alannah drifted in escalating ecstasy. She accepted his touch and reciprocated, stroking his chest, feeling the thrust of his muscles along her thighs as he moved against her. She let her hands rove over his body, exploring the strength of his buttocks and the might of his shoulders. She slid his shirt off, then gasped as his naked chest contacted hers. His flesh was cool, yet burned with heat, and frissons of energy swept through her. Without thinking, she lifted her hips at his urging and let him remove her skirt. For a moment he left her, then immediately returned to her, nesting his naked thighs between hers.

Their individual sensations merged and, instead of two separate people, they became one. Touching each other in the bliss of darkness, they responded to each other's quivers; they felt each other's shivers. Xanthier stroked down her sides, just as fascinated with the curve of her hip as he had been with the curve of her breast. He kissed her there, in the indentation, then licked her navel. She moaned, her body aching for him, eagerly reaching for him.

He throbbed, needing to join with her, and his body told her, asked her. She opened to him, spreading her legs in invitation. Resting his head against hers, he pushed against her, seeking the connection he knew could exist between them. As the head of his hardness nudged her, he could feel the sweet moisture that signaled her acceptance. She wanted him as much as he wanted her.

She cried out, lifting her knees. "Xanthier!" she moaned.

He slid one inch inside, then panted with the incredible sensations her core evoked. She was tight and firm, yet slippery and hot. Tiny ripples of pleasure already pulsed along her channel, and he could feel every movement. He pulled out, then captured her mouth in a searing kiss. As she arched to meet his mouth, he plunged inside, bursting through her maidenhead and sinking deep within her core.

Her knees fell apart as waves of delight washed

over her. The twinge of discomfort caused by his possession was swallowed in the wealth of joy that filled her, and she lifted her hips to meet his in an ancient ritual between man and woman. He slid in and out, relishing each movement, wanting to show her the beauty he could give her as he partook of his own pleasure.

His pace slowed as he held himself back, waiting for her to meet him, but she urged him faster, unwilling to delay the ecstasy waiting for them. She gripped his shoulders, digging her nails into his skin, holding on to him as if she feared she would fall deep into the earth without his ballast. She gasped, moaned, then screamed as ripple after ripple of emotion spiraled around her, then merged and burst, erupting into a climax that shattered her senses and left her floating in a cloud of happiness.

He felt her grip him, deep inside, pulsing and clinging. He shouted triumphantly, burying himself within her, exploding. He collapsed, unable to keep his weight off her, while waves of pure bliss washed over him and poured into his heart.

For long moments they lay still, each weak with satisfaction. Finally, after his heart settled back into an even beat, he rolled to his side and wrapped her in his arms. She lifted a languid hand and pulled the blindfold from his eyes, but he kept his eyes closed, enjoying the world of sensation they had entered together. He would never be the same. She had shown him another side of reality, a place where nothing mattered but touch and feel, smell and sound. He had no regrets. He did not want to go back to the world from whence he had come, where brothers fought for land and people battled for power. Here, in this woman's arms, he had found peace for the first time in his life.

Chapter 8

"Tell me about your family," Alannah said as she snuggled in Xanthier's arms several weeks later.

"Why? The past is behind me."

"I am curious. I have no past, no family other than Grandmother."

Xanthier nodded slowly. "I suppose it is understandable that you would be interested, but the truth is, there is little about my past that is commendable."

"Nonetheless, I want to know," Alannah insisted, unwilling to let Xanthier avoid her question.

Relenting, Xanthier pulled her closer and rubbed his cheek against hers. "I had very little love and support growing up. My father raised me after he sent my mother into exile on the day of my birth. My father was a very hard man—he did not allow any demonstration of weakness. From the moment I could walk, I was taught to fight."

"Why? What purpose did fighting serve?"

Xanthier laughed deprecatingly. "I cannot explain. You will not understand because our motives do not exist on this island. In Scotland, I fought for power and wealth. I fought for respect and infamy. I did not feel alive unless I was fighting someone or something. I had a companion . . . His name was Kurgan and he, too, fought in order to live. We spent months roaming the hills, searching for something to wreak havoc upon, anything to maim or destroy."

"What happened to him?"

"I don't know, nor do I care. We are not friends and, in fact, he has great animosity toward me. We were both in a battle a few years ago that went poorly. I pulled my men out of the village when I saw women and children hiding inside. Kurgan did not. He ordered the village burnt to the ground, and all the people perished."

"How terrible!"

"Aye. But do not think I was a hero that day. I left the battle because I did not think the reward worth the risk."

"I don't believe you. You did not want to hurt the helpless," Alannah insisted.

Xanthier leaned his forehead against Alannah's. "I wish what you say was the truth, but you do not know me. I have cared for no one but myself all my life. That day was no exception. As for Kurgan, we served each other's purposes, but once I received my sailing commission, we parted ways."

"What happened to your mother? I have always wondered what happened to mine."

"My mother . . . my mother raised my twin brother in a secluded retreat in the Highlands. She raised him to be everything opposite of me. My twin is kind, loving and considerate. I am not."

"Yes, you are," Alannah protested. "You are a fine man! I dislike it when you speak deprecatingly about yourself."

"Alannah, you only say that because you know me here, on this island. If you had met me before, you would have despised me. My twin despises me.

He tries to accept me, but he is repelled by my character."

"Surely that is not true."

"It is. I know it because we have a deep connection with each other. We can feel each other's emotions. I know what he thinks of me."

"That must be very troubling."

"It is the truth. Why be concerned about something that cannot be changed? He and I will never come to terms with each other. I have done many terrible things, and he will never forgive me."

"How did you take to the sea?" Alannah queried, trying to change the subject.

"I had to escape Scotland. I had no land to call home, no family to sit beside. Even marauding had ceased to interest me. I had nothing. King Malcolm sent for me and gave me my commission. He gave me a ship and the right to raid the seas in his name. It was a new frontier. The open ocean was like a mother, welcoming me to her hearth. In a few years, I had captured several ships and added them to my command. I now have five—although I don't know how many sank in the storm. Still, I have immense wealth and extreme power. I am respected and feared."

Alannah laughed. "So you try to tell me! To me, you are simply a sailor who was shipwrecked on my island."

"You mock me," he growled as he nibbled her neck.

Alannah shook her head and pressed a kiss on his cheek. "Did all this fighting make you happy?"

"Never. I was constantly restless as if I was looking for something more. I thought it was more wealth and more power. Now I realize that I was searching for you."

They sat in silence for a moment. "Your life must have been wildly exciting," Alannah finally murmured.

"Hummm," Xanthier replied as he continued a leisurely exploration of her throat. "I guess you could say that. I was always doing something, acting on something."

"It is not like that here," Alannah said softly. "Here, one day merges into the next. Except for the storms, life is relaxed and predictable."

Xanthier smiled. "Aye."

"Won't you yearn for that life again? Won't you want more excitement? What about the women? Weren't they beautiful? No one was blind or crippled, were they?"

Xanthier pushed Alannah to the ground and playfully nipped her shoulder. "You bring me all the excitement I need. I have lived that life and have rejected it. I want to be with you."

Alannah smiled in return, but a frisson of concern wedged into her heart. She wrapped her arms around his neck and squeezed, hoping that his words would stay true.

Tilting her head, Alannah listened for Xanthier's movements. The spring season was passing by, and in its wake was a vibrant summer that warmed the meadows and calmed the seas. Several new foals scampered through the tall grasses and a new batch of rabbits nibbled on the clover. The cove was warm enough for swimming, and the streamed of butterflies now hummed with dragonflies. As the weeks passed into months, she learned to judge Xanthier's moods by the timbre of his voice and the briskness of his actions. Her extrasensory perceptions were attuned to him.

He was complex. Some days he was mellow and easy to be around, but other days he was angry with pent-up frustration. Despite his avowals to the contrary, Alannah worried that he would eventually need more than a peaceful, idyllic existence. What he had revealed about his family made her aware of how his past haunted him. He had taken to the ocean to escape not only them, but also himself.

She knew that her island offered him a respite from the trials of his life. Grandmother had told her enough about the outside world for her to appreciate the differences he must be experiencing, and the few visits by Gondin had made her somewhat aware of the complexity of other people's lives. She wondered what life must be like in civilization. She wondered how people talked, how they interacted, how they spent their days. Before Xanthier, she had barely thought about the outside world. Now she thought about it constantly.

Today was one of the days when Xanthier's turbulent nature was boiling just underneath a veneer of calm. Alannah felt his body tighten with anxiety as he moved away from her in order to expend his energy in physical labor.

"We need wood," he said, his voice clipped and short.

Alannah murmured assent, knowing that a pile already existed behind the cottage. Concern made her silent, and she left him and went to find her white stallion.

"Are you ready, Claudius? I find I need your solace. Xanthier is unhappy, and I fear I am the cause of his dissatisfaction. He is a man of the world, whereas I am just a blind peasant girl on a deserted island."

The stallion snorted in response, his body tense with suppressed power. Although controlled in her presence, he was easily agitated and would explode if riled.

"Stay still," she scolded him when he danced away from her. "You are becoming too unruly!"

The stallion dropped his head and shifted back up to her, and Alannah was able to pull herself astride. The moment her light weight settled upon his back, he surged forward, hurtling toward a fallen tree that formed a natural obstacle. Alannah gripped his mane, and her legs wrapped around his middle. He gathered his muscles, and she balanced herself as they flew over the log and landed on the far side in perfect harmony.

Galloping madly, they swept down the narrow path past Xanthier. Alannah crouched low, flowing with the horse, urging him to run fast, faster, but her worries still chased them. They swept over the low meadow and onto the beach, the stallion's strides confident and proud. Alannah clung to his back, wrapped within the white mane that cascaded around her. She buried her face against the brisk wind and listened to the thud of the stallion's hooves pounding the wet sand.

Stride by stride she let the joy of her equine companion soothe her soul. Xanthier repeatedly told her that he was satisfied with his new life. He told her daily that he wanted to stay with her. She needed to believe him, despite her fears. His constant solicitation and kindness should be proof of his feelings for her.

Alannah breathed deeply, trying to let go of her anxieties. She still missed Grandmother, but Xanthier's passion filled the nights and her sadness was muted by the blossoming love she felt for him. She sat upright and opened her eyes wide, reveling in the sting of the wind. She urged the stallion further, and they raced until the stretch of beach ended and the sharp smell of leaves warned her that the forested hillside lay ahead.

She pulled the horse to a controlled canter, and then they loped up the hill. The stallion carefully avoided low-hanging branches, and Alannah pressed her body close to his. The cool shadows caused fine goose bumps along her arms until they broke out of the trees and onto the barren cliff that overlooked the ocean. The signal tower still stood where Xanthier had built it many months ago, but it was deserted and no fires burned there.

Xanthier did not use it anymore. That was proof enough. They were meant to live together on this island. She should stop doubting him. No ship would come and disturb them, and she and Xanthier would continue to share a blissful, isolated life.

Claudius stopped, his breathing heavy but steady, and pricked his ears forward as he scanned the endless blue. His tail swished. He felt his mistress relax, and peace enfolded them both. He trumpeted, a stallion announcing his territory, and twitched his tail again in response to Alannah's pleased chuckle.

She rubbed his sweaty neck, then leaned back, arching her torso until her head rested on Claudius's rump. She flung her arms wide, welcoming the heat of her horse beneath her and the sun above her. She rested with him, unaware that the stallion's big brown eyes gazed thoughtfully at a small speck on the horizon.

*   *   *

That evening Xanthier found the amulet bag. "What is this?" he asked. He had been fixing the shelves when the bag tumbled to the floor.

Alannah held her hand out to feel what he was talking about. As her fingers closed on the item, she grew withdrawn. "It is something that Grandmother found in my blankets when I was set adrift."

He opened the bag and sifted through the contents. "There is gold in here."

"Aye. That is what Grandmother said. Perhaps it was a bribe for someone to take me in if they found me."

"Alannah, these gold medallions are very valuable."

"How could that matter to me?"

Acknowledging her statement with a shrug, he continued to look in the bag. "This is an exquisite necklace. It looks like an heirloom. I cannot imagine someone sending this off as a bribe. It has a partial engraving on the back . . ." He stared at the engraving, his brow knotted with anxiety. The crest looked familiar, but it was so faint, he could not be certain.

Unaware of Xanthier's scrutiny, Alannah continued to talk. "When I was young, I would rub it, trying to memorize the lines and re-create them. In time, I rubbed the markings down. Grandmother said that the stones are the same color as my eyes. Is that true?"

The note of wistfulness in Alannah's voice made him pause, and he glanced up at her. Placing the remaining items, the key and the letter, down on the table, he came over and cupped her face in his hands, tilting her head up toward his. "The stones are called emeralds, and they are one of the jewels of the gods. They are a rich, deep green, the same color as the leaves and seaweed. It is the color of life. Your eyes are also green, but they glow with even more brilliance than these stones, for you, too, are the essence of life and beauty."

Alannah lifted her hands and touched his cheeks, feeling the scarred side contrast with the smooth one. It was like him. Part of him was rough and ugly, while another part was soft and kind.

"What color eyes do you have?" Alannah asked, trying to keep his attention.

"Gray."

"What color is that?"

"Do you remember the day of my shipwreck? The sky was full of clouds that were heavy with rain. The sun was hidden behind a heavy blanket just before the storm exploded. That is gray. The color of storm clouds."

"Storms are exciting . . . powerful. You are like a storm." She slid her hand down his chest suggestively.

"I will show you what power is," he growled as he lifted her into his arms, the amulet bag momentarily forgotten. He pushed her down onto the ground, and nudged her thighs apart with his knee. "I can teach you about strength and passion right on this cottage floor. I am the stormy sea and you are the innocent dolphin. I toss and turn, surging around you, pulsing through you . . ."

"What do I do?" Alannah asked breathlessly.

"You tell me. What do you feel? Play the dolphin for me."

"I feel playful . . . clever . . . sleek. I feel your fingers stroke my velvet skin as I swim through the current."

"I wrap around you, encasing you in my immense size. I cuddle and hold you, supporting your weight as you dance in the water."

"You frighten me but at the same time, you give me life. You are my element and without you I would die."

"Without you, I would be meaningless . . ." Xanthier bent his head and kissed her lips.

She opened her mouth, welcoming him as her arms reached around his shoulders and drew him closer. Energy sparked between them and they both gasped. "Take me . . ." she whispered, her head tossing. "Take me now before I perish with need!"

Growling in appreciation, Xanthier lowered his body over hers, but he did not enter her. He rocked against her, the head of his cock stroking her most sensitive flesh.

"Xanthier!" she cried. "Don't tease me! I want you now!" Still holding back, he rotated his hips, taunting her mercilessly. Frustrated beyond explanation, Alannah gripped his shoulders and dug her nails into his muscle. Then, without asking, she pushed him off and rolled on top. "I told you," she murmured at Xanthier's stunned reaction. "I told you not to tease me anymore."

Using her own strength, she held him down, then straddled his hips. "It is my turn." She leaned down and brushed her lips over his chest, stroking his muscles and sweeping gently over his nipples. "How does that feel?" she asked. "Or this?" She moved down his torso, alternately nibbling and licking until she reached his navel. Suddenly distracted, she dipped her tongue into the indentation, then blew softly.

Xanthier groaned and cupped her head in his large hands. "What are you doing?" he asked huskily.

"Mmmmm . . . tasting you. I want to taste more of you." She abandoned his abdomen and moved lower, exploring his body with her mouth.

"Stop," he demanded, but his voice trembled and Alannah smiled.

"Not quite yet," she whispered in reply, then swept her fingers down his strong thighs. "I want more of you." She followed her fingers with her mouth, kissing his sensitive skin at the crease of his groin. She sucked.

He groaned.

She shifted and breathed against his testicles, teasing him. Rubbing her cheek against his muscles, she licked them, then blew cool air against them.

He groaned again, this time gripping her head tightly. He tugged on her, trying to pull her away, but she resisted. "You don't need to . . ."

"Yes, I do. I want to experience every part of you. I want you in my mouth."

"Yes!" he cried as she swept her tongue up his shaft, then swirled around the tip in a tantalizing taunt. He delved his hands deep into her hair, holding her in place, forgetting his gentlemanly restraint of moments ago.

She licked him in quick darts, starting at the base and progressing upwards. His member pulsed and throbbed under her ministrations. It swelled and Alannah switched her rapid licks to long, smooth strokes. When she swirled her tongue once again around the sensitive peak, he arched his hips upwards and pulled her mouth down.

Alannah bent her neck and opened her mouth, welcoming his oral penetration. She wrapped her lips around him and sucked.

Xanthier cried out, the sensations overwhelmingly powerful, beyond sensual. He gripped her head and pulled her down, forcing her to take more of him. He groaned at her acceptance, feeling her tongue rippling against him even with her mouth closed over him. It was tight, warm, intense . . . he had never felt anything so exquisite. He rocked against her, moving her head up and down in a perfect rhythm.

Alannah felt supremely powerful as she enclosed him in her mouth and pleasured him. She felt him surrender to her even as he controlled her movements. Waves of delight washed over her as he filled her. She wanted to please him and in doing so, she was pleased.

He began to shake, his entire body tensing. His motions grew erratic, and Alannah was required to maintain the rhythm, sliding her mouth up and down his shaft as his fingers dug deep into her hair. He groaned again; then suddenly he was quiet except for his panting breaths. He jerked, his body spasming, and he abruptly tried to lift her away from him so that he would not ejaculate in her mouth.

Alannah fought his motion, sucking harder and wrapping her fingers around the base. She squeezed him softly, then stroked as she licked him, and suddenly he could not resist. He exploded with a shout, his tumescence bulging and pulsing, pouring his seed as Alannah drank of his essence.

Xanthier's torso lifted off the ground as he came, and every muscle in his body rippled with tension. Then, as the waves of climax swept through him, he sank back, completely relaxed.

Alannah slowly lifted her head. Her brilliant eyes were wide open, and her pupils were dilated with pleasure. She stared through him, focusing her extra senses on every nuance of his ecstasy. She felt his heat, his fine trembling, his blood pumping. She heard his rapid breathing and heart beating. She felt his utter contentment. Smiling, she curled up on his chest and slept.

Xanthier stared up at the roof, his body still singing with sensation. A scrap of paper caught his eye and he remembered the amulet bag and its contents. Carefully reaching out so as not to disturb the slumbering Alannah, he unfolded the letter.

He scanned it briefly, then read it more carefully. His relaxed expression transformed into one of fury. *No!* he cried silently. It could not be! If the truth revealed in the letter were ever discovered, it would tear them asunder.

He disentangled himself from her sweet form and carried the letter to the fireplace. He stared at the flames, debating. Then, with an oath, he flung the paper toward the fire and stalked out of the cottage.

Behind him, the letter fluttered to the ground. A greedy flame reached out and touched the letter, caressed it, singed it, but then drew back, leaving the incriminating proof intact.

PART II

The Kingdom of Scotland

Chapter 9

When dawn broke, sending streaks of pink and orange across the horizon, a ship dropped anchor just offshore of the island. The captain stared at the coastline, frowning in concentration.

The first mate joined him. "It appears no different than the other islands. He is not here."

"Someone built the signal tower."

"That could have been years ago. If the commodore were here, he would have kept the fires lit."

"Nevertheless, we will explore the island just as we have all the others. He is a survivor, and we have an obligation to find him. Believe me, if we do not, and he *is* alive, he will hunt us down and make us pay. Have no doubt, the commodore is not a man to be trifled with. Let the other ships give up. We will not."

"Aye, Captain Robbins," the first mate replied. Turning to the crew, he shouted, "Lower the boats!"

As the rowboats were dropped into the water and the men piled in, Captain Robbins continued to scan the island. Making a sudden decision, he opted to join the crew, leaving his first mate to watch the ship.

A ring of coral protected the island, and a peninsula jutted into the sea, forming one arm of a beautiful cove. He set the men rowing into the sheltered area. A burst of sound drew his attention, and he saw a herd of wild horses racing across a high meadow. Stunned, he watched the creatures until they circled and came to a stop. A towering white stallion led them, his coat gleaming in the fading sunrise.

"I have never seen such a sight," breathed one of the men. "Fancy seeing a bunch of horses on a deserted isle!"

"They'd be worth a fortune," stated another. "Look at them! Look at the stallion!"

Captain Robbins nodded, equally impressed, but he was uneasy about their presence. Such tall, lithe horses were not the wild ponies of Scotland. These looked like the highly bred beasts of a lord's stable. He narrowed his eyes and looked around again, seeking evidence of human habitation.

"We will search the tower first," he said. "Leave two men to guard the boats."

The men turned to him in puzzlement. "Why should we guard the boats? No one is here."

Captain Robbins turned on his men with a frown. "I told you to leave two men to guard the boats. I don't trust this place."

The boats were pulled ashore, and two men stood next to them, their swords drawn, while the rest of the crew crossed the rocky prominence to explore the signal tower. Robbins reached it first, noting the strength of the rope that lashed the various logs together.

"The rope is not old. Someone built this tower a short time ago. The commodore was here." He climbed inside. The fire pit was cold, but remnants of coals still littered the floor. A horrible suspicion

entered his mind, and Robbins feared that something had happened to the commodore after he had
landed on the island. "We will spread out and
search."

Xanthier walked through the woods, his blindfold securely fastened around his head. A bird
swooped down to his right, and he ducked, barely
avoiding the creature. "That bird!" he exclaimed.

Alannah laughed. "It seems to favor you. How
did you know it was diving today? It usually gets
a peck on your head before you notice him."

"I am becoming more attuned," Xanthier grumbled. He moved carefully, taking care not to trip
over fallen branches or stumble into rodent bur-
rows.

"You are doing marvelously," Alannah assured
him. "But I am not sure why you persist in practic-
ing with the blindfold."

"I want to know your world. If I can function
without sight, I can understand you better."

"You understand me perfectly! You are the one
who is incomprehensible!"

Xanthier shook his head and unerringly reached
out and pulled Alannah close, enfolding her in an
embrace. "Alannah, you are a fascinating person.
You intrigue me like no other. I know you have
feelings for me, but sometimes I worry that you are
holding back. That scares me."

Alannah shook her head and pulled away. "You
have nothing to be afraid of." She strode gracefully
through the forest. "Except perhaps that grumpy
bird."

Xanthier grabbed her hand and pulled her back.
"Alannah, I don't think you understand what I am
saying. I want to know everything about you. I

want to understand you. I want to be one with you."

"And you feel that you can do that when you close your eyes?" Alannah questioned.

"Yes! When I separate myself from the visual world, I become a new person. I feel like I have entered a new existence that you created just for us."

Alannah flushed, then wrapped her arms around his neck. "You and I have both created this paradise we share. We are both sides of the world merged together."

"Yes. You are everything to me." He bent his head, finding her lips easily. "My beautiful Alannah," he whispered between kisses, "let me show you what I can do blindfolded . . . you will see that I can be quite skilled in the darkness . . ."

They sank onto the forest floor, wrapped in each other's arms, their lips clinging.

"Your hands do not need to see . . ." Alannah murmured.

"I want you, Alannah. I want you so much."

"Mmmmm . . . I want you, too," she replied as she arched her back, begging for his attention. Without hesitation, he bent his head, brushing his lips over her thrusting nipples, wanting her as much as she wanted him.

Suddenly, Xanthier froze. His head snapped up, and he listened intently.

"Xanthier," Alannah whispered. "Touch me again . . ."

"Shush." He pulled his blindfold off and peered around.

"What? It is only the horses. Come back . . ."

"No. Listen."

Alannah sighed, then propped herself up on one

elbow. She frowned, then scrambled to her knees. "I hear it," she said quietly. "It sounds like cloth flapping in the breeze. You must be getting very good with the blindfold if you could hear that before me."

Xanthier kissed her on the head as he rose and pulled her up beside him. "Stay behind me." Concern filled him as the words in Alannah's letter raced through his mind. He glanced at her, a frown creasing his brow.

"Why?" She leaned over and picked up the staff Xanthier had carved for her. It fit snugly in her hand and she felt comfortable with it in her possession.

"I am sworn to protect you. Until we know who has invaded our isle, I prefer to keep you safe."

"It comes from the beach."

"Yes, it is the sound of sails. A ship's sails. Every day and every night for many years I have lived with that sound."

Alannah tilted her head, hearing the nervousness in Xanthier's voice. She shivered with anxiety, then teased herself for her silly fears. *It is only a ship,* she mused. *Nothing is going to change. Xanthier wants to stay here with me.*

They crept through the trees, retracing their earlier footsteps. As they approached the coast, the fluttering sails became louder, and several human voices reached their ears. Alannah bit her lip, aware that with every step they took toward the ocean, Xanthier became more and more excited.

A new sound reached them, like two hard objects scraping against each other, and the result was a high-pitched whine that made Alannah wince.

"Swords," Xanthier whispered. He breathed harder, memories coming back to him. Flashes of his past reminded him of battles, of one-on-one combat when the feel of a sword in his hand was as natural as the feel of blood on his palm.

They finally reached the beach and Xanthier touched Alannah's hand. He kissed it softly. "If it is them . . ." he started.

"Yes?" she asked.

"If it is them, don't worry. I will not break my promise to you."

A chill swept through Alannah. She reached out to stop him, wanting to ask him what he meant, but he moved away and stepped out into the open. Instantly, the scraping sound ceased. Tension filled the air. She swallowed and gripped her stick firmly. Who was it? Who had made that sound and now was silent?

The man sharpening his sword froze as Xanthier and Alannah walked out of the forest. Their appearance was so unexpected, so unprecedented, that he held his breath in stunned amazement.

The sailor next to him was equally startled, and they looked at each other, then back at the pair.

"Commodore?" one asked slowly. "Is that you? What happened to your face? So many scars . . ."

Xanthier glared at the two men, his rage erupting. "Is that your comment upon seeing your commodore after months lost at sea? What took you so long to get there?"

"Commodore!" the other sailor gasped. "You are alive! We found you! Captain Robbins said you would survive. We found one other from your ill-fated ship, but he died several days after we rescued him."

"Well, I have no intention of dying."

"No, sir. Of course not." The sailor stared at Xanthier's healed wounds in fascination, but he forbore to comment on them again. He swung his gaze to Alannah.

"We can see that you had entertainment while stranded." The sailor laughed. "What a fancy piece of flesh!"

Xanthier leaped forward, swiping the sword from the unsuspecting sailor and pressing it to his throat. "You go too far! How dare you speak to the commodore's woman as if she were a harlot!"

"I had no idea she was yours, Commodore. I would never disrespect her if I knew!" He swallowed nervously.

"You should not speak to any woman like that!"

The sailor looked at Xanthier in confusion. "But you taught us the law of the sea, Commodore. Whatever we find, we take. I thought she was an island girl you used for temporary pleasure."

Xanthier cringed and lowered the sword in disgust. "What is your name?"

"Douglas, sir."

"You are demoted, Douglas. From now on, you will scrub the decks, eat last and be thankful I do not kill you outright."

"Aye, sir!" Douglas cried, his gaze flicking to Alannah with intense dislike.

"You," Xanthier said as he pointed to the other sailor with his sword. "What is your name?"

The sailor averted his gaze. "Tanner, sir."

"Do you share your friend's assumptions?"

"No, sir."

"Good. Signal the captain."

Chapter 10

Alannah turned to him, trying to calm her heart and steady her breathing. "You threatened to kill him," she whispered.

"Are you not listening? That man insulted you."

"I never heard your voice so angry."

"He needed to be punished."

Alannah spun on her heel and left the beach, forcing Xanthier to follow her. "It was ugly and unnecessary."

"Alannah! I was protecting you!"

"I don't need that kind of protection!" she cried as she broke into a run.

"You should be grateful!"

"Why? Why should I be grateful?" she asked as she paused.

"Isn't it obvious?"

She turned around. "No," she said slowly. "Why should I be grateful?"

"Any woman would be pleased to have a protector."

She shook her head, her brows drawn together in confusion and anger. "Is that what you think you are to me? A protector?"

"Of course! I promised Grandmother that I

would be available for you and I have proved my faithfulness."

"I thought you felt more for me than simply duty."

"What are you talking about, Alannah? There is no greater emotion than the protective feeling of a man for a woman. Are you daft? Don't you understand?"

"All I understand is that you see me as a duty you must fulfill, and I want no part of it. I don't need anyone's assistance!"

"Yes, you do! How could you say you do not? You are blind, or have you forgotten that fact?"

"Leave!" she screamed in fury. "Leave my island! I don't want you and I don't need you!"

"Alannah? What has gotten into you?"

"I am fully capable of surviving alone, and even if I am not, I would rather die than be a recipient of your protection."

"You need me!" Xanthier shouted back. "Even more now than ever! If you only knew . . ."

"Really? You think I cannot survive? You think I am helpless?"

"You are twisting my words. I only meant to say that you should be pleased to accept my protection."

"Have you learned nothing on this island? Have you learned nothing of me?"

"I know more of reality than you do," Xanthier replied, infuriated. "You live in a dream world. I have lived where men are warriors and women are vassals. Those sailors do not understand your ways, but they understand mine. I showed them how to behave and they responded to my threats. In the real world, power is based on strength, wealth and success. We fight in contests and we compete in wars. It is a matter of who is the strongest. No one gives quarter, not for anything. I have survived because I understand those rules, and I play by them well."

Alannah sank to the forest floor, tears filling her eyes. "Answer this," she murmured, her voice so soft he was obliged to step closer. "Do you think I need you?"

"Yes, I do."

"Why?"

Xanthier was silent.

Alannah nodded. "You see, that is why I am upset. You are set on protecting me, but you do not understand why. If I needed something from you, it would only be your love."

Flinging his hands up, he walked away.

Captain Robbins sat across from Xanthier and Alannah in the cottage. He drank from the seashell, and scooped some fish into his mouth. The fish was wrapped in fragrant leaves and flavored with unusual spices.

"This is delicious," he commented.

"Thank you," Alannah answered as she, too, took a bite of fish.

"How do you do it? Cook, I mean?"

"What do you mean?" Alannah asked.

"How do you cook without seeing the fire?"

Alannah flushed and averted her face. "Practice, I suppose," she mumbled.

"Enough," Xanthier commanded. "There is no need to comment on her impairment."

"I was complimenting her, Commodore."

"She doesn't need that either," Xanthier growled.

Alannah lifted her face, her sea green eyes snapping in anger. "I have learned how to do a great many things, Captain, even with my 'impairment.' "

"Do you ride the horses?"

"Yes."

"They are incredible beasts, Mistress Alannah. They look swifter than any I have ever seen."

She smiled. "Indeed, they run faster than a diving seagull."

"They would win a fortune racing."

"Racing?" Alannah asked.

Xanthier rose and stirred the fire. "The captain speaks of horse racing. Me, I prefer the great ship races across the ocean straits."

Captain Robbins nodded. "Absolutely fantastic. When the ships sail, the ocean is like a seething stretch of canvas and wood. Incredible."

"But what about the horses? How and why do they race?" Alannah asked.

Xanthier turned and stared at her. "They race for money and fame. A person is nothing without one or the other."

Alannah bit her lip and rose hurriedly. "Are you saying I am worth nothing because I have neither?"

"Excuse me," Captain Robbins interrupted. "I fear I have entered a conversation for which I do not have all the information. I will return to the ship—"

"Don't bother," Alannah broke in. "I was just leaving." She snatched her staff and strode out the door, her back stiff and unyielding.

Xanthier glared after her, his teeth clenched so tight, his scars stood out as white streaks against his tanned face.

"I did not mean to cause trouble," said Captain Robbins.

"There is no cause for apologies. Alannah is the one causing trouble," Xanthier said as he nodded at the captain. "Feel free to finish your meal. I am concerned about her, and your arrival has only complicated matters. There are things I have recently learned that make me realize that retreating in isolation on this island is not possible. I must bring her to Scotland."

"With all due respect, Commodore, the woman is blind. She would be ostracized, stoned or worse. Perhaps it is best that you leave her here and ignore whatever information you came across."

Xanthier stared around the room, looking at the sea treasures that decorated the walls. Beautiful seashells, skillfully woven hangings, bundles of herbs . . . the amulet bag. The cottage was a haven. He dropped his head in his hands. "I wish I could. Perhaps I will be able to remedy the situation, but"—he lifted his head—"most likely it is impossible."

"I have never seen you admit defeat before a battle," Robbins replied.

"You are right. I will not admit defeat. I surrendered my home, my land and my title. I gave away my daughter and my pride. For the first time I have found something I want, and I will not stop until I have taken full possession of it."

Captain Robbins stood at attention. "With your permission, I will return to the ship. Do you have instructions for me?"

"Ready the ship for a return trip to Scotland. I will speak to the king. He commissioned my original ship, and I must bring him the treasures I collected in his name."

"And then?"

"Then we will distribute the goods, sell the ships and divide the profits among the men."

"That is all? What about Mistress Alannah?"

"I will tell her that she must come with me for a short voyage."

"Does she know about the situation you discovered?"

"No. And I have no intention of telling her."

Xanthier stalked through the forest, searching for Alannah. Finally locating her in the meadow near the horses, he walked up behind her and put his arms around her waist.

"Alannah, there is no point in arguing. Whatever I have done, I apologize. My only goal is to make you happy."

"I do not believe you. You are holding something back from me. I can sense it. You think that you can be secretive, but you have forgotten that I perceive things that no one else can see. What are you hiding?"

Xanthier looked away. "Nothing," he mumbled. "You are nervous over nothing. In fact, I came here to resolve our conflict and ask you to come with me on a brief trip to Scotland."

"Scotland? Why?"

"For many reasons, the foremost being that I do not want to leave you here alone."

"Do you really think I am helpless?" Alannah asked softly.

"No. I think you are brave and spirited. And beautiful."

"But you think I cannot survive on my own because of my blindness."

"Alannah," he replied in exasperation, "it is not

only your lack of sight that makes you vulnerable. You are a woman, you are young, you are lacking in knowledge. Why do you fight the realities? Why not accept that we can create a partnership together?"

"A partnership requires two people with strengths that complement each other. Grandmother and I were partners."

"We can be partners, too. We complement each other in very special ways." He ground his hips against her buttocks.

Alannah pulled away. "What strengths do you see in me?"

"You are gorgeous, uninhibited, fascinating . . . you are what I need."

Frowning in frustration, Alannah turned to face him. *"What strengths?"* she insisted.

"You don't need strengths. I will be your strength and you will be my peace. That is our partnership."

"I do not see how that is equal."

"Of course it is not equal. Where do you get these odd notions? If you had been raised in a regular household, you would not speak like this. Men and women are not equal. You are supposed to love and honor me and I am supposed to protect and support you."

Alannah turned her head to where the horses were grazing. "They do not relate to each other like that. The stallion is certainly the strongest, but he offers more than his power to the herd. He offers his wisdom, his experience and his cooperation. The lead mare is not simply a broodmare. She is a clever, sure-footed and intelligent member of their family. She finds the food; he figures out how to get to it. He feels the weather and she determines where to shelter from it. They are equal partners."

"Surely you are not equating us with the beasts?"

"Why not? They are the creatures I understand."

"Exactly! You do not understand people! This is the way of the world. Men are men and women are women. Accept it!"

"I do not have to accept anything!" she shouted. "You are suddenly changing everything between us. What happened to the respect you gave me yesterday? What happened to the sharing and giving that we created between us?"

"I have changed nothing!" he yelled back. "You are the one who is being stubborn and unreasonable. I made a vow to your grandmother to protect you for eternity, and that is what I will do. If you find that repulsive, I have no other answers! I can be stubborn, too!"

"Ohh!" Alannah glared through him, her eyes flashing with emerald fire. "Go away! I suspected you would leave and now I am proved correct. That is what you are afraid to say, isn't it? You want to go back to your world and fight and pillage and bed beautiful women who can gaze into your eyes with perfect vision! What we had between us meant nothing to you."

"How can you say that?" he asked, his voice cracking with a mixture of hurt and anger. "I want you. I want this world. I want your love. I intend to spend the rest of my days in your arms. But we have to make a trip to Scotland. I have responsibilities there that I must carry out."

Alannah whirled around, turning her back to him. "No. Absolutely not."

Xanthier frowned. "You must. There is no other way."

"I will not leave my island!" she shouted.

"Earlier you told me to leave immediately. Don't make this difficult."

"Please. I know something is happening. I can sense it. Don't ask me to go."

"You are coming with me regardless," he stated harshly. "I would rather you went willingly, but you will go either way."

"You wouldn't dare! I would hate you!"

"It will only be for a fortnight. We will be back before the next flowers bloom. The storms of spring are over and the summer will be uneventful. You speak about your ability to survive so often. Now is your chance to prove it in a foreign country." Frustrated with her stubbornness, Xanthier grabbed her shoulders and spun her back around. He pulled her flush against him. "We will go there and be back to paradise before you realize it. Please understand that I cannot leave you alone on this island. Trust me, I have my reasons." He held up his hand as Alannah attempted to interrupt. "I know you have lived here for sixteen years, but that was before you met me and I found you. I cannot risk losing you to some misfortune. Anything could happen to you while I am gone. You could fall from your stallion and plummet down the cliff. You are mine, and I will not take any chances!"

"You are making a terrible mistake! You say you will not take chances, but you are willing to give up my love for this ridiculous show of protection that I do not need or want."

"The discussion is over. You will come."

"I will not!"

* * *

Alannah screamed, flailing her hands against Xanthier's immense chest. "Leave me alone! Leave me be! I hate you!" Then, as Xanthier lifted her and flung her over his shoulder, she started to sob. "How can you do this to me? I thought you cared for me . . ." Her brilliant green eyes shimmered with tears as they cascaded down her cheeks. All night she had pleaded with him, and now her voice was cracking.

"I have no choice," he snapped as he walked away from the cottage. Moving as briskly as he could without actually running, he headed down the path toward the beach. As he passed the bush he had tripped over when she had blindfolded him, he stumbled. Waves of pain filled his heart, but he ruthlessly crushed the feelings as he tightened his hold on his charge.

"You have no idea how harsh the world can be. I do not want you exposed to it."

"How can you say that?" she shouted at him "You are the one who is showing me such harshness. You are the one causing me distress!"

She pummeled her fists against his back. A sharp whinny startled her. "What is happening to Claudius?" she cried. "Is he hurt?"

"No. I am having him loaded onto the ship. I thought you might want him near." They reached the coastline and Xanthier dropped Alannah into a boat, then quickly followed her before she could scramble out. "Think before you try to escape me," he growled. "With Claudius aboard my ship, you would be on the island without your best friend."

"Why are you doing this to me? Why?"

Xanthier signaled his sailors to push off, and the rowboat was launched. Within moments, they had pulled out past the coral reef and bumped against the ship's hull.

Gripping Alannah's squirming body in his strong arms, Xanthier scrambled up the rope ladder and attained the deck. Glaring at any sailor who looked at his bundle askance, he strode rapidly to his cabin and dumped her on his bed.

Alannah leapt up and ran for the door.

"Stop!" he commanded. "What do you think you can achieve?" He jumped in front of her, forcing her to collide against his chest. "If you press me, I will lash you to the bed frame. Now, promise me that you will stay put."

In response, Alannah jerked out of his hold and reached blindly for the door.

"You fool!" Xanthier growled. He caught her as she stumbled. Swearing, he dragged her back to the bed and pulled a length of rope from the canopy. He wrapped it around her wrist and then tied her to the solid bed frame. As he finished tying the knot, he looked down at Alannah's frightened face. "Alannah," he said softly. "I do not want to harm you. I want to take care of you."

"I will never forgive you," she answered dully, then dropped her head down and cried as she heard him quietly exit the cabin and shut the door behind him.

Xanthier stared at the island as the anchor was lifted. Seagulls swooped on the air currents, reminding him of the beautiful butterflies—both real and metaphorical—he was leaving behind. Betraying her trust and abandoning the mystical Isle of Wild Horses was harder than anything he had ever done—harder even than relinquishing his homeland, harder than severing all ties to his family. She had brought more to him than he had ever thought possible, but he had sworn to protect her, and he would do so, no matter what. Within one fortnight they would be back, and they would live in complete happiness.

Captain Robbins followed Xanthier's gaze. "Are you sure it is appropriate to force her to come?"

"I have no choice. I want to protect her. She is sometimes too reckless. It wouldn't be right to leave her here all alone. I am also concerned about the island. Now that other people know about it, it is only a matter of time before someone tries to claim it as their own property. While I am in Scotland, I must lay claim to it for her. Until then, swear the men to silence. If anyone speaks of the isle—or of her—they will feel my wrath. When I return with her, I want no further interruptions from visitors."

"Commodore, the horses are worth a fortune, and everyone knows that you kidnapped her. We cannot trust the men to keep silent. It is an impossible request. They will spread tales of the island and relish the story of her reluctance. The island and the girl are unclaimed. Someone will try to take either or both."

"I know that!" Xanthier grumbled. "Why do you think I am doing this?" He paced around the deck, his agitation inflaming the scars that marred one side of his face. Whereas he had been a formidable man before the shipwreck, now he was visually frightening. His scars made him look dangerous, and the crew was more leery of him than ever.

"Where are the other ships? Were any others shipwrecked in the storm?"

"Only yours perished. The other ships are scheduled to dock in Scotland this month to reconvene. We separated to search for you with more efficiency."

Xanthier ached for Alannah already. He could not bear to think of how angry she was, and he dreaded to think how long she would maintain her fury. He unhappily contemplated the next two weeks, and prayed that his business would be quick and successful. He wanted to live on her enchanted island, without the past finding and destroying them. He had matters to resolve, but her anger was torturing him, and he closed his eyes against the agony. No matter how much she pleaded, no matter what she said, he was convinced that taking her to Scotland was the only thing he could do.

Only two weeks, he repeated silently. By the rise of the next full moon, they would return, unfettered. He gazed out across the sea and watched a lone albatross fly over his bow.

She sat on the bed, her dark red hair a furious mess around her pinched face.

"I see that you have not accepted your situation," Xanthier commented.

"I despise you. You think that you can haul me over the ocean upon a whim as if my wants are of no importance. You told me how you used to be a thoughtless, mean-hearted warrior and I contradicted you, time and again. I now see that you were right. You are high-handed, uncompromising and completely monstrous. I will never forgive you. And to think that I thought I loved you."

Xanthier clenched his teeth. "I am doing what I have to do in order to help you. If you would simply trust me—"

"I will never trust anything you say again. Bring me to Claudius."

"I cannot. I do not want you running around the ship. You could trip and fall overboard."

Alannah narrowed her eyes angrily and sprang upright. She took a quick step forward before her bound wrist pulled her to a stop. "Give me my staff and let me free!"

"Promise me that you will not do anything foolish. We are in the open ocean and the sails are full. We are traveling very quickly and the sea is not smooth."

"I will promise you nothing!"

"You must cease this stubborn resistance!" he yelled in exasperation as he paced up to her and attempted to gather her in his arms.

"Don't touch me!" she screamed in response.

He shook her. "Never shout at me. Never refuse me. I will not allow it."

"Then it is time you learned new ways of handling disappointment, for I will resist you with every fiber of my body."

Infuriated, he shoved her against the bed frame and ground his lips against hers. She twisted out of his grasp, kicking him. "Stop!" she shouted. "I never want to feel your mouth again."

"You have no choice," he snarled as he captured her again and held her face still. He kissed her roughly, trying to dominate her rebellious spirit.

She bit his lip, drawing blood. As he jerked back she shoved him. "Would you rape me?" she cried. "Would you do what you have done to others simply because you have the greater strength? Are you as much a monster as your scarred face suggests?"

Stepping back as if burnt, Xanthier stared down at her in shock. "We are lovers. It is not rape between us."

"It is now. Leave me be and never touch me again."

Frustrated, his shaft throbbing with need and his

heart breaking, he yanked at her bonds and freed her wrist. "Then go. Fend for yourself. Walk about the ship and keep your balance as the waves toss us to and fro. See your beloved horse and make friends with the sailors. I have done what I must, and you are ungrateful. You say that you will not forgive me. I say that I will not forgive your lack of trust. Good day."

Chapter 11

Alannah stumbled across the deck, her land legs wobbling precariously as she attempted to traverse the slanted boards. She held her staff out in front of her with one hand, and used the other to grasp nearby objects for balance. She was flung sideways and gasped in fear. She blinked rapidly, trying to maintain her equilibrium. Steadying her steps, she took a deep breath. She would achieve nothing by tottering around. She must concentrate on using her abilities.

She felt the wind, absorbing its energy. She felt the deck rock back and forth as it cradled the ship. Just as when she navigated the island, she must learn to become one with her environment here at sea. She gradually became used to the waves and could hear the rippling water before it crashed against the wooden hull or swept downward, pulling the ship into a trough.

Alannah understood the power of the water, for she had always lived beside it. There was something incredibly erotic about floating atop the sea, as if the ship was somehow conquering the ocean by virtue of skill and stealth. Alannah reached the railing and bent her head into the wind. It skated across her cheeks, enveloping her in a seductive caress.

Soon she would arrive in Scotland. Her blindness would hinder her, challenge her. She was being forced to travel to a land that had rejected her. Frissons of fear rippled up and down her spine. What would await her in this far-off country? She did not know what she would do once she reached the shore, but she was determined to face each trial with dignity and pride.

Captain Robbins walked up to her and smiled sadly at her fierce expression. "Alannah, you look so ferocious. Do you intend to battle the sea serpents?"

"I am only thinking of the days ahead. I know that they will be difficult. I am afraid of leaving the island."

"You are an unusual woman, and I see strength in you. I know you will do well. Have no fear."

"Never," she whispered. "I will never show fear."

"Showing fear is not wrong, only succumbing to it is. Perhaps you should share your anxieties with the commodore. He would know better how to comfort you."

"I do not want his comfort. I would rather be alone." Perhaps it would have been better if she had never known the beauty of Xanthier's touch or the power of his companionship. But it was useless to wish that she did not know what she knew. She knew the joy of waking up in his arms and feeling his gaze caress her skin. She had already experienced the rapture of his nearness when the breeze whispered through the trees or the sun drenched the grassy meadows. She had loved him, and it was impossible to forget what that had felt like. Alannah turned back into the wind, for despite her brave words she was still afraid.

"I would ask something of you," she said.

"You have only to say the words," Captain Robbins replied seriously.

"I would like to learn about Scotland. The intricacies of the dinner table, the beauty of the dance, the subtlety of conversation . . . I know there are many things I need to know."

"Of course, Alannah. I would be honored to show you."

"And I have one other request. I wonder if you could help me find out something about my family."

"Your family? I thought you were orphaned on the island."

"I was, but when I was set adrift, I had an amulet bag with several items. Only a day before you arrived we were looking at it. When I put away the items, I placed the bag around my neck and it still rests underneath my dress."

"Are you sure you want to seek your family out? Sometimes skeletons should not be disturbed."

"I have thought about it for a long time. I have wondered about them and why they cast me away. If I am to be forced to travel to Scotland, it may be fate. I feel compelled to find out what I can."

"I will, of course, help you any way I'm able."

"Thank you." As Captain Robbins walked away, Alannah shivered. How was she to find her family? What would they say once she faced them? Grandmother had believed that they had abandoned her because of her blindness. She had warned Alannah that people were frightened of differences and would shun her presence. Most likely her family would not be happy to see her, but as she felt the wind rush through her hair, she pressed her lips together and lifted her chin. It was time to face the unknown.

Xanthier found her leaning against Claudius's stall. He approached slowly, not sure of his reception. Without turning, Alannah tensed. "What do you want?"

His anger flaring at her cold tone, he spoke to her shortly. "We will be sailing for the better part of a week. I have invited Captain Robbins to dine with us. Dinner will be served shortly. I will be sleeping in the crew's quarters, as I have no wish to be around you while you act so childishly."

"I hardly think my anger is childish. If you will recall, you are the one who acted the tyrant and gave me no options. I am pleased that you have found other sleeping quarters. Your nearness would only serve to make my night sleepless. I want nothing to do with you."

Growling under his breath at her obstinacy, he stalked away, and despite her strong words, Alannah almost reached out to draw him back.

That evening Captain Robbins nodded appreciatively. "You learn very quickly, Alannah."

"My blindness fostered a very good memory. Grandmother used to remark on it."

"After dinner, shall I show you some dance steps?" Captain Robbins asked. "With your permission, Commodore."

Xanthier nodded curtly, displeased that Alannah had not spoken to him once all evening. She seemed so comfortable talking with Robbins. He narrowed his eyes in jealousy.

Alannah smiled in Captain Robbins's direction.

"Yes, I would love to dance. Grandmother actually taught me many steps."

"I did not know that you liked dancing," Xanthier interjected.

Ignoring him, she continued talking to Captain Robbins. "Pray, tell me more about the societal customs and gatherings."

"There is much food and wonderful entertainment. Sometimes there are storytellers or acrobatic acts. In fact, the biggest event of the year is coming up within the fortnight. It is the annual festival of the king."

"What happens then?"

"Contests, jousts, games, races, dances—"

"Races? What kind of races?"

"Horse races," Robbins clarified.

"You told me that my stallion could race."

"Yes, he is of superior speed and strength, but he could not enter the contest."

"Why?"

"He is untamed. No one could ride him."

Alannah frowned. "I can ride him."

Captain Robbins shook his head and laughed. "You could not ride him in the race. You are female. But come, come and dance with me."

Xanthier glowered at them but did not interfere. If dancing made Alannah happy and distracted her from her situation, he was willing to allow it.

After an hour, however, he was feeling less considerate. Drinking cup after cup of ale had made him slightly drunk, and watching her supple body sway to imagined music had made him more than aroused. Finally he rose and braced his hands against the table. Looking at Captain Robbins over Alannah's head, he jerked his chin.

Robbins nodded silently, and when the steps of

the dance drew them apart, he moved aside. Xanthier stepped into his place.

Alannah twirled in place, her lips curved with pleasure. She stepped forward, then back, then dipped in a curtsy. "Robbins," she chided, "I can tell you are not dancing. Don't stop yet. I want to finish this one . . ." She reached out, expecting Robbins's hand to join hers and guide her in a promenade.

Xanthier gripped her hand instead.

She tried to draw back, his touch making her instantly wary. "Where did Robbins go?" she asked.

"It doesn't matter." He pulled her forward, continuing the intricate steps. Alannah stumbled, her pulse fluttering and making her dizzy. "Don't be a coward, Alannah. Can you not dance with me yet maintain the distance you profess to want?"

"Of course," she replied, but inwardly she quailed.

Xanthier stepped close to her, brushing his body against hers. She moved away but he caught her waist and spun her around. "Your body betrays you, Alannah. I can feel your arousal."

"You are imagining something that is not there."

"No. I know you better than that. I feel the heat of your body and see the flush against your skin. You want me."

Alannah abruptly ceased dancing. "You taunt me. If you have even a shred of gentlemanly behavior in your soul, you will stop this assault."

"Aye, I will stop for now, but you are fooling yourself if you think you can stop me forever."

Alannah swallowed, all too aware that his words rang true.

That night she tossed and turned in the large bed, frightened, insecure and desperate with need. She had never slept anywhere but on the island and waves of homesickness assailed her, disrupting her rest and turning her dreams into nightmares. Unfulfilled desire made her restless and she cried out in her sleep.

Within seconds Xanthier was at her side, staring down at her tortured face. Always before she had slept peacefully. He had never seen her so knotted with anxiety in the midnight hours. He knelt beside the bed, moving softly so as not to wake her, and gently stroked her face. She cried out again, breathing rapidly, and kicked the covers off her legs, but Xanthier stroked her face again, seeking to offer the comfort she would not earlier accept.

Her cries softened, and she turned her cheek toward him. He used two fingers to smooth her wrinkled brow. Touching her soothed him as well, and he lowered his head to the bed and stared at her. She was so lovely. So unique. He ran his fingers over her forehead and down her temples, communicating his emotions through touch. Soon her tossing head stilled and her face relaxed. She purred in her sleep and nuzzled her cheek against his hand. He smiled and closed his eyes, joining her in slumber.

"Alannah, prepare to go down below. We will be docking in a few hours," Xanthier said coldly before walking away from her. For the duration of the voyage, Alannah had not relented. She still refused to speak to him and only accepted his caresses at night when her sleeping body could not resist. He always left before she woke.

"What will happen once we land?" she asked.

"I will take care of my business. Then we will sail back."

"What am I supposed to do during that time?"

"You will stay here and wait."

Alannah pressed her lips together and turned away. She would say nothing. If he thought she would wait complacently on his ship while he gallivanted around, he was ignorant as well as tyrannical. "Nothing is that simple," she said. "Will you tell me what business you must conclude?"

"It is not necessary for you to know."

"I see." She shook her head, disgusted with him. It would serve him right if she turned his plans upside down.

Alannah took a deep breath, hearing his angry strides as he paced away from her. Already she could smell the difference in the air. A whiff of green grass came to her and she tilted her head back and breathed deeply. She welcomed the landing, for Claudius stomped with pent-up energy.

Xanthier barked orders to his crew as the ship docked. Alannah sat inside her cabin, listening to the ruckus outside. The sailors were unloading piles of riches from the ships and packing them on ox-drawn carts. The port was seething with people and the stench of unwashed bodies and floating refuse made her wrinkle her nose in disgust.

Above deck, Xanthier also reacted to the terrible smells.

"Not quite like your island paradise, is it, Commodore?" Robbins remarked.

"It is revolting. I have three days to settle my affairs. Find out where the king is spending the summer. I intend to travel there immediately. Alannah will stay on the ship. Lock her door for her safety."

"If I may, I would like to accompany you. The first mate can stay and watch over her."

Xanthier turned to Robbins in surprise. "If you wish."

"Your goal may be more difficult than you assume. The king will not be happy to part with your services."

Xanthier growled under his breath. "Find some horses and ask what sailors know how to ride. We must take at least ten to guard the treasure. With an offering like this, the king should give me anything I want. I will ask for ownership of Alannah's isle in order to protect it from any who seek to inhabit it. A small island off the coast will seem like nothing to King Malcolm. The trade will be well worth it."

"Perhaps the king will agree," Robbins replied. "And your other business?"

"I will deal with that privately. And I will set aside a dowry for my daughter, Istabelle."

"Do you intend to see your daughter while you are here?"

"No. I have not seen her for five years, since the week of her birth, and I have no intention of seeing her now. I will do my duty but that is all. I hold no affection for her."

Robbins watched the tightening of Xanthier's face and averted his eyes. "What about your twin brother? Will you say good-bye to him?"

"I did that five years ago. We have no reason to speak again." As he said the words, emotion washed over him. He sensed Brogan. Whenever either of them experienced major upheavals, each could sense the other's anxiety. In the last few months, their twin connection had dwindled, for he had felt peaceful and content. Now, as his worry surged and he braced for trouble, the connection hummed to life and he knew that Brogan was aware of his arrival. "My brother is content with his wife, Matalia, their son, Mangan, and my daughter. I have no need to see him. Now, if you truly intend to accompany me, get things organized while I say my good-byes to Alannah."

"Aye, Commodore."

After a frustrating and unrewarding parting, Xanthier's mood was fouler than before. The ride to the township where the king and queen were residing had taken a day longer than he anticipated and he was nervous about Alannah's sudden passivity. When he had taken his leave of her, she had even smiled mysteriously.

Xanthier strode into the hall of the royal court, well aware of the horrified gasps that echoed in his wake. Since he'd left the island, the reality of his facial disfigurement had become unavoidable. He was half-handsome, his unblemished side still showing the strong lines of his lineage, but the other side was scarred and twisted, making him frightening to look upon.

A woman glanced up at him, screamed and fell to the floor in a faint. Her friend fanned herself rapidly, ignoring the prostrate woman as she gazed avidly upon Xanthier.

"That is Xanthier O'Bannon, bad twin of the O'Bannon brothers, isn't it?" she whispered. "Brogan, the other twin, is the Earl of Kirkcaldy. I have heard that Xanthier has become fabulously wealthy! He has enough riches to rival the king's!"

"His reputation alone terrifies me," another woman said as she pressed closer to the aisle. Her eyes were wide and she took several quick breaths. "His visage is grotesque, but he holds a certain fascination . . ."

"Indeed! But his past transgressions cannot be discussed in polite society," whispered the first lady. Then, ignoring her own words, she continued. "The worst offense was the sudden death of his wife, Isadora of Dunhaven. She plunged to her death from the towers of Kirkcaldy during the brothers' struggle for power. In addition, Xanthier's daughter, Istabelle, is now in the foster care of Brogan and his wife, Matalia. It is said that Xanthier has had no contact with her. He has abandoned her completely."

Such rumors were recirculated as Xanthier walked through the assemblage, causing the volume of voices to rise. King Malcolm glanced up, curious to see who had generated such strong interest.

"Margaret," he murmured to the queen, "it appears that the O'Bannon brother has returned."

Queen Margaret clasped the cross that hung prominently from her neck and smiled. "It is good that he has come. I have heard many stories about him. It is said that he was lost at sea for several months. I am pleased that he did not lose his bounty."

"Yes, it is time to replenish our coffers, especially with the festival commencing in three weeks."

"I will send for his brother to come to the festival as well. That family has suffered too many years of strife and it affects the balance of power in our country." Margaret turned to her husband. "Perhaps it is, indeed, fortunate timing. The brothers have been estranged for too many years and Xanthier has obligations he has ignored."

Malcolm nodded, pleased as always with his English princess. Although her Roman beliefs often conflicted sharply with those of the Celtic church, she was unfailingly devoted to her husband, and he did not regret rescuing her after she had been exiled to Scotland. He, too, had known exile, but his time had been spent in England. Consequently, the two monarchs understood each other as few noble spouses could.

Xanthier approached the chairs where King Malcolm and Queen Margaret were seated. "Your Majesties," he stated as he bowed.

"Lord Xanthier, we are pleased to see you. It has been a long time. Some believed that you perished at sea, along with my ship."

Xanthier looked at the king warily, gauging his temperament. "As you can see, I survived and am well. My caravan has arrived and I have brought many items of value. Perhaps the queen would like a gold chain studded with rubies?"

Margaret raised her eyebrows. "Such a gift would be well appreciated," she answered.

King Malcolm leaned forward. "We will be receiving in our chambers in one week's time. Perhaps you should seek an audience."

"I thought to speak with Your Majesty immediately," Xanthier interjected.

"We would not think highly of any request before a week's time," King Malcolm reprimanded him.

Xanthier nodded and backed away. Although he was anxious to complete his required visit, he would have to be patient. Thinking of Alannah cooped up in the ship's cabin, he felt a moment of guilt.

As he walked back through the people, with Captain Robbins at his side, he clenched his teeth. The women shrank away and pulled their skirts from him as he passed, and the men subtly dropped their hands to their sword hilts. The unfriendly atmosphere made his already short temper flare, especially when one lady remarked upon his visage.

"I see that the Lord Xanthier's mean spirit is erupting from within. Such a disfigurement would only be cast upon a man whom God places in disgrace. He looks like a monster."

Xanthier froze, then turned to confront the bold woman. "Lady Catherine of Dunhaven," he stated, recognizing the rotund form of his former mother-in-law.

"I daresay that you should be ashamed to show your face here," Lady Catherine snarled. "After what you did to my gentle daughter . . ." She trailed off, frightened of the fierce look on Xanthier's face.

"I will speak no ill of the dead, m'lady, so I shall say nothing of Isadora. But keep in mind that I have few scruples, and am more than likely to change my mind should you persist in bringing the topic up."

"Well!" Lady Catherine gasped. "Such a distasteful man! I never liked you, and only let my daughter marry you because she had her heart set on it."

"Your daughter, madam, was set on becoming a countess."

"A shame then that you lost your inheritance, is it not? She died in disgrace because of you."

Xanthier narrowed his eyes, glaring. Rage boiled within him, and he had the urge to pick the woman up and toss her into a chair where he could force her to face the truth about her daughter. But he was not going to defend himself, and he was not going to explain.

"I can see where Isadora learned her manners," he growled as he turned away from her. "Captain Robbins," he said to his companion, "let us quit this room. It has begun to reek."

Captain Robbins bowed briefly to the people who surrounded them. Their faces showed both shock and fascination, and he silently agreed that Xanthier should avoid their presence as much as possible over the next week.

"The game room," he murmured, motioning to an arched doorway. Women were banned from entering the men's room, and he hoped that Xanthier's reception there would be warmer.

Xanthier and Captain Robbins exited the royal receiving room with mutual sighs of relief, but were on guard almost immediately when they spotted the tabards of several other clans.

"Traveling with you seems to be a challenge," Captain Robbins remarked as a few men rose and stared at Xanthier with stony faces.

"You do not have to stay, my friend," Xanthier answered. "I warn you that I am not well liked in my homeland."

"I am sorry to tell you that you are poorly liked in every land. I see it is no different here than it was in France or England or aboard the ship. I seem to be the only fool who hasn't figured out what is wrong with you."

Xanthier grimaced. "I don't know why. You

seem to be a fairly intelligent man. Why you persist in staying around is beyond me."

Captain Robbins looked at Xanthier, knowing that there was real pain behind the mocking words. "You spared my life, Xanthier, at a time when you had every right to kill me."

"What are you talking about?"

"Several years ago I was a drunken fool with no sense. I attacked you one night, looking for funds. You set me straight that evening. I will always remember the glint of the knife you held to my throat." Even though he did not say it aloud, he also remembered Xanthier's cold gray eyes and expressionless look when he had released him.

"I don't remember."

"I was convinced that I was going to die by your hand. But you did not kill me. Instead, you carried me to an inn and put me in bed to sober up. You told me to find a purpose in life."

Xanthier stared at Captain Robbins. "You never told me this story before."

"Although it was a turning point for me, it was irrelevant to you. By morning, I decided that you were right. Drinking and carousing were only habits that I had developed to add adventure to a dull existence. You lived an exciting life. Your wide travels and vast experiences intrigued me. I waited several days, then came to your ship asking for work."

"I do remember that. You told me that you had no experience but you were willing to work hard. You did, Robbins, and you advanced quickly. I have always been impressed by you. It is rare for a man to make captain in such a short time."

Robbins laughed. "I never would have if you

hadn't captured so many ships! You were desperate for crews and it gave me a golden opportunity.''

"Aye, that is part of the truth, but you have done well and I am pleased.''

"I seem to be one of the few people who has generated your pleasure. Surely no one here at court appears friendly.''

"One other person besides you has given me great pleasure.''

Captain Robbins nodded. "We will go back to the ship soon, Commodore.''

"I wish I were there already," Xanthier grumbled, then walked fully into the game room. He glared at one man and placed his hand on his sword. "Do you have something to say?" he growled.

The man rose, his face turning red. "Your reputation precedes you," he muttered. "I have no wish to tangle with your sword." Xanthier was a feared warrior, and his years in self-imposed exile aboard the sailing ships had only honed his skills. The man stepped carefully back, then turned and fled the room.

An auburn-haired man stood and faced Xanthier. "Old friend! I had heard you were lost at sea!"

Xanthier glared at the man. "Never call me friend, Lord Kurgan. We were battleground allies, which is a far cry from friends." Boiling anger threatened to burst forth and Xanthier was forced to clench his fists in order to keep from strangling Kurgan.

"As you wish. But with your new scars, I would think you would be grateful for the few people who can still stand to be near your visage.''

"I never liked you," Xanthier growled. "I suggest you stay as far from me as possible.''

Kurgan narrowed his green eyes and glared at Xanthier. Jealousy swamped him. At every battle the two had stood as competitors, with Xanthier winning most often. Kurgan had been inordinately pleased when he heard that Xanthier had died, and his disappointment at seeing the man in the flesh could not be keener. But Kurgan was well versed in court manners, and he hid his animosity well. He bowed with a flourish.

"I, on the other hand, intend to stay close beside you. You came back for a reason, and I will discover it. Once I do, expect me to interfere." He flashed a cold smile, then sauntered from the room.

Xanthier stared after him, disgusted with himself. Of all the people he should not have antagonized, Kurgan was the most important. He glowered at the other men who had overheard their conversation.

Some of the men nodded at Xanthier respectfully, several men departed, leaving only a few remaining lords. When it was clear that there was no one else who was threatening, Xanthier took his hand from his sword. "Well, Captain Robbins, you have now witnessed how beloved I am in my own country."

"Aye. But I had expected a cold reception."

Xanthier chuckled wryly and motioned to an empty table where they sat down and were given tankards. He took a deep draught and his present anxieties drifted away. Wiping the foam from his mouth, he stared at the wall behind Captain Robbins's head. Thoughts of the past flitted through his mind. Instead of thinking about the king and queen, he remembered the berry juice Alannah made, and the laughing way she had shown him how to find the ripest berries with the best flavor.

Instead of worrying about the men at court, Lady
Catherine and the multitude of other enemies he
had cultivated throughout the years, he thought
about the love Alannah had given him so freely.
He yearned for her soft purity. She made him feel
cared for in a way he had never dreamed possible.
He wanted to return to her and the island. One
week before he could speak to the royals. It
seemed like forever!

Chapter 12

Alannah spent eight days waiting for him, but by the end of the ninth day, her anger had changed to determination. He had talked about protecting her, but instead he had locked her on the ship, ashamed of her. It was a familiar pattern. Her true family had set her adrift. Grandmother had hidden her from the world, even when Gondin's visits had afforded her the opportunity to return to the mainland. Now Xanthier had left her, indicating that she would be unfit for the outside world.

She sat in the cramped cabin, swamped by loneliness. He had left her. All his words of affection meant nothing. He had used and discarded her. Just as she had feared, he had returned to his world and forgotten her completely.

Alannah had no desire to be concealed any longer. She was willing to brave the outside world. In fact, she wanted to explore new lands and experience new people. She wanted to find her family! She would not let anyone limit her life because of her lack of vision. Xanthier was wrong. She would not be an outcast. She would not let people ostracize her. She had many other gifts, and she was ready to share them with confidence.

As the sun set, she gathered her belongings, taking with her the amulet bag, a blanket and her staff. While orange and red streaks cut the evening sky, Alannah carefully listened at the door. Then, when she could not hear anyone, she lifted the latch and opened the portal. She closed her eyes, asking her senses to guide her. She heard the ship creak as it rocked against the pier, as well as the seagulls as they swooped overhead, searching for a twilight meal. Down the corridor came the unmistakable sounds and smells of supper preparation. Alannah could identify the cook, the first mate and at least two other sailors.

Using her staff as quietly as possible, she glided down the gangway and placed her free hand against the hatch. She could feel the vibrations of hundreds of other palms that had touched the wood as if their energy was intertwined in the ship itself. She caught her breath, sensing Xanthier's essence. Waves of longing swept through her and she bit her lip in indecision. Should she go? Should she wait?

Her reverie was broken by Claudius's sharp whinny. Alannah exhaled. She must go. She would not wait for Xanthier's return like a penned sheep, meekly abiding by her master's orders.

She pushed the hatch open a few inches, then halfway, and wriggled out. She paused, searching the area with her senses . . . but only she was above deck. Claudius neighed again, and Alannah moved swiftly toward his stall, an enclosed, oversized box bolted to the deck.

"Claudius," Alannah whispered. "Make no noise, for tonight we will set foot on land." She fumbled with the latch, finally opening it, and stepped aside.

The white stallion leapt out and dashed across the deck, then skidded to a stop at the ship's far railing.

The men below decks suddenly ceased talking, alerted by the clattering hooves. The first mate shouted, and Alannah's heart raced in fear.

"Claudius!" she yelled as she scrambled after the horse. The stallion spun around and trotted back to her, his hooves sliding on the smooth surface. Alannah grabbed hold of his mane and swung up on his back. He instantly reared, whinnying again, and Alannah leaned forward to keep her balance. "Hold!" she demanded. The stallion shook his head, tossing his mane back and forth. He stamped his feet and swung his tail in agitation, but obeyed Alannah's command. As his feet touched the deck, she turned him toward the dock.

The hatch sprang fully open and the sailors tumbled out of the gangway. "Stop!" the first mate shouted as he ran toward the pair. Frightened, the stallion bolted forward.

"Stop!" the first mate cried again. "You will crash through the railing!"

Alannah clung to Claudius's back and squeezed her thighs. Fear shivered through her as she felt the stallion gather his muscles. She wrapped her legs around him. "Jump," she whispered. "Jump!"

The stallion leapt over the rail and crashed onto the slick dock. He stumbled to his knees, unsteady on land after so long at sea.

Shouts reverberated up and down the dock. The stallion screamed, scrambled to his feet and shot forward in fear. Within seconds, he was racing down the narrow streets of the village, leaping minor obstacles and crashing through major ones. Alannah clung to him, praying fervently for his eyesight to lead them through the unfamiliar territory.

The stallion wove through the cobbled streets, sliding on the uneven surface. He galloped madly, not knowing where he was going and only responding to his instinct to flee an uncertain situation. Chest heaving and legs flashing, he powered through the streets until he finally spied a length of uninterrupted road leading out of town. He veered to the right, aiming for it.

Alannah felt the stallion stumble as he swung abruptly sideways. Far behind them she heard the sailors ringing an alarm. She kicked Claudius, asking him to go farther, faster! The white stallion laced his ears back, stretched his nose out and flattened into a headlong, uncontrolled gallop.

After ten minutes, they reached a forest. Racing around a sheltered bend, the white stallion suddenly whinnied in fear. He planted his front legs and skidded on the graveled surface. A child screamed in terror just beneath the stallion's hooves.

"Stop!" Alannah shouted as she frantically wrapped her arms around the white stallion's neck. "Stop!"

Alannah felt the swish of Claudius's front hooves as he pawed the air over the child's head and she screamed again. The white stallion twisted in the air, then lunged sideways in wild fury. Alannah slipped, her arms flailing. She gripped with her thighs, terrified to be atop her enraged stallion but more petrified to fall beneath his flailing hooves.

Alannah slipped further. "Help!" she cried as she felt herself falling. Her senses spun as she tried to orient herself, tried to keep her balance, but the scrambling stallion fell to the ground amidst the terrified cries of the child. Alannah tumbled off the white stallion's back, feeling the quick rush of the air against her skin a second before she crashed onto the road and pain blasted into her head and thundered through her body.

Alannah opened her mouth, trying to breathe, but her wind was gone and she could only gasp. Her head pounded and she could not feel her legs. She tried to roll over, but she could not, and she gasped in horror. Pain rocked through her, like barbed needles piercing her flesh. Her back quivered from the high-impact landing, and it spasmed, effectively paralyzing her.

"No," she whimpered. "Please don't let this happen." Opening her blind eyes, she stared blankly into the darkening sky above her.

Then, like a soft caress, a child's hand touched her face.

Chapter 13

Istabelle stared down at the beautiful woman lying on the road. The powerful white stallion had almost trampled her, but somehow the woman had pulled him away without bridle or saddle. Normally unimpressed by anyone save her beloved cousin, Istabelle was enthralled by the mysterious woman.

Istabelle was only five years old. Today, in fact, was the day to celebrate her birth. That very celebration had sent her riding her pony outside the gates of her family's coastal home, alone and unattended. She detested festivities and hated the pomp that attended such a day. Unfortunately, she had fallen from her pony and severely injured her ankle. The pony had dashed for home, leaving her stranded.

When the stallion had thundered around the corner and almost trampled her, she had been certain that her short life was about to end. Now the woman lay breathing heavily, eyes closed and clearly in pain. The stallion had scrambled to his feet and was now nuzzling his mistress in a show of concern.

Alannah felt the evening surround her. She listened to the insects and concentrated on the slow change in temperature as the cool air drifted down from the mountains and sank into the lower valley where she lay. She could sense both Claudius and the child staring down at her.

Bit by bit, she moved her toes, then stretched her back. After taking time to let the immediate pain fade, she was able to move each muscle carefully until they all began to function together once again. Slowly, making sure that she did not strain anything, she rose to her hands and knees and crawled to the side of the road.

The horse and child followed her.

She felt for her stick, but could find nothing but twigs and gravel. Helplessness washed over her, and she shivered. She was frightened.

"Are you looking for something?" the child asked.

Alannah turned toward her. "I need my staff," she said after a pause.

"It is to your left," Istabelle replied. She stared at the woman curiously. "Can't you see it?"

Alannah's hand brushed against the staff, and she gripped it eagerly. Rising, she stood and stretched her back. "No," she said. "I cannot see anything. I am blind."

"Oh." Istabelle frowned. "I have never seen a blind person before."

"Neither have I," Alannah answered with a grin, and Istabelle giggled at her joke. "My name is Alannah."

"I am Istabelle."

"Pleased to meet you, Istabelle. I sense that you are hurt."

Looking ruefully down at her ankle, Istabelle nodded. "I fell from my pony and twisted my ankle."

"Where is your pony now?"

"He ran away."

"How will you get home?"

"I don't know." Istabelle shrugged.

Alannah tilted her head, hearing in the child's voice the insecurity that she hid from others. She sensed the child's loneliness and her feelings of abandonment. She seemed like an orphaned lamb that wanted to act like a tigress.

"If you point the way, I will take you back," Alannah offered. "I have no desire to stay here, either."

"All right," Istabelle answered.

An hour later, they crested a hill that overlooked a coastal valley. Istabelle described it to Alannah. "Our castle is to the right. It has a stone wall that encloses the inner towers. The left tower is taller than the right one because when my uncle's grandfather built it, they couldn't level the ground. I like it."

"I am sure that if it is as beautiful as your heart, Istabelle, it is a fine home."

Istabelle laughed. "I don't think anyone has ever said that I have a beautiful heart. Normally they say I am like the devil and can't keep out of mischief."

"I think you want them to think that."

Istabelle looked over her shoulder at her new friend and stared at her, perplexed. The blind woman was unlike anyone she had ever met. "Will you come inside? Meet my aunt and uncle?"

"I . . . I am not sure . . ."

"Come on," Istabelle insisted. "It is getting dark. You helped me. I should help you, as well. And your horse will need food."

The words echoed in Alannah's mind as she

thought back to the day she had met Xanthier. Tears sprang to her eyes. Despite her anger, she missed him. "Very well," she said, more to combat the loneliness than because she wanted to.

"Good!" Istabelle replied. As they rode toward the castle, an entourage suddenly burst out of the gates and galloped toward them. Dipping her head, Istabelle groaned. "My pony must have made it home. That will be my uncle and his men. You will have to tell them where you come from and how you got here."

"Yes, I suppose I must."

Alannah entered the hall with careful but confident strides, Istabelle at her side. The echoes of footsteps and voices, the tinkle of utensils and pottery, the swish of dresses all combined to form an immense overload of sensory input. The castle smelled different—there were so many bodies within the enclosed space. Bread baked in the attached kitchens, dry rushes lined the floor. Even the air felt unusual. It was shadowed and cool, similar to walking underneath a large tree, yet colder and less personal.

But despite the strangeness of the castle, Alannah felt comfortable. She swung her stick gently as she walked alongside the young girl. The smells, sounds and feelings that surrounded her were just another set of new experiences. She welcomed the challenge.

Servants, soldiers and lesser lords and ladies paused to watch Alannah's progress. Her regal bearing was stunning, and her wealth of thick auburn hair struck envy in many hearts. She made no attempt to hide her lack of vision. Indeed, it was clear that she was not self-conscious about it at all.

Curiosity quickly turned to admiration as she walked with Countess Matalia and the Earl of Kirkcaldy, Laird Brogan O'Bannon. Istabelle guided her and together they ascended the steps to the raised platform above the lower table.

At the top, the earl turned to address the assemblage. "People of my house, may I present Mistress Alannah. She has come from far across the sea. I wish everyone to bid her welcome. She rescued our Istabelle, and brought her safely home. We are in her debt."

A chorus of greetings followed the earl's announcement. A small boy ran up to Istabelle and tugged on her hand. "Cousin," he said, "why are you limping?"

"I fell off my pony, but I met the most magical woman. Meet Mistress Alannah. My cousin, Mangan."

"Honored," Alannah said, sensing the boy's strength. He was destined for something special. She reached out and stroked his head. "You had best take care of your little cousin. She needs you."

"Yes, mistress. I know."

Matalia laughed. "Go on, children. Let me help Mistress Alannah settle in for the night while you have early supper."

As the children scampered away, Matalia touched Alannah's arm and led her off the platform toward the stairs. "Come, let me bring you to your room so you can freshen up and rest. Please excuse the children. They are excited. Relax, and tomorrow we can talk. And I thank you, once again. Istabelle is difficult to control. We would like to offer you anything you wish as our way of saying thanks."

Alannah nodded, aware of all her aches and

bruises now that exhaustion was overtaking her.
"For now, I am only concerned with finding a bed."
Her stick bounced against the stairs and she
stepped up, only to find that the steps continued.
"Where are we going?" she asked, suddenly
nervous.

"Up to your room. There are about thirty steps
before we reach the landing. Will you be able to
climb them?"

"Of course," Alannah replied, even though she
felt inner trepidation. Heights did not scare her.
She had been climbing upon the cliffs and clamber-
ing up trees forever. But this was a man-made
structure, and she did not understand how it was
supported. Despite her concern, they made it safely
to the next floor, and Matalia led her to a small
guest room where a warm fire was already crackling
in the hearth and a platter of food was waiting.

"Will you need assistance?"

"No, thank you. I am suddenly very tired." She
wondered what Xanthier would think about her escape, and whether he would seek her out.

"As you should be," Matalia said. "Rest well and
I will see you in the morning. Then we will talk."

Alannah nodded gratefully. As soon as the door
closed, she explored her surroundings, quickly discovering the bed, the table, the chairs, the trunks
and the window. With her bearings adjusted, she
ate some food, then sank into the soft mattress and
fell into a deep but uneasy sleep.

Chapter 14

The next day, Xanthier thrust his sword at his opponent, his anger and frustration increasing his power and accuracy. The sun was rising above the royal castle, and Xanthier was furious with his delay. He wanted to return to the ship and Alannah. Captain Robbins fell back, parrying swiftly, but Xanthier advanced, his face a twisted mass of scars as he snarled his wrath.

"Take care!" Robbins shouted as he leapt back.

"Hold your sword up! Is there no one who can stand up to me?" Xanthier pushed Robbins back and pressed his blade to his friend's chest. The others who watched shook their heads. They had no wish to face Xanthier's fighting fury.

"Remember, 'tis not with me that you find fault," Robbins reminded him.

"Augh!" Xanthier dropped his blade and spun away. "Why do they delay?"

"You have an audience today."

"No doubt they will cancel it again, as they have the other two times."

"Nonetheless, you should rinse off and get ready. I do not think Queen Margaret will appreciate your stench."

Disgusted, Xanthier stalked away, seeking his

quarters. Every day he spent here confirmed his desire to leave. He wanted to escape the people, the smells, the chaos that reigned in the royal city. He wanted to go back to the solitude and tranquility of the island, and Alannah.

What must she be thinking about his extended absence? Was she all right? How were the horses, the meadows, the butterflies? As he stripped off his sweat-drenched clothing and pulled on fresh items, he thought about her. He had never mentioned love. In all the times they had lain together, in all the times they had held hands and felt the sea breezes, he had never told her that he loved her. The moment she was in his arms again, he swore to himself, he would express his feelings.

As night took over the land, he walked down the hall to the king and queen's chambers. With a heavy hand, he knocked. To his surprise, the door opened.

"Commodore O'Bannon." The servant nodded. "Their Majesties are awaiting your presence."

Xanthier strode in and bowed. "King Malcolm. Queen Margaret."

"We have heard many rumors, Xanthier O'Bannon. Is it true that you are seeking to give up your commission?"

"Aye, Your Majesties. I wish to give up the fleet and settle down."

"Where do you intend to settle?" Queen Margaret asked.

"There is an island off the coast. I would ask to purchase it."

"Does it hold value?"

"Only to me. It is small and unfit for farming."

The queen looked at her husband, lifting her brow. King Malcolm shrugged. "The festival is coming soon. It would be best for us to think on this matter and decide after the festival."

"Your Majesties," Xanthier interjected angrily, "I have waited for weeks! I must ask you to think on the matter immediately. I have another, vastly important matter to discuss—"

"We are not unaware of your desire for haste. However, there are many matters we must consider," King Malcolm said. "Your brother, the earl, has indicated concern for your welfare. Your daughter, Istabelle, is growing up. The island is not a land we know anything about, and we need to decide how to bestow it. In addition, you have been a great asset as a commodore. We are loath to see you desert your post."

"I have been a loyal subject! I implore you. You must hear me out."

"Indeed. We appreciate your concern. We will think upon it. Until then, please join the festivities."

As Xanthier was forcefully pulled out of the chamber, his anxiety erupted into seething rage. He strode through the great hall, ignoring the gasping ladies.

As several women stumbled out of his way, a sailor touched his sleeve. "Commodore," he said hesitantly, "there is something I must tell you . . ."

As the sailor whispered into Xanthier's ear, Kurgan of the Serpents, standing a short distance away, watched Xanthier pale, then stride rapidly from the room. Something was clearly wrong. Desire to thwart his enemy pulsed in Kurgan's blood and he narrowed his eyes in concentration. He rubbed his forehead, feeling the tingling sensation that overtook him when his thoughts took form and gave him new ideas. Underneath his black cloak he wore his family tunic, embroidered with the insignia of the serpent. His uncle was Lothian, known murderer and pillager, and it was from him that Kurgan had learned to take what he wanted without caring for the consequences.

It might be worthwhile to discover the reason for Xanthier's apparent distress.

He rose from his seat. Xanthier's presence was like an oozing sore in his backside, and Kurgan could not stand the festering disquiet. He would follow the sailor and determine what was going on.

That same day, long after the sun had risen and the dew had burned off the fields, Alannah sat with Brogan and Matalia. The long table in the great hall stretched across half the room, but the three people sat close together at one end.

"Tell me what we can do for you," Matalia said as she sipped her morning drink.

"I would like your help in finding my family," Alannah said softly. "I would like to find out who my mother was and perhaps why she cast me away."

"Certainly," Matalia agreed, though she creased her brow in concern. "Do you know anything?"

"When I was left adrift in a small boat, there were several items in an amulet bag attached to my blankets. Grandmother kept them for me throughout years."

"What is in the packet?"

"A letter, a key and a necklace. It also contains some coin."

"Can I see the letter?"

"Yes, I brought it with me this morning." Alannah handed the old piece of paper to Matalia. "It recently was burnt and I am afraid some of it is

now missing. I hope it can be read . . ." She held
her breath with anticipation.

"Oh dear. So many of the words are gone. I am
not sure . . ."

"Let me look at it," Brogan demanded. "I will
read what I can."

> *Dear stranger,*
> *Please . . . my special daughter . . . cannot*
> *protect . . . My life has been a terrible . . . I want*
> *more for her. Take the coins . . . tell her . . . My*
> *home in Clarauch . . . be careful!*

"Clarauch?" Matalia said. "That was a small village over the hills nestled among three estates. The
ownership of the land has passed from family to
family depending upon the fighting strength of the
current owners. However, it was abandoned fifteen
years ago after being burned in a raid."

"Yes. The history of that area has been rich in
violence, but there are some peasants who settled
nearby," Brogan added.

"Of course. Perhaps someone in the area will
recognize her."

"Matalia, the letter ends with an exhortation to
be careful. I do not think it wise to brazenly ride
over there and announce that we are looking for
Alannah's lost family. There must have been a reason why she was sent away in a boat. The letter
says that the writer's life was terrible. We must
use great caution." Brogan looked at his wife for
confirmation.

She nodded. "We will send someone to ask dis-
creet questions and glean information without raising suspicions."

"Aye. That would be wisest," Brogan agreed.

"It will take some time before we hear of any responses. Within the week we will be traveling to court where the king and queen are holding a festival. We were wondering if you would like to come with us."

"Someone once told me about festivals," Alannah said slowly.

"Many contests will be held, including jousting, wrestling, gaming and dancing, but the biggest event is race day."

"I have heard of races with horses."

"Yes!" Matalia exclaimed, excited. "That is the best part of the festival! The king always makes the purse something extravagant, something new. One year it was a ruby the size of your fist."

"Another year, he bestowed a title upon the owner," Brogan said. "Younger brothers, aspiring squires and penniless lords can suddenly increase their fortunes."

"You make it sound like a charity event." Matalia laughed. "It is not as if just anyone can win. It is highly competitive. Horses train for it year-round."

"But the thrill of this race is that anyone can enter," Brogan insisted. "That is what makes it different from the others. It gives everyone an opportunity to reach for something that would otherwise be unattainable."

"I always have a horse in the race," Matalia said proudly. "And my horse won two years ago, although I must admit, your stallion is magnificent, perhaps even more impressive than mine. It is a shame he is so untamed. If he could wear a bridle and saddle, and be guided by a rider, he would have a very good chance!"

"My blindness . . . perhaps I should not go among so many people . . ."

"Nonsense," said Brogan. "You will be our official ward. While under the protection of our name, you will be untouchable. Your ability to function so well makes you commendable, and I will tell that to any who dare to comment. You saved our niece. As far as we are concerned, you are family."

Making a sudden decision, Alannah grinned. "I want to go to the festival with you. I want to experience this race you speak of with such excitement. It sounds like a fascinating experience. I would like to go."

Nodding, Brogan and Matalia leaned back and agreed.

Then Brogan rose abruptly, and Alannah turned toward him, curious. Frowning, he said a quick good-bye and left the room. Striding outside, he looked across the fields toward the Highlands. Something was happening. Xanthier.

The twins had been estranged for so many years, he doubted they would ever reconcile. The betrayals . . . the intrigue . . . so much had come between them. They were two men connected by an invisible cord that could never be severed, yet they could not exist in the same room without going to swords. Brogan bowed his head. If only the pain of their childhood could be erased. Brogan had found Matalia, and through her love he had found surcease. Xanthier had not been so lucky. He had struggled under the yoke of duty and the chains of a loveless marriage. And now there was more strife. Brogan could sense that something was threatening Xanthier.

Inside the hall, Matalia leaned forward and gripped Alannah's hand. "Something else is upsetting you."

Alannah turned aside, not answering.

"Alannah, you came from somewhere. What happened?"

"I . . . I was taken from my home . . . by a man."

"Did he hurt you?"

"No. Yes. In some ways. I was escaping from his restraint when my horse almost trampled Istabelle."

"Who is he? I will send my husband after him and we will punish him severely."

Alannah stood up, agitated. She did not want Xanthier hurt. She shrugged. "He never told me his name." As she walked away, she realized that she spoke a partial truth. Although she knew his first name, she did not recall him ever telling her his surname or the names of his family.

Several days later, Xanthier stared at the ship, his heart throbbing in pain. How could she do this? Why had she left him? Had he really done something so terrible that she had felt the need to run away in a land that was hostile to women like her?

He closed his eyes, letting his horse drop his exhausted head almost to the ground. Memories of her flooded his mind, and for once he did not fight them. He welcomed her imagined presence, pretending that she was seated in front of him and his arms were wrapped around her. He recalled the spray of the ocean waves and the sting of the beach sand as they galloped along the coast. He breathed deeply, smelling her hair, her neck, the tang of her sweat.

Snapping his eyes open, he bellowed into the wind, howling his regret and his yearning into the elements. God! He wanted her so badly! He missed her so profoundly! Where was she now? Was she thinking of him? Was she smiling? Was she crying?

Tears welled in his eyes and he dashed them angrily away. She was the magic that lit the world like a candelabra shimmering with millions of sparking candles. What had he done?

Finally getting his emotions under control, he turned to his companion. "Robbins," he said, roughly, "send a search party out to find her, but be careful. There are things I do not want revealed, and I must return immediately due to the king's command." He turned away. "I have never felt so helpless. Please find her."

"Yes. I will send out a party immediately."

"If the king does not answer me by the end of the festival, I will not stay at court, no matter what he commands."

"And once she is located?"

"We will have to sail away immediately."

"I thought as much. I will send one of the ships to a small port in the north to await your instructions."

"Make sure the ship is prepared to depart at a moment's notice. If I leave without the king's permission, I may be in a hurry." Pausing, he added, "I need her, Robbins. I cannot imagine life without her. I pray that she is safe. If the powers that be have any compassion, I pray that they will watch out for her."

"We will find her, Commodore," Robbins replied, while silently asking God to watch over Xanthier as well.

Chapter 15

Alannah held the reins tightly, feeling the stallion's prancing excitement as she sat sideways on him—the uncomfortable position that the O'Bannons had explained was absolutely required. There were so many smells in the air—so many sounds! Everything was new and fascinating. She was convinced that she had done the right thing in escaping the ship. Her pain at Xanthier's actions still ripped at her heart, yet she was trying to move forward. She needed more than the island. She was not ready to live alone and isolated. The promise of new experiences made her feel alive. She shivered with excitement as she rode with the O'Bannon caravan as it traveled to the royal court.

Several people passed their convoy, and Alannah heard their friendly greetings. The O'Bannons were warmly regarded, and many talked gleefully about the upcoming race.

"One would think Alannah had horns on her head and was wearing bearskins," Brogan grumbled after another person glanced at Alannah's attire with surprise before riding on.

As Alannah flushed, Matalia glared at her husband. "Don't mind him. He is just nervous about going to court. We still have a few weeks to prepare and I think you are doing fabulously. We will find patterns for court clothing and selections of fabric with which to make several gowns."

"I have no need of another dress. Mine is still quite serviceable."

"Heavens, Alannah! You can wear whatever you like to ride, but when in court you will have to wear appropriate clothing. Now, let me see . . ." Matalia muttered to herself as she sat back in her wagon and shut the curtain, leaving Brogan and Alannah to ride their horses alongside her.

Brogan sighed. "She is right. Going to court makes me queasy. I hate dressing up in those silly outfits and prancing around like a peacock. I think it is Matalia's exotic blood that makes her so happy to preen."

"Is she beautiful?" Alannah asked.

"Aye. She is exquisite."

"Perhaps a bit of your reluctance comes from jealousy?"

Brogan snorted. "If I would admit to that, you and my wife would have my innards on a platter! But, yes, perhaps you are right. I do not like sharing her with any other."

"You two are very much in love."

"She is my life. One day, you will find someone to love as well."

Alannah shook her head sadly. "I do not think so. My heart is no longer open to love."

Brogan stared at Alannah curiously. "You have been hurt," he stated. When she did not reply he frowned. "How could you? I thought you lived alone with the woman you called Grandmother. Isn't that what you told us several nights ago?"

"There was someone once . . . he was on my island for some time before he left. I do not think that love is for me. My stallion is my best friend. Just as I can live without sight, I can learn to live without love."

Brogan looked up as Matalia poked her head out and chattered about making a gold-threaded burgundy satin dress. With startling clarity he realized that any injury to himself would mean nothing compared to the loss of his wife. He would accept being crippled, infirm or even blind as long as it meant he could still feel her presence every morning and know that her love surrounded him every night.

He placed a brotherly hand on Alannah's shoulder and squeezed. She deserved to find the same peace he had found. "We will see," he answered softly. "I am thinking that court might be a good place to go after all. With all the people coming to the festival, perhaps you will find that special person. Join my wife and be a female. Make clothes and try perfumes. Enjoy yourself."

"Brogan!" Matalia chided. "I was talking! We must concentrate on the details. I am so excited. It is like having a daughter! We must present Alannah to the king and queen."

"Really, Matalia, that is not necessary," Alannah interjected. "I am quite content to stay on the periphery."

"Absolutely not! You will eat from silver plates and dance with Scottish lords. Have you heard about Queen Margaret? She was exiled from England before our king took pity on her and married her. She is quite religious and is becoming well known for her charitable acts."

"Hummm." Alannah lifted her head and smelled the air, already uninterested in the discussions about the king and queen. While Matalia and Brogan talked about the devout Queen Margaret and the religious changes she was encouraging, Alannah continued to enjoy the newness of her surroundings. It was both fabulous and frightening!

Alannah thought about the people traveling to the festival. Was it possible that Xanthier would be there? Alannah bent her head, her heart in turmoil. She was so angry with him, so hurt, but she trembled at the faint possibility that he would attend the festival. She shook her head, trying to dispel her thoughts. She had other concerns now, just as he clearly had other concerns too. She needed to find her family and determine her origins.

And a new thought surfaced again despite her attempts to quash it. If Xanthier had ever truly cared about her, he would have searched for her when she ran away. The fact that she had heard of no inquiries proved that he had ceased to be concerned about her safety, her survival or even her presence. Alannah sighed, stifling the pain that welled up within her as she stroked Claudius's neck. At least she had her friend.

They rode into town just as twilight spread over the houses and occasional lamplight flickered in windows. On the cobbled street, the horses' hooves clattered loudly down the alleys.

"For tonight we will stay at a tavern," Matalia said. "Their Majesties will not appreciate our late arrival. It would be better to refresh ourselves and see them in the morning."

Alannah smiled, amused by the nervous twitter in Matalia's voice. "Surely they are not so frightening as all that," Alannah said.

Matalia regarded Alannah seriously. "Please, Alannah. You must understand. Our king and queen are very powerful. If they are displeased with you, they have the power to imprison you, strip you of everything or even kill you."

"How terrible! How can two people be that important?"

"That is the way of the world. Will you be careful?"

"I will be cautious," Alannah answered, more to reassure Matalia than because she comprehended the power of the monarchs.

They arrived at the tavern and Brogan spoke to the innkeeper while everyone dismounted and stretched their legs. With an exchange of precious coin, the innkeeper motioned to the barn and Brogan nodded appreciatively.

"The innkeeper says that he will set a guard in the barn overnight to protect the horses."

"Good," said his wife. "I will sleep better knowing that someone is watching over them. There are people who would do anything—even harm a horse—in this township."

Alannah shook her head. Her island had been so simple, and this land confused her. "How could anyone hurt a horse? They are so gentle."

"I know it sounds horrible, but we must protect them carefully. Brogan will also make certain your stallion is well guarded."

Brogan smiled and slipped his arm around his wife. "I would do anything for you, darling," he murmured. "I want you to be happy."

Matalia gazed up at him and smiled warmly in return. "I will always be happy as long as I am married to you," she whispered.

Brogan squeezed her and turned to Alannah. "Would you like to see . . . er . . . ah . . ."

"I would love to see the stable," Alannah replied, laughing. Using her carved staff, she took several steps toward the barn. The laugh died on her lips. The staff reminded her of Xanthier, but she firmly pushed his memory aside. She must forget him.

She swung the stick back and forth and followed the sound of the horses' hoofbeats. As soon as she heard them step on hard-packed earth, she knew they had entered the structure. She swung her stick to verify the edges of the entranceway, then carefully stepped inside.

The rest of the entourage was getting organized when a gray-eyed man and his companion strode into the courtyard. The O'Bannon men-at-arms nodded respectfully and moved out of their way. One nudged his friend. "Do you know who that is?" he asked.

"Yes, who doesn't? He is the wicked O'Bannon twin, Xanthier, the one who left Kirkcaldy to Brogan O'Bannon. And that is one of his captains, Captain Robbins."

"What do you think happened to the commodore's face? With those scars, he will not be popular with the ladies anymore."

"That just leaves the field open for other, more fortunate men!" The two soldiers laughed and shoved each other, but abruptly sobered when Xanthier glared at them. The men both bowed, showing their respect, but Xanthier stalked up to them and narrowed his gaze upon them.

"Did I miss something amusing, gentlemen?" He had just returned to the king's castle and had recently partaken of several tankards of strong ale. The smell of alcohol surrounded him, and the men swallowed nervously. Xanthier was dangerous enough without the added influence of spirits. They had no idea what he might be capable of when drinking.

Suddenly Brogan turned and faced his brother. "Xanthier," he said. "I was not aware that you would be here."

Xanthier glared at Brogan. "I have no desire to stay. Especially now."

Nodding in acknowledgement of their mutual animosity, the twins backed away from each other. "You may join our table, if you wish," Brogan offered. "Istabelle would like to see you."

"No," Xanthier replied quickly. "Do not speak of my presence to the child. I do not want to see her." He spun around and motioned to Robbins. They strode out of the tavern yard and entered the drinking establishment, never noticing the stricken expression on the face of a little girl who stood behind Xanthier's brother.

Xanthier walked into the main room and dropped into a chair as Robbins followed. Xanthier's flare of irritation quickly faded and he stared moodily around the room, thinking of Alannah. He was furious that he could not leave to search for her, for day after day of searching had revealed nothing of her whereabouts. If she were dead, he would know, which meant she must be somewhere. Somewhere, but not where she should be.

He slammed his fist on the table. He must be in control! She should do as he told her! She should have waited on the ship for him, and he would have taken care of everything. Now he must contend with Brogan's presence as well.

He closed his eyes, aware that his thoughts were unreasonable but feeling them all the same. He missed her so much, and felt helpless at this delay.

Every moment made him more and more frustrated, and he found it easy to lash out at those around him, punishing strangers for his inner tumult.

When he heard her voice and the swish of her stick, he dropped his head to the table. The memories were overwhelming—they seemed so real. He could imagine her stepping into the hall next to the common room. He could even smell her. Then, as his imagination took over his sane mind, he could hear her footsteps as she tapped up the stairs and left him alone once again.

Alannah paused in the hallway, sensing Xanthier's presence. She tilted her head, listening, wondering if what she felt was real, but all she heard was the low rumble of several men talking and the thud of cups hitting wooden tables. She stepped forward, but Brogan came up at that moment and gripped her elbow.

"This way. We should avoid the common room. It gets unruly as the evening progresses. There are people there we should avoid." He looked over Alannah's shoulder at Xanthier sprawled at the back of the room. "No need to stir up trouble." Unaware that the cause of Xanthier's torment was standing next to him, Brogan guided Alannah to the base of the stairs where Matalia waited. "I will have supper sent up to you, ladies."

Matalia thanked him and preceded Alannah up the stairs, taking care to stay ahead of the tapping of her stick as Alannah felt the stairs and ascended them gracefully.

Upstairs, Matalia was pleased to find an elderly seamstress already awaiting their arrival. "Your husband sent for me, m'lady," the woman explained as she curtsied.

"Very good," Matalia replied, and motioned toward Alannah. "My dear friend will be meeting the queen and I wish her to be dressed appropriately."

The woman turned to look at Alannah and her eyes widened. "By my saints," she whispered. "She is the spittin' image of . . ." The seamstress trailed off, aware that Matalia was staring at her with irritation.

"I do not think her lack of sight should shock you, old woman. Monies will spend the same regardless of who wears the dress."

The woman shook her head vehemently. "The mistress's vision is not my concern, m'lady. I was simply surprised by her looks. She is lovely."

Matalia nodded, somewhat mollified. "See that you treat her well. A dress is in the trunk that I think you can alter to fit her. If you have any questions, see me. I will be in the next room." Matalia stepped over to Alannah and lowered her voice. "Are you comfortable with her, dear? Do you want me to stay and help you?"

Alannah shook her head. "She seems very kind. Have no worries."

When Matalia reluctantly left, Alannah approached the seamstress. "What is your name?" she asked.

"I am Effie. And you, mistress? What should I call you?"

"My name is Alannah."

"Is your family with you?" Effie watched her carefully for a response.

"No. I am here with friends. Shall we get started? This seems to be important to Lady Matalia."

Effie stared at her, wondering. Was it possible? She looked just like Zarina. But no, it was not possible. Zarina was old and the babe had been lost long ago. Still, she looked just like her . . . "Here," she said finally as she pulled the dress out of the trunk and removed the papers that lay between the fabric folds. She helped Alannah put the dress on, then stepped back and surveyed her critically. "It looks a bit too large in the waist, and perhaps too short. One will be easy to correct, the other . . ." She trailed off, mumbling to herself as she poked and prodded. "I will have to add a bit here and tuck some there." She pulled out some pins and began her alterations, muttering constantly. Mistress Alannah was just like Zarina! The same figure, the same coloring, the same walk. It was worth investigating. The wizened man in Clarauch would know. Perhaps she would send her son to speak to him.

After pulling on the dress's hem with disgust, Effie leaned back on her heels. "I will need to do much sewing to alter this for you. Should I make a few other dresses as well?"

Alannah shrugged, not sure that she cared. "If it is appropriate, I will commission other dresses."

Effie pulled Matalia's dress off Alannah as she nodded. "Indeed, mistress. It will be for the best. You'll see."

Alannah put her old dress back on and faced the seamstress. "I am sure that Matalia promised you some coin."

"Aye," Effie answered warily.

"I would like to pay for my own clothing. Will you let me?"

Effie raised her eyebrows. "I have no care who pays me, mistress."

Alannah searched briefly and pulled out one of her gold coins. "Please use this to make me presentable."

Effie gasped. "This is enough to purchase twenty dresses, mistress! Are you certain?"

"I want to learn all about court life. I want to experience the dances, the games, the food and the traditions. I want to learn everything. If dressing like the other women will help me in my endeavors, then I will do it."

"Aye. Wonderful!"

Alannah smiled. "Thank you, Effie. Thank you very much."

Effie stared at her, awestruck by the beauty of her smile. She smiled just like Zarina. There could be little doubt. But Effie had survived fifty years because she knew how to keep her mouth shut, and she would continue to hold her silence. If there was some reason Mistress Alannah did not know her identity, far be it from Effie to change anything until she understood the consequences.

In the tavern, Xanthier stared up at the ceiling, missing Alannah terribly. He wondered if he had done right by her. He believed that he needed to claim the island so no one could ever take it from her. He wanted to protect her and her identity. He did not want her in this world of intrigue and deceit.

Yet, by running away, she had left the security he could provide for the dangers of an unknown future. Mayhap she did not want him. Perhaps she, too, was disgusted with his terrible past and his facial scars. At court, women cringed at his scarred appearance, and held their skirts away when he passed. Catherine of Dunhaven had all but accused him of murder in front of the king and queen. The worst of it was, she was nearly right. Although Isadora's fall from the tower ramparts had not been his doing, he had felt little remorse when he beheld her broken body.

And what about the men? Everyone was ready to fight, and most would be pleased to run a sword through his rotten heart. This was no place for a beautiful spirit like Alannah's.

A man accidentally bumped Xanthier's arm, spilling some of his ale into his lap. Pulled forcefully from his recollections of Alannah, Xanthier rose with a roar of fury. He swung, smashing the unsuspecting man in the face, fracturing his nose. The man stumbled to his knees and ducked behind another man, who was the unfortunate recipient of another punch from Xanthier.

In moments, the tavern room erupted into a brawl, men crashing against the furniture and swinging their fists at anything that moved. The barmaid screeched and raced from the room.

The woman's cry made Xanthier pause. He had heard many screams on the battlefield, but now he thought of how Alannah would feel if she was the person being hurt. He stepped back, suddenly contrite, but a soldier who had taken several hard punches saw his opportunity and shoved his fist into Xanthier's chin, sending him staggering back. *Alannah!* Xanthier cried silently, ignoring his attacker. *Where are you? I don't want to fight anymore. I want you back!*

Catching him unawares yet again, the soldier hit him, this time smashing a chair over his head. Xanthier collapsed with a splinter of wood. Thoughts of his beloved winked out and he slipped into unconsciousness.

Chapter 16

The next morning, Matalia and Brogan received word from the man they had sent to Clarauch. Excited, they called for Alannah and met her in the tavern's common room.

"There was an unknown woman several years ago who was said to have been searching for her lost child. Her identity was kept secret," the servant reported.

"Can we determine who she was?" Alannah asked. "What did she look like? Where does she live?"

The servant shook his head. "I don't have those answers yet. However, it was clear that the woman was frightened, and did not want her search to be widely known. I think it is important that we continue to proceed carefully."

Alannah frowned, anxious to find answers. "Is there nothing more to report?" she asked with frustration.

"Well, there is another update. It is not related directly to your family, Mistress Alannah, but I think you will find it worthy of note."

"Indeed?"

"I met a man who was very interested in your tale. He is waiting outside. Shall I bring him in?"

Alannah nodded quickly as she gripped Matalia's hand. The servant ducked out and returned momentarily with a man dressed in the king's colors.

Brogan invited him in. "Rest and take a meal with us. We are eager to hear your news. You appear to be a king's man."

"Aye, I am honored to serve King Malcolm with my sword. Greetings, Laird O'Bannon. M'lady Matalia." The man nodded at Alannah, then flushed with embarrassment when she did not respond. "Mistress," he mumbled.

Matalia stepped forward. "Mistress Alannah is newly returned to Scotland. She, too, is excited by the opportunity to hear from you. As you can see, she has no eyesight, and one must speak to her in order to communicate with her."

Alannah gave a brief curtsy as Matalia had shown her. The man glanced at her, surprised at her beauty and grace. He moved away, feeling slightly uncomfortable as his heart beat erratically. She was incredibly beautiful! Her auburn hair was thick and luxurious and her dark green eyes were luminous. He swallowed nervously.

Brogan motioned for everyone to sit, and the assemblage settled on benches around the fireplace.

"What is your name?" Alannah asked the man.

"Gondilyn, mistress, at your service." He stared at her, watching for her response.

Alannah stilled. Straining her ears and vainly attempting to hide her excitement, she asked, "And your father? Who was he?"

"Gondin," he answered.

"Did Gondin travel the seas?"

"Aye. Although only a merchant, he traveled by sea once every three to five years."

"Does he still live?" Alannah asked, her voice breaking.

"No," Gondilyn replied. "He died five years ago. Did you know him?"

"Yes," Alannah whispered. "I lived on an island . . ."

"It *is* you!" he breathed as he rose and knelt next to her. "I know you! You are the child my father spoke of. You are the one who lived with Mistress Anne! How came you to be here?"

"You know of me?" Alannah replied, ignoring his question as her thoughts whirled. "You really are the son of Gondin?"

"Aye! I wanted to come to you. Father spoke of you often, telling me tales that fascinated and beguiled me. I desperately wanted to continue his visits to your island, but I was unable. He died while at sea and never left a map to the island. Can you forgive me? Where is Mistress Anne?"

"I believe your Mistress Anne was the woman I called Grandmother. She passed away this year. I mourn her deeply."

"I ache with you, Mistress Alannah. I am so sorry I could not sail to you. My father's ship was lost so many years ago, I had given up hope of ever seeing you with my own eyes. I feared for your continued well-being."

Matalia spoke up. "If your father was a merchant, how came you to be a soldier?"

Gondilyn shook his head sadly. "I am abysmally bad at numbers but a very good fighter. I was never able to barter like my late father. It was his idea that I go to court and find a place for myself that would be better suited to my skills."

"And Grandmother? Do you know anything

about her? Do you know anything about me?"
asked Alannah.

"I do not know much about you other than that
they found you adrift, but I know about Mistress
Anne. She was the love of my father's life. She was
my mother."

Long after Matalia and Brogan had gone upstairs
to their rooms, Alannah and Gondilyn talked about
Mistress Anne and Gondin.

"Marriage between them was forbidden due to
their differences in social standing," Gondilyn explained. "My father was forced to wed another
while Anne remained a spinster. However, their
love could not be denied and they formed a bond
that, though not sanctified by the church, was deep
and meaningful."

"Grandmother told me some things about Gondin. I knew she loved him deeply and eagerly anticipated his visits. When he stopped coming, she was
greatly saddened."

"Gondin treasured his visits to your island."

"What about you? How did she come to be your
mother?" Alannah asked.

"Gondin and Anne met secretly. Unfortunately
for Anne, a child was created from their illicit
union. That child was me. Gondin took me into his
home, telling his wife that I was a foundling, and
raised me while arranging for Anne to live in a
small cottage nearby," Gondilyn explained. "The
arrangement was not perfect, but it sufficed. Anne
was safe, my father did not abandon his responsibilities, and I was well loved. Once a month, Gondin
took me to visit Anne, which brought her great
joy. But as the years passed, Anne developed a
reputation for healing that began to strike fear in

the local bishop. He constantly belittled her, mocking her unwed status and remarking on her ungodly ways. When the bishop's unwed niece gave birth to a stillborn, the bishop sentenced Anne to death. Risking everything, my father purchased a small ship and sailed away from Scotland with her, trying to find a truly safe place for the woman of his heart."

"And he found the island?"

"Yes. He told me that he chose that island because of the wild horses. A Viking ship had wrecked off its shores years before, and the only survivors were the powerful steeds. He decided that if the horses had chosen to settle upon that island, then it must have all the things a person would need as well. He hated leaving her, but he could not abandon his family. He had ten children, eleven counting me, and his legal wife to care for."

"What a sad story. He must have been an unhappy man."

"No. He was sad, but he always told me that a few moments of bliss were worth years of toil. He loved his wife in a different way, and he adored all of us. I think he always felt guilty that his actions had caused such problems for Anne. He tried very hard to make up for it, but things happen that are out of our control. The shame of the situation is that he sailed that last time with the intention of staying with you and Anne. His wife had died of fever, and my halfbrothers and halfsisters were all settled in homes of their own."

"Grandmother waited for him. For years she stared out to sea, waiting for his ship."

"I am sorry I could not come and tell you. Please accept my undying devotion from this day forward. I will not fail you again."

"It was through no fault of yours. We will discuss it no more."

"You are not only the most beautiful woman I have ever seen, but also the most gracious. I would be honored to be your friend and ally."

"I would like us to be friends," Alannah agreed.

Gondilyn pressed her hand. "With pleasure. Alannah, please allow me to accompany you to the festival."

"I fear my blindness will cause strife."

"If it does, I will stand beside you. With my sword, and the earl's friendship, you will be accepted."

Something had been bothering Xanthier ever since the tavern fight yesterday. Something or someone. Perhaps he was just sensing things that were not there, like some of the crazy people did in the darkest alleys. But despite trying to taunt himself out of his odd feelings, he still glanced over his shoulder for a fourth time. It was almost as if there was something he should be seeing but could not. He thought that his strange feelings were due to Brogan's presence, but he sensed that there was something else still tugging at him. It felt like Alannah.

In frustration, he swung up on his horse and motioned to Captain Robbins. "I am ready for a run. Care to race?" Without waiting for a reply, Xanthier kicked his steed and set him galloping madly down the cobbled streets. The horse slipped and skidded, trying to keep his balance, but Xanthier rode him expertly, driving him forward until they reached the packed earth of the side streets. Then he leaned forward and let the reins fly, asking and receiving immense speed from the maddened animal. The steed was faster than most despite his large size, which made him ideal for battle. In addition, he was strong enough to carry a man's weight while armored, and swift enough to outrun most lighter specimens. Xanthier was pleased that the stable he had hired to house and exercise the horse while he was at sea had done an exemplary job. The stallion was in prime shape.

Within moments, Captain Robbins was far behind and Xanthier was galloping alone. His horse tripped, and Xanthier, normally the best of horsemen, tumbled to the ground. Emotionally exhausted and physically drained, he rolled into a ditch and did not attempt to rise. His head pressed against the soft loam. The earth beneath him and the wide sky above him held him in a comforting embrace, and he relaxed, drifting into a memory-laden doze as his horse galloped away.

Alannah rode slowly along the hard-packed lane, letting Claudius pick his pace. She had wandered out of the inn and chosen to take a ride. Guilt assailed her and she wondered if she should have stayed at the ship. Perhaps she should send a message, letting Xanthier's men know she was safe. Claudius occasionally stopped to graze, yanking fragrant bits of grass and chewing them with relish. Earlier they had raced along the lane, but now they meandered peacefully while Alannah pondered what to do.

As she was thinking, she heard a faint groan from nearby. She pulled the stallion to a stop and tried to locate the source of the sound. Hearing it again, she nudged her horse to the side of the road where a ditch dropped down. The sour odor of alcohol wafted up to her and she grimaced in distaste. Without a word, she turned away and continued down the lane, feeling sorry for the poor man who lay in the grass in such misery.

She felt an almost overwhelming urge to go back, to help the man, and she even stopped to consider it. But Matalia had warned her about strangers in the town. She had informed her that most people were not to be trusted and she should not interact with anyone she did not know. She backed the stallion up a few steps, then paused indecisively. The man was in agony. She could feel it down to her bones, and for some reason she could not bear to leave him helpless.

She took a skin of water from her waist and tossed it into the ditch where it landed near the drunkard. She hoped the water would help him clear his head, or perhaps wash him of the sickening smell of fermentation that oozed from his skin. Satisfied that she had done something, Alannah urged her stallion into a trot and headed back toward town.

As the afternoon ended and the sun began to sink, Alannah returned to the tavern yard.

Matalia frantically awaited her arrival. "Where have you been? We've been waiting for you for hours!"

Alannah dismounted and bowed her head apologetically. "I am sorry to have distressed you, but I needed to go for a ride this afternoon."

"The king and queen are going to announce the prize for the race this year! I am so excited! What do you think it could possibly be?" When Alannah did not respond, Matalia continued. "Well, go up to your room and change. Effie is waiting for you. She would not show me your dress. She said I would have to wait until you were wearing it. What impertinence!''

Alannah giggled. "Do not be angry with her. I am sure you will be well pleased.'' She felt along the stable wall for her stick, and after locating it, moved with authority toward the inn. Several tavern workers watched her with a mixture of awe and superstition. In their experience, blind people were useless cripples. They did not walk with pride and grace. Moving respectfully out of her way, they watched her reach the door, find the latch, lift it confidently and step over the doorjamb with ease.

One boy turned to another and said, "If'n I didn't see it wit me own two eyes, I'd'a never believed it!''

"I know," the other boy responded. "She's a bit like an angel.''

"Hah! A Scottish angel with red hair and green eyes?''

"Well, there is no saying that an angel canna be red-haired. I'm a'thinkin' that she might be an angel walking this earth, but since this world is so much uglier than heaven, she was struck blind.''

His companion nodded, thinking that his friend might be right. They traded a few more thoughts, then drifted back to work. Meanwhile, Matalia followed Alannah up the stairs, continuing to berate her.

"I wish you would not go out alone. There is no telling what sort of person you might run across.''

Alannah bit her lip, remembering the man she had left in the ditch. She had really wanted to help him, but caution had held her back. "I am trying to be careful," she responded. "But really, Matalia. There is no need to worry. My stallion can outrun any horse." She walked away from her, suddenly immeasurably lonely. It was a feeling she did not like, and she tried to bury it immediately. But the loneliness surged forth, along with the knowledge of Xanthier's abandonment. It was odd, she thought. Odd that in the midst of so many people she was lonelier than she had ever been before.

She leaned against the door, wishing that someone would come up to her and enfold her in a warm embrace. She thought of Grandmother. The world seemed very strange without her constant presence. Then she thought of Xanthier. For a moment she let her mind wander, remembering the glorious days when they had worked as one, thought as one, felt as one. There had been no loneliness then. Instead, there had been a feeling of completeness.

Alannah sighed. It was useless to remember, for it only brought pain. He was gone and she was not going to let him ruin her new life. She was done with him. She had other concerns now. She had located Gondilyn and was seeking her family.

She stood up and raised her chin. It was time to get ready, and Effie was waiting for her. Alannah forced a smile. She was going to meet the king and queen of Scotland!

Chapter 17

Xanthier stared moodily at the throng of people filling the royal banquet hall. If he had had any choice, he would have been out searching for Alannah tonight instead of listening to empty conversations and looking into vapid faces. There was still no word of her whereabouts. Unfortunately, the king had anticipated his avoidance and issued a request for his presence.

People stood around him, pressing against him as they jockeyed for position. Tonight the contestants for the various games would officially register, and everyone was eager to see who would or would not join the lists. Disgusted, Xanthier leaned against the wall, trying his hardest to ignore everyone.

"Oh!" gasped a young maid as she tripped over his feet. She held her hand to her mouth in fascinated horror as she beheld Xanthier's scars. "Ohhh! It is Commodore O'Bannon! He is so manly. So handsome in a rough kind of way. So . . . so . . ."

Her mother quickly grasped the girl's hand, holding her upright when she would have collapsed in a faint. "Now, now, child," the mother scolded. "You had best keep your breath. There is nowhere to sit, even if you do feel light-headed. Come now. We need to get closer."

The mother hustled the girl along, clucking disapprovingly when she looked back over her shoulder and gasped once more.

Annoyed, Xanthier glared at her, making his already intimidating face look overwhelmingly frightening. The girl screeched and rolled her eyes upwards, then fluttered them closed as she slumped to the floor.

"Heavens!" cried the mother as she fanned the child. "Your dress will be ruined! Get up!"

Xanthier turned away, bored. Gauging by the influx of people, he estimated that he could slip out the back door within the hour and never be missed. The trumpets sounded three times, signaling the jousting entrants. Men moved toward the dais and announced their names while presenting their tabards. A clerk rapidly wrote their names in a log and checked the tabards for appropriate size, then nodded at the king. When the king nodded in reply, the men bowed and moved aside for the next entrant.

Xanthier became aware of a man standing next to him. The hair on the back of his neck lifted and his muscles tightened. Xanthier turned to face him.

"Xanthier O'Bannon," the man said in greeting.

"Kurgan of the Serpents," Xanthier replied. "We meet again."

"You have been avoiding me," Kurgan accused.

"Perhaps," Xanthier replied.

"Last time I fought with you, it was on a battlefield in the Lowlands."

Xanthier nodded. "The battle at Knott's Glen."

"Glorious fight, was it not? Glorious!" Kurgan's

face glowed with malicious enjoyment at Xanthier's discomfort.

Xanthier clenched his teeth. The battle had been bloody and senseless, and had harmed the locals more than anyone. Fifty or more farmers had been slaughtered and over a hundred soldiers had fought until their body parts littered the ground and their life force soaked the earth.

Speaking softly, Xanthier leaned closer and stared at Kurgan. "I forget, Kurgan. Did we win or lose?"

Kurgan frowned and rubbed his head. "We won, of course. Don't you remember?"

"And what, exactly, did we win?"

"We won the battle. That was our goal. We fought to fight!"

Xanthier closed his eyes briefly, then pulled away from Kurgan as if he could not stand his stench. "I do not fight so senselessly now," he finally said.

Angered, Kurgan stepped closer and pushed his chest into Xanthier's. "You think you have somehow become better than us? The five of us were terrors of the Lowlands! Before your brother came back and stole your land, we ruled! No one dared to lift their eyes when we rode through their villages! We took what we wanted and killed anyone who got in our way. Are you so different now? You, the commodore of a commissioned fleet? Look at you—your face is ruined. You are scarred inside and out. It does not matter what you try to do, you can never be redeemed for what we did. Give up trying! Come back and fight alongside me again. Murder whoever displeases you and rape those that catch your interest."

Xanthier balled his hands into fists, infuriated

with Kurgan. "Your madness is spreading, Kurgan. I knew that day at Knott's Glen that you were losing your mind. Raiding, yes. Looting, yes. Showing power and strength, yes. But I never raped and murdered for no reason, like you did."

Kurgan spit on the floor at Xanthier's feet. "But you were there, Xanthier," he whispered, "and you raised your sword just as high as I did that day. You are tainted already." He stepped back and rubbed his head again, messing his hair. He twitched, his head jerking in tiny spasms. "Don't forget that, Xanthier. You are already tainted. Nothing you can do will erase that!"

Before Xanthier could reply, Kurgan ducked into the crowd and disappeared. Xanthier breathed heavily. The area around him was infused with a sheen of red and he found it hard to focus. Kurgan's words echoed in his mind, and Xanthier could not shake them, for he feared that they were all too true. He was evil. Everyone knew it. Xanthier turned and pounded the stone wall with his fist. Pain burst through his hand as his knuckles bloodied the stones. Another maid gasped and shrank away from him.

The trumpets sounded again, calling for the next event. Xanthier felt claustrophobic as a surge of people dragged him forward. He spun around, ready to punch anyone who dared shove against him, and caught a glimpse of beautiful auburn hair across the room.

He froze, staring at the place where he had seen the vision, but it was gone. Agony welled inside him. Not again! He could not bear to be beset by memories again! He struggled to exit the crowd, faintly hearing Queen Margaret announce the horse race contestants. The people swarmed around him, hindering his escape. He needed to get out! Now! Looking up, he saw another flash of her hair and even the curve of her cheek. He gasped, desperately needing air. Twisting, he tried to go the other way, away from the apparition, but the crowd would not let him.

The people became agitated, whispering among themselves, placing bets and pressing closer. Xanthier pushed a man aside, glaring at him with such fury that the man let him pass. But another was right behind him, and another and another. Duncan, McGregor, Lithfin . . . Name after name was announced and the people got more and more excited. They could not wait to hear the king announce this year's prize.

Xanthier was able to get halfway to the door before he saw her again. This time he felt his heart stop. She was standing with regal grace, her form encased in white lace decorated with tiny silver and green beads. She glittered, catching and holding his eye as if she were magical. Her auburn hair flowed down her back, accented by emerald-colored clips and rippling ribbons.

It could not be her! How could she be in court, dressed like a princess?

The auburn-haired woman turned as if she could sense his gaze, but a swarm of maidens suddenly blocked his view. He shoved someone aside, staring at the place where she had been standing, but she was gone. Xanthier's heart thudded into motion again, sending blood rushing to his head. It could not be her!

Hurkin, Quinn, Murphy . . . The announcer continued his list, but Xanthier paid him little attention. He would prove to himself that he was not as crazy as Kurgan, seeing things that were not real.

He would go up to the woman and touch her. He would force his mind to stop this desperate imagining. He would no longer allow himself to imagine her presence wherever he went.

He moved with the crowd, seeking to reach the front dais where he knew she would be. The people parted for him, strangely aiding him, whereas before they had hindered him. He was propelled forward, weaving through the crowd with ease.

Mackenzie, Clarken, Gerrak . . . The crowd paused, and Xanthier burst through the front line, reaching the dais just as another family ascended the steps. Tap, tap, tap. The woman in silver and green used a wooden staff to test the steps as she walked.

". . . O'Bannon, and lastly, Kurgan," the announcer stated, and the crowd buzzed with excitement. "If no others are ready to come forward, the king is prepared to make a proclamation."

The crowd cheered, then abruptly stilled as the king rose.

Alannah trembled. This was the moment! This is what Matalia and Brogan had told her to expect. She paused, feeling something behind her. She almost turned to see what was pulling her, but Matalia took her elbow and nudged her forward. Carefully tapping her staff, Alannah walked up to the front, then listened intently.

"I have thought long and hard about this year's prize," said the king. "I have debated many options, but I believe I have found something truly unique and valuable. I am going to bestow a section of land upon the winner!"

The noise of the crowd rose instantly, as the people whispered guesses as to the land the king was putting up. Property! Nothing was more valuable than a place to call home.

"Silence!" the king roared. "This land I speak of is an island off the coast of Scotland, sheltered by reefs and rich in soil. It is a lush land that supports sheep and horses. It is called the Isle of Wild Horses, and our very own Commodore Xanthier has captured it for Scotland."

The crowd went wild, screaming and shouting, as the ladies turned and pointed at Xanthier and the men nodded in appreciation of his apparent vigor and valor.

Xanthier felt light-headed. He shook his head, making sure that the nights of drinking had not corrupted his brain, but no, the king was staring at him, clapping and smiling. The island? He was giving away the island Xanthier had been trying to claim? He swung his stunned gaze back to the woman who looked like Alannah, and saw her face pale, saw the fine trembling that overtook her hands.

It *was* her! It was Alannah! By some miracle she was here, only footsteps away! Thoughts of the island fled his mind and he focused upon her presence. He could touch her and kiss her and sweep her into his arms! He stepped forward, a smile beginning to form on his lips, when he saw her turn into the arms of a young soldier.

Rage filled him and he growled in fury. Terrified, people around him stepped hastily back.

Alannah gasped, clinging to Gondilyn. "No! That is not possible! That is *my* island!" She shook her head and turned to the king. "You cannot do that!"

King Malcolm looked down at Alannah and reprimanded her gently. "Mistress, watch your tongue around the king and queen of Scotland. Unless you have something appropriate to say, say nothing. Xanthier brought word of this island's existence and it is within my power to claim it and bestow it upon whomever I wish."

The crowd fell silent. Everyone seemed to hold his or her breath in anticipation. Alannah swallowed, realizing with dawning comprehension that her beloved island was soon to be given over to another. She opened her mouth, mouthing the word *please,* but said nothing aloud. There was nothing she could say.

Alannah grasped Matalia's hand. "This cannot be happening," she murmured. "It cannot be so!"

Xanthier recoiled at the look of pain on her face. He had to help her, had to help the woman he loved. Hoping that he was not making things worse, he stepped forward. "The island is hers," Xanthier stated. "I speak on her behalf."

The crowd whispered madly again, delighted at the new turn of events.

The king glared at Xanthier. "How dare you speak of ownership! You came to me attempting to claim property you found while in service to the king. This matter is no longer your concern. If you have issue with her, take it up privately."

"You!" Alannah cried. "You betrayed me, Xanthier! You were staking a claim, intent upon stealing my island all along!"

"No, Alannah. That is not how it happened—"

"Silence!" the king thundered. "No more will be said! Bring forth any final contestants so we can close the lists."

Alannah swayed in shock. Each time either Xanthier or the king spoke, she flinched as if they were striking her. Her emotions surged. Pain, hurt, fury all vied to be expressed. She had accepted Xanthier's abandonment, but she had never considered this betrayal! The island was her home, her haven. How could he do it?

Xanthier shook with barely suppressed rage, but his head moved in a semblance of a nod. He was furious with the king, but equally angry with Alannah. How could she think that he would steal from her? He had spent so much time in agony, protecting her interests!

Xanthier grabbed her, but she jerked her arm out of his grasp. "Don't ever come near me!" she hissed under her breath. "I am nothing to you, and you are nothing to me. Let us both remember that!"

"Stop this, Alannah, and listen."

"No! This cannot be happening!" she cried again. "It cannot! I cannot lose my island! You are a terrible, awful beast!" Hurt welled inside her, and she fought her tears with supreme willpower. "I never want to talk to you. Never! Ohhhh . . . What can I do?"

Xanthier closed his face, hiding his emotions. He did not want anyone to see the pain in his soul. Somehow she had made it across the land and was standing in the Scottish court. She was safe! His heart ached. He loved her so much! His eyes swept her form, remembering the creamy flesh that had quivered under his hands. He recalled the smell of her satisfaction, the sound of her moans. He had to make this disastrous situation better. Turning to the king, he said, "I will enter the race. My horse comes from strong stock and has always been one of the fastest on the field."

"And win *my island*?" Alannah cried incredulously. "Never!" She abruptly turned to Gondilyn and gripped his arm. "Will you ride? My stallion is faster than any other horse! Will you ride him in the race and win my island back for me?"

"I . . . if that is what you want, Alannah. I will ride the race in your name, upon your steed."

Xanthier stepped back, infuriated. How dare she let another man ride the white stallion! It was the final insult. With a snarl of disgust, he turned away and stalked through the crowd.

Matalia watched his retreating back as she wrapped Alannah in a warm embrace. "Are you all right, Alannah?" she asked.

She nodded shakily.

"How do you know him? What just happened? Is that the man who hurt you?"

Alannah dashed a tear from her face. "Yes," she whispered. "I hate him."

Matalia stared after her brother-in-law's retreating back and frowned. She knew she should tell Brogan, but she wasn't sure what she shoudl say.

Music played and people formed lines for structured dances while others gossiped. Fancy candles lit the room and cast the smell of tallow along with their flickering flames. Bursts of laughter erupted here and there, and an occasional shriek indicated a too bold suitor.

The evening passed in a blur. Alannah was an instant celebrity. Her beauty combined with her uniqueness made her fascinating, and the queen favored her with unqualified approval. Most people who met her found it amazing that she functioned so well without her sight, and many commented upon it. At first Alannah felt proud, but as the night wore on she yearned for someone to appreciate her for what she was and not for what she was not. She wanted them to acknowledge her blindness and respect it without commenting on how "unblind" she seemed to be.

When she had lived on the island, it had never been a matter of pretending to be visual. She was blind and that was that. Instead, she had utilized her other senses and to some extent, had felt that she understood the world better than sighted people did. Grandmother had taught her to feel that way, and even Xanthier had seemed to understand her special gifts. Neither had used phrases that compared her to someone who could see. They appreciated her for who she was.

Xanthier's betrayal echoed in her mind. The shock of hearing his voice had been hard enough, but hearing it speak such devastating sentences . . . she had not known how to respond. She had set out from the ship to expand her knowledge and—she must admit—show Xanthier that she was fully fit to function in society. Although she wanted to find her family, part of her really wanted simply to find him. Whatever fantasy she had had about their meeting, however, was dashed. It made sense, of course, that he would be here at court for the festival. Nonetheless, she had not expected to see him.

A gentleman interrupted her thoughts. "You are magnificent, Mistress Alannah. I swear I have seen you before. Where else have you been presented?"

Alannah turned toward the man and shook her head. "I have not been anywhere else."

"Surely that is not true. You look so familiar . . . I am Kurgan. Your auburn hair and emerald eyes are striking."

"I think you are teasing me," Alannah replied nervously.

"No! I think you are absolutely beautiful. It is just that I think I have seen you somewhere. You remind me of someone . . . Forgive me if I am too forward, but would you care to dance?"

Kurgan smiled as he pulled her onto the dance floor where a new line was forming. He had never seen Xanthier so distressed as when this woman had flung insults at him and rejected his attempts at communication. It was fascinating.

For years, Kurgan had wrestled with being unable to crack Xanthier's hard exterior. Kurgan disliked everyone, but Xanthier irritated him more than most. When they had battled together, Xanthier had always been the better fighter, the wilier strategist. Time and again Kurgan had been forced to smile and acknowledge Xanthier's superior skills. When Xanthier had deserted the field at Knott's Glen, Kurgan had initially felt triumphant. For once he had fought longer and harder than Xanthier! But then people had started saying derogatory things about the battle and about the soldiers who had fought it. Kurgan's reputation as a fierce warrior had been tainted with disapproval.

It was ridiculous! Warriors should be able to do anything they wished. Chivalry and honor were rules to mock. After the battle, it had been Xanthier who had received the sailing commission, Xanthier who had become successful and revered while he had been sent home to watch over his uncle's estate.

Of course, now that he had not only inherited the estate but also the title to go with it, Kurgan was of higher rank than Xanthier, but it still rankled that his former colleague had amassed such a fortune. It was time the tables were turned. Perhaps, with Mistress Alannah, he had found the key to making Xanthier squirm!

Xanthier was tortured by the vision of Alannah dancing with other men. She floated, her beaded dress sweeping behind her as she danced with partner after partner. And Kurgan! How could she stand his evil touch upon her waist? Xanthier glared at them, unable to drag his gaze from the dance floor. She was amazingly graceful, executing the dance movements with flair and elegance.

Xanthier swallowed more ale from his tankard. This was worse! Before, he had only wrestled with his thoughts. Now she was only steps away. Longing for her overwhelmed him and he escaped to the gaming room. He could not bear it. He could not see her with someone else, especially Kurgan. He couldn't even stand to see her talking with another!

He swiped a new drink from a passing servant, then strode over to a game of dice. He flung a pile of gold coins on the floor. The other players looked at him with surprise.

"You have done well for yourself," one remarked.

"If you worry that I cannot meet my debts, have no fear," Xanthier growled. "I have several ships in harbor filled with treasure. I'll take the next throw." He reached for the dice and tossed them against the wall. He hardly watched the pieces as they tumbled to a stop. Instead, he looked through the entranceway and stared at the dancers. She was so easy to pick out, like a beacon.

"Toad's warts!" a player exclaimed as the numbers came up. A swift exchange of coins resulted in an increase in Xanthier's pile and they motioned for him to roll again. Dragging his eyes from her, he threw the dice again. She was more relaxed now, even smiling occasionally. People were flocking to talk to her. Xanthier gripped his sword hilt when one dance partner grew bold and touched her shoulder as if he was brushing her hair back from her neck.

"Lord Xanthier, you won again. Care to count your coins?"

Xanthier started. He looked down at the floor and saw the mound of coins. He wanted to lose them all! He wanted to punish himself. He shoved the entire pile into the center with his boot.

"Don't be a fool," Captain Robbins muttered behind his shoulder, but Xanthier ignored the wise advice. He rolled the dice, praying for a bad combination. The other players leaned forward, eager to regain their losses. The dice tumbled against each other, bouncing against the far wall, until they rolled to a stop at Xanthier's feet. The other players stared in shock.

"How can that be possible?" someone shouted.

"Toad's warts!" the other cried again.

"God's breath," Xanthier growled, disgusted at his good fortune. He turned around, looking for her again. She was standing in the midst of several men. Bile rose in his throat.

He wanted to kill them all, kill anyone who dared to stand near her and stare into her green eyes. He would gladly murder any fool who leaned close to her or had the audacity to hold her hand. Rage boiled inside him, and he struggled mightily with his temper. A year ago he would have acted on his impulses. But something inside him had changed over the last several months.

He turned away and stalked from the room, abandoning the coins and the sight of her. He would leave, he decided. Forget the king and queen.

Forget the meeting they had granted him tomorrow to discuss his other concern. Forget her. He would go tonight. The ships were ready and it would only take a few hours to round up the sailors.

He strode onto a stone walkway, then entered a shadowed area where the dance lights were blocked by potted trees. He paused and leaned against the railing. His rage twisted, became something new and different. It was pain brought about by jealousy. He wanted her! He wanted to feel her flesh next to his and feel her surrender to his—no, *their*—passion.

He closed his eyes and dropped his head.

Alannah subtly pulled away from Kurgan even though the steps put them close together. His hand was hot and he smelled sweaty. She could feel the heat of his gaze on her shoulders, and it made her slightly ill. She longed for the music to end. Smiling with forced gaiety, she nodded at his stream of trivial comments without listening to his words, and breathed with relief when they broke apart to travel separately down the line. At last, the music ended and she could escape.

"Please," she murmured to Kurgan, "could you find Matalia and bring me to her?" Dancing had taxed her ability to function without stumbling over everyone, and she needed to rest.

"Certainly, my dear," Kurgan said as he picked up her hand and patted it familiarly. "But tell me first about how you met the commodore."

Alannah shook her head. "I do not want to discuss him, ever!"

"Of course. How could I be so unfeeling? It is clear that you are upset with him. When one is shocked by the actions of a close friend, it is painful."

"Yes, it is very painful," Alannah admitted.

Kurgan grinned again, pleased that he had guessed correctly. There had been a relationship between the two, and it would give him a perfect opportunity to thwart his enemy. "I would not drag you through this throng. Wait here, by the window. I will bring Matalia to you." He picked up a cup of mead and pressed it into Alannah's hand. "Drink this," he breathed. "It will make you feel better."

Alannah nodded and gratefully took a swallow. The sweet mead relaxed her.

"See?" Kurgan said. "Isn't it wonderful? It is fermented. Drink up and I will be back shortly." He moved away, returning moments later with Matalia and Brogan. He stayed by her side for an hour, trying to woo her. Other admirers swarmed around her, too, asking her to dance and vying for her attention.

As the sounds and scents overwhelmed her, Alannah excused herself and leaned against the wall. It was so much to handle. She needed time to think. She had spoken rashly to Xanthier, yet she could still hear the king's words like little knives in her heart. In the excitement of meeting the king, she had managed to put Xanthier in the back of her thoughts for a moment, but now he was here, filling her mind with a vengeance. Raising her hands, she rubbed her temples, trying to erase the ache there.

She felt the whisper of fresh air against her cheek. With relief, she felt along the wall until she found the source of the breeze. It was an open doorway leading outside. Without pausing, she ducked out and moved to the right, out of sight. She pressed against the stone wall and breathed deeply, grateful to be away from all the people.

Chapter 18

Xanthier turned slowly after hearing a soft sigh, stunned that Alannah was standing only two steps from him. She glowed in the moonlight, her dress sparkling like hundreds of fireflies. He stared at her, letting his gaze rove over her. She was his! He had found her on a deserted island, and no one else should have her. He growled under his breath.

The sound caught her attention and she froze, hoping that she was invisible in the dark. She did not want any more bland conversation. She did not want to sidestep any more pointed questions. Using her senses, she tried to locate and decipher the person she heard.

"You're mine," he whispered.

Alannah gasped. "Xanthier!" He took a step forward, stalking her as she cringed away from him, terrified of her own longing to leap into his arms.

"You . . . are . . . mine," he repeated, dragging the words out so that there would be no mistaking them.

"No," she cried. "You left me! You betrayed me! You have no claim anymore."

Xanthier took the last step and wrapped his hands around her throat. He smoothed his thumbs over her fluttering pulse. "Why did you run away?"

Alannah tried to pull back, but her limbs would not obey her instructions and she stood silently like a lamb waiting to be devoured by the wolf.

"Hummm? Why did you leave the ship after I was delayed? Were you looking for me?"

She shook her head.

Xanthier squeezed gently, tilting her neck. He brushed his lips across hers. "I've wanted to do this since the moment I saw you . . ." Shifting his hands, he cupped her head and pushed her fully against the wall. He nibbled her lower lip, tasting her mouth, then slanted against it and kissed her fully, sliding his tongue inside.

Alannah sighed and he groaned in response. He gripped her waist and pulled her flush against him, showing her how aroused he was. He ground his hips, needing to get close to her, wanting, *needing,* to be inside her.

Almost instantly Alannah felt her desire spiral out of control. All thoughts of resistance disappeared in the ambrosia of his kiss and she wrapped her arms around his shoulders.

He swooped her into his arms and dropped his lips to her neck, then lower to the valley between her breasts. He would not give her a second to think, a moment to remember. He would overwhelm her senses and make her helpless with yearning. He carried her away from the banquet hall and out to a torch-lit garden.

Locating a cushioned bench, he placed her gently down and leaned over her. The torchlight cast flickering shadows and golden firelight over her bared shoulders. He drew in his breath, stunned by how gorgeous she was, sprawled beneath him. Her mouth was open slightly as she breathed, and he could see her breasts heave.

He reached for the ties on her dress, unwinding them as quickly as he could. Each time one was loosened, he dropped his lips to her, licking and sucking on her revealed skin. A wave of passion surged through him, and his patience was ended. He gripped the edge of her hem and tossed it upwards, finding the silken haven of her thighs. He grabbed her ankles and yanked her to the edge of the bench, pressing her against his swollen phallus.

He slipped his hand between her thighs, found her most sensitive place and stroked it softly, reveling in her instant reaction. She gasped and sank back on her elbows, her hair tumbling. Moisture coated his fingers and he smiled with satisfaction.

Frantic now, he yanked his own clothes apart, releasing his rod, which pulsed and strained. Spreading her legs, he forcefully held her knees apart and opened her for his plunging entrance.

She cried out, immersed in the emotions he alone could evoke. She felt helpless beneath his assault, yet at the same time incredibly powerful. She felt his control slipping away and knew that she did this to him. Her body, her scent, her touch made him wild.

She arched her back, lifting her half-bared breasts. He responded instantly, burying his face in her flesh, wrapping his lips around her cloth-covered nipple. He sucked firmly, wanting her to feel him, and she moaned in pleasure. Holding her with his mouth, he sank into her, sliding deeply within her. She gasped, squeezing him with her inner muscles, feeling him slide easily within her slippery cocoon.

He pulled out, then sank in, watching her face. Giving her pleasure was . . . exquisite. Seeing her transported with desire . . . there was no way to describe it. He stroked her, sliding in and out, watching the sensations build within her, feeling her tighten with escalating ecstasy. She burst, her thighs falling apart, her eyelids flickering. Her skin flushed and she collapsed back against the cushions.

But he would not stop. He flipped her over, baring her buttocks to the torchlight. He pulled her against him once again, spearing inside her swollen confines. Holding her waist, he slammed into her from behind, forcing her replete body to awaken, to rise to meet his passion.

Alannah felt him take over, felt him guide her body into the rhythm he wanted. She was pliant, giving, willing. Then the flickers of excitement flared and she was moaning with need once more, gripping the iron railing of the bench to brace herself, to assist his pounding invasion.

He felt it coming and he paused, not wanting to end their closeness. Panting with effort, he reached around and touched her, playing with her sensitive parts with a mixture of rough possession and sweet adoration. She twitched, trying to get him to move again but he held back, touching her, stroking her.

Suddenly her hand joined his and she wrapped her fingers around the base of his cock, encircling it tightly. He gasped, the surge of ardor flooding his body with need. He pulled back, relishing the slide of her fingers while the rest of him lay buried within her. She squeezed slightly, urging him to come back to her, and he complied immediately, sinking deeply. He grabbed her hand and pulled it to where he had been touching, interlacing her fingers in his as he stroked her.

She moaned, the mixture of sensations both inside and around her overtaking her inhibitions and releasing her from earthly constraints. She soared, flying high above the garden as wave upon wave of delight suffused her.

Xanthier clenched, shuddering as he sank as deeply into her as he could, trying to become one with her, to meld with her. He shuddered, feeling the surge of his ejaculate sweep down and flood her, drenching her with his essence. He held her buttocks tightly against him, relishing every pulse, every twitch, every instant of the long, beautiful climax they shared.

As the sparks faded and he could function again, he turned her back over and gazed into her dazed face. In their passion they had trampled some flowers, and the pungent odor of their crushed blooms filled the air. A small candle sputtered in a sconce that some careless guest had left on the bench, its wax spilling down the candlestick in rippling layers. Xanthier was reaching to snuff it out when Alannah gripped his hand.

He looked down, surprised by her uncanny accuracy. She pushed him gently and he knelt at her feet as she sat up. Her disheveled appearance instantly aroused him and he put his hands on her hips, pulling her closer.

Alannah smiled and pushed his shirt off, baring his chest. Then she took the candle from its resting place and held it over him. With one finger, she nudged him back until he lay on his back underneath her. She dipped her nail into the hot wax, then stroked it down his chest, making a thin cream-colored line that hardened as it cooled.

She did it again, making a design, scratching him lightly while the heated wax burned his skin. His passivity excited her, and she grew bolder, tipping the candle and splashing the wax. He gasped but remained still, submitting to her game. She leaned down and kissed the reddened area, laving it with her tongue. He groaned, her hot breath burning more than the melted candle.

She felt around and collected several petals, then used them to brush against his sensitized skin. The velvet softness of a rose, the tickly delicacy of hawthorn, the raspy sensation of heather . . . she played with all of them, stroking his skin and taunting his flesh.

He lifted his hips, pushing her own hips toward his mouth. "Let me taste you," he whispered as he urged her upwards. The beads on her dress glimmered in the moonlight and he was reminded momentarily of her new, sophisticated role in the Scottish court, yet her rumpled appearance made her seem like a sultry faerie whose magical powers could entrap and enslave him forever. He closed his eyes and lifted her as he moved underneath her spread legs.

She grasped the bench once again, balancing on her knees and holding herself upright by the iron bars. His tongue flickered out and he licked her. Shards of delight broke through her and she teetered. He gripped her firmly, holding her upright, and licked again, searching for the place that would give her the greatest pleasure. She cried, tears springing to her eyes as he found it and cherished it, licking and sucking, stroking and soothing. She tried to pull away because the sensations were so intense, but he held her still and continued his ministrations. She dropped her head, giving over to him, offering herself into his care.

The feelings spun and circled, making her feel as she had never felt before. He slid a finger inside her, stroking her as he licked, and the tears came fully, trailing down her cheeks and dropping like pearls into the earth.

She gasped, then held her breath, almost fainted . . . then it burst over her, exploding so forcefully she screamed and wrapped her hands around the iron bench so hard her knuckles turned white.

He plunged his tongue inside her, wanting to taste her climax, wanting to drink her pleasure.

Then she collapsed. He held her tightly, pulling her down, then turning her around. He lifted her dress once again and sank inside her, stroking quickly and firmly until he climaxed within seconds, filling her as her rippling ecstasy still fluttered around him.

"Oh, Alannah," he murmured. "Let's go. Let's leave tonight and go away from all these people. I want to return to the island and do nothing but love you."

Alannah frowned, his words dragging her back to reality. "What do you mean?" she asked.

"You don't belong here. Let me take you back to your rightful place. What do you say?" He lifted her so he could see her face.

She frowned deeper. "I have things to do here," she said slowly. "The island . . . the search for my family . . ."

"Forget them," he replied angrily. "They mean nothing. Let's leave now, this moment!"

Alannah pulled away from him. Her head swam and her limbs were weak. She stumbled to the bench and sat down as she tried to straighten her clothing. "I cannot forget my family. I want to know about them. And I must compete in the race. My island is the prize."

"I will win it for you. And even if I don't, I will defend the island from anyone who dares to step upon it," he shouted. "Come with me now!"

Alannah gazed up, her sightless eyes peering into the darkness. "You still think you can take my island?" she asked. "It should be mine, not yours."

"Don't be ridiculous," he replied furiously. "I want to protect you. This is a confusing, violent world with plundering men and cruel ambitions. Women do not own land. Men own land and protect their women."

"You should know me better," she said softly. "You should have known my feelings before. I was right when I told you to stay away from me. You are not good for me. I will win my island. I do not need your protection or your help."

Xanthier glared at her, infuriated beyond comprehension. How could she turn away from him after such blissful intimacy? All he wanted to do was protect her! Wasn't it his role to shield her from harm? Wasn't he supposed to take care of her? She should be grateful!

She stood up. "Please go away. Leave the race and leave me. Go back to the sea. Do whatever you want to do, but stay away from me and my island. I do not want you."

He stumbled back as if stabbed. She could not be saying these things! "Alannah!" he cried, but she shook her head.

"You created this situation through your single-minded need to own and command. My island is free. It has no lord or allegiance. It loves me and I love it. You seek to change that."

"How can you think that? I tried to claim it so it would never change! I only wanted to put my name on the map so the island would be safe from any others. There are reasons why that must be done."

Alannah relaced her gown and straightened her hair. "You still think that I need your protection. I hope someday you will realize I don't."

Xanthier took a step back and glared at her. "Maybe you are right. Maybe I am fearful for you and am overly protective. But hear this, Alannah. One day you might have to acknowledge that you need some protection after all. When you are ready, I will be there for you."

Chapter 19

Kurgan stared into a still pool. Moonlight reflected gently off the water, highlighting the trees and flowers that made up the queen's garden. His face, too, was reflected in the natural mirror. His hair was a deep, rich red, and while his pale green eyes were lost in the darkness of the pool, he could see the slope of his own cheekbones and the curve of his neck.

He twitched, seeing something he did not want to see. Although his image was familiar to him, it was not himself he saw in the water. He saw another whose auburn hair trailed down her back and whose cheek arched in aristocratic splendor. He touched the pool surface with his finger, causing ripples to distort the image. He waved his fingers back and forth, creating chaos in the formerly peaceful reflection.

Beside him lay the body of a young man. Although he had tried to keep his secret, torture had a way of making even the bravest man speak out. Although his body now lay in a pool of blood, he had already delivered his message to the one person Kurgan never wanted to receive it. That person had spent the last ten years in a secluded cottage in the Highlands. Gweneath Zarina Serpent, widowed wife of Lothian. His reluctant aunt.

Kurgan glared at the water's reflection, wishing he could push Zarina underneath the water and drown her in the murky depths. He had to make a decision quickly, for in one month he could lose his power, lose his title, lose his lands. Everything.

A sound caught his attention and he looked up to see a sparkling figure race down the path and head toward the hall. Alannah! Abandoning his water game, he padded swiftly after her. With sudden clarity he determined that he could still remedy the situation. He could kill her. Her death would assure that what he most feared was never realized.

He saw her again, and altered his path to intercept her. Grinning gleefully, he leaped ahead and gripped his sword.

Alannah froze, hearing the quick breathing of another person approaching. It was definitely not Xanthier, for the tread was light and rapid rather than firm and measured. Also, by the pattern of its approach, it seemed that the person was hunting. Her extra senses vibrated. Danger!

As fear raced down her spine, Alannah backed up against a tree. What—who—was hunting her? What did he want from her?

She touched the bark, then felt along the trunk until she found a low branch. Making a sudden decision, she grabbed hold of the branch and swung herself upwards. Her dress hindered her progress and for a moment she almost gave up, but a sound in the dark infused her with determination and she managed to climb upwards until she was well above the pathway.

The footsteps crunched on the gravel and came

around the path until they were underneath her hiding place. The hiss of swinging steel frightened her, and she bit her lip to still its trembling. With heightened senses, she could feel her pursuer's madness, detect his insane desire to hurt and plunder. She did not know why he had fixated upon her, but she prayed that he would find another victim and leave her alone.

Kurgan glared into the darkness. Where had she gone? He clenched his teeth and swung his sword back and forth in the air. It would be so simple to slice her throat! She would never see it coming! It would solve his problem and infuriate Xanthier at the same time.

A snapping twig to his right drew his immediate attention, and Kurgan ducked behind some bushes and followed the sound. A rock tumbled, making Kurgan excited. She must be just ahead! He ran forward, leaving the graveled pathway and following a less frequented path around a corner of the castle.

Alannah heard him leave with immense relief. She took a deep breath and pressed her head against the tree.

"What are you doing, Alannah?" Matalia called out from beneath the tree. "Why are you in the queen's ash tree?"

Alannah tilted her head, locating Matalia by her voice. There were no other sounds, and Alannah sighed gratefully. "I fear I have torn my new gown," she said as she clambered down.

"Indeed! Why did you go up there?" Matalia reached out and helped Alannah manage the final steps until she dropped to the ground.

"I thought I heard something," Alannah replied.

"Don't be ridiculous. There are no wild animals

in the queen's garden. Don't do that again. You never know what might befall you."

"Hummm," Alannah said noncommittally.

"I wanted to find you to tell you that I am going to my room to get some rest. The queen has granted us a small room in the northern wing, and I had our belongings moved over. The younger set is still dancing, but I find that I must retire a bit earlier these days. You can stay if you'd like."

"No," Alannah replied quickly. "I would rather go with you." She reached out for Matalia's arm and clung to it with uncharacteristic nervousness.

Matalia looked at her rumpled hair and flushed face with concern. "Alannah, are you all right?" she asked for the second time that night.

"Yes. I just want to go," Alannah answered and smiled pleasantly when Matalia guided her out of the garden and toward the northern chambers.

From the shadows Xanthier watched them go. His hand was dirty from throwing the rock that had distracted Kurgan from searching for Alannah. He had purposefully led Kurgan astray by snapping the twig and tossing the rock, but he knew that she would not appreciate his interference so he did not reveal himself. As he watched Matalia and Alannah walk away, he discreetly followed them, assuring himself of their safety until they were indoors once again. Then, with a grim look, he peered into the darkness where Kurgan was still searching. He must have learned something about Alannah. Xanthier did not know how Kurgan could have discovered the truth so soon, but he was not pleased.

By morning, there was another O'Bannon who was not pleased. Brogan O'Bannon, Earl of Kirkcaldy and twin brother of Xanthier, glared at the missive in his hand.

"Why are you rereading it, husband?" Matalia asked in exasperation. She pulled her horse to a walk and looked at him. They were on an hour's pleasure ride, but for the last twenty minutes, Brogan had been complaining and she was getting irritated with him. Istabelle and Mangan rode behind them, but Alannah had chosen to remain with Gondilyn to train for the coming horse race.

"Because I cannot believe the words that are written here," Brogan exclaimed. "Why would the king demand my presence at a meeting with Xanthier? He knows that we are not on good terms."

"Brogan, you are being bullheaded. The missive is clear and I understand the king's concerns. We do not want another fight over Kirkcaldy. Xanthier's daughter, Istabelle, is . . . let us say that she has strong emotions and a stronger will. If she set her heart on Kirkcaldy, we would have another war on our hands."

"Our son, Mangan, loves his sister. There will be no fight."

Matalia nudged her horse closer to his and took a deep breath. "Istabelle is not Mangan's sister. They are cousins."

"They are very much like brother and sister," Brogan argued, glancing behind him at the pair riding their ponies.

"Bah! They are like the moon and the sun. I love them both, but Mangan is sweet, considerate and gentle, whereas she is wild and unruly, God bless them." Matalia kicked her horse into a gallop, leaving Brogan to grumble in private.

Soon Brogan chased after her and grabbed her horse's bridle. "They know no other life. You cannot doubt that they love each other," he said as the beasts slowed their pace.

"Yes, I know they care deeply for each another, but Istabelle is your brother's child. Xanthier has a right to her."

"He gave up that right when he left her with us on the night of his wife's death five years ago."

"Surely you are not as unreasonable as you sound," Matalia rejoined. "He left because it was the best thing to do. He left because he had no other choice. You should honor him for his courage. It takes a great man to know when to let go of a dream. He fought just as hard for Kirkcaldy as you did—harder even—but he came to realize that you would be the better earl. You must admire him for that."

"Aye. I understand. I know it took great strength to walk away from his home. Nonetheless, he left his infant with us and I do not see how giving her back would be good for her."

"Xanthier is Istabelle's father," Matalia insisted. "She needs a mother."

"Aye, I am sure the queen understands that. As I have said a thousand times already, I am sure that is why we have been invited to speak with him. Undoubtedly the king has chosen a bride for Xanthier and wishes him to rejoin the Scottish nobility. *With his daughter.*"

Brogan pulled his horse to a stop. All morning he had been plagued with the conviction that something was threatening Xanthier. Once again the sense of danger surged through him.

Matalia looked at him and bit her lip. "Is it he?" She glanced at the ponies that carried Mangan and Istabelle, assuring herself that they were near.

Brogan nodded, knowing that Matalia understood.

"Is he well? Has something happened?"

Brogan shrugged and nudged his horse forward again. The ride had been pleasant and he was not looking forward to returning to the bustle of the castle. As they maneuvered back through the village streets, it was important that they stay together. Istabelle had a tendency to wander away. "He is there, but I cannot figure out what is going on. I have never before felt such confusion from him."

"You have not seen each other for a long time. Perhaps it is just the changes that come with life."

"No. There is something specific, but I am at a loss to understand it. I only hope that he is not plotting something that he is deliberately hiding from me. I do not like this at all."

Matalia frowned and moved closer to her husband. She, too, was devastated by the royal command, for she did not want Istabelle to be torn from her home and placed in an unknown household, even if it was run by the child's true father. But she could not voice her concerns. She had to be strong to help her husband. He had enough worries to wrestle with, and her love for him demanded that she keep up a strong façade. She would stay firm. She would support the transition. If it was what the king ordered, she would place Istabelle in Xanthier's care, despite her fears. It would be like losing a daughter, yet a royal command could not be ignored.

Suddenly, Mangan raced his pony up to Brogan and Matalia. "Mother! Father! Istabelle ran off! She heard you talking and she jumped off her pony and ran into the forest!"

"Which way, Mangan? Which way did she go?"

Mangan pointed to the right, his small face scrunched up into a worried expression. "She should stop doing things like that. She is going to get hurt."

"Yes, darling, I agree. Istabelle is strong-spirited and has a mind of her own."

"I would never run away."

"No, you would stay and confront your problems, but you are very like your father while Istabelle is more like *her* father."

"She doesn't think anyone loves her even though I told her I love her and am going to marry her one day."

"Silly. You will marry some sweet lady, not a hellion like Istabelle. Especially if she cannot control her temper. Now wait here with me while your father looks for her."

Xanthier stared at the king and queen in shock. "Marry?" he asked incredulously. "You want me to marry the Lady Serena?"

"Yes." King Malcolm nodded. "It is time for you to wed again. You are a strong and wealthy lord. You have a daughter who needs gentle raising. The lady Serena has a dowry property in the south that needs a master and I will grant it to you upon your marriage."

Xanthier stared at the impassive royal faces in complete astonishment. Of all the events he had pondered, he had never considered the possibility that they would insist he remarry. "Your Majesty," he said carefully, "I told you what property I want—the island. And have you forgotten that I was wed five years ago and I have done my duty by Scotland? There is no need for me to—"

"I have heard tales of your daughter, Istabelle."

"Oh?" Xanthier was momentarily distracted. "Does she fare well?"

"Have you no contact with her at all?" the queen demanded.

"No, Your Majesty. She is under the good guardianship of my brother and his wife."

"That is not acceptable anymore," the queen stated. "Having children generates a sense of peace and stability, which is what Scotland needs. You will take Istabelle into your home and obtain a wife to help raise her."

Xanthier rose angrily. "I must protest," he growled. "I am a poor father and a poorer husband. I live on the seas. I have no time for a wife or for abandoned lands in southern Scotland."

"We are not asking you to give up your life," the king replied. "We ask only that you take a noblewoman to wife, and do right by Scotland. I gave you your first ship, your commission and a reason for living after you lost everything to your brother." The king stared at Xanthier coldly, displeased by his arguments. "You are obligated to obey my dictate."

"I have repaid you a hundredfold. Your coffers have swollen from the treasures I captured for you."

"You do not seem to understand," Queen Margaret interrupted. "We are not denying your accomplishments. We simply feel that you have neglected certain aspects of life. It is time to marry and take Istabelle into your home."

The king, far less tolerant than the queen, rose and glared at Xanthier. "I insist that the matter be resolved by the festival's end."

"I cannot!" Xanthier shouted. "I have other concerns, which I have been trying to discuss with you for weeks!"

Quickly interrupting him, Robbins stood up and bowed. "I have no doubt that the king and queen know what is best. Lord Xanthier is overwhelmed. Land! What a boon! Come, Xanthier, we must celebrate the good news."

Xanthier yanked his arm out of his friend's grasp and clenched his teeth. He bowed to the king and queen. "Your Majesties," he gritted. "I wish to be heard."

A page raced into the room and brought a parchment to the king. The letter had the bold crest of the Serpent emblazoned on the seal. The king broke the seal and scanned the document. Leaning over to his queen, he murmured inaudibly to her.

Xanthier watched them with concern. As they talked quietly together, thoughts whirled in his head. How much had Kurgan discerned? Could he know everything? Xanthier waited for the king to turn on him.

"As you were saying, Lord Xanthier?" King Malcolm finally said, his face betraying nothing out of the ordinary. "Is there something else you need to discuss?"

Xanthier stared at the king. The king stared back. Xanthier snapped his jaw shut and shook his head. The king smiled. "Perhaps we should finish our discussion with your brother present. I have already asked him to meet with us shortly. In the meantime, remember, I expect you to announce your betrothal to your new bride immediately."

His anger barely held in check, Xanthier strode away. "Why? God in heaven, why?" he hissed as he and Captain Robbins left the audience chamber. "I have no desire to marry some stranger! I will not! For the first time in my life, there is something I want—the island and Alannah—and the king is taking every measure to ensure that I can have neither!"

Captain Robbins pulled him through the crowd in the hall and dragged him outside. "You had best keep your voice down, Xanthier. I can understand your reluctance, but it is not seemly to voice your opposition so loudly. The king and queen of Scotland have given you a command. You have become complacent in your superiority as a commodore of the high seas. You must remember that there are those above you whom you must obey."

Xanthier rounded on his friend. "And if I do not? If I leave?"

"That would be a very bad decision. You would have no home, no family. You would have nothing but your ships. The royals of all the nations would turn against you. You would find no safe port."

"I have had no home and no family for a long time. It would be no different." Xanthier's voice softened with a hint of sadness, and Captain Robbins looked at him with dismay.

"You would be banned from the Isle of Wild Horses," Robbins reminded him.

Xanthier countered, "If I could have Alannah, I would not need anything else."

"Is that possible?" Captain Robbins asked.

Xanthier turned away. "Not now. Not legally. Not now that I know who she really is. Or until she comes of legal age and is free to act on her own."

"Why not be with her without the formality of marriage? If you care for her so much . . ."

Xanthier shook his head. "Believe me, when I found the letter, I debated all night about its significance. I thought to cast it in the flames and erase its words from this earth. But I know what it says, and I know what a good man would do. He would not marry Alannah without her family's permission and blessing. He would not deliberately place her in a shameful position for his own selfish reasons.

"I have lived without honor all my life. She showed me how to appreciate beauty, love and perhaps most importantly, honor. She worships the horses, the lands, the seas . . . she honors the world around her and expects that the world will honor her in return. Her family would never allow us to marry." Xanthier spun to face his friend, his face twisted in agony. "What am I to do?" he whispered. Robbins averted his gaze, unable to answer.

The image of Brogan flashed in Xanthier's mind as he stood in the courtyard. He contemplated the turn of events that had placed him in this predicament. His twin, his connection. The other part of his soul who walked this earth and breathed in tandem with him. He shook his head, but the images kept flickering in his mind. The two had come from the same seed but had been ripped apart within hours of their birth. They had grown up in completely different environments—Xanthier in a house of intrigue and strife, Brogan in a haven of love and reassurance. They had fought against each other in an inevitable battle for the title and lands that had once been their father's, but in the end Xanthier had walked away and left the property to Brogan.

Many speculated about why Xanthier had left. Some surmised that he had determined that Brogan would be a better ruler. Some thought that Xanthier had murdered his wife and had had no other choice. Very few knew that Xanthier's wife, Isadora, had poisoned the ailing earl and plotted to murder Brogan and his family. Xanthier had been the one to stop the horror. Xanthier had deflected the other warriors who had been sent to disembowel Brogan and his beloved bride, Matalia. He had ensured their safe escape.

But that was another story, from another lifetime. Xanthier did not acknowledge his past deeds, nor did he care to be reminded of his twin brother. It was all best forgotten. He had run away from his life five years ago, and he was no more ready to face it now than he had been then.

A stallion's whinny caused him to look up, and he saw Alannah and a guardsman riding past him. Her blind gaze swung by him, paused, then seemed to peer into him. He shivered, wanting suddenly to be held within her arms. He longed for her peaceful presence and her beautiful spirit. She, who could not see, was the only one who had ever really seen him. He took a step forward and opened his mouth to call out to her, but a flurry of activity suddenly blocked his view as all the horses for the upcoming race were brought forward to be measured.

He jumped back, embarrassed by his own need for her, and flushed red.

"Are you all right?" Captain Robbins asked, but Xanthier did not answer. Instead, he stalked away, his thoughts spinning with images of his past, memories of his twin brother and desire for his Alannah.

Chapter 20

Alannah held her stallion as the clerk measured him, noted his markings and diligently inscribed them into his book. The same clerk would check the horses daily, and double-check them on the morning of the race. She did not understand why the procedure was necessary, and thought that Matalia's explanation of horse switching and identity changing was preposterous. But there was much in this world she did not understand.

"He will have to wear a true bridle and saddle for the race," the clerk cautioned. He glanced at the barebacked stallion with apprehension.

Alannah turned fearfully to Gondilyn. "A bridle and saddle?" she asked.

"Aye. We will need to teach him not to fear the leather, then teach him to obey my commands. I am not sure it will be possible, Alannah. We have only a few days."

"Claudius will do anything for me," she assured him. "If I ask him to wear tassels and gilt and bear you upon his withers, he will."

Effie trailed after her, carrying a light shawl made of dark blue velvet trimmed in silver fox. The servant had decided to attach herself to Alannah, and Alannah was just as perplexed by that as she was by everything else. When Effie snatched a glass of flavored cider from a stand set up for the ladies of the court and presented it to Alannah, she shook her head reprovingly.

"Effie, I told you to stop waiting upon me. I am a simple woman. I do not warrant such attention. You should find someone worthy of such solicitation."

"I am pleased to serve you, mistress. I would be much offended if you sent me away."

Alannah sighed in exasperation and took the drink. She was thirsty, and it seemed silly to argue with the older woman. She did not know why Effie was so strange, but perhaps it was just her custom.

The clerk stepped back and nodded, then reddened when he realized that Alannah could not see his head motion. He cleared his throat and bowed, then turned purple at Effie's look of disgust. "Go ahead," he said, embarrassed by his ineptitude. He did not know how to address someone who could not see. "I'm finished, mistress," he added. "All done. No more—"

"Thank you," Alannah interrupted. "Shall we go to the road outside the village and start teaching Claudius?" she asked Gondilyn.

The clerk gratefully turned away from them and approached another horse and rider with relief as Gondilyn voiced his agreement. "Yes. Let us begin by having you ride him with a blanket on his back. Once your horse is accommodated to the sensation of the cloth, we will try a saddle."

After purchasing a small, unadorned saddle blanket from a vendor, Gondilyn showed Alannah how to place it on her horse. He then gave her a cloth band to tie around the stallion's girth to hold the blanket in place. After Alannah tied it on, Claudius swung his head back and sniffed the strap. To Gondilyn's amazement, Claudius then lowered his head to nibble the ground, searching for grass.

"See?" Alannah said. "He will do anything for me."

"He practically ignored it," Gondilyn exclaimed. "I am impressed. Ride him for awhile, then meet me by the road and I will have a saddle."

As Alannah began to move away, Kurgan stepped from the crowd and intercepted her.

"Alannah," he purred. "I am so pleased to see you this morning. You still intend to enter your horse in the race?"

"Yes," she replied. "I have no choice."

"This island where you were raised must be very valuable."

"It only holds value to me."

"I think not. Xanthier appears to want it . . ."

"No matter what, I will never let Xanthier win my island," Alannah said angrily. "My stallion will win this race, and the matter will be settled, forever."

"Things are often not as simple as they appear," Kurgan warned her. He slipped his hand under the saddle blanket and stroked Claudius's hide. The stallion stomped his foot furiously and shifted away, his ears laced flat against his head. "You are a beautiful woman. You made me feel like I was floating on a cloud when I danced with you last evening. I hope you can find a place in your heart to accept my admiration."

Alannah blushed, unaccustomed to such flattery. Xanthier had never said pretty phrases to her. His assertive personality did not lend itself to sweet compliments. Kurgan's words made her smile.

"I enjoyed dancing as well."

"Perhaps we can repeat the experience?"

Alannah nodded and was about to reply when Gondilyn cleared his throat. "We shall see," she said after a pause. "For now, I have duties to attend. Gondilyn, I will see you this eve," she said as she prepared to take Claudius for a run. "Good day, Kurgan."

"You will be in my thoughts," Kurgan answered.

Alannah turned away and approached her horse. She vaulted onto his back. Immediately he reared up, striking out with his hooves, and Kurgan leaped back in fear. "Claudius!" she exclaimed. "Stop dancing around."

"Be careful," Kurgan responded. "I want to stay in one piece. Otherwise I will not be able to be dance with you tonight."

Alannah, uncomfortable with Kurgan's comments, leaned forward, and her steed sprang ahead, eager to leave the courtyard. He swished his tail at the saddle blanket, but for the most part ignored it. They galloped out of the milling throng and sped up to the dirt track. Alannah breathed with relief as the sounds of the village faded away. The steady beat of the stallion's galloping hooves reverberated in her mind and she bent down, trying to relax. *One-two-three . . . one-two-three, barrrrumpt, barrrrumpt . . .* the galloping hooves echoed and she focused on them, pushing away all other thoughts. *Crash, swish . . . crash, swish . . .* she pretended that she could hear the ocean waves hitting the sand and sliding back out to sea. She longed for the peace of the island.

Suddenly she felt the blanket shift and she sat up to adjust her balance. The stallion pinned his ears back and bolted forward, confused by the unfamiliar movements. The blanket slid again, twist-

ing around his belly as the cloth strap sprang loose.
Alannah screamed and grabbed Claudius's mane as
she desperately tried to pull him to a stop, but he
was frightened and began to buck.

Alannah struggled to stay upright, feeling the
rushing wind sting her cheeks as the white stallion
surged into full, racing speed. The blanket rolled
under him, dragging Alannah until she was pulled
partially underneath him. Her hair snagged on
bushes and ripped out, leaving trailing auburn
tresses along the path. She screamed again, truly
frightened, and tried to scramble back onto the
horse's back.

Claudius abruptly turned off the track, leaping
over a ditch and bounding up the forested hillside.
Alannah was tossed backwards, but she clung to
the animal's neck. Squeezing hard, she pulled herself upright, and was able to grasp his mane. With
determined concentration, she forced Claudius to
slow, until he finally broke his headlong gallop and
drew to a stumbling halt.

Alannah breathed with relief and slid off safely.
She felt for the cloth strap and found the knot unraveled. She frowned, knowing that she had secured it herself. She stroked Claudius, soothing him
with soft sounds until he finally relaxed and rested
his head upon her shoulder. Alannah's breathing
slowed as she, too, calmed down.

Then suddenly a branch snapped above her.

She tilted her head and listened intently.

From her hiding place in the trees, Istabelle
stared down at Alannah. Ever since their first meeting, Alannah had seemed to Istabelle like a creature out of a legend. The woman's auburn hair
cascaded down her back like fire and her face was
breathtakingly powerful. Istabelle stared into her

eyes, knowing how unusual they were. It was not simply their color, although the green hue was unique. It was as if the woman had eyes that could see everything that everyone else could not.

"Who is there?" Alannah demanded.

Istabelle remained silent, keeping her hiding place secret. Her tiny heart was broken and she wanted to escape from everyone. But Alannah intrigued her. She watched the woman curiously, interested to see what she would do.

Alannah turned slowly back to her stallion. She could hear a child breathing up in the tree. By the pattern of her breathing and the smell of her skin, Alannah guessed that it was little Istabelle. There were no sounds of others approaching. It seemed strange that the child would be this far from town without parental supervision. Perhaps she had run away again due to some problem her five-year-old soul could not solve.

Crooning softly to her stallion, Alannah rubbed the white coat and dried the patches of sweat. She worked slowly, leisurely, allowing her speeding heart time to recover so she could focus on the little one nearby.

Istabelle shifted, becoming anxious. It was hard to stay still for so long! Her stomach rumbled and she clutched it with a smothered giggle.

"I'm hungry, too," Alannah remarked.

Istabelle glanced down but said nothing.

Alannah shrugged and set about finding nuts and berries. As the stallion followed her, she walked carefully, searching the ground with her fingers. "This is a walnut tree," she said out loud. "I know the walnuts will taste good this time of year. And over there I can smell some blackberries . . . yum." She sauntered over to the hidden bush and pushed some ferns out of the way. A small blackberry bush peeked out, loaded with succulent fruit.

Istabelle scrambled down. "Can I have some?" she asked. Her voice was high and girlish, but possessed of stubborn strength. Alannah smiled, pleased that the child had joined her.

"Of course. But if you are to share my dinner, I should know why you are out here, all alone."

"My father doesn't want me," she answered. "I heard him say so, and Uncle Brogan agrees. It makes me angry. I get so angry I have to run away every once in a while."

"Is that what you were doing the day I met you?"

"Yes. One of the other children told me that I wasn't good enough to be loved by a father and that is why he left me." She tiptoed around Alannah to the other side to sneak some extra berries. Since Alannah said nothing, she continued. "I saw you riding your stallion. You are a very good rider, like me. Most people would have fallen off." She reached out to pick a particularly enticing red berry.

"Thank you. I am trying to teach my horse how to take a saddle and bridle. I don't think you will like that one, Miss Istabelle."

Istabelle paused, incredulous. Lowering the berry, she looked at Alannah suspiciously. "I thought you couldn't see," she complained.

"I can't," Alannah replied as she carefully selected only the ripe berries from the bush. "But I can hear and I can smell. Do you want this one?" Alannah held a black one out to her.

Istabelle snagged it and popped it in her mouth. "Ummm," she mumbled, and held out her hand for more.

For several moments, they picked and ate fruit in silence. Soon both of them were full and Alannah motioned to the horse. "Do you think it is time to go back?"

Pouting, Istabelle looked at her newly found best friend. "I would rather stay out here with you," she said.

"Hummm. I can understand that. I would rather stay out here, too. I find that I am less interested in civilization than I thought. I miss my solitude, but we do have obligations. I am sure someone is worried about you."

"No," Istabelle insisted. "No one cares about me."

Alannah raised her eyebrows as she lifted Istabelle on the stallion's bare back. "What about your mother?"

"My mother is dead."

"I think my mother is dead, too," Alannah answered. "I don't know anything about my father."

"Not even his name?" Istabelle asked.

"No, not even his name." She climbed up behind the girl and squeezed her thighs. The stallion walked down the hillside, picking his way carefully through the trees.

"I know my father's name."

"Really? See, you know more than me. What is his name?"

"Xanthier. Xanthier O'Bannon."

Alannah gasped. "Who?" she cried. "Did you say Xanthier?"

As the name echoed through the forest, a man, hidden within the trees, suddenly sprang in front of the riders. Istabelle screamed. The man swung a large branch against Alannah's temple.

Pain exploded in her head, bursting out to engulf

her in white shards that streaked out and darkened into blackness. Alannah tumbled to the forest floor, blood soaking her auburn hair. Istabelle screamed again as the man wielded the weapon at Alannah a second time. Her high-pitched voice startled the sensitive stallion and he sprang forward, dancing with anxiety. She clung to his mane, terrified.

"Get on with ye!" the man shouted as he flung his hands up in the stallion's face. The stallion reared and the man swung the stick at him. Infuriated, the stallion lunged forward, snapping with his teeth while striking out with his front hooves. The man stumbled back, swinging the branch. A loud *thwack* reverberated in the forest as the branch crashed against the stallion's foreleg. The horse whinnied and dropped back.

The man grinned and flourished the branch again, forcing the stallion to limp backwards. "This witch has a hundred lives! I'll make sure she is done this time!" He grabbed the unconscious Alannah by her lax hand and started to drag her toward a nearby stream.

"What are you doing?" Istabelle screamed. "What are you doing to her?"

The man glanced back and laughed evilly. "The same thing I am going to do to you, you little brat, if you don't keep your mouth shut!" He pulled Alannah to the water and dunked her head beneath the rippling stream.

"Stop!" Istabelle cried. "She'll drown!" Never known to be considerate about others, Istabelle was suddenly compelled to protect her new friend. Alannah's mysterious skills fascinated her. She had never felt such instant caring for anyone—except her cousin, Mangan—and she was furious that the man was intent on harming the blind woman.

She kicked the stallion and he responded by spinning and striking out with his hind legs. The man ducked, barely avoiding the dangerous hooves. He scrambled to grab his branch, but the stallion kicked again. This time his hooves connected and he flung the man several feet, where he crashed into a tree. The man gasped, trying to collect his breath as Istabelle and the stallion advanced. "You horrible man! Leave her alone!"

The man dragged himself upright and swung the branch at the stallion once again. It connected, thudding against the horse's legs, but the stallion arched his neck and bit the man's shoulder. Holding him with his teeth, the stallion tossed the man back and forth, until the man hung limp and defenseless. Then, with a twist of his body, the man yanked himself away from the stallion and raced away through the trees.

Istabelle stared after the man in horror, then turned to locate Alannah. "Oh!" she gasped as she saw that Alannah was being pulled into the stream by the rippling current. Rocks littered the bed and the water flowed swiftly, looking dangerous to the five-year-old child. She scrambled down off the horse and yanked Alannah's hand, pulling her partially out of the river. Staring at Alannah's ashen face, she knew the woman needed help.

She dragged Claudius by his mane toward a stump, climbed on his back and thrummed the powerful horse with her tiny heels, kicking him mercilessly until he flung his head up and snorted in irritation. "Go!" she shouted. "Run! Run like you did before. I saw you race like the wind. I know you can do it!" She kicked him again, crying in her desperation. "We have to get help before she dies!"

The stallion took a step and faltered, his foreleg buckling. He shook his head angrily at the pain.

"Please," Istabelle cried, large tears tumbling down her face. "Please . . ."

The stallion took another step and whinnied his distress. His leg would not support his weight. His big, brown eyes swung to Alannah's prostrate form. He tucked his legs under him and hobbled forward another step. The child urged him, her light weight inconsequential but her plaintive cries pressing. He pricked his ears forward and listened to her urging as he tried to limp down the hillside.

Chapter 21

For the second time that day, Xanthier stood before the king. This time, Brogan had called the meeting, but he was not interested in the political maneuvering. Instead, he desperately sought assistance to search for Istabelle.

Xanthier glared at Brogan from the opposite side of the royal dais. They had identical faces, identically colored eyes, identical expressions, except that half of Xanthier's face was twisted and scarred. Distrust and anger filled the air.

"You lost her?" Xanthier growled in disgust. "She is but three years old!"

"Five. She is five," Brogan snarled back.

"Five then. And you still lost her!"

"Do you even care?" Brogan shouted. "I am the one who raised her. You don't want her."

"You are correct. I don't want her. This is certainly not my decision. I want nothing of this arrangement." Xanthier narrowed his eyes and dared anyone to reprimand him.

Brogan blinked, feeling something different coming from his brother. *He is lying!* Brogan realized. *He is lying to himself! That is the strange confusion I have been sensing lately. He is trying to convince himself of something that is not true. What else has he been lying to himself about?*

Brogan took a step back and turned away, masking his expression. If Xanthier did not understand his own feelings, it was not up to Brogan to explain them. "This is not helping matters," he said with a measured tone. He was the Earl of Kirkcaldy, and he was obligated to act with restraint. Turning toward his anxious wife, he motioned her forward. "My wife and I request a search party to assist in locating Istabelle. Night is falling and we are fearful for her survival."

"We cannot reduce our defenses simply for one small child," King Malcolm disagreed. "You will have to use your own people, but I will excuse you from the evening's events."

Matalia stepped up. "If we could just have ten more men . . ."

"I have given my answer," King Malcolm replied. "I will, however, demand that Xanthier and his man assist you. She is, after all, *his* daughter."

"I have other obligations," Xanthier grumbled.

"At the tavern? At the gaming tables? With a jug of ale? Forgive me if I do not think they are important," Brogan countered.

Xanthier glared at his brother, but before he could argue, the queen spoke. "Xanthier *will* help locate the girl. I insist."

Both Brogan and Xanthier gritted their teeth. They glanced at each other in mutual discord, but Brogan turned aside first. He was truly worried about Istabelle and desperate to find her. If Xanthier could help, so be it.

They left the chambers and stood on the outside steps. Taking a deep breath, Brogan started to explain where they had already looked. "We searched the woods near the road. We have also looked down by the market and have turned over every stand. We explored each tavern and stable. We have even knocked on every door. We cannot find her."

"The festival grounds?"

"That is where we'll go next."

Xanthier nodded and mounted his horse. "Then I will check the forest."

Brogan shook his head. "I already told you we searched that region."

"For God's sake, brother," Xanthier exclaimed, "I will not sit on my ass while my child is missing. Go to the festival grounds and I will start on the woods. If I was a little girl trying to hide, I would head for the trees."

Matalia touched her husband's arm in reassurance. "I believe him, darling. Trust him for the moment."

"I am unworthy of that trust," Xanthier interjected.

Brogan and Xanthier stared at each other for a moment, listening to the inner communication that raced between them. Brogan heard Xanthier's sad loneliness and Xanthier heard Brogan's confusion. Despite all that had passed between them, a secret longing still filled them both. This time Xanthier turned away first. No matter how much he wished that they could be true brothers to each other, it was not meant to be.

He pointed his horse toward the hillside and started looking in ditches and under bushes where he presumed Istabelle might hide.

Night fell swiftly and with it came a chilling wind. He pulled his cloak around his shoulders and frowned. This was not good weather for a little girl. He wanted to go faster, but was afraid he would miss her if he was not careful. He swung his horse back and forth, zigzagging up the hillside until he was deep into the trees.

He tried to ignore his worry, tried to stifle his rising concern. She was only a child. She meant nothing to him, despite their shared blood. Still, he worried as he scanned the forest.

A flash of white caught his attention. He peered through the trees and tried to make out the shape. It moved with laborious steps, grunting in pain. Stealthily pulling his sword, Xanthier urged his horse forward and approached the creature.

The white stallion! Xanthier gasped upon seeing the magnificent creature haggard and wounded. He took tiny, painful steps as he held up his right foreleg, which was clearly swollen. Upon the horse's back was the trembling form of a little girl, her tear-streaked face pinched with fear.

"Istabelle?" he said softly.

The girl turned toward him. "You aren't Uncle Brogan," she said uncertainly.

"No, I am not. I am Xanthier, Brogan's brother."

"Then you are my father," she said.

Xanthier could not answer her. He searched her face, looking for evidence of the awful night five years ago. He expected to see accusations in her eyes, revulsion in her expression. He expected to see the disgust he felt for himself reflected in her, but she stared at him innocently, her gaze clear and sweet.

"Will you help me?" she asked.

He nodded.

"The lady . . . the lady Alannah is hurt."

Tension surged through him. Thoughts of the

past whisked away and he stared at the stallion with dawning comprehension. Alannah had ridden him out of the courtyard this morning and had not returned. Now her stallion was injured and Alannah was not with him. "God, please take pity! Don't take her . . ." he prayed.

"She is in the stream, but she won't wake up. A man hit her over the head."

"Where, Istabelle? Where is she?"

"Up there." Istabelle pointed. "In the stream."

Debating quickly, he leaped off his steed and dragged the girl off the stallion. The sky was deepening to black, and he knew that time was limited. He placed Istabelle on his own mount and gave her the reins. "This is a big horse, but you were riding an even bigger one. Do you think you can ride it back down the hill?"

Istabelle started to cry and wrapped her arms around his neck. "Don't leave me!" she sobbed. "Don't leave me again!"

"I'm not leaving," he replied, taking her weight into his arms. "But your aunt and uncle are worried and you should go back to them. I'll find Alannah."

"No!" Istabelle screamed. "No! Don't leave me!"

"Fine!" Xanthier shouted, then with extreme effort calmed his voice. "Fine. Show me where she is."

Istabelle pointed up the hill and Xanthier nodded. Holding her awkwardly, he walked to the trembling white stallion and stroked his neck. "Lie down," he whispered. "You did your duty. You found help. Lie down now and I will come back for you."

The great stallion collapsed to the ground, dropping his head with a heavy sigh. Pain streaked up his leg and his mind was becoming cloudy, but he knew this man. This was the man from the island, the man his mistress loved. He could rest now. The man would help her.

Xanthier gave the stallion one last pat, then swung back onto his own steed. "All right, let's go," he said to Istabelle as he settled her between his arms. They moved quickly through the trees, following Istabelle's directions. They crested a small hill and Xanthier saw a quickly moving stream winking in the moonlight through a thick screen of woodland. "Is that it?" he asked as he guided his horse down the slope.

"I think so," Istabelle murmured. She clung to him like a burr, as if she would never let go. Xanthier shifted, trying to loosen her grip, but she squeezed harder. "Near the rocks," she said as she stared up at his face.

Xanthier turned his head so his scars were pointed away from the child. He was certain they were frightening and he wanted to spare her. She had already endured much tonight.

Istabelle winced, feeling that he was turning away from her. She buried her head in his chest, terrified that he would abandon her again. She started to cry.

Suddenly Xanthier spotted Alannah. She had pulled herself out of the stream itself, but had managed to crawl only a few feet before she had collapsed. Xanthier leapt off his horse and dragged Istabelle's arms from around his neck. "Wait," he said harshly, then ran the remaining feet and knelt at Alannah's side.

"Alannah? Please, Alannah. Oh, God!" He stroked her head, feeling the sticky blood that matted her hair.

Alannah stirred and opened her eyes, staring sightlessly at Xanthier. "You?" she asked incredulously. "You . . . came for me?"

"Can we forget for the moment all that has come between us? Can we not just let it go for the eve? Let me take care of you. Let me show you . . ." He scooped her up and carried her to his horse. He saw her discarded saddle blanket and paused.

Istabelle noticed his glance. "The girth was loosened," she informed him. "She almost fell but she didn't. She is a very good rider."

Xanthier looked down, almost forgetting the five-year-old. "Yes," he said quietly. "She is a very good rider. I've never seen a better one."

"He's a nice horse, too."

"Aye. I agree. Let's go back to where he is resting and set up a fire. Alannah will want to tend to him."

Istabelle nodded.

Alannah rested gratefully against her rescuer. Her head swam and she could not concentrate on anything. It was hard to remember things. She knew she was upset about something, but it took too much effort to recall what it was. It was so much easier to curl up in Xanthier's strong arms and let him take care of her.

The fire crackled. In the distance, they could hear wolves howling. Alannah sat within the warmth of Xanthier's embrace, her back pressed against his chest. She rested her head wearily against his neck. The acute pain had faded but her sense of disorientation persisted. Despite the injury, she felt an overwhelming sense of peace. Something seemed so right, and she knew that it was the man she was leaning against who made her feel that way.

Here, far from the court, he was relaxed. He was gentle and considerate, just as he had been on the island. His breath flowed evenly in and out, and his hands stroked her head in soft, rhythmic patterns. Sleeping several feet from them was the child, Istabelle. Alannah thought there was something she should remember about her, too, but again, her head pounded too much to delve into it.

The white stallion lay on the far side of the fire, his injured leg wrapped in a mud poultice. He groaned occasionally and lifted his head, only to drop it back down again after spying Alannah. Each time, he was assured of her safety and he dozed off again.

The firelight flickered over the trees, enclosing them in a cocoon of mellow light. Alannah felt Xanthier's heart beat. She felt so perfect, curled against him. In a natural gesture, Alannah turned and placed her lips on Xanthier's neck. His hands froze and he held his breath. Emboldened, she kissed him again, softly, reverently.

"Alannah?" he whispered. "Your head?"

"Shush." She kissed the other side of his neck, then trailed her lips down to his collarbone. She licked him, tasting the maleness of his flesh, a unique mixture of salt, musk and strength. She turned to face him.

He gazed down at her exquisite face, but her outer beauty did not move him as much as her inner radiance. He captured her head between his palms and tilted it upwards. Bending slightly, he brushed his lips against hers. "You have no idea how pleased I am that you are well."

"And you have no idea how happy I am at this moment," she whispered in response.

His eyes glowed and he wrapped her in a tight

embrace, then pulled her to her feet and led her out of the firelight, away from the sleeping child. They remained hugging, touching each other in the darkness, breathing with each other, until Alannah gently pushed him down and kissed him again. She ducked her head, finding the opening in his shirt. Using her teeth, she nibbled the shirt open, exposing him to her questing tongue.

He shifted and sat back against a tree and she moved, too, placing her knees on either side of him. With him guiding her, she rubbed against him as she kissed and licked, finding delectable ways to increase his mounting excitement.

Slowly, lovingly, they helped each other pull their restrictive clothing out of the way. Then she rose up and slid down on top of him, pressing his maleness deep inside of her.

He hissed through his teeth and closed his eyes, entering her world of sensation. He concentrated on the warmth of her wetness, the rippling tightness of her core. He slid his hands up her thighs, squeezing her and urging her to sit deeper, to slide higher. He was in heaven, and she was his angel.

Alannah welcomed him, feeling herself open to him as he filled her stroke after stroke. She reveled in his surrender as he allowed her to mount him, and she relished the power of his hands as he held her to an even, ever-increasing tempo. She cried out softly, dipping her head down, and her hair covered them both in a silken cloak.

He lifted one hand and sank his fingers into her abundant hair, tilting her head so he could devour her mouth. Gasping, he arched his hips upwards as she sank downwards, and they met in sweet unison.

She cried out again and he moaned, dropping his hand back to her thigh and urging her to move faster. She gasped, feeling the climax building inside her, but she held back, forcing her body to teeter on the precipice.

He pumped faster, moaning aloud, knowing she was so close, wanting to join her, praying that they would reach bliss together. "Oh God!" he gasped, and she moaned too.

"Yes!" she whispered. "Now! Now!"

"Yes!" he repeated and they exploded together, stars bursting behind their closed eyelids, heat and fire shattering their bodies in blessed ecstasy. Wave after wave rolled over them, washing them in warmth, peace and glory.

PART III

The Race for Love

Chapter 22

By morning, she remembered everything. She stared down at his sleeping face and frowned. Istabelle was his daughter. He had a daughter. He had never mentioned a wife and certainly never spoken of a child. Hurt spread through her, deeper than before. He had lied to her from the beginning. He had a family that he had never told her about. And then, just to add more insult, he had made sweet love to her with the child of another woman sleeping only feet away.

Alannah blinked, fighting back tears. She knew she had initiated their encounter last night. She knew she couldn't blame him completely. She blamed herself as well. She could not control her desire for him. Consider last night. Think about the night in the garden. Although she knew he was inappropriate for her, she still tumbled into his arms.

The stallion was standing, the poultice having worked wonders overnight. She felt along the bone, cringing when the huge steed flinched at her gentle touch. Slowly, silently, they walked away from the slumbering Xanthier and Istabelle, the horse limping but able to walk, and the woman wounded but able to survive.

An hour later they reached the base of the hill and exited the forest. She was immediately hailed.

"Alannah! Have you come from the woods?" Brogan asked her as he rode up. His voice was tight with worry.

Alannah nodded wearily. "Aye. My horse is injured and he had to rest."

"You, too, seem injured. Do you need a surgeon?"

"No. I am well. My thanks. I am sure you are wondering where Istabelle is. She is safe, in the forest." Alannah turned away.

"Thank heavens! Is she hurt? Where is she?"

"She is with her father." Silence greeted her remark and Alannah waited, feeling Brogan's tension rise dramatically. "Is her father, Xanthier O'Bannon, your brother?" she asked, fearing the answer.

"Aye."

Alannah swallowed. Her heart split, and she struggled not to scream in fury. "Do you know why he came to the festival?" she asked.

"I presume he came in order to marry. I heard that he intends to wed Lady Serena."

So Istabelle's mother must be dead. Still, a rush of pure hatred filled Alannah's heart before she forcefully stamped the emotion down. It was not the woman's fault. It was Xanthier's. He was the one who had lied. Alannah clenched her hands and moved away. She could not bear to be near anyone for even a second longer.

How could he have done such a thing to her? He had a family—a child—and was seeking a wife. He had no need for a blind woman. Well, then she had no need for him! Alannah blinked rapidly, keeping her tears hidden as she rode away. She would only stay until the race was over. She would ensure that her island was secure; then she would leave Scotland forever.

The cold woke him. It was not a blistering cold, or even a shivering cold—it was the coldness of loneliness. Xanthier reached out, searching for her body. He squeezed his eyes shut, hoping that her warmth would suddenly appear and his suspicions would be proved wrong, but he could not conjure up her presence. Finally opening his eyes, he stared at the leaves on the ground that had been flattened from her sleep. Alannah was gone.

Sadness overwhelmed him and he could not drag his gaze from her natural bed. A few strands of her hair wove in between the brush, and he could still smell her presence.

He was devastated; he was furious! After everything he had done for her, she still refused to surrender to him in all ways. She had left him with no word of explanation.

He had shown her his feelings—with his kisses, his fingertips . . . his entire body. Why had she left him? Could she not see how much he loved her? He tried to show her with his touch. He made love to her as an expression of his emotions. Every stroke, every caress was designed to worship and please her, to make her realize how much he cared even though he could not express himself in words.

A sound made him look up, and a rush of hope filled him. His gray eyes searched the glade until they paused at the sight of Istabelle huddling against a tree. Her gray eyes stared back at him, hauntingly familiar. His own eyes, his own daughter.

"Good morning," she said softly.

Xanthier looked past her, searching for Alannah.

"She left," Istabelle said. "She took the horse and went down the mountain. I stayed with you."

Xanthier returned his gaze to Istabelle and frowned. "You should have gone with her. Brogan and Matalia will be waiting for you."

Istabelle glared at him. "You are my father. I am going to stay with you."

"Don't be silly, Istabelle. Brogan has raised you. If I have any say, you will remain with his family."

Istabelle shook her head and rose. "I don't care what you say. I will stay with you."

Giving up, Xanthier went over to his horse and started to saddle him. "If little girls are this stubborn, I would prefer to keep my distance. Unfortunately, I have no choice but to ride with you now, so come on and mount up." A small smile softened his gruff words and Istabelle grinned and ran over to him. Within moments, she was seated in front of him and they were riding down the hill.

In less than an hour they exited the woods and rode over the bare fields. Xanthier could sense his brother's restlessness, and he altered his path to intercept him. Moments later, Brogan and Xanthier came face-to-face.

Relief flooded Brogan's heart and he held his arms out to Istabelle.

"I am well," she murmured as Brogan clasped her in a hug and kissed her head. The position was awkward and Xanthier leaned away, indicating that Brogan could take Istabelle from his horse, but Istabelle pulled back and wrapped her arms around Xanthier's neck. "My father found us. Isn't he wonderful? Isn't he brave?" She smiled up at Xanthier adoringly.

Brogan stretched his lips into an answering smile and nodded with his teeth clenched. "I am glad

you have been found, no matter who found you,"
he said. Glancing at Xanthier, he added, "My
thanks."

"I do not believe I have ever received thanks
from you, twin. It is a day I will remember," Xanthier replied mockingly.

"It is a day I will not forget," Brogan replied.

As Brogan and Xanthier sparred, their words
slicing back and forth like swords, Alannah walked
her stallion back to the royal stables where he was
to be kept until the day of the race. In the yard
she was pleasantly surprised to encounter Gondilyn.

"Alannah! I have been looking for you! What
happened? You never came to the field."

"I am pleased to hear your voice, Gondilyn. I
had an accident and slept overnight in the forest."

"That is dangerous!"

She shook her head. "I have spent all my life in
the wild. Believe me, one night there could not
harm me."

"You are too beautiful to sleep in the dirt."

"Don't be ridiculous, Gondilyn. I am not fragile."

"Promise me that you will take better care. What
if someone had come across you last night? Think
what could have happened."

Alannah ducked her head, embarrassed. She
would not tell him of her attack.

Unaware of Alannah's discomfort, Gondilyn continued. "What happened to your horse? He is
limping."

"Yes. His foreleg is injured. I must tend to it."

"But the race is in only a few days. How will we
be ready?" Gondilyn followed her into the stable.

Alannah slid off the stallion's back and handed

the blanket to Gondilyn. Without speaking for several minutes, she brushed Claudius, removing the dirt and fine dust from his white hide. The stallion's head hung low. He was clearly in pain.

"Alannah? Will he be ready for the race?" Gondilyn repeated.

Alannah shrugged. Thoughts of past events were swirling in her mind, but foremost was the pain of believing that Xanthier had deliberately lied to her by withholding knowledge of his daughter and upcoming nuptials. Leaning her forehead against the horse, she expelled a pent-up breath.

"I hope he will be sound. The race is very important to me. I do not want anyone else—especially Xanthier—to have any right to my island."

Gondilyn tried to approach the stallion, but the horse bared his teeth at him. "I have my doubts, Alannah," Gondilyn said nervously. "I do not think your horse will let me ride him. And even if he does, how will I control him?"

Alannah picked the brush back up and vigorously groomed the stallion. "He must enter the race."

"I—"

Alannah rounded on Gondilyn and interrupted angrily. "You must ride him!"

"What if I can't?"

"You can if you believe you can."

"I hope you are right, Alannah. I should not have doubts. You have shown resilience that is truly remarkable and I admire you immensely. If I could have a tiny grain of your character, I would be a better man."

Alannah flushed and turned away. The tone of his voice was reverent, and it made her uncomfortable. "Would you get a bucket of cold water for me?" she asked, changing the subject. "I want to wrap my horse's leg in a cold compress. I collected some herbs on my way down the mountain and I will need to make them into a tincture."

"Of course, Alannah. I would do anything for you."

Mumbling her thanks, Alannah ducked out of the stable and went to collect more materials.

Later that day, she worked with the white stallion, placing a leather bridle over his head and stroking him with the saddle leather. Gondilyn stayed with her for a few hours, until his duties called him away.

She made a liniment that she applied alternately with the cold packs, and she wrapped a bandage around Claudius's lower leg to help keep the swelling down. She mixed some powders into his food to reduce the inflammation and relieve the pain.

After Gondilyn left, Matalia came by, scolding Alannah soundly for worrying them last night. "Brogan and I were very concerned about Istabelle. Where were you? How did you find her?"

"I went for a ride and along the way I found her. Because my horse was lame, we had to stay the night. I am sorry I caused you anxiety."

Matalia frowned. "Alannah, are you all right? You seem . . . upset."

Alannah patted the stallion and picked up her walking stick, indicating that she was ready to leave the stable. "He should be better tomorrow. Today he should rest."

"You are avoiding my question. Is it the stallion? Are you upset about the race?"

"Yes, partly. I am uneasy about a great many things, some of which I can tell you, others I cannot." Alannah and Matalia walked outside. Matalia blinked at the bright sunlight but Alannah smiled at the warmth.

Lending her an arm to hold on to, Matalia questioned Alannah further. "Tell me what troubles you. Let's sit in the garden."

"Do you promise to say nothing? I do not want anyone . . ."

"I understand. Sometimes one wants to keep things private. But, Alannah, it is often better to confide in someone. Talking about your troubles can make them seem so much lighter."

"Perhaps. But promise that you will not tell anyone, even your husband."

"I promise," Matalia replied.

"There is one thing that puzzles me. Someone attacked me last night. He hid in the trees and hit me with a branch, knocking my head so hard that I lost consciousness. He hurt Claudius as well."

"Oh! How terrible!"

"That is not all. I believe the cinch holding my saddle blanket was deliberately loosened. The blanket slipped, and it was only by the grace of God that I did not take a bad fall. I fear that someone is trying to harm me."

"Oh my! Who would ever do such a thing?"

"I wonder if it has anything to do with the messenger you sent to Clarauch. Have you heard anything?" Alannah asked.

"Nothing more. It is as if you never existed. Perhaps we should leave immediately."

"No." Alannah sighed. "That is exactly what I will not do. I will not let some villain force us to alter our plans. But I do think some precautions are in order. I will need your help."

"Alannah, we must tell Brogan."

"No! You promised! He will only insist that we leave."

"But how will we protect you without his help? And I still think we *should* leave."

Alannah rose. "Am I to regret telling you?"

"No," Matalia replied hastily. "I will stay true to my promise, although it worries me greatly. We will have to tell someone, however. You will need a guard, and we will need someone to stay with the stallion."

"There is no need to say anything specific to the horse's guard. I still have some coin. We will hire someone to watch Claudius day and night. We will tell the guard only that we are concerned because the stallion is valuable."

"Aye. That makes sense. And you? What about you?"

"Effie can stay with me."

"Alannah! You need someone bigger and stronger than an old woman. How about Gondilyn? He cares for you."

"Well . . ."

"There is no one else. Either we tell him, or I tell Brogan."

"Very well," Alannah reluctantly agreed. "I will tell Gondilyn."

As they rose, Matalia turned and placed her hands upon Alannah's shoulders. "Alannah," she said softly, "is there something else? Is there more that is troubling you? Could it be about Xanthier?"

Alannah dropped her head, veiling her face with her auburn hair. The words bubbled in her mind. Xanthier, Istabelle, the woman she presumed to be his bride . . . Alannah struggled to form thoughts, to make sense of her conflicting feelings, but in the end she could only shake her head. Watching her with growing concern, Matalia enfolded her in a hug, rocking her gently. "It will be all right," she whispered. "Whatever ails you, whatever else you cannot say, remember that I am your friend."

Alannah pulled back, thinking of Xanthier. He had once been her friend, too.

Chapter 23

Kurgan watched Alannah leave the garden. Her tall, willowy figure was striking, and her long auburn hair danced around her perfectly formed face. He hated her.

He turned to the man beside him. "Why is she still alive? I thought I made my desire clear."

"Her horse!" the man whined. "It fought me!"

Kurgan glared at him with disgust. "Horses are stupid beasts of burden. They do not protect people."

"You weren't there," the man replied sullenly. "The horse attacked me. I pulled the woman into the river and she should have drowned. It is the horse's fault."

"What about the girl?"

"She is only a child. She won't remember anything."

"Just the same, stay low for awhile. Until we find out if Alannah reports her accident, we will have to be patient."

The festival crowd surged around them. Music played in several locations, creating an air of frantic activity in the yard. Jugglers cavorted in and around the guests, and several animals dressed in colorful garb gamboled about. Queen Margaret and King Malcolm sat on a covered stage, watching the antics as they imbibed flavored wines and nibbled on exotic fruits.

Alannah pressed close to Gondilyn. The noise, the activity, the rising energy of the people made her nervous.

"How much longer?" she whispered for the third time.

Gondilyn bent his head and murmured back, "As I said, Alannah, you must not insult the royals by leaving too soon. The race is tomorrow. If we leave now, and the king or queen notices our absence, they might disqualify our entry."

"Yes, yes, I know. You said that before. But how long must we stay? We need to study the race course."

Gondilyn sighed and patted her hand where it rested on his forearm. "A few hours, maybe more. Then I can try to ride your stallion once again. Perhaps the next time he will let me stay astride."

Alannah groaned and rubbed her temples with her free hand.

"Besides," Gondilyn said, "you are more safe in the crowd than alone in the stables."

Alannah nodded reluctantly, wishing that she had not confided her fears to him. Gondilyn had become extremely protective, and while she appreciated his nearness in the throng, she preferred her solitude.

She tilted her head when a familiar voice hailed her.

"Alannah," Kurgan called out, "I have been searching for you. How do you fare? I heard that you were lost in the woods last night, and only made it back this morning."

"It was nothing," Alannah murmured. "I had a mishap but all is well now."

Kurgan smiled. "You have no idea how pleased I am to hear that. Could I convince you to change escorts? I would be honored to show you around the festival grounds while the guardsman returns to his duties. I am sure you would not want him to be reprimanded for neglecting them."

"Is that true, Gondilyn? Will you be punished for spending time with me?"

"Do not worry," Gondilyn replied, but his voice betrayed his nervousness and Alannah wrinkled her brow.

"Perhaps you should go," she replied. "We could meet later."

Gondilyn looked at Kurgan with concern, but Kurgan ignored him as he deftly took Alannah's arm and led her away, saying, "Spending even one hour in your presence will make my day complete. Excuse me if my comments seem too forward, but I can hardly contain myself. You are all the beauty and elegance I ever dreamed was possible in a woman."

Alannah flushed. "Have you forgotten that I am blind?"

"No," Kurgan assured her. "Your blindness only adds to your allure."

A strident female voice carried through the throng, and Alannah paused to listen.

"He is seeking a bride? With his manly scars and exciting reputation, not to mention his wealth, he will be swarmed with hopefuls. The field should not be limited to Lady Serena. I wonder what I can do to gain his attention . . ."

"Don't be such a ninny," another female voice

replied. "He is not likely to fall for any of your tricks."

A third voice joined the conversation. "He frightens me," she said, "and he has made it clear that he has no desire to remarry, despite the king's demand. I, for one, would be nervous if I caught his eye. Consider the consequences. Remember what happened to his last wife."

"Ach, but think of the marriage bed. With his strength and power . . . his sense of command . . . his vast experience . . . I would marry Xanthier O'Bannon in an instant. I doubt he will have trouble finding a bride."

The women walked away, still talking about the various merits of a union with Xanthier. Alannah felt frozen. "Kurgan," she whispered urgently, "do you know much about Xanthier O'Bannon?"

"Yes, of course. Why do you ask?"

"Is he betrothed? Does he have a bride?"

"Heavens, no! His wife died five years ago shortly after the birth of his child. Since then, no woman has wanted to link her name with his."

"He is not betrothed?" Alannah repeated dumbly. Waves of guilt assailed her, and thoughts of what Xanthier must have felt when he awoke to find her gone swirled in her head.

"No," Kurgan said. "I have heard many terrible things about him, however. He is not a good man, Alannah. You would do well to stay clear of him."

"Do you see him?" she asked breathlessly, wanting to be near him again, wanting to feel his hand clasped in hers. Joy overwhelmed her and she dragged Kurgan forward as she smiled happily. He was not going to be married! He had not lied to her!

"Alannah!" Kurgan hissed, furious that she was

ignoring his overtures. "What is it about this O'Bannon? How do you know him? God help you, for he is an angry and violent man. Stay away from him. He is more likely to hurt you than care for you."

Alannah turned and touched Kurgan's face. "Do you know him?" she asked softly.

"Yes, I know him and I know his reputation." He caught his breath, surprised by the feather-light touch of her fingers. "I have fought with him and can tell you tales of his brutality."

"He is not as horrible as you think. He has depths to him that he does not show. It is true that he can be irritating, overbearing and thoroughly frustrating. But he is also tender and considerate. I would like to find him and talk to him."

Kurgan narrowed his eyes. "You sound like a woman in love, but I strongly caution you to steer clear of him. He was supposed to inherit a powerful title, but he lost it to his brother. His fleet is feared and his men are considered very dangerous. There are many uncertainties about him, while you are a saint. You are soft and gentle and need special care. Everything about you is delicate and ethereal. Your beauty is unparalleled, whereas his scars are disfiguring. It is not a good match, Alannah. You should find someone who would take better care of you. Someone who would love you with the sweetness you deserve. Someone like me."

"Kurgan, you are saying things you should not. I can hardly explain my relationship with Xanthier, for I do not understand it myself. He was shipwrecked on my island and spent many months with me. I will admit that I do not understand him, and I am unsure of my feelings for him. One moment I am so angry I cannot stand to hear his name, whereas other moments I want to be near him and hear his voice."

"Have you forgotten that he tried to take your island? Can you trust him?" Kurgan took her hands, pulling her gently close to him. He shut his eyes, feeling the sweetness of her body pressed against him. She *was* beautiful, he thought. There was something about her that truly *was* intriguing. Perhaps murdering her was not for the best. He could achieve all he wanted as well as taste the pleasure of her flesh if he could convince her to marry him. As his thoughts swirled around the possibilities, he slowly released her. He glanced across the yard and stared straight into the steely gaze of Xanthier O'Bannon.

Kurgan froze. Xanthier's fury was palpable. A slow smile spread over Kurgan's face. Alannah could not see Xanthier, and it was the perfect opportunity to exact some revenge. Kurgan placed his arm around Alannah's shoulders and guided her toward a flower stand. Selecting a lovely white rose, he carefully placed it in her auburn hair.

"This flower cannot compare to your beauty," he whispered.

"Your words are extravagant," Alannah replied with a smile. "You will spoil me with such compliments."

"As I intend to do. Perhaps I will be afforded the opportunity to spoil you for a long time."

Alannah laughed. "While we are walking, will you keep a look out for Xanthier? I must speak with him."

"I will watch," Kurgan said as he cleared his throat. "Believe me, I will watch for him."

Xanthier clenched his teeth, his jealousy raging. Alannah smiled at Kurgan as if he was her lover!

She touched him and walked beside him with easy familiarity. Xanthier's impulse to approach her and demand an explanation for her disappearance that morning faded. Once again he was stymied by her contradictory signals. Her warm loving of the previous night warred with her unexplained departure and conflicted with her budding relationship with Kurgan.

Xanthier glared at both of them. Of all the people she could have chosen! Fingers trembling with the desire to punch his enemy, he squeezed his fists closed. He needed to fight. He needed to expel his anger. Spinning around, he headed for the wrestling competition that was commencing on the eastern field.

Istabelle trailed after him. "Father?" she asked.

Xanthier glanced down at her in surprise. "What are you doing here?"

"I wanted to play with you," she said.

"Go on, Istabelle. I am going to a place where children are not allowed."

"But Father! I want to play!" She stomped her foot in a display of temper. The antics always worked on her Uncle Brogan. If she put up enough of a fuss, he would laugh and let her do whatever she wanted.

Xanthier frowned and knelt down, looking at her eye to eye. "Istabelle, that is not ladylike behavior. You should respect an adult when he says that you cannot do something. Obedience is not just for convenience. It is also for your protection. Think about when you got lost in the woods. Had you listened to your aunt and uncle and stayed close to them, you would have not wandered off."

"But I *want* to play with you!"

Xanthier shook his head, perplexed. "Don't you

have other children to play with? What about your
cousin, Mangan? I'll tell you this . . . if you are
good today, I will seek you out this evening."

Istabelle pouted and Xanthier frowned back. Finally, seeing that Xanthier was not going to relent,
Istabelle flung her arms around his neck and
squeezed. "You promise?" she begged.

Uncomfortable with her public display, Xanthier
pulled her arms free and stood up. "If I said I will,
I will," he replied. "Now go on and find someone
to entertain you. I need to work off my own frustra-
tions." He turned and walked away, but a tiny part
of his anger had dissolved and he half smiled at
the memory of her pleading gray eyes.

Istabelle skipped away, searching for a playmate.
Mangan saw her and was walking over to join her
when Istabelle spotted Alannah. Smiling, she raced
up and grabbed Alannah's hand. Mangan paused
and watched Istabelle thoughtfully. She was more
than his cousin; she was his best friend, and he
knew her better than anyone. Seeing her reach out
to the blind woman made him curious and a little
sad.

It was the first time Istabelle had chosen someone else to play with. Mangan sat in the shade, his
eyes filling with tears, but he wiped them away as
quickly as they formed. He knew that Istabelle was
overflowing with hurt and pain from the abandonment of her father. It was good that she was opening her heart to someone new. Deliberately turning
away, he did not interfere.

"Mistress Alannah?" Istabelle called out.

Alannah grinned and gave Istabelle a kiss on the
forehead. "You seem none the worse for wear. Is
your father near?"

"He just left. He is going to the wrestling grounds."

"Oh." Alannah frowned. *He must not have seen me.*

"Tell me, what is it like to be blind?"

"Child!" Kurgan scolded irritably. "Don't be so inquisitive. Show Mistress Alannah more respect."

"No," Alannah interrupted. "Such a question is natural. I could ask the same. What is it like to see?"

"Everyone knows what it is like to see," Istabelle said, then paused and cocked her head. "Everyone but you . . ." she added, trailing off.

"Exactly. Close your eyes and try it. We can explore the festival together, discovering all the scents and sounds that make it so fascinating." Alannah took a deep breath, remembering when she had blindfolded Xanthier. Sharing her unique world seemed so easy with these two. Istabelle reminded her so much of Xanthier, Alannah was surprised she had not realized their connection earlier.

"And later I will tell you everything and you will experience the festival as if *you* could see," Istabelle said.

"Very well." Alannah giggled.

Kurgan hung back, disgusted with Alannah's familiarity with Xanthier O'Bannon's child. "I can see that you are occupied. I will leave you two as long as you promise to join the dance with me tonight."

Alannah nodded at Kurgan, then turned her complete attention to Istabelle. "No, silly," she said to the child. "You must be more clever than that. You see, it takes a great deal of restraint to function without sight. You must remember everything. You must consider every step. You must think before you leap. Those are things I believe you have little experience in doing."

Istabelle held her hands out but within seconds she bumped into a cart. She opened her eyes and bounced back. "Sorry," she mumbled.

The cart's owner looked at Alannah nervously. Her blindness was obvious, but she was dressed in fine clothes and he was unsure of her station. Nodding to the little miss, he pushed his cart away.

"Why did he act so funny?" Istabelle asked.

"He is uncomfortable being around me," Alannah replied.

"But that is silly," Istabelle grumbled. "You should be adored, not avoided."

Alannah laughed. "Such wisdom in a small girl! I wish that you could share your thoughts with those who are narrow-minded."

Istabelle glanced up at Alannah, hearing the wistful note in her voice and correctly interpreting the edge of hurt. "You are a very brave lady," she said softly. "I hope that I will be as brave as you when I grow up."

Alannah gasped and pulled Istabelle into a fierce hug. "You are already very brave, Istabelle. Harness your wisdom, control your intelligence, balance your impulsiveness and you will become a woman whom people will write stories about."

"Look! I mean, *smell* that? Custard bread!" Istabelle dashed away and raced up to a baker who had several sweet treats in his basket. The smell wafted down to Alannah and she smiled. Within moments, they were munching on the bread and heading toward the next attraction.

Mangan was not the only person who noticed Istabelle's preoccupation with Alannah. Matalia O'Bannon pointed it out to her husband.

"Brogan," she said, "look at Istabelle. She seems to have taken a firm liking to Alannah."

"I don't believe it. Istabelle is rude and unpleasant to most everyone. I doubt anyone but us could tolerate her for more than five minutes."

"Nonetheless, she is enjoying herself with her new friend."

Brogan peered through the crowd and finally located Alannah and Istabelle where they were working as a team to throw hoops onto a set of pegs. Istabelle could not throw them far enough, and Alannah could not see them, but together they were doing quite well.

"Indeed," he said, amazed. "That is the last thing I expected. I would have thought Istabelle would be at her worst with someone hindered by a physical ailment."

"It is good to see her thus," Matalia murmured as she slid her hand into Brogan's. Mangan rose and slipped his hand into her other one, nodding in agreement.

But Lady Catherine, Istabelle's grandmother on her mother's side, was not so pleased. "Why is my grandchild near that unfortunate?" she exclaimed to her servant companion. "Her reputation is sullied enough by her mother's death and her father's abandonment. I'll not have her associating with lepers, too!"

Her companion nodded in agreement, forbearing to point out that lepers and the blind were hardly the same. It also did not escape her that Lady Catherine had given the child no concern for the last five years, abandoning her as fully as Lord Xanthier had done.

"It is a crime, having that blind creature walk

with civilized personages! I will not lower myself to acknowledge her existence," Lady Catherine said loudly. "And I think her horse should be struck from the race. Surely only *normal* people should compete in such a prestigious event."

Her companion nodded again, but glanced at the beautiful blind woman with compassion. Lady Catherine's views were shared by many of the aristocratic ladies, but within the servant class, Mistress Alannah was respected. And a rumor was starting to circulate among the serving folk, a rumor that had started in the town of Clarauch and would be sure to make people like Lady Catherine quiver in dismay.

Chapter 24

Queen Margaret motioned imperiously to Xanthier and Captain Robbins, demanding that they approach the dais. "Have you spoken to Lady Serena?" she asked Xanthier.

"Your Majesty, I ask you once again to release me from this request. I would give the court half of my coffers to maintain my freedom."

Queen Margaret glared at him. "Although I am pleased that you are willing to support your monarchy, I must insist on your marriage. Young men like you will be led to ruin without the calming influence of a wife. Tell her soon, or I will do it for you."

Xanthier bowed, keeping a tight rein on his temper. The last thing he needed was a wife to pester him, to annoy him and make demands on him. He had had one already, and the experience had not made him respect the institution. A memory flashed in his mind, and he saw Isadora falling from the tower as he watched helplessly from the top of the stone structure.

He did not feel the guilt that he should. There had been no love between him and his former wife, only anger and hate. He did not regret her death. She had not wanted a girl child and had ascended the tower intending to kill the baby. Although he had never held the infant, had kept his heart withdrawn from her, his instincts had taken over, and he had snatched Istabelle from Isadora's hands just as she was poised to drop the infant. Isadora's own momentum had sent her over the edge, and she had plunged to her death. In saving his daughter, Xanthier had inadvertently killed his wife.

A man cleared his throat. Surprised that anyone would approach him, Xanthier lifted an eyebrow and stared at the stranger.

"Me name is Guinness. I live in the Highlands."

"Guinness," Xanthier acknowledged warily.

"I have a daughter who needs a husband, if'n you don't like the Lady Serena."

Xanthier blinked as another man stepped before him.

"Before you hear his offer, Lord Xanthier, I think we should talk. I, too, have a daughter and she comes with a healthy portion of fertile land."

"Sir," someone else interrupted, "not only does my daughter have land and money, she is far more attractive than the daughters of either of those two."

Xanthier stepped back, stunned. "I don't understand."

Captain Robbins chuckled. "I told you that you were more eligible than you thought. General knowledge of your wealth mixed with the ladies' fascination with your dangerous allure makes you the most desirable man here."

Politely excusing himself from the men, Xanthier moved away. "What is this all about?" he asked of his companion. "Are these people stupid? I am the worst of all men. They should not entrust their daughters with me. I have nothing good to offer."

Captain Robbins shrugged. "Perhaps you are not as terrible as you'd like us to believe. Look over there. A whole bevy of hopefuls trying to catch your eye. You are blinder than the blind woman. With very little effort, you could have your betrothed at your side by festival's end, just as your queen commands."

"How disgusting," Xanthier said. "I want nothing to do with any of them." Just then he saw Kurgan, and he forgot the hopeful brides. He narrowed his gaze, remembering Alannah and Kurgan dancing and talking together. Afterwards Alannah had walked at Kurgan's side and allowed him to touch her with easy familiarity. Didn't she know that she was Xanthier's? Didn't she understand that he had laid claim to her? How dare she consort with another man! Without thinking, he strode over to Kurgan, intending to warn him away from her. People leapt out of his way, startled by his forceful tread.

Just as Xanthier was about to reach Kurgan, Captain Robbins caught up with him and placed a restraining hand on his shoulder.

Furious, Xanthier spun around and dropped his hand to his sword hilt.

Stepping back, Captain Robbins held up his hands in a show of nonaggression. "I only caution you, my friend. There are many people about. Do you want to say or do something in front of everyone?"

Xanthier glanced around, noting that many guests were watching him avidly.

Captain Robbins stepped closer and lowered his voice. "I am aware of your turmoil, but you must not do anything foolish. If you fight openly with Kurgan, the king may send you away. Then what will you do? How will you gain the island? Or the girl?"

"Why is he courting her?" Xanthier replied softly. "It does not make sense."

"She is exquisitely beautiful with her green eyes and heart-shaped face. Perhaps he is attracted to her as you are," Robbins suggested.

"I have a difficult time believing that Kurgan would be moved by Alannah's grace. He is fond of violence and domination. She is not to his taste."

Captain Robbins shook his head. "She has a radiance that is hard to ignore. Every man within ten feet of her feels her aura and is drawn to her, but I respect your caution. However, you cannot focus on her right now. You must seek your bride. Find a wife, bed her and put Alannah out of your thoughts."

Xanthier glared at Captain Robbins. "What are you saying?"

"Perhaps it is time to let her go."

Xanthier's breath seemed to catch in his lungs. He felt faint. He felt sick. He stumbled to the edge of the room and leaned against the wall. His hands trembled and spots floated in front of his vision. Never! He would never leave her! Not now, not when he was trying to do the honorable thing for the first time in his life. She was beauty and light, purity and grace. On the island, everything had all seemed so right. A marriage of the heart. Xanthier felt waves of agony overpower him.

Another hand descended on his shoulder, and Xanthier looked up, too weak to fight. Gray eyes met gray eyes as he stared into the concerned gaze of his twin brother.

"Come," Brogan said. "Let's go outside."

The sickness started to wane and Xanthier felt the blood rush back into his arms. He took several stabilizing breaths. His emotions were so raw, he could not resist. Stumbling, tripping, barely able to keep upright, he leaned on the man with whom he had fought for over two decades. Their mutual animosity was suddenly gone, and Xanthier accepted Brogan's support gratefully.

Once outside, Xanthier slumped to the ground and buried his head in his hands. "She tears me up inside," he whispered. "I want her so much, but she angers me! I came here to lay claim to her island so that she would forever be safe, yet she is furious with me. I tell her—and show her in no uncertain terms—that I want her, yet she runs off with my enemy. What am I doing wrong? Is it the sins of my past come to haunt me? I came here to tell her tale to the king, and then claim her as my own, but nothing is happening as I thought it would. I have done so many terrible deeds . . . perhaps she deserves much more than I can offer."

Brogan squatted down and stared at his brother. He did not refute Xanthier's statements, for he knew that Xanthier had done things that had hurt innocent people. He knew that Xanthier had plotted and fought throughout his life to gain power and wealth. But something had changed in him, and Brogan could feel it.

"Brother, our lives can never be relived. We cannot go back and start again, nor can we change what we have done. You are who you are and you have lived as you have lived. What is it about her that makes you regret your past?"

Xanthier looked up, his face haggard and drawn. "She showed me a sense of peace. When I was with her, I felt that I was not terrible. I felt worthy of her smiles and deserving of her cries of joy. If I lose her, I fear I will lose myself forever."

They sat in silence for several minutes and Brogan shifted position to sit next to him. They stared at the horizon, felt the breeze and listened to the hum of insects.

"I never had her, though," Xanthier finally said. "She was never meant to be owned. Her spirit is strong and bold. She can see the world in a way we can never comprehend. I feel like a village idiot trying to woo a princess. And now I must marry a titled daughter. How can I ask Alannah to stay with me after I wed another?" Xanthier turned and stared at Brogan. "I cannot. I cannot marry anyone but her."

"And you cannot marry her?"

"Exactly. Her guardian would never allow it."

"Who is her guardian?"

Xanthier shook his head. "I cannot say."

"Then run away with her," Brogan suggested softly. "I understand love. I would have done anything to keep Matalia at my side."

"Don't you think I have asked? She will not. The impending horse race forces us to remain at odds. If I do not win the island for her, she will hate me forever, yet if she wins the race, she will never realize that I always meant to give the island to her."

"And if you win?"

"I don't know. She may still hate me for controlling her life. I cannot win. What torment! She lies in my arms one moment, then flees the next. I try to show her how much I want her, but she says that I am not understanding her. I am at a loss."

Brogan smiled. "Well, then welcome to the world of men! If you understand women, then you don't love them. I still cannot comprehend my wife. She speaks in ways that baffle me and acts in ways that confound me, but I love her with all my heart."

Xanthier grinned. "I guess it is my just reward."

"Indeed. You have chosen a very complicated woman, and I would be foolish to give you advice. But I do know one thing. If you love her, nothing should stand in your way."

"You are right. She means too much to me. I will speak to the king."

"Are you daft? Are you both idiots?" Matalia stomped her foot in vexation. "How can such an intelligent man make such a stupid mistake?"

"I don't understand. I thought you would be proud of me," Brogan said, his confusion evident.

Matalia sighed. They were walking down the corridor to the king's receiving room. It was early in the morning the day of the great race. Matalia sighed again, venting her frustration. "You men! You think you can arrange everything and we women will fall at your feet in gratitude!"

Brogan flung up his hands. "Explain it to me then," he growled. "What did we do wrong?"

"You'll see," Matalia promised. "Xanthier should have spoken with her first. You have placed her in a difficult situation. I know what I would do."

"What?"

"I would throw your proposal in your face and never talk to you again!"

Brogan grabbed Matalia and pressed her against the wall. He bent his head and ground his lips

against hers, making her remember the hour past
when he had covered her body with his and made
love to her in the dawn.

She gasped and wrapped her arms around his neck.

"Would you? Would you leave me forever if I
made a blundering mistake?"

"Perhaps not," she whispered. "I might give you
a second chance."

Brogan nodded with satisfaction, then dragged
her back down the hall. "Come, Matalia. We
mustn't be late."

She shook her head in exasperation, but followed
him. The poor O'Bannon family had made so many
mistakes in dealing with their women. They had a
knack for ruining perfect love. She hoped that Xanthier was not about to do the same thing.

When they reached the chamber, Xanthier was
already there. His scarred face was tight, and his
steely eyes were hard. Scanning his countenance,
Matalia could see little evidence of his love for
Alannah. It was incomprehensible to her that anyone would open her heart to such a cold man, but
as she knew, love was the most powerful of all
emotions. She was not about to gainsay it.

Many people filled the chamber. Xanthier and
Captain Robbins were there, but there were several
others who made Matalia nervous. Kurgan, nephew
of Lothian the Serpent, was also present. His uncle
had destroyed her father's family, murdering her
grandfather and grandmother as well as her many
aunts. Lothian's lust for gold had been unappeased,
and he had burnt her mother's homeland in an effort to locate a legendary treasure. Although the
uncle was now dead by her own father's hand, his
insidious greed still festered in Kurgan, and Matalia
had always maintained her distance.

She leaned next to Brogan, who wrapped an arm around her comfortingly. There were several others in the room, including Gondilyn, the elderly servant, Effie, and three others she did not recognize. Finally, sitting in the far corner was a woman covered in a green veil.

Xanthier glanced at his twin. Brogan held Alannah's amulet bag in his hands, presumably taken from her room and brought here at the king's command. The only person not yet present was Alannah. Xanthier, too, was nervous about the unexpected number of people. He had requested a private audience and had been stunned when his request had been granted so quickly. Now he wondered at the reason.

The king motioned Xanthier forward. "You wanted to speak with us," he said formally. "We are waiting."

"I had thought to speak privately," Xanthier replied.

"Everyone in this room is intimately connected to the issue at hand."

Xanthier frowned. "I do not see how you would know what I need to speak about . . ."

"We are aware of all that occurs in our kingdom. Speak now or leave."

Clenching his fist, Xanthier took a deep breath and approached the throne. The door to the chamber opened, and Alannah entered, waving her carved staff in front of her. She was dressed in a purple velvet dress with silver threads. A silver circlet covered her head and her auburn hair looked luxurious. Xanthier paused, wanting to go to her, but the king cleared his throat.

Xanthier spoke. "I would like to present my choice of a bride. As Your Majesties are well aware, I have been resistant to marriage since my first wife met an untimely death. However, you have commanded me to marry and provide a home for my daughter, and I have considered my choices very carefully. Although I am aware that you hand-picked Lady Serena for me, I would humbly beg you to accept Mistress Alannah as my choice."

Alannah gasped and Matalia rushed to her side. "What?" Alannah whispered. "What did he say?"

Queen Margaret spoke. "Alannah, dear. Had you no knowledge of this man's proposal?"

Alannah shook her head, bewildered. "I don't understand . . . Did he say that he wants to wed me?"

"Then I may safely assume that you have not accepted him or given your word?" Queen Margaret interjected.

"No, he said nothing to me, nor I to him. We never spoke of marriage." Alannah trembled, joy starting to bubble inside of her. He wanted her! He wanted her enough to ask for her! He hadn't lied! He had wanted her all along!

"How old are you, Alannah?" the king asked. "You must get the permission of your guardian before I can grant a request of marriage."

"I am but sixteen, and the only woman who could be considered my guardian is dead," Alannah replied.

"What about the rest of your family? Have you spoken to them?"

"I do not know who my family is. I am an orphan."

Xanthier glanced nervously around the room. He finally looked at the king who stared down at him with a lifted brow. "Does anyone in the room have

any information about Mistress Alannah's family?"
the king asked.

"Perhaps," the woman in the corner said softly.

The king motioned to her. "M'lady, please
come forward."

The woman who sat in the shadows stirred. She
walked slowly, carefully, as if a great load were
weighing down her steps. The servant, Effie, ac-
companied her and steadied her arm. The woman
patted Effie's hand, then stepped up to the
throne alone.

"Mistress Alannah, would you come forward as
well?" the king asked.

Alannah turned to Matalia in fear. "What is
going on?" she asked.

"I don't know, but the man we sent to Clarauch
is also here," murmured Matalia. "You had best
approach the king."

Alannah bit her lip, unable to make sense of
what was going on around her. The only thing she
could focus on was that Xanthier wanted to marry
her. She did not care who else was in the room, or
about the older woman who stood so quietly at
the throne. Learning about her family was suddenly
unimportant compared to Xanthier's words.

Using her walking stick, she stepped up to the
dais and reached out to seek Xanthier's hand,
wanting reassurance.

He tried to step forward, but the king motioned
him back with a frown.

"Alannah?" the woman in the green veil whispered. "Is that your name?"

Alannah turned to face the woman. "Yes," she
said slowly. Something about the woman caught
her attention, and she focused all her senses. She

smelled the woman's unique scent and listened to her soft voice. "My name is Alannah."

"Were you always called that?" the woman asked.

"I am not sure," Alannah admitted after a brief pause.

"Tell me your tale," the woman requested. "Tell me what you know about your family, your beginnings."

Alannah reached out again. This time Xanthier ignored the king's warning and came forward to clasp her hand. "What is this all about?" she asked him.

"No matter what happens, Alannah, know that I love you," he replied. "I have wanted to share my life and my name with you in order to show the world how much you mean to me. Perhaps my needs were too grand. Perhaps I should have been content to stay hidden away with you. But I wanted to prove my love by putting a circle of gold upon your finger. I wanted to marry you."

"You never asked me," she whispered.

"I couldn't. Not after I found out about your family. That is when I knew I had to come to the king for his permission. Answer the lady's questions, and you will soon understand."

Alannah nodded. Addressing the woman, she replied, "I know nothing of my family or origins. I was set adrift in the ocean, whether in the hope that I would live or perish, I know not. A man who was sailing the sea on the way to visit his lost love rescued me and brought me to an island. The woman on that island was Mistress Anne, but I always referred to her as Grandmother. She raised me as her own."

"Who was this man who found you? Can his story be corroborated?"

"He was Gondin, the merchant. He has since died. Grandmother also passed away several months ago."

"What proof do you have of your beginnings?" the queen asked gently.

"I have nothing save the things that were with me when I was found. A letter . . ."

"May I see it?" Queen Margaret asked.

Brogan pulled the burnt letter from the amulet bag and presented it to the queen. She scanned it and passed it to the king. "This is suggestive," she said to her husband.

Gondilyn stepped forward. "I can affirm that her tale is true. My father was Gondin, and he told me of the infant he found lost at sea. He told me that he brought her to the island where Mistress Anne lived in seclusion."

"Did he describe the infant?" Queen Margaret asked.

"Yes. She was pretty, with reddish hair and green eyes. He said she could not see."

The woman raised her hands to her veil. With hesitant motions, she grasped the edge and lifted the concealing cloth. As her chin was revealed, then her nose and finally her eyes, all in the room fell silent. The whisper of silk filled the chamber as the woman fully removed her veil and stared at Alannah.

The woman's hair was dark red, streaked with silver. Her face was heart-shaped with strong cheekbones. And her eyes . . . her eyes were a glowing, unusual shade of green that shimmered with unshed tears.

Alannah turned toward her, and everyone present could see the resemblance between them. The woman took a step forward and lifted her hands to Alannah's face. "I am your mother," she whispered.

Chapter 25

Touching Alannah softly, the woman stroked her daughter's brow and lovingly cupped her cheek. Then, with a moan of relief, she pulled Alannah into a warm embrace.

"You were not abandoned, darling. I did not care whether your eyes saw the physical world. I loved you more than life itself. I wanted to keep you, to raise you, to love you like a mother should, but I could not. I put you in that boat in order to save you."

Alannah pulled back, shocked.

"You are my daughter," the woman continued. "Your name is Adeline, and you are beloved. You have always been beloved. You come from a great family and are heir to the Serpent fortune. And next month will be your eighteenth—not seventeenth—birthday. In one month you will inherit it all."

"You were my uncle's whore!" Kurgan shouted, all pretenses gone. "Just because you bore the girl does not confirm that she shares the Serpent blood. She could be the bastard child of anyone. The land is mine! The title is mine! He was my uncle and I am the rightful heir!"

Effie darted forward and bowed in front of the

king and queen. "Your Majesties," she said as she curtsied low.

"Speak," King Malcolm commanded.

"She has this," Effie replied as she snatched Alannah's amulet bag from Brogan's lax hand.

"What are you doing with that?" Xanthier said as he took a step forward to retrieve the item. "That is Alannah's bag. You have no right to rifle through her belongings."

"No, let her show the king," Alannah said. "I want to know. Grandmother always said that the necklace inside would show me a new world. Even you said that it looked like an heirloom."

"Aye," Xanthier said quietly. "I remember the faded crest on the back." Fear clouded his eyes as he watched Effie pull out the necklace. What had started so simply—a beautiful woman on a deserted island—had become twisted and convoluted. Xanthier scanned the people in the room, noting the differing expressions. The O'Bannons were stunned, as surprised by events as he. Kurgan was furious, his face turning shades of red and purple. The servants looked triumphant, as if they were unveiling a secret that had remained hidden for too long.

And the woman—she was blissfully happy, staring at Alannah with overflowing love. She hardly glanced at the necklace, for she appeared certain already. She had found her long-lost daughter, and there was not a more exquisite moment in her life than right now.

The king held his hand out and Effie gave him the emerald necklace. He peered at it, nodded, then handed it to the queen. "Lady Zarina?" he asked the woman. "Do you remember this necklace?"

"Yes, it is the same one that I placed in a velvet bag and sent with my infant, the infant I birthed to Lothian."

"She could have stolen it! Or bought it from a dealer! The necklace alone does not prove anything!" Kurgan sputtered.

"Do *you* recognize it?" King Malcolm asked.

Kurgan glanced around, trying to evade the direct question.

Another servant came forward. "I have been in the family for sixty years, and my mother was with them for seventy years before she passed away. In the portrait room, in the eastern wing, there is a picture of Lothian's mother, Lady Circe. She is wearing that necklace in the portrait. The necklace was in the family for centuries until it came up missing almost twenty years ago, at the same time Lady Zarina tried to leave the castle. She tried to escape Lord Lothian, and she did, for a while. But after the birth of her baby, Lothian found her again and brought her back."

"Still, it means only that she stole the necklace," Kurgan argued.

"Yes, I stole the necklace when I ran away from Lothian. I took it to give to my infant so she would have some valuables. I hoped that whoever found her would sell it for her care." The woman looked at Kurgan dispassionately. "You remind me so much of Lothian. Your mind is tainted. I would give anything to say that Adeline does not carry the same blood, but I cannot lie. Adeline— Alannah—is your cousin. She is Lothian's and my child."

"Clarauch . . . that is near the Serpent stronghold," Brogan stated. "Lothian must have taken Zarina from her home in Clarauch."

"Aye . . ." Zarina whispered. "I was but a peasant girl. He stole me, impregnated me and then married me in order to gain control of the babe, but I made sure he never got his evil hands on her. But I hid her too well, and I couldn't find her once Lothian was gone. I looked . . . I looked for so many years!"

"And a key," Effie said as she withdrew the final item from the bag. Everyone stared at it. The key's handle was carved and embellished. It was the key to the castle—the key that was given to the mistress. Lothian's Serpent emblem was boldly scrolled upon it.

Queen Margaret took the key and directed her question to Alannah. "Were you aware of the significance of these items?"

Alannah shook her head. She started to shiver and Xanthier came up behind her, wrapping her in his protective arms.

"The letter, the key and the necklace leave no doubt," said the queen. "She is Lothian's issue. Lord Kurgan, step forward and hand me your signet ring."

"I am her guardian," Kurgan said quickly. "Until she is truly eighteen, she is my legal ward. I deny Xanthier's request, and instead, request her hand in marriage for myself."

"How dare you!" Xanthier shouted. "You do not want her! This is only a strategic move to retain control of your lands! I see now what you have been about. You knew, didn't you? You knew who she was before today!"

"Xanthier," the king snapped. "Restrain yourself!"

"Your motive for marrying Alannah is suspicious

at the very least!" Xanthier shouted. "You plotted
to harm her!"

Kurgan stood chest to chest with Xanthier. "You
only want her because she is blind and cannot see
your disfigured face," Kurgan sneered. Xanthier
slammed his fist into Kurgan's chin, causing him to
stumble back, his eyes flashing with fury. "You will
regret that," Kurgan growled softly.

"Cease!" the king shouted. "Gondilyn, separate
the two."

Gondilyn stepped between the two men as Captain Robbins gripped Xanthier's shoulder and held
him back. "You must ignore his taunts," Robbins
murmured. "Focus on the issue at hand or you will
lose everything."

Nodding reluctant agreement, Xanthier turned
back to the king. "Your Majesty! I love her! Do not
let one month come between us. Please let us unite."

"What is happening?" Alannah cried, frightened
and confused by the events around her. "I don't
understand."

"Lothian had no children," the queen explained.
She stared at Alannah with compassion. "He
feared any issue he had would try to overthrow his
authority. It is common knowledge that he beat any
girl who became pregnant until she miscarried. In
the very end, he wed a peasant girl named Zarina
and no one knew why."

"I had my child," Zarina replied. "I was the only
one who got away from him and I birthed my baby,
although his beatings left her blind. I actually
thanked God for her blindness, for it seemed a
small offering to give for her life."

"Why did he marry you, Lady Zarina?" queried
the queen.

"After he caught me and returned me to his household, he became obsessed with wanting to sire a child. His mind was warped and he could not tell right from wrong. He was bent on searching for gold, and then realized that he would need someone to bequeath his riches to. Because I had given birth to his child, he married me. In so doing, he made the child legitimate. Despite his efforts, I never became pregnant again, which made our missing baby the heiress to Lothian's castle, land and wealth. Kurgan gets nothing. All that he obtained as the closest relative to Lothian is nullified. Alannah receives all."

The king nodded, then turned back to the stunned group of people. Addressing Xanthier, he said, "Kurgan has every right to deny your proposal to Lady Alannah. I will, however, let Alannah make her own decision about whether she will accept his proposal. Regardless of her decision regarding him, she will not be able to marry you."

"But you can make an exception! I came to you for help. Kurgan does not understand her special requirements. She is blind, and needs someone who will stand by her and be proud of her."

"Indeed, Lord Xanthier," the king replied, "I do not care if she grows toads upon her brow, you will not wed her. Kurgan has made that decision. However, you are a very wealthy lord of the realm. There are many matches that would be appropriate. I recommend you seek out the woman I selected for you. The pair of you should live quite comfortably together. One woman is as good as another."

The queen turned her head toward her husband. Her gaze grew frosty and her spine rigid.

"In fact," King Malcolm added, "if we consider

the best interests of the realm, Kurgan would be a good match for her. It would allow him to continue to rule the lands he has commanded, and give our new heiress a young, virile husband."

Chapter 26

Hours later, Alannah leaned against the stable wall, her eyes closed, and breathed steadily, deeply, concentrating on keeping an even rhythm. She smelled the straw, the grain, the horse sweat, the manure, the freshly trimmed hooves. Even the wood and dirt had a unique odor.

Walking with the aid of her stick, she moved down the aisle, listening to the sounds of each horse as she passed his or her stable door. Some pawed, some slept, some munched steadily on hay.

At one stall she paused. The horse within shifted his weight, then snorted as he moved his head up and down. She heard the tossing of his mane and the soft smack of his lips as he nodded, then shook his entire body.

"My big, beautiful stallion," she murmured. "What craziness we endured. You have been my best friend, yet I have hardly spoken to you in the past days. I have been so wrapped up in the events around me, I forgot to pay attention to one that is so important."

The white stallion snorted, then rested his chin on the half door so Alannah could stroke his muzzle.

"What has happened to me? Everything I have

known has been turned upside down. I thought my mother despised me and abandoned me because of my eyes. Now I find that she has always loved me, and has been searching for me for years.

"I always assumed I was like Grandmother, peasant born. She told me of the fancy people, and I have moved among them comfortably. But I never thought I was one of them. I thought I never *could* be one of them. Yet look at me now." Alannah raised her signet ring, showing it to the horse. She touched it with her other hand, tracing the lines of the Serpent seal. "Is this really me, friend? Is this really happening?"

Alannah stepped inside the stall and began brushing her beloved beast. She used her hand to rub his familiar hide. She smoothed his hair, wiping away all traces of dust. Leaning down, she lifted his hooves and picked them clean, making sure that no pebble was embedded in the soft *V* of his inner foot.

"Is your leg going to hold?" she asked. "I don't want to do anything that will hurt you. Will you wear the saddle blanket? Will you wear a bridle and reins for me? Will you let Gondilyn ride you?"

The stallion blew softly. His ears pricked forward and he focused his big, brown eyes on Alannah's face. He could not understand her words, but her confusion and fear were clear to him, and he was concerned for her. He swished his tail, frustrated that he could not find his mistress's enemy and fight. Fight or flight. Those were his only responses. He rubbed against her, wanting to help her. He would do anything for her. He would race for her.

Alannah released his hoof and started on his mane and tail. She combed them thoroughly, straightening all the tangles. Then she carefully braided the mane into many plaits that interlocked with each other down the crest of his neck.

"Do you know what else happened?" she whispered. "He came here to ask for me. Xanthier went to the king and queen to ask for me! He was not embarrassed by my blindness. He never abandoned me. All along, he wanted to announce to the world that he wanted me by asking me to join with him for eternity."

Alannah paused and smiled. "Imagine! He did want me! After all my doubts and fears . . ." She picked up the saddle blanket and placed it carefully on the stallion's back. The sound of the stall door opening made her turn.

"I love you," he said.

"And I love you!" she breathed, and stepped into Xanthier's arms.

He held her close, squeezing her. "God! I have wanted to say those words, hear them for so long. I love you so much! You are incredible, beautiful and powerful and gentle."

"Stop." Alannah giggled. "You are acting foolish."

"I don't care. I will act foolish around you if it will make you smile. I would do anything to make you laugh."

"Do you really love me?"

Xanthier cupped her face, staring at her seriously. "I love you more than there are waves in the ocean, more than there are clouds in the sky and more than there are butterflies in the world. You are everything to me. When I am without you, I am lost. My old life ceases to exist; it has no meaning. Since I met you, I have become a new man. You have given me gifts you don't even fully realize. I love you."

"Xanthier," Alannah sighed. "I have missed you. On the island, you completed my existence. You opened my eyes."

"Opened your eyes?"

"Yes! You made me see what life and love were all about. You gave me adventure and excitement. You gave me ecstasy. You showed me love."

"I didn't mean to hurt you by leaving you on the ship."

"But you left me for so long . . . you caused me so much distress," she scolded him softly. "I was so alone."

"I brought you to Scotland both to try to gain rights to the island, and to try to convince the king to let us officially wed. I did not want to love you like I did, yet not have our union sanctified by God. But I was wrong not to tell you. I should have confided everything to you. In my arrogance I thought to marry you and give the island to you as a wedding gift, not understanding that I risked everything. Will you forgive me?"

Alannah was silent, absorbing his words. She tilted her head and brushed her lips across his scarred face. "You have shown me how to forgive," she murmured. "You forgave my angry words, my running away from you without explanation. Your single-mindedness has shown me that you love me. I learned from you."

Xanthier shook his head. "How can you turn my faults into favors?"

"I see no fault in you. Every part of you is what makes you the man I love. Your past, your stubbornness, your scars . . . everything about you. I love it all."

Xanthier groaned, burying his head in her neck. "What are we going to do?"

"We must win the race; then we will sail away, just as you suggested. I have no intention of letting anyone hinder my happiness."

"But, Alannah, Kurgan and the king have forbidden it. And you have a mother now, one who loves you and wants to get to know you."

Alannah frowned and pulled away. She lifted the saddle and placed it carefully over the blanket on Claudius's back, then reached under and grabbed the girth. She murmured to the stallion, soothing him until he accepted the heavy weight. Then she plucked the bridle headpiece from the pole and placed it over his head.

"My mother has lived for seventeen years without me," she said as she stroked Claudius, rewarding him for his docility.

"Alannah, I could not take you away from such an important person. I lived without a mother. I know the pain it causes. I do not want those wounds left unhealed in you."

"Are you making choices for me once again? Are you deciding what is best for me? Like Grandmother? Like you did on the island when you forced me to sail away?"

"I just want to help you."

"Then let me decide."

Xanthier leaned back, watching Alannah's movements as she led the stallion toward the stable door. She walked with confidence, not hiding her blindness. She accepted it. She was a lovely, intelligent woman. "You are right," he relented. "You will make your own choices. I will respect your decisions. We will do as you desire."

"Thank you," she whispered. She brought his face down to hers and pressed her lips against his, showing him how much she appreciated his acceptance.

He gripped her shoulders and deepened the kiss, opening her lips with his and plunging his tongue inside her mouth. He devoured her, loving her and worshiping her.

"Oh!" Alannah gasped.

"Now," he whispered as he pushed her back into the stall they had just vacated. "I want you."

"Here?" she whispered back. "Anyone could come in! Anyone could hear!"

"Then be quiet," he commanded. He lifted her skirts and deftly slid his hands into her silken undergarments. He brushed her, sweeping his fingers across her most sensitive flesh, then gripping her buttocks to lift her onto the wooden partition.

"Oh!" Alannah gasped again as she held onto his shoulders. Her thighs opened and she quivered. He knew just how to touch her . . . he made her melt with desire. His fingers danced upon her, around her, teasing her until she was liquid, then his finger dipped inside her. She cried out but silenced her moans when Xanthier grumbled a warning.

"Shush," he said, "else I will stop."

"Don't stop," she pleaded. "Not now!"

He played with her, rubbing his thumb over her, sinking his finger inside her one inch, then two, then as deep as he could. He could feel her surround his hand in moist acceptance, but he wanted more . . . he wanted her helpless with yearning.

He lifted her skirts farther and bent his head. He blew softly upon her, taunting her further while still touching and stroking her.

"Please!" she cried.

"Please what?" he growled. "Tell me what you want."

"I can't say!" Alannah whimpered as his breath warmed her thighs and she arched upwards, seeking his tongue.

"Tell me," he insisted, "or I will stop."

"No!" Alannah shouted, then covered her mouth in horror. "No," she repeated in a whisper. "Whatever you do, don't stop."

"Then tell me . . ."

"Kiss me," she pleaded. "Kiss me and love me!"

He groaned as he complied, touching her intimately with his mouth as his fingers sank deep within her, rhythmically drawing her into a swirling abyss of ecstasy.

"Yes," she sighed between her fingers that covered her mouth. "Like that!"

Then, just as she was about to climax, he pulled away from her. "No!" she cried, but his body replaced his mouth as he sank his cock fully into her trembling core, hardly missing a beat.

"Oh, yes!" he replied as he bucked against her, supporting her weight as she weakened. He drove into her, his member swollen, hard and pulsing. He closed his eyes, relishing the beauty of their union, trying to hold back his explosion. Stroke . . . stroke . . . He clenched, paused, tried to hold back.

Alannah wrapped her legs around his waist and lifted her hips to a new angle. They both gasped . . . gripped each other close . . . stroke, stroke . . . His motions became frantic, frenzied and she cried out, forgetting to be silent. Deeper and deeper, she arched into him and screamed as stars burst around her and frissons of heat and sensation filled her, then swept through her and left her limp with repletion.

He bent his head against her, feeling her rippling orgasm, controlling himself, wanting to experience every moment of the pleasure he could give her. Then, as her body relaxed, he, too, sought the pinnacle and poured his essence deep inside her.

Claudius reared, his white coat glistening in the moonlight, and Gondilyn tumbled to the ground once again.

"Augh!" he groaned. He remained on his back for several moments as Alannah soothed the stallion, then slowly rose for the tenth time. He hobbled to the side of the road and sat down, exhausted. "That stallion is too wild, Alannah. No one will ever be able to ride him."

"Don't be ridiculous. He is as tame as a kitten. Let me show you again." Alannah mounted, carefully settling into the saddle. "Shush," she murmured to Claudius. "I know you don't understand a lot that is happening, but it is very important that you behave. You must wear this saddle, and you must let Gondilyn ride you."

The horse snorted and stamped his foot.

"I can't tell if he is agreeing with you or not," Gondilyn whined. He was irritated because the fabulous beast would submit to Alannah and not to him. "Alannah, this is not going to work. I have no intention of being thrown in the dust in front of the king and queen."

"It must work! How else am I to win my land? The island must not fall into another's hands."

"Why does it matter anymore? You are heiress to lands much more vast and valuable than a simple island. Let it go and enjoy the benefits of your windfall."

Rounding on Gondilyn angrily, Alannah rode

Claudius over to him and towered above his prostrate form. "You do not understand! I care nothing for any land but my own! Kurgan can take the property for all I care. I want the island!"

"I cannot ride your horse," Gondilyn shouted back.

"Fine! Then I will ride him!"

Gondilyn laughed aloud. "You are being preposterous. No female can ride in the race."

"Why not?"

"Because. It simply is not done."

Alannah clenched her teeth. "There is much in the world that I am not fond of. There must be a way that I can ride."

"Not unless you suddenly grew a beard . . ." Gondilyn's words trailed off as he watched Alannah break into a wide smile.

"That is what we will do. I will disguise myself as you!"

"No," Gondilyn whispered. "Don't even consider it. The race can be violent. It is risky. If we were discovered, we would be punished beyond imagining."

"It is the only way," Alannah concluded. "Claudius will never allow you to ride him. He barely accepts the saddle and headstall. During the commotion of the race, you will never stay mounted. If I am to enter him and win my island, I will have to ride him."

Sighing, Gondilyn approached the white stallion and gazed up at Alannah's beautiful face. Her sea green eyes shimmered. Relenting, he bowed his head. "Please be careful. Stay clear of the other riders."

"I know. You do not need to tell me."

"You cannot let anyone know."

"I understand," she answered curtly.

He touched her leg gently. "We will have to practice the course so you know where to go."

Alannah nodded, then giggled with excitement. "I will win!" She grinned at his snort and added, "I will!"

"Of course. I would expect nothing less."

Many hours later, after Alannah and Gondilyn had ridden the course four times and Alannah had memorized every obstacle and every turn, they said good night and Alannah rode Claudius back to the stable. As she dismounted, a man materialized out of the shadows.

Alannah whipped around. "Who goes there?" she demanded.

"Fear naught, Alannah. It is I, Kurgan."

Guiltily touching her sweaty stallion, Alannah nodded a hesitant greeting.

"Amazing turn of events," Kurgan said softly. "Do you realize how long I have labored over the Serpent properties? And now, with the arrival of one slip of a girl, they are lost. Amazing."

"I had no idea," Alannah murmured, feeling uncomfortable. "I do not want the lands. You can keep them."

Kurgan laughed, and there was an ugly tone to his humor. "It is not as easy as that, Alannah. Inheritance laws cannot be changed. You are the rightful heiress no matter how unsuitable you are. Our marriage will right the wrongs of our birth."

"I have no intention of marrying you, Kurgan. Xanthier asked me, and I want to marry him."

Kurgan draped his arm over her shoulders. "Don't you know about Xanthier?"

"What do you mean?" Alannah asked, nervous

at Kurgan's proximity. He had been courteous and gentlemanly, yet now her extra senses were picking up strange vibrations from him. She trembled, suddenly afraid.

"Xanthier has stayed at court in order to find a bride. Although he says that he wants to wed you, he is only making excuses. He wants your land and your island. He wants a title. You can give him all that."

"What are you trying to tell me?"

"Don't you find it strange that Xanthier only asked for your hand after finding out that you were an heiress?"

"That is not true! He asked *before* Zarina came forward!"

"Don't be naive. Recall that he knew about your identity all along, but withheld the information. Don't you find that suspicious? He asked for you simply because of your title and lands, but he wanted to gain them without your knowledge."

"I don't believe you."

"That is your heart speaking and not your head. Think about it. At least I have been honest. I want you so that we may merge our assets. Xanthier has lied. He has fooled you into thinking that he wants you whereas in reality, he wants the same thing I want—your property."

"No . . . Xanthier cares for me," Alannah insisted, but her voice lacked conviction. Past hurts welled up, and she remembered her sense of betrayal.

"Simply think it over, Alannah. You must decide whether to use your heart or your head. It is your future. Do you think you should base a decision that will affect the rest of your life on your emotions? Think logically. Make a decision based upon facts. I know who you are and I want what you have. I have been honest with you."

Alannah swallowed, thinking about her fears and insecurities. With Xanthier, every moment was fraught with high intensity. With Kurgan, she would not have to wonder about his feelings. She would know that their association was based upon mutual need.

"I will think upon it," she finally said, "if you will reconsider your refusal to grant me my choice."

"Very well." He glanced at the saddled stallion, noting the new trappings, and Alannah's dusty face. "Your horse is well behaved for you," he remarked. "Yet I have not seen your rider successfully gallop him on the course. How is he faring?"

"What do you mean?" Alannah replied quickly as her face flushed.

Kurgan stared at her silently, then smiled. "I will be amazed if Gondilyn stays mounted for the duration of the race."

"He rides Claudius quite well," Alannah lied as she turned away.

"I see," Kurgan grinned, suspecting the truth. "I believe tomorrow will be very interesting."

Chapter 27

Early the next morning, Gondilyn sneaked into Alannah's room with a brown robe and a fake beard. "Will you reconsider?" he begged one final time.

"No. Help me get ready. We don't have much time."

Giving up, Gondilyn helped Alannah, pulling the robe over her head and covering her delicate face with the contrived facial hair.

"You will not be able to use your staff," Gondilyn warned her.

"I know. I will mount Claudius as soon as possible and let him guide me."

Gondilyn donned a similar robe. "I will wait for you at the end of the race. If—when—you win, dismount and head to the privy. I will wait for you there with your clothing. Then I will come out and accept the award on your behalf."

"Perfect," Alannah agreed. "We have no time to lose."

The pair swiftly descended the stairs and exited the castle. They entered the stable without encountering anyone. Gondilyn breathed with relief. "God is helping us!"

*　　*　　*

The O'Bannons waited for Alannah, but when she did not appear they went down to the race grounds without her, assuming that she was somewhere in the festival courtyard. They stopped off at the warm-up area and sought Claudius and Gondilyn. Brogan watched the stallion apprehensively.

"Are you—" Matalia said.

"Is he—" Brogan started. Both spoke at once, and then looked at each other and laughed. "I'm sorry. You first," Brogan said.

"Are you ready, Gondilyn? Will Claudius be kind to you?"

Gondilyn grunted an affirmative.

"Is he sound enough? He was injured only days ago," Brogan said.

Again, Gondilyn grunted a reply.

Matalia and Brogan looked at each other again, surprised at how untalkative Gondilyn was being. Matalia leaned against her husband. "He must be very nervous," she whispered. "He looks so thin . . . so frightened."

Brogan nodded. "Perhaps he is being superstitious," he replied in an undertone. Then, loud enough for Gondilyn to hear, he added, "Good luck. Ride the stallion well and Alannah will be forever in your debt."

Alannah nodded, then, without another word, rode Claudius away from her friends. She *was* frightened! She could only navigate by sound, and noise was reverberating all around her. Horses were trotting back and forth, warming up, and she was terrified that she would run straight into one of them. Several sharp reprimands informed her of how close she came to realizing her fear.

People filled the tents. The bright morning sunshine flooded the area and blazed against the silken clothing of the assemblage. The king and queen sat on raised thrones and motioned to various horses as they talked together.

Alannah could not see the colors, but she could feel the light. She was warm, inside and out. She was finally in charge of her own destiny! She was not an infant floating at sea, or a blind child stumbling around an island. She was a woman taking control of her future. She nudged Claudius toward the starting track.

An angry whinny to her right caused her to flinch. Claudius tossed his head and whinnied back. As Alannah shushed her horse, she heard Kurgan laugh.

"My beast is a mighty stallion," he said to someone who was staring at his furious horse in awe. "I will win. You should place a bet on me."

The person looked up at Kurgan and said, "He is a very big racehorse. I am quite impressed, but I have already placed a bet on the white stallion."

"Then you are a fool!" Kurgan snapped, and kicked his horse. The animal reared up, then sprang forward before Kurgan pulled him to a halt by viciously sawing on the reins.

Alannah frowned as she sensed Kurgan's horse's anxiety. No human should treat a horse like he did. Horses gave their strength to their masters because of their hearts. The beasts did not have to submit. They could easily escape. When they allowed a person to tame them, they were giving a gift. Shaking her head, Alannah wished that Kurgan would appreciate the beauty of the animals he commanded.

She felt Xanthier several horses away, sensing his firm but relaxed manner upon his horse. He was an excellent rider and his horse was strong and swift. He understood how to communicate, not dictate to his horse.

Xanthier shifted his steed closer to Gondilyn's, and whispered to the rider, "Hear me carefully. I want you to win. This race is for Alannah's island, and she, more than anyone, deserves to claim it. I have remained in the race only to ensure that nothing foul occurs, as I do not trust Kurgan. Are you going to be able to stay mounted?"

"Aye," Alannah murmured while turning fully toward him. "I think I can manage." She smiled into his stunned face.

"Alannah!" he whispered urgently. "This is no place for you! You could be injured, maimed or worse. For the love of God, don't do this!"

"I must," she murmured back. "I want my island. It is my home."

"I will win it for you."

"Can you guarantee that you will win? Do you believe that your horse has a better chance to win than Claudius?"

Xanthier frowned. He could not refute her statements. The horses were being led to the starting line and he could not continue to plead with her without revealing her disguise. He clutched his reins with white-knuckled fear. He had vowed to protect her and so far, he had done a poor job of it. This time, nothing would stop him from making sure that she rode a safe, fair race.

Alannah lifted her chin and listened to the crowd. Voices tumbled over one another and it was difficult to make out individual conversations. She could feel people watching her and she ducked her chin down, shielding her eyes. She was about to ride in a race! Excitement coursed through her and she trembled.

The stallion pranced and Alannah turned her concentration to the race. Other riders jockeyed for

position, and Alannah shifted with them, feeling
the rising excitement.

"Hold the line!" a man shouted. "Hold the line!"

Claudis whinnied and pawed the ground. "Stay
calm, friend," Alannah whispered. "This is a time
to work together. Be my eyes. Be my legs. Be my
strength."

The stallion gathered his muscles, and Alannah
tensed. A hush spread over the people, and all she
could hear was the snorting and pawing of the
racehorses.

Then the flag snapped down.

Alannah squeezed her thighs and Claudius burst
forward in an explosion of speed, swirling dust and
thundering hooves. The other horses leaped forward and set out in a dangerously chaotic gallop.
They bumped into each other. Whips swung, legs
became tangled and two horses and riders tumbled
to the ground only feet from the starting line. The
rest of the pack surged around the fallen men and
stretched out along the racetrack.

Xanthier set his steed behind Alannah's, keeping
her in sight. She rode with such grace, her form
floating above her horse's back. Desire whispered
through him, then pride overwhelmed him. She was
so beautiful to watch!

Claudius jumped a sinkhole and landed jarringly
on his forelegs. He tripped, then struggled to retain
his balance. Xanthier gasped, but Claudius maintained his footing and Xanthier briefly closed his
eyes with relief.

A gray racehorse swerved to the right, bumping
against the white stallion's haunches. Because she
could not see him, Alannah couldn't react quickly
enough and Claudius was shoved off the packed
area. He floundered for a moment on the soft grass.

Alannah struggled to help her horse, and they were able to get back onto the track. They had lost the lead, but were only a length behind.

Infuriated, Xanthier nudged his steed next to hers, trying to shield her from the other competitors.

Alannah's confidence wavered. Everything was happening so quickly and the pounding hooves echoed around her, making her sense of hearing all but useless. She shouldn't have done this. She should have listened to Gondilyn and stayed out of the dangerous competition. Another horse swung ahead of her, causing Claudius to shorten his stride. Alannah bit her lip, frustrated, discouraged and fearful.

The race course turned as it circled the village. A series of jumps peppered the next phase and Alannah crouched down, letting the stallion set his own pace. The first jump came up amazingly fast, and the field flowed over it like a river moving over a submerged log. Many villagers cheered and shouted encouragement from the sidelines. Alannah took several even breaths. She had to keep her faith, her sense of peace, if she was going to stay in the race.

Several other natural jumps came up, and Alannah and the stallion leapt them with ease, yet they remained trapped behind the front-runners. Alannah's confidence trickled back and she urged Claudius to gallop faster. Ahead of them were four others, including Kurgan's black stallion.

The track turned sharply uphill, and the horses abruptly slowed. Their shoulders bulged as they pulled themselves up the slope. Once again, the white stallion was forced to stay back, following the others. One horse kicked up a rock, and it flew backwards, thudding into Alannah's chest. She cried out, but then leaned forward, trying to help balance her stallion as it raced up the hill.

They reached the other side, and suddenly the horses were skidding and sliding, trying to stay upright as they tumbled downhill. No audience littered this area, and the race was a lonely, heaving mass of horseflesh. Alannah heard the breathing, the straining, the occasional strike of a hoof against rock. Thoughts of the isle whispered through her mind. Thoughts of when the herd of wild horses raced together for fun, for the thrill of running. Alannah smiled, feeling the glory of the race as the wind whipped through her hair and snapped against her cheeks. Slowly, inch by inch, Claudius began to move forward within the pack.

The horses reached the bottom of the hill and plunged into a marshy, wet flatland. Water sprayed upwards as the horses' hooves crashed into pools of water. The horse that had pushed the white stallion from the field hesitated, frightened of the water. Taking immediate advantage, the white stallion swept past him and gained the lead next to Kurgan while the other horses flagged, exhausted by the grueling pace.

One other steed kept pace with the white horse. Xanthier bent low over his bay horse, asking him to stretch his massive muscles and match the stallion, stride for stride.

Kurgan turned, noticing the other horse's appearance at his side. He kicked his own horse, sending the beast into another burst of speed. They bounded out of the water and reached another flat area. They had circled three-fourths of the way around the village and were heading toward the homestretch. He snarled under his breath and whipped his horse mercilessly.

Losing was not a possibility. He must win, for by winning he could gain possession of the island Alannah wanted. It would give him the leverage he needed to force her to agree to his plans. And then, once she consented to marry him, he would have the ultimate revenge upon Xanthier. He would have the woman, the island and the power to ensure his enemy's total defeat.

Welts appeared on the black hide of Kurgan's horse as it strained with increased effort. But the white stallion continued to gain, outdistancing even Xanthier's horse.

Within seconds, the white stallion drew even with Kurgan's animal, then surged ahead. His white legs flashed in the sunlight. Sparks flew from his hooves as he struck rocks and gravel. His speed was remarkable, beyond imagination.

The stallion was Alannah's strength, her vision. She was the horse's stability and safety. They were partners as only a beast and his mistress could be. Their interdependence was cherished; their mutual love was accepted. As they rushed headlong into the wind, nothing mattered except the joy of running.

Kurgan's and Xanthier's horses raced neck to neck, several lengths behind the white stallion. Kurgan's face turned ugly. He pulled a rock from his saddlebag.

"You think you can beat me!" he shouted at his enemy. "I would rather see you dead!" He flung the stone at Xanthier's head.

The granite thudded against Xanthier's temple, stunning him, and he teetered in his saddle.

Alannah heard the shouts, felt the pain in Xanthier's head, felt him drift toward unconsciousness. She screamed in horror and thoughts of the race were swept from her mind as her love for Xanthier surged forth. "No! Xanthier!"

She leaned back, slowing her stallion. She needed to reach Xanthier! Claudius shook his head angrily but obediently slowed, and they began losing ground. The tents making the finish line were visible in the distance.

The three horses thundered toward the festival grounds, Claudius tossing his head in agitation as he was held back, the black stallion laboring under Kurgan's cruel whip, and the bay steed careening out of control without his master's guidance.

Alannah pulled Claudius even slower, forcing him to fall behind Kurgan's horse. "Xanthier!" she cried. "Don't fall! Please!"

Xanthier blinked as he swayed in the saddle. His head swam as pain shot through his temple like lightning smashing against the sky. His tenuous hold on consciousness slipped and he leaned out of his saddle. The ground was rushing by with dangerous velocity.

"Wake up!" Alannah shouted, realizing how precarious his situation was. The other horses were racing behind them and would soon trample them. Kurgan was far in the lead.

Tears welled in Alannah's eyes, but she did not cry for the loss of her island. She sorrowed for the evil in the world, for her lover's pain and for the loss of her innocence. But with the realization that maliciousness abounded, she also reveled in the knowledge that within her was a power greater than any evil. She had found love.

Alannah reached for Xanthier's horse's bridle and gripped it tightly. She pulled back, slowing him, then pushed him off the track. The other horses thundered past them as they stumbled off the race course and slowed to a canter, then a trot, and finally, to a stop.

She touched Xanthier's forehead, finding where the rock had hit and wiping away the blood that soaked his hair. She stroked his face, feeling his shallow breathing with great concern. "Xanthier," she whispered. "I am not ready to lose you."

He blinked. He groaned.

She leaned forward, pressing her lips against his neck. "I love you."

He leaned against her slight frame. "Keep talking to me," he murmured. "I want to hear your voice."

"I love you. I want you. I need you. I never want to lose you." She kissed him again.

"You will never lose me," Xanthier swore as he opened his eyes and stared at her beloved face. "And certainly not today, thanks to you."

Suddenly Gondilyn rode up to them, galloping frantically from where he had waited at the edge of the course. "What goes on? Who is injured? I saw Xanthier's horse falter, then Alannah's horse lose heart."

Alannah smiled gratefully at her friend. "Xanthier needs some medical attention."

"Aye, I can see that. Alannah, I will take care of him if you change out of your disguise and hurry back to the tents. You cannot be found on Claudius. Ride my steed back and I will walk your stallion home."

"Who won?" Alannah whispered, although she already knew.

Gondilyn looked away, then took a deep breath. "Kurgan. Kurgan won the race and your island."

Tears filled Alannah's eyes once again. "Don't worry," she said softly. "It doesn't matter. We did our best." She pulled her disguise off and handed the items to Gondilyn.

As Alannah rode slowly toward the festival grounds, she held back her tears. The island was her home. There she had first learned love and patience, care and understanding. She was terribly disappointed.

Kurgan left the winner's circle after accepting congratulations from the king and queen. He stalked over to Alannah, glowing with self-satisfied smugness. "I have your island, Alannah. If you want it, you will have to marry me."

She stilled. "Do you think I would agree to wed you based on a piece of land? No matter how much I want to claim that island for myself, I would not betray my heart to do it."

His face contorted with fury. He grabbed her sleeve and whispered to her under his breath, "If it hadn't been for you, I could have killed that miserable bastard, won the race and had everything I wanted. You have resisted my every intention. But since you foiled my plans, you will pay my price. I can see that you care for him, so hear me clearly. If you do not agree to announce your marriage to me, I will find Xanthier and murder him in his sleep. Do you understand me?"

Alannah trembled, frightened and stunned by Kurgan's evil. "How could you?" she whispered but Kurgan shook her.

"Trust me, I will do as I said. Announce the marriage and make everyone believe it or I will make sure your lover doesn't live to see tomorrow's sunrise." Releasing her, Kurgan rode away and was lost in the crowd.

Alannah couldn't move. He would murder Xan-

thier. He had already tried. Suddenly the events of
the past week rushed through her mind and everything made sense. Kurgan had known all along.
Kurgan had intended to stop her from inheriting.
He had attempted to distance her from the only
man she could truly trust by making her doubt his
love. It had all been Kurgan. Perhaps Kurgan had
also convinced the king to put the island up for
a purse.

Xanthier had tried to help her from the beginning. It was she who should be ashamed that she
had not understood his reasons. Time and again he
had tried to tell her of his love, of his honorable
intentions, but she had ignored him. It was time to
do something good for him as he had done for her,
time and again. She could save his life.

Xanthier searched the crowd for Alannah. His
head throbbed but he was recovered enough to
walk unassisted, and he wanted to hold her in his
arms. The people swarming around simply irritated
him and he wished they would all disappear. He
wanted to see her and assure himself of her well-
being. He wanted to lay claim to her as his wife.
Nothing was going to stop him anymore. He didn't
care what the royals said. If Alannah would have
him, he would be the happiest man in the world.

Suddenly he saw her. She was walking carefully
through the throng, her staff swaying in front of
her as she took small, measured steps. Her auburn
hair shone with deep red highlights and her sea
green eyes gazed at the people with her unique,
penetrating but sightless stare.

Suddenly, Kurgan appeared at her side and took
her arm. She smiled nervously up at him.

Xanthier stood in confusion, frozen in shock as the pair approached the dais together and nodded to the king and queen.

Galvanized into action, Xanthier walked forward and grabbed Kurgan's shoulder. "Get away from her," he growled. "Don't sully her skin with your touch!"

"Careful, Xanthier. Before you start making a fool of yourself, you should listen to our announcement."

"What announcement?" Xanthier answered, his anger overflowing, but the king interrupted him by rising and addressing the populace.

"What courage! What a powerful example of Scottish strength! Cheers for Kurgan, Lord of the Serpents!" the king shouted. "A race well run!"

The people screamed in response. Alannah stood quietly, facing the royals. She shivered. The race had been won by cheating, yet she could say nothing. Any protest would result in Xanthier's demise. She felt his presence nearby and ached to run to him, but she could not. She needed to protect him.

"I am pleased to give you my personal acknowledgment," the king said. "From the throne, I commend you."

Alannah shook, her head swimming. She felt faint. It was almost time.

"As the prize of this race, I give the ownership of the Isle of Wild Horses to Lord Kurgan. May you use your property well." The king smiled as the crowd cheered. Then, raising his hand for silence, he spoke again. "And I hear that the lord and lady wish to make an announcement?"

"Aye. The Lady Alannah wishes to speak," Kurgan said as he nudged Alannah forward.

Taking faltering steps, Alannah made her way to

the dais and knelt. Bending her head, she murmured so softly that the queen had to lean forward to hear her.

"I want to announce my acceptance of Lord Kurgan's proposal of marriage. We wish for the banns to be posted immediately," she murmured.

"No! I forbid it!" Xanthier shouted.

The queen sat back and stared at Alannah. "It was my impression that you preferred Xanthier. Have you carefully considered your decision?"

Alannah nodded. "Yes. Kurgan is my choice."

The king nodded happily. "It is as it should be," he said. "Their union is the best political arrangement. Bless the marriage!" But the queen remained silent, staring at Alannah with concern.

Gondilyn, too, watched Alannah with drawn brows. He was not sure what was happening and he didn't know if he should interfere or not. He wanted Alannah safe, but he was unsure about either Xanthier or Kurgan. Both men were unpredictable and tended toward violence. He rubbed his head, his feelings in turmoil.

"Alannah? What are you doing?" Xanthier shouted. "I thought you cared. In the race . . . you lost the race because of me!"

Alannah rose from her curtsy and forced a disdainful look upon her face. "I don't know what you are talking about. Gondilyn lost the race because he is an inferior rider to Kurgan. There has been too much strife between us and I have chosen Kurgan as my intended."

"You can't do this," Xanthier growled, but Kurgan stepped forward and grinned at Xanthier's furious face.

"You are making an idiot of yourself. Accept defeat. I won the race, and I won the lady. I have vast lands and a high title. You have nothing except a floating piece of wood. Think about that every night as you watch the waves crash against your ship's hull."

"I will never forgive you," Xanthier said in a low tone. "I will not rest until this wrong is righted." Then, enraged yet helpless, he left the courtyard and stalked away.

Chapter 28

As Alannah listened to Xanthier's footsteps fade into the crowd, she barely contained her tears. He was so hurt, but she had only meant to protect him. Why had everything become so complicated? She felt numb. The words she had spoken clogged her throat and made her nauseous, yet she had said them in order to save the one man she truly loved.

She knew Xanthier would never forgive her, and would never understand why she had deserted him, but that was not important. His life was the most precious thing she could imagine. Perhaps, one day, he would find someone else he could love.

"Come, daughter," Zarina murmured. "Come away from the crowd."

Alannah stumbled after her, sick to her stomach after Kurgan's perfunctory kiss sealing the engagement. It was such a mockery! She felt nothing but distaste for Kurgan, yet here she had declared her devotion to him. Tears welled in her eyes.

Zarina pushed people out of the way and led Alannah away. The king detained Kurgan and congratulated him again as Alannah and Zarina escaped.

"Thank you," Alannah whimpered. "That was so difficult . . ."

"Yes. You are embroiled in such a convoluted situation. And you have spent so much time in isolation. All of this must be overwhelming at times."

Alannah nodded. "You are right. The people seem so loud and overpowering. I try so hard to do what is right, yet everything keeps going astray. I long for silence and peace. I miss the crash of the ocean waves and the twitter of the birds. I want to return to my simple life. It is all so confusing."

They reached the stable and Alannah walked the stallion over to a bucket and collected her emotions. She could not falter now. She had made a choice and she must stand by it or Kurgan would follow through on his threats and murder Xanthier. She sluiced her stallion with water, then scraped his hide clean. As Zarina stood by, Alannah remarked, "Claudius wanted to win. I, not Gondilyn, was riding Claudius, and he would have won if I hadn't held him back."

"Is that what happened? Did you go back to help Xanthier? Perhaps you did not think winning the race was worth the cost. Some, like Kurgan, think winning is everything. You don't. You are wiser."

Alannah wrapped lengths of cloth around the animal's forelegs, then put him in a stall to rest. She did not respond to her mother.

"So, you will wed Kurgan."

"Yes."

"Can I ask why?"

"No."

"Ah. I see." Zarina stood by as Alannah continued to tend her stallion. Finally, breaking the silence, Zarina stated, "I am afraid of horses."

"Really? How strange." Alannah turned and focused on her mother. She suddenly realized she knew nothing about this woman who had birthed her. She did not know what foods she liked, what season she loved, what activities she enjoyed.

"Do you want to talk?" Zarina asked. "Not about Kurgan or Xanthier, but about flowers and sunrises?"

"Yes," Alannah answered slowly. "I'd like that very much."

Xanthier slammed his personal items in a saddlebag, then crashed his fist against the mantelpiece.

"That witch! She has confounded me time and again with her incomprehensible shifts of emotion! She acts as though she loves me, then tramples my feelings as if I mean nothing to her." He kicked a chair, shattering it, then picked up the pieces and threw them into the fire. As sparks tumbled out of the grate, he flung his head back and howled with rage.

With fury fueling his actions, he strode down the stairs and exited the castle with his saddlebag flung over his shoulder. He was finished with her. From the moment he had met her, she had done nothing but turn his life inside out and upside down. If she wanted that beast, Kurgan, he was not going to fight for her. Let her wallow in the misery of her own making. He had ships to command and seas to conquer.

He crossed the courtyard and swiftly saddled his horse. Although tired, the bay stallion whinnied and tossed his head.

"This is it," he muttered. "I will leave this blasted place and never return. I never want to see her again." He tied his bags across the horse's back and mounted. As the horse clattered over the courtyard stones, he looked up at Alannah's window. Pain shuddered through him.

Suddenly Istabelle spotted him and raced to his side. Reaching up, she tugged on Xanthier's boot.

"Father? Father!"

He glanced down. Istabelle had clung to him since the moment he had left the royal dais. He had managed to avoid her when he escaped to his room, but somehow she had found him again. Her big gray eyes stared up at him, and Xanthier felt a tug at his heart. Something about the way she looked at him made him feel like he was the most important person in the world. He was not sure he liked the feeling.

"You found me again."

"Yes! Father, did you see her? Did you see Lady Alannah? Did you know that she is a lady now? Did you see her horse? Did you know that she is an heiress who was lost a long time ago? Did you know that she is going to marry the awful man, Kurgan?"

"How do you know all these things, Istabelle?"

"I listen," she replied airily. "I hear many things. You ran in the race! I am so proud you are my father!"

"Thank you," he said with a small smile. "I did ride in the race, and I know about Lady Alannah, and I think you've eaten too many sweets today."

"You are very handsome when you smile, Father."

Xanthier's laugh died and he stared at Istabelle. "I have not laughed often in my life," he said.

"I know. Uncle Brogan said you had a very unhappy childhood, and that Alannah's betrothal will be a terrible blow upon your bruised spirit."

"You are too young to repeat such complex thoughts."

"Uncle Brogan also said that you will probably

give up and run away like you always do. Like you ran away from me."

"He said that?"

"Are you going to? Are you going to let Lady Alannah marry that mean man?"

Determination surged through him. Alannah loved him. She could not wed Kurgan. He would not allow it. He stared at Istabelle's clear gaze and shook his head slowly. "No. You are right, little one. It is time I stood up for what I want. I am not going to give up this time."

"You gave up on me. You never came to visit me."

Xanthier sighed and looked away. "I'm sorry, Istabelle."

"It doesn't matter. Now I will come live with you."

Xanthier knelt down beside her. "Istabelle, I want you to listen carefully to me. I . . . I think you are a wonderful little girl. I once saved your life at the risk of my own, and I have never regretted it. I did not leave you with Brogan because I did not want you. I left you because I was not a fit father. I sail the seas, I have no home and I have no wife. I live a dangerous life. I know nothing about little girls—or any children for that matter. Your uncle is a good man. I knew you would be treated fairly. I left you with your aunt and uncle because that is what I felt was best for you. Do you understand?"

"No, but I will try to."

"I did not abandon you or give up on you. I placed you in Brogan's care for your own good. And I am going to have to leave again."

"No!" Istabelle shouted.

"Shush! You must not speak so loudly. I tell you

this only because I do not want you thinking that I am leaving you again. This is a great secret and you mustn't tell anyone. I am going to leave Scotland."

"Why? Why are you leaving?"

"I . . . I am supposed to get married, but I do not want to marry just anyone. I want to be with Alannah."

"I like Alannah, but she will be marrying the Serpent."

"I like her, too, and I cannot let her wed him."

"So you are leaving Scotland with Alannah?"

"Yes, whether she wants to join me or not. Do you understand? It is not because of you. It is because of politics. I once brought her here and now I am going to take her back."

"I want to come with you."

Xanthier shook his head. "I already told you. I am not a good father, and I will be living a dangerous life. You will be better off here with your aunt and uncle."

"I hate you! You are terrible!"

"Istabelle!"

"I do! You are the meanest person in the whole world! You aren't my father! You never were! I hate you!"

"Please . . ." Xanthier whispered, sorrow filling his soul. He felt strange emotions for this small child, and it pained him to hear her berate him. "Please understand."

"No, I don't understand! All I understand is that you are leaving me again." She spun away and raced off, ducking in between people so quickly, she was instantly swallowed by the surrounding masses.

Xanthier stared unhappily after her. He had not

anticipated feeling this badly about leaving her. A long time ago, he had cut her from his heart and pretended that she did not exist. What he had told her was true. He had left her because he had felt unworthy. But there was another part that he had not revealed. He had not told her how he had felt that day when he had pulled her from the air and saved her from plunging to her death.

At that moment, he had felt weak and out of control. At that moment, he had felt that his infant daughter was more important than anything. The realization had warped his mind and shaken his soul. It was frightening to feel such overwhelming love for something so delicate. The tiny baby had been so helpless. She had depended completely upon others to feed, clothe and support her.

The responsibility had been too mammoth. The feelings had been too intense. He admitted it. He had fled in fear. He was terrified to be a father because he was certain he would ruin everything. He had no pattern to follow. He had no father figure to mimic. When he had held his daughter in his arms at the top of the tower, the night wind pouring around them, fear had paralyzed him.

Xanthier looked up and saw his twin brother enter the courtyard. A connection hummed between them and for once Xanthier did not resent it. They were twins, and they felt each other. Xanthier knew that Brogan sensed he was upset. He smiled at Brogan reassuringly until his brother nodded. Then Xanthier left the yard and started making plans.

Istabelle raced through the crowd, tears streaming down her face. Fury warred with pain as she ducked and dodged, trying to escape. Once again, her father was leaving her. She broke through the outskirts of the crowd and dashed from the safety of the festival grounds into the unfamiliarity of the village.

The dwellings stood close together, shutting out the sunlight, and the streets were narrow. Grass changed to dirt, and the sweet smell of the countryside switched to the cloying scent of overcrowded humanity.

Istabelle ignored everything. She ran down one street, then another, weaving in and out until she was deep within the village. Tears flowed freely and she sobbed uncontrollably. Finally, completely exhausted and out of breath, she collapsed against a wall and curled into a ball.

What was wrong with her? Why did her father hate her? He would not leave her if he loved her. He must hate her. Istabelle cried harder, her small shoulders heaving. She could barely gather breaths between her sobs.

There must be something terrible about me. Something so terrible no one will tell me. Otherwise, people would not always abandon me. First my mother left me by dying . . . then my father left me at Kirkcaldy while he sailed the oceans. And Uncle Brogan and Aunt Matalia—they brought me here to get rid of me! And now, once again, my father does not want to take me with him. I must be a horrendous, hideous, despicable person!

She rolled back and forth, her small arms wrapped around her waist as if she was in agony. Her clothes were covered in dirt and her face was streaked with dust and tears. Her black braids soon came unraveled, and the ribbons Matalia had carefully tied became limp.

*   *   *

A barmaid was walking swiftly to work when she happened to see a little girl. Despite the mud and mess, she could see that the girl was from a wealthy family. She glanced up and down the street, looking for the child's parents.

"Whot you doing, miss?" she asked.

Istabelle cried harder and turned away. "Don't talk to me," she whimpered. "I am a terrible person. Everyone hates me."

The barmaid looked up at the sun, noting its downward path. She would be late to work. "Well, then . . ." She hesitated. "You all right then?"

Istabelle broke into harder sobs, then pounded her tiny fists on the dirt street.

"Humm. Well, then," the maid repeated. "You canna stay here. Come on then." When Istabelle ignored the summons, the woman picked her up and held her awkwardly in her arms.

"Let me go!" Istabelle shouted. "Leave me alone!"

"Humph," the woman said. She held the struggling child tightly and continued on her way to the tavern. Within moments she arrived at work and was greeted with a barrage of angry curses.

"I told you, Mary! I told you once and I told you twice. You're gonna lose your position with the way you always show up late."

"I have a reason this time," Mary grumbled as she dumped Istabelle on the floor. "Look whot I found on the street. A little miss."

The tavern keeper peered suspiciously at Istabelle, and Istabelle glared back. "Dirty little thing."

"She done run away. Thinks the world hates her."

The tavern keeper nodded. "Aye. I know the feeling. One of the royal soldiers is having a spot o'er there. Bring the girl to him and see if he'll take her back. You got work ta do."

Mary dragged Istabelle to the corner where a man sat moodily looking into his ale. "Sir?" she inquired. "Sir? Are you from the castle?"

"I am Gondilyn," he replied glumly.

"I have a little girl who has gotten lost. Think you that someone would give me a coin for bringing her back?"

Gondilyn glanced up and stared at Istabelle. He nodded slowly. "I know you. You are O'Bannon's little child. The one who got lost before. You have a tendency to run off, don't you?"

"I don't see why it matters," Istabelle grumbled. "No one cares about me anyway."

Gondilyn pulled out a coin and gave it to the barmaid, who grinned and pocketed it, then went about her own business. "I'm sure someone cares. What about Lady Alannah? I saw you playing with her yesterday."

"I thought she liked me, but now I know she doesn't either."

"How do you know that?" he asked.

"Father is taking her away and leaving me behind."

"What?" Gondilyn asked in stunned amazement.

"I am being abandoned again. You see? No one loves me."

"Xanthier is taking Alannah? Is that what you said?"

Istabelle looked up and stared at the shocked look on Gondilyn's face. She remembered what her father had told her about keeping everything a secret. Flushing, she looked away. "Nothing," she muttered. "I didn't mean anything. Forget it."

Gondilyn sat back. His doubts about Xanthier

surged to his mind, and he wrestled with his confusion, not sure what to do.

For long hours, deep into the night, Gondilyn struggled with his decision. Then near dawn, he sought out Lord Kurgan.

Chapter 29

Matalia sat in the window seat, staring into the twilight. "I don't think this is right," she whispered.

Brogan came over and sat next to her. He picked up her hand and held it to his lips. "We cannot interfere, Matalia. Alannah made her own decision."

"Oh, I know. I admire her very much, but my admiration does not convince me that this is the right choice for her. When we were in the royal chamber, she seemed so happy that Xanthier wanted to wed her . . . Why turn her back on him now?"

"I don't know, but everything will work out as it should."

Matalia buried her head in Brogan's chest as she nodded. He held her and rocked her, hoping that his words would come true.

Zarina stood at Alannah's door and glared at Kurgan. "Do not dare cross this threshold. I do not know how you convinced my daughter to marry you, but I am sure you used nefarious means. Your uncle was an evil man and you have the same look about you that he did."

"Remember," Kurgan hissed, "you are only a

peasant whore who managed to marry a lord. You are nothing!"

"Peasant or princess born, I know filth when I see it. Heed my words well."

"You can do nothing to me. When I marry Alannah, I will once again be the official ruler of all the Serpent lands."

"No. Alannah will control the properties through the entitlement, and as her mother, I can advise her to watch you carefully."

Kurgan narrowed his eyes and stepped back. "She will be my wife. She will do as I say."

Zarina crossed her arms. "She has the tender concern of the queen. If you do anything to upset her, the queen may very well block the marriage. Now leave while you still can."

"You may impede my access to her today, but when I wed her, you will no longer be able to dictate my actions," Kurgan replied angrily.

"Each day that I can spare her your company is worth the trouble." Zarina smiled grimly, aware that what he said was true. While in the castle she could protect her daughter, but once they married, Alannah would be at Kurgan's mercy.

As Matalia murmured her concerns to her husband and Zarina argued fiercely with Kurgan in the hallway, Xanthier scaled the outside wall and slipped through Alannah's window. He was silent, his boots strung over his shoulders and his hands cloaked in woolen gloves.

Alannah was brushing her hair, her brow drawn with worry. She turned, sensing someone enter the room. She was partially undressed, and candlelight shone through her linen underclothes, highlighting her curves.

"Is someone there?" she asked hesitantly. She tilted her head and inhaled. She could smell another person, but her senses were fooling her, for she thought she smelled Xanthier. "Who is it?"

Xanthier wanted to choke her! What idiocy had made her choose Kurgan? He was done with giving up and running away from conflict. He had relinquished his home, his daughter, his birthright . . . He was not about to let his woman be with another man. This time he was going to take what he wanted and curse the consequences!

"Disappointed?" he asked snidely. "Awaiting your betrothed with open arms?" He stalked fully into the room and glared at her.

Alannah gasped and stepped back. "Xanthier! What are you doing here?"

"You are mine. I told you that once before and apparently you forgot."

"I am not yours. I am promised to Kurgan now. Go away and never come back!" Her voice broke. If Kurgan found out that she was talking to Xanthier, he would kill him. Her sacrifice would be for naught.

Infuriated beyond reason, Xanthier grabbed her and yanked her against him. "Your betrothal is a farce. I am the one who found you. I am the one who introduced you to the pleasures of the flesh. I am the one who sat with you as you mourned your grandmother. Kurgan is nothing!"

Alannah struggled against him. "Stop! Don't say those things."

"Tell me the truth, Alannah. Do I really mean nothing to you? Are you willing to throw me away?"

She kicked him, then pounded her fists against his chest. "Yes! You mean nothing and you must leave. Leave now."

Xanthier leaned back, avoiding her flailing fists. He quickly released her arms and gripped her waist. He lifted her and tossed her over his shoulder, putting her rump in the air. "I don't believe you," he said flatly. "You lost the race for me. You came back and helped me. Whether you are willing to admit it or not, I know you care for me." He strode to the door.

"If you take me out there, I will scream."

"Scream and soldiers will come. Is that what you want?"

Alannah hesitated.

"Very well." Xanthier dumped her on the floor, on top of a throw rug. Without pausing, her rolled her up in the rug, hiding her completely. "I intend to get to the bottom of this." He smacked her hind end in emphasis and Alannah emitted a muffled squeal.

He opened the door and peered down the corridor. No one was present. Glancing back into her room, he took Alannah's staff that was propped against the doorway. It was the one he had carved for her. Then he moved swiftly down the corridor until he came to the stairs. Pausing to listen, he ducked into an alcove as two people ascended the steps, chatting about the race. The couple walked on, never noticing Xanthier standing in the shadows with his oddly shaped rug.

Xanthier used her staff to push open the servant's ground floor door, then stepped out into the moonlight. Everything was silent. Pleased that no one had seen or heard them leave, he moved silently to the garden where the white stallion was tethered next to the bay steed.

He lowered his bundle to the ground. Unwrapping Alannah, he gazed at her disheveled face with a mixture of anger and concern. "Now, tell me what is going on. If you really want me to leave, I will ride away and be gone, but if there is something else, you had best tell me now."

Alannah rose to her feet, her linen chemise askew and her hair a riotous mess around her shoulders. Her sea green eyes stared at him— through him—as they had the day they had met on the island beach. "Kurgan . . ." she said hesitantly.

"Kurgan is not here."

"He vowed to kill you if I did not agree to wed him," Alannah admitted softly.

"Is that all? Alannah! He has been vowing to kill me for a decade! I do not fear him. God in heaven! Is that why you consented to marry him? To protect *me*?"

"Yes!" Alannah breathed. "I love you and I cannot bear the thought that I might cause your death."

"And I love you more than there are stars in the sky. Nothing should come between us. Nothing!"

"But I have ruined everything. I cannot break my betrothal . . ."

"I don't care. We love each other. Grandmother and Gondin hid their love, living separately and without intimacy. I will not repeat their mistake. You and I will go find a new island and live together. We need nothing else."

"What about the excitement of society . . . the thrills of civilization . . . ?" Alannah asked. "Don't you want that?"

"I have had my share of them. I want you. I want to make a family with you. We will not live in complete isolation. I will keep my ship and Captain Robbins will sail by every six months. If you want to go to France, I will take you there. If you want to travel to a distant shore, I will set sail to please you. But in the end, I want to return to the island and build a strong home for us to live in for the rest of our years. Will you come with me?"

The smell of the night air surrounded her, and she was enveloped by his loving declaration. Worries and concerns drifted away and she closed her eyes and felt him. He was strong, committed and honest. He loved her and wanted nothing but her. She knew she wanted him, too. She wanted to live with him, romp in the meadows with him and grow old with him. She intended to show him how much she loved him every day of the rest of her life.

Xanthier stood in the midst of the flowers, breathing their heady scent. She was like these flowers, rich, vibrant and exotic. Like the flowers that came to life every spring, she was like a miracle. He waited for her answer. His self-hatred was fading. With her love, he could see what was beautiful in the world. He could believe in goodness and decency. He had realized that love and family were more important than any fight or struggle for power.

Through Alannah, he was not ugly and scarred. His past transgressions were not written on his face, and the blood of innocents no longer dripped from his hands. He was reformed. Because of her, he was no longer filled with hatred and revulsion. He was at peace. He was a man in love with a beautiful woman.

She took the last step toward him and tilted her head up. "I will go wherever you go," she whispered. "You are my heaven."

"Alannah," he sighed as he kissed her softly,

gently. Her lips were ambrosia. They tasted like strawberries and honey and he sucked on them, licked them and kissed them again.

"Xanthier," she answered as she leaned against him. She stroked his face, caressing his cheeks and tracing his familiar scars. "You are so wonderful," she whispered. "So handsome to me . . ." She felt him grin and knew she had pleased him, which pleased her. She ran her fingers along his neck and then slid her hands inside his shirt. "I want you," she murmured.

Xanthier pulled her hands free and shook his head. "We must go." Alannah nodded and he took her hand and led her through the garden to the darkest corner where he had tethered the two horses.

"Kiss me," she pleaded and he enfolded her in another embrace, covering her face with leisurely kisses.

"I love you," he told her. "I can't wait to spend the rest of my life with you." He released her reluctantly and glanced around. There was no movement, no sign of anyone who might be aware of their presence. "Everything is well," he reported. "No one knows."

Alannah went up to her white stallion and stroked his nose. "Thank you for bringing him."

"I know how much he means to you. I would never separate you from such a loyal friend."

Alannah nodded and pulled the saddle and bridle from Claudius. "Be free," she whispered. "Be as you are naturally! I should never have forced you to give up your wild spirit, even for one day."

"And I don't want you to ever be anything other than who *you* are," Xanthier echoed.

Claudius snorted and tossed his head, then trotted around them in a circle as he arched his neck and swished his tail.

Xanthier grinned and lifted Alannah up on his bay steed, then strapped her staff to the saddle before he swung up behind her. She sat sidesaddle, cuddled between his strong thighs as Claudius pranced beside them.

They rode out of the garden, their faces brushed with starlight. For several hours they traveled toward the coast, wrapped in the miracle of their reunion. The radiance of the evening reflected the twinkling in their eyes as they moved toward their future together. The white stallion clip-clopped alongside Xanthier's horse, his head high and his steps firm. A night bird whistled and its mate sang in response.

"Ever since I met you, the night has become special," said Xanthier. "I love the darkness, the richness of relying upon my other senses."

Alannah laughed. "The day is equally wonderful."

"No. The night is the best. Come here." He snuggled her against his chest. "I am sorry that I left you on the ship. I should have brought you with me but I didn't want to share you with anyone. I thought I could survive a short while without you, but then the night would come, and I would be beset with memories."

"Tell me more," Alannah asked softly.

"I could not forget the way you felt. In the dark, I would remember how your breasts curved and how your nipples would pebble in my palms. At night, I would recall how you smelled when I buried my nose in your hair while you slept. When sight no longer dominated my senses, I became overwhelmed with how much your essence filled me with peace. The night was my greatest friend and my worst enemy."

"I, too, had troubles at night."

"What did you think about?" he asked.

"I thought about your hands, and how they wrapped around my waist and held me close. I remembered the sounds of your breathing, and the way you sighed when I curled up against your back. I—"

Xanthier pressed his lips against hers, unable to wait any longer. "I know we should not stop yet," he murmured, "but no one is following us, and I need you. I need you now." He nuzzled her neck, then slid off his horse. He held her atop the steed, and gently spread her thighs. "I want to taste you, here, in the night, where I am not distracted by anything else." He pushed her dress up and followed the hemline with his lips, kissing her. "Your skin tastes so wonderful . . ."

Alannah gasped and gripped his shoulders. "Your lips feel so marvelous," she replied.

Pushing her dress up to her waist, he nibbled her thigh, then suckled her sensitive skin a hair's breadth from her mound.

"Xanthier!" she whimpered, wiggling to encourage him.

"Not yet," he murmured as he circled her, taunting her.

"Please," she begged, and he lifted his fingers to her, delicately brushing his hand over her. "Yes!" she gasped. "Please! Quickly!"

Using his fingers, he opened her, brushing her center with his fingertips. She twitched, moaning with pleasure. They were focused upon each other entirely. The rest of the world ceased to exist. No one and nothing was important except his fingers and her pleasure.

Teasingly, he touched her, then slipped one finger inside her. She trembled and arched her hips, and the horse danced sideways. Xanthier pulled her down and laid her on the grass. Her body glistened in the moonlight and Xanthier bent his head. Swiftly, precisely, he tasted her inner secrets as his finger moved inside her. Alannah tossed her head, surrendering her body to his ministrations, giving her heart to his care.

Licking her, sucking her, he raised her excitement and she cried out, wanting him more. He moved his hand more quickly, responding to her need, and she bucked beneath him. Pleasure suddenly rippled over her and she gripped his shoulders, pulling him tighter.

He flicked his tongue faster and she moaned, then cried, then screamed his name. He plunged another finger inside her and she screamed again, pleasure swirling through her body. Then he pulled back, leaving her bereft for one moment, until his body covered hers and he sank deep inside her.

He groaned, feeling her inner muscles grip him. Her body made love to him by welcoming him and holding him, wrapping firmly around him so that every stroke was a motion of bliss. She felt another orgasm climb, and she let the feeling flow through her, let it erupt within her.

He grinned, feeling her body respond as it tightened and relaxed, and he began moving against her powerfully. He gripped her thighs and pulled them apart, opening her fully, then plunged inside time after time. She screamed again, climaxing again, unable to stem the flow of pleasure he created, and he pulled her arms around him, wanting to feel the rasp of her nails as she lost control.

He made love to her, feeling her, loving her, finding ecstasy in her arms as his rhythm increased, then went wildly out of control and he slammed his body into hers. Faster, harder, faster, and then he paused, stunned by the starlight bursting within him, by his intense feelings, and then he poured into her. His entire body shook as he filled her with his seed and he clutched her tightly. He let the waves of delight swim through him, relishing the glory of their union. Then, completely exhausted, he collapsed on top of her.

Tears filled his eyes and he buried his head in her neck, embarrassed, but she stroked him softly, crooning to him, letting him know that he was safe with her. They lay together, he holding her tightly, she cradling him gently, until, little by little, they both relaxed and fell into a sweet slumber.

Chapter 30

Kurgan's men rode silently through the trees, their horses' bridles muffled by strips of cloth and their horses' hooves wrapped with canvas. The men's expressions were grim, for they were well aware of Xanthier's warrior skills. Everyone knew of his powerful sword and swift feet. In the past, he had fought with little regard for the rules of combat. He was ruthless and unpredictable. In short, every guardsman wished they were searching for anyone but Xanthier O'Bannon.

Kurgan did not have such concerns. He twitched and rubbed his head, angered to the point of madness. Sweat beaded his forehead and he wiped it with the back of his sleeve. He could feel the end coming. Xanthier and he had finally reached an impasse where fighting was the only solution. Now he had an undisputable reason to avenge his hatred. Stealth was not necessary. Xanthier had kidnapped an heiress and wife-to-be of another noble. Even the king would frown on that. It surpassed any deed that could be excused. When Xanthier was caught, no one would blame Kurgan for killing him.

The men were serious, their faces drawn in lines of worry and dismay.

In the very back of the procession, a mercenary held Istabelle, bound and gagged. The mercenary's orders from Kurgan were to hold the child hostage until she could be used. Xanthier must be captured at all costs, and Kurgan had no compunction about using the child for his own purposes.

The men moved silently through the forest, following the subtle signs of Xanthier and Alannah's path. A broken twig, a crushed leaf, a chipped stone . . . all the markings of their passage pointed the guardsmen forward. Moving like silent hunters, they spread out to form a net with which to capture their prey. The moon rose, the night birds quieted and an eerie dread filled the forest.

Xanthier blinked. Something was wrong. He rolled off Alannah and stared up at the night sky. Straining to see, he saw nothing but the moon and the stars. Again it came to him—danger. He closed his eyes and listened. He heard nothing.

Seeing nothing in the dark was to be expected. Hearing nothing was not. He sat up and reached for his sword. Slowly rising, he listened intently, searching for a sound that would give him a hint of what was wrong. A horse's soft whuffle sounded to his right, about a hundred lengths behind him.

"Alannah!" he whispered. "Get up. Get up now!"

"What?" she whispered groggily.

"There are riders in the woods."

She rubbed her face, then listened carefully. Her heightened sense of hearing helped her pick out the muffled clop of many hooves and the occasional snort of several horses. She gasped and leapt to her feet.

"What do you hear?" Xanthier queried urgently, trusting her hearing better than his own.

"Twenty, maybe more. They are in a line and they are walking toward us."

"How did they find us so soon?" Xanthier asked as he flung his clothes on and tossed Alannah's underclothes to her. As she yanked her chemise over her head, he grabbed her hand and pulled her toward Claudius. He flung her aboard, then mounted his own horse.

"Come on," he whispered. As silently as possible, they urged their horses through the dark, weaving in and out of the trees. Within moments, Alannah and the stallion took the lead, for although Alannah could not see, she was more attuned to riding in the dark than Xanthier was.

Alannah was filled with dread. She feared that Kurgan was chasing them, and while she did not care what happened to her, she was deathly afraid of what would happen to her beloved. She urged the stallion faster, asking him to trot. Responding immediately, the white stallion moved swiftly through the forest.

Behind her, Xanthier nudged his horse, risking the sound of their hoofbeats while hoping that increased distance would save them from the search party.

A shout signaled the scouting party's discovery of Xanthier and Alannah's trysting place. The men could feel the warmth of the ground where the lovers had lain in each other's arms only moments before. The thunder of hooves echoed through the trees as the party galloped after their quarry.

"Mercy!" Alannah cried as she kicked her horse into a gallop.

"Run!" Xanthier shouted. "Run!"

They sped through the trees, then broke out into an open field. Leaning over, Xanthier shouted at her. "Go on! Your stallion is faster! Ride and don't stop for anything. Promise me!"

"Promise you will stay with me? No matter what?" Alannah shouted back.

"I promise!"

Nodding, they leaned forward and raced through the grass, their horses leaping over heather and soaring through the night air. The guardsmen spotted their fleeing forms the moment they exited the trees, and they, too, broke into a gallop.

Xanthier and Alannah fled, chased by the mercenaries. The white stallion easily outran Xanthier's bay, but Alannah pressed on, convinced that Xanthier would stay with her. She pulled away, the white stallion's hooves flying.

Suddenly, Kurgan's black horse broke from the pack. His red and black Serpent banner snapped in the air as he whipped his steed forward. Xanthier's heart raced with fear for Alannah. Kurgan's bloodlust was all too well known. She must not be captured! Turning to her, he shouted, "Run, Alannah! Run! Kurgan is following us. Go through the forest and meet me at dawn. You go left and I go right. If we split, they will have to separate as well."

"No! I will not go without you!" She sat upright, slowing the white stallion.

"Please, Alannah! For once do as I say! If you love me, if you believe I love you, race like the wind!"

In horror, Xanthier saw the black horse gaining on them.

"Run, Alannah! Run! I will meet you on the

other side of the forest! My ship is anchored off the coast!''

Gasping, Alannah leaned forward and kicked, sending the white stallion shooting forward. She bent to the left, asking her stallion to shift direction. She heard Xanthier go right, and she prayed that his tactic would work.

Kurgan grinned, evil thoughts tumbling around in his head. "Go after him!" he commanded his soldiers as he veered after Alannah. This was what he lived for! This was what he desired. Fight! Chase! Mayhem and destruction. It was in his blood and it rotted in his brain.

Exultant, he whipped the black horse harder. He had beaten the white stallion in the race and he could beat it again, capturing its rider. Although Alannah was bent over her horse and flying through the meadow, it was only a matter of time before he caught up with her and dragged her from the stallion's back. Kurgan cackled, then slashed his horse with the whip and drove him forward. If he captured her, Xanthier would be at his mercy.

Stride by stride, the black horse gained upon Alannah and her white stallion. Alannah heard Kurgan's straining breath, felt the ground tremble as he got closer and closer. Within seconds he would reach her.

Alannah wrapped her fingers in the stallion's mane. Closing her eyes, she concentrated on the stallion's movements, feeling the muscles as they rippled and rolled beneath her thighs. "Race," she whispered. "If ever I have asked you, I ask you now."

The white stallion flicked his ears back. He stretched his nose out. He flung his legs forward. A burst of incredible speed exploded from his body. In seconds, he was drawing away, a white blur against the night meadow.

"No!" Kurgan screamed, but the sound faded as Alannah escaped.

On the other side of the field, Xanthier was not faring as well. His horse was still exhausted from yesterday's race, and he soon realized he could not outdistance his pursuers. Electing to use strategy instead of relying upon speed, he sent his horse into a sharp right turn and headed for the river that flowed alongside the meadow.

The river was fast, with very steep banks. It was also wide. Xanthier did not pause. He sent his horse flying over the embankment and plunging into the water. He and the horse sank immediately, but they scrambled upwards and managed to get their heads above the waves. Thrashing madly, they swam through the swirling water, crashing against rocks and tumbling against floating debris.

Xanthier clung to the horse, urging him forward, and inch by inch they swam toward the other side as the current swept them downstream.

The mercenaries skidded to a halt at the edge of the river, then turned and followed his progress downstream. None dared plunge into the dangerous water.

Istabelle saw her father braving the furious current, and she struggled to be free of her bonds. The soldier holding her swore as she was able to pull her hand free, then rip her gag off. Suddenly, the river took a sharp turn and a huge rock loomed up. Istabelle gasped in terror.

Xanthier felt the river shift and he looked ahead. There was no possibility of avoiding the enormous boulder that blocked his way, and at the speed he

was traveling, it would likely crush his skull if he
hit it head-on.

He couldn't give up! Alannah had done her part;
it was up to him to finish his. He bent down and
kicked his horse, hard. The horse grunted and
tossed his head, but swam faster. "That is not good
enough!" Xanthier shouted and he kicked again.

The horse leaned forward, churning his legs as
fast as he could. Then, just as the rock reared up,
Xanthier and the horse caught the trailing edge of
an eddy and were spun backwards, away from the
dangerous granite. In the abrupt calm, the horse
surged forward and scrambled to shore.

Fatigued, the horse and Xanthier stood for several moments, trying to regain their breath.

On the other side, Kurgan's men watched Xanthier's struggle with awe. His reputation as a fierce
warrior was already assured. Now he would be
known as a brave and courageous man, one who
would risk everything for love. The men looked at
each other, not sure what to do. Xanthier was on
the far side of a river they had no intention of
crossing. As far as they were concerned, he had
escaped.

A child's scream echoed over the riverbank.

Xanthier's head snapped up. Peering across the
water, he saw Istabelle struggling to be free of a
soldier's arms. What was she doing there? Why was
she with Kurgan's men?

"Father!" she screamed.

Xanthier stared at her across the seething river.

"Father, are you hurt? Father, are you *hurt*?"
she shouted.

Xanthier shook his head.

"Don't leave me," she cried. "Don't leave me!"

She jumped off her captor's horse and darted toward the river.

Xanthier gasped.

Glancing up and down the river, Istabelle took a tentative step forward.

"Stop her!" Xanthier shouted. "Someone stop her. She is a child!" In agony, he watched his daughter take a step into the river. The rushing water sucked at her feet and she fell to her knees, starting to cry.

"Help her! Don't let her drown."

The mercenary grabbed Istabelle's hand but did not pull her from the water. "Come back," he commanded. "Come back and I will save her," the man called.

Xanthier's heart slowed, then stopped altogether. His breath was swept away. His muscles melted. He fell to his knees. No! This could not be happening! Not now. Not when he had escaped and Alannah was free. Not when he had finally accepted her love and given her his devotion. Not when he could be with his love forever, if he only walked away. Not now!

Istabelle's sobs carried across the water. She scrambled to keep her footing, but the current was too strong and she fell once again. Only the man's hand kept her from being swept downstream.

Xanthier took a deep, long-awaited breath. His heart started to race, thudding loudly in his ears. He had promised Alannah that he would stay with her, no matter what. He had begged her to follow his plan based on their mutual love and trust. As much as it tore him to pieces, he had to break that promise. He knew she would never forgive him. She would ride away and disappear. There would be no forgiveness, no third chance.

He put his hands flat against the earth and bent his head. Visions of her lovely face flickered behind his closed lids. Peace and security, love and acceptance, all gone. He had promised to protect her. He was bound to protect those who needed his strength. But he had no choice. Istabelle was his daughter, and he could never live if he caused her death. Once again, he was willing to toss his life away to save his child.

He looked up and nodded.

The soldier pulled Istabelle up from the water, and waved at Kurgan, who was riding toward them.

One man shook his head in dismay. He looked across the river at Xanthier who would need to recross the river. It would be just as dangerous the second time as the first. He stared at Xanthier in stunned amazement. "I . . . I . . . can't believe he is doing it for a daughter he abandoned years ago."

The men held their collective breath, amazed that Xanthier was making another attempt to cross the treacherous current. This time Xanthier went carefully, swimming alone, taking his time, but the river still swept him under and halfway across, his head was submerged. Fighting, he resurfaced, but crashed against more debris and fell forward. Rocks and logs battered his body, but still Xanthier struggled onward, circling with his arms and kicking with his legs. He had almost reached the smoother water, but a wave knocked him down again, slamming him against a rock. This time, when he fell, he did not get up.

The river swept his body downstream.

Kicking his horse, one of the soldiers raced after Xanthier's form. He managed to get downstream, then waded out into the water's flow. As Xanthier floated by, he used a stick to snag Xanthier's belt and drag him to shore. He turned Xanthier over and slapped his back, making Xanthier cough.

"Father!" Istabelle cried again as the rest of the party joined the soldier. She raced over to Xanthier, and knelt beside him, kissing his cheek. "Thank you, Father. You are the bravest man in the whole world. I love you."

Xanthier's eyes flickered open and he stared into Istabelle's gray gaze just as he had done the day he had rescued her from the tower. He thought briefly of Alannah. Although he had chosen his daughter over escaping with Alannah, it had been Alannah who had taught him that he had the strength to make this kind of decision. He had few regrets. He could have done nothing else. He smiled at Istabelle and opened his arms.

Chapter 31

Kurgan kicked him and Xanthier jerked in pain. Blood dripped down his forehead, and bruises already covered his bare chest. His hands were strung above his head, tied to the thick branch of a tree, and his sword lay at his feet.

"You thought to humiliate me," Kurgan raged. "Ever since you walked away from the field at Knott's Glen, you thought you were better than all of us. Who is the victim now? Who will you save this time?" Kurgan punched him in the ribs, grinning when he heard a satisfying crunch of broken bones.

"What do you expect to accomplish by this," Xanthier hissed. The camp firelight danced across his face in a grotesque display, highlighting his scars, his glittering eyes and his facial wounds. The mercenaries shrank back, afraid of him even though he was tied securely.

"I will see you crumble," Kurgan replied. "I will watch death creep across your face and know that I put it there. My satisfaction will be your demise."

Istabelle hid in the shadows, her eyes tightly closed against the horror in front of her. Waves of unrelenting guilt assailed her, for she knew that

Xanthier had come back for her. He would have been free had she not leapt into the river.

Xanthier did not look in her direction. He glared at Kurgan, focusing his energy on his enemy. Anger boiled in his blood. He was not ready to die! He had things to do and a life to live! He wanted to lie on the beach with Alannah, and see his child grow to be a woman. He had ceased to run from his problems and his responsibilities. He wanted to fight for justice and beauty, for his family and his life.

As Kurgan pummeled him again, Xanthier closed his eyes and concentrated. In a way he had never done before, he deliberately focused on his twin. He pictured Brogan's face . . . then his thick arm . . . then his sword. He sent his brother a silent message, asking for help.

Far away, Brogan awoke from a deep sleep and stared into the darkness of his castle room, a frown creasing his brow.

At the edge of the forest, Alannah trembled with fear. Kurgan had almost caught her, but her stallion had saved her. It had seemed like a miracle until she realized that Xanthier had not been as lucky. Kurgan's men must have captured him.

When she determined that Xanthier was not coming, she had chosen to try to retrace her steps. Unfortunately, she was unsure of where she was. For one of the first times in her life, she felt truly hampered by her blindness. She did not know this area, and she was frightened.

Sitting in the dark with her white stallion standing silently beside her, Alannah knew she had to go back. Xanthier would not want her to. He would want her to go to the ocean, find his ship and sail safely away. He would want to know she was safe and protected. But she had to go back.

Alannah climbed off her stallion and ran her hands lightly over the dirt until she felt an impression. She traced it, determining that a deer had made the track. Deer enjoyed high grass and succulent feeding grounds like meadows. She felt several inches farther until she found the next indentation. Following both the tracks and her instincts, she prayed that they would lead her closer to the grassland where she had last seen Xanthier.

Soon another, smaller set of deer tracks joined the first set. Crawling along the forest floor, Alannah moved slowly but carefully. Her stallion followed behind, his heavy footsteps clomping on the ground, churning the leaves and obliterating the deer tracks as he laid down his own. Alannah prayed that another animal was not doing the same somewhere ahead of them, for if she lost the tracks, she would truly be astray.

Wind swept upon her, chilling her. Alannah pondered the wisdom of proceeding, but she did not stop her forward momentum. Xanthier might need her assistance and she would do anything to help him. He had claimed her and shown her his love. It was her turn to prove her own devotion.

Tinkling water sounded in the distance and Alannah tilted her head to listen. The stallion raised his head, too, his ears cocked forward. As one, Alannah and the stallion turned to peer into the grass to their left where a creature was rustling. Recognizing the sounds and smells, Alannah smiled. The doe and yearling she had been following were bedding down for the night. They were circling and pawing, making a comfortable place for themselves.

"Thank you," she whispered, not wanting to disturb them. "You brought me to the river. I can follow it upstream to the meadow. May you live a beautiful life, my forest friends. You have given me a chance."

The deer ignored her, unperturbed by her presence, and they finally folded their spindly legs, dropped their heads and dozed.

Alannah remounted, nudged the stallion into the water and began traveling upstream. Excitement filled her and flowed into the white horse. They were going to find Xanthier! A sense of urgency forced Alannah to keep moving, and she fervently hoped she was not too late.

Brogan padded stealthily through the dark halls. Xanthier needed him. He was certain of it. Just because Xanthier had never asked him for anything before did not make his silent message any more mistakable. His twin brother needed help and he intended to answer the call.

Matalia, as always, had understood him. When he had woken her and told her his thoughts, she had sent him on his way with a kiss. Although she was not close to Xanthier, she understood her husband's bond and supported his need to find out what was wrong.

He knocked on Xanthier's door, but discovered the room abandoned. All Xanthier's personal effects were gone. Brogan frowned, trying to figure out what to do. He sat down on Xanthier's bed and closed his eyes, trying to feel what his twin had felt when he last slept there. Image after image of Alannah filled his thoughts. A flash of them riding the white stallion together. Alannah frolicking in the waves. Then a black picture of Kurgan.

Brogan scrambled to his feet, his sense that

something terrible was happening to his brother increasing. He raced down the halls until he reached Alannah's room, but it, too, was empty. There were signs of a struggle and the rug was missing.

Chasing down his last lead, Brogan headed toward Captain Robbins's sleeping quarters. After quietly entering, he stepped among the other sleeping men until he found Robbins.

"Captain," he whispered.

Robbins woke with a start and reached for his sword.

"Come outside with me," Brogan commanded softly. "Your commodore requires your assistance."

Robbins swung out of his trundle and dressed rapidly. Years at sea had taught him to wake quickly and to be alert instantly. He slung his sword belt on and nodded to Brogan, and the two left the room and exited the castle. "Tell me what is going on," Robbins said as soon as they were out of earshot of the inhabitants.

"Xanthier and I share a . . . a special bond that allows us to sense what is happening to the other."

"I don't understand."

"We communicate with each other, even when we are separated by the vast sea. It is a silent, unspoken method of feeling each other. At times over the last fifteen to twenty years, we have both resented this ability. We have both been annoyed by it. Tonight, I am greatful. I believe he is calling out to me for help."

"Why would he do that?"

"I think he and Alannah are both in trouble, and Kurgan may be the cause. If they were to run off together to avoid him, do you know where they would go?"

Robbins stared at Brogan, silently debating. His eyes grew guarded as he analyzed the situation. Brogan had never shown undue love and concern for his brother, nor had Xanthier spoken highly of Brogan. "If they left, it is their business where they have gone, m'lord."

Frustrated, Brogan ran his hand through his hair. "I know you do not trust me or my motivations, but I assure you they are pure. I sense that Xanthier is in great need. Are you willing to risk his life on the chance that I am not being honest with you? I know he requires assistance, and we are most likely his only hope."

With a brief nod, Robbins relented. Motioning to the stables, he preceded Brogan there and saddled a mount. "There is a port to the north that has a ship prepared for immediate departure. If Xanthier is leaving, he would go in that direction."

Relieved that Robbins would help, Brogan saddled his mount as well and they set out of the courtyard in a flurry of hooves. The darkness of deep midnight cloaked the forest and they were soon forced to shorten their horses' strides in order to find their way. Brogan grew more and more tense as the minutes slipped away.

Istabelle's screams reverberated through the night, waking the forest creatures and rousing Xanthier from his stupor.

He yanked sideways, barely avoiding the dagger Kurgan swished toward the back of his neck. "Even trussed, you still seek to kill me with a blade to my back," Xanthier growled derisively. "Do you fear me so much?"

"I fear nothing!"

"Then prove it. Cut my ties and face me like a man. Blade to blade. To the death."

Kurgan glared at him, knowing that his soldiers were listening to Xanthier's challenge. He quickly reckoned his chances. Xanthier was battered and beaten. His ribs were broken and his arms were undoubtedly weak with lack of blood from being tied above his head for so long. His chances of fighting well were slim, which gave Kurgan the advantage he wanted.

"Very well. But if you try to escape, my soldiers will kill your child."

"What do you intend to do with her?"

Kurgan cast his gaze upon the frightened girl. "I will keep her and find . . . special uses . . . for her."

Fury swept through Xanthier, and his eyes turned into two chips of ice. The soldiers shifted uncomfortably until the one who had held Istabelle spoke up. "Lord Kurgan, slay him now. Do not set him free."

Kurgan rounded on the man. "Do you doubt my ability to fight?" Raising his sword, he held it at the man's neck. "Have a care what you imply."

"Aye," the man replied as he jerked back. He pulled his knife from his boot and walked over to Xanthier. Leaning close, he whispered to him, "If you think by killing Kurgan you will be free, you are wrong. I have been paid to protect his life, and my reputation relies on me completing that task. I will run a sword through you myself, should I find the need."

"Not a very fair fight," Xanthier replied mockingly.

"No. It isn't meant to be." The mercenary sliced Xanthier's bonds and stepped back.

Xanthier crouched to the ground, rubbing his arms to regain feeling in them so he could hold the sword lying at his feet. His fingers were numb, and he was light-headed. His ribs pierced his chest with pain, and swelling around one eye hindered his vision. Glancing up, he realized that he had only seconds to prepare, for Kurgan was already advancing.

Alannah heard Istabelle scream. She gasped, and kicked Claudius into a headlong gallop up the river's edge. They were going to be too late! She ducked low onto the stallion's back, urging him to race like the wind, and Claudius crashed out of the water and surged up the bank. A fire gleamed in the night and Claudius swerved toward it just as Alannah smelled it.

"Hurry!" she implored her friend, and Claudius responded by galloping faster than ever before. The clash of swords rang through the night and the scent of blood filled the air.

Xanthier sensed Alannah's presence, and he faltered. "No!" he shouted. He stumbled back, his concentration divided. Kurgan pressed his advantage, his sword flashing in the firelight like a reflection of hell upon a blade forged from dead souls.

Suddenly Claudius burst into the camp. Alannah's hair whipped around her face, mingling with the white stallion's mane, and her unnerving gaze pierced through Kurgan as cleanly as a thrown dirk.

"Leave him be!" Alannah screamed, her voice echoing across the glade. Her stallion reared, his hooves striking the air in a display of fury.

Xanthier was galvanized into action. Her nearness infused him with strength and he thrust his sword at Kurgan, catching him unawares.

It was Kurgan who stumbled back this time, parrying Xanthier's attack desperately. "Kill them!" he shouted to his minions. "Kill them all! Kill the child, kill the woman, kill the horse!"

Xanthier leapt forward, rage giving him herculean strength. But a thread of despair also snaked into his mind. No matter how well he fought, he could not possibly kill all the soldiers before they managed to inflict harm on the two he had vowed to protect.

"Focus on me!" he shouted. "I am your enemy. Istabelle and Alannah are only pawns in your game. They should not be made to suffer the consequences of our fight." He lunged, his sword drawing Kurgan's blood. "Let us go and I will spare you," he growled.

Kurgan cackled with insane hatred, and struck back, his sword vibrating. Again and again he attacked, forcing Xanthier to block his thrusts repeatedly. "Know that not only will they die, but they will suffer greatly before they do," Kurgan taunted.

"You are wrong!" Alannah cried as her horse struck out with his hooves. She lifted her staff and briefly, within a fraction of a second, she called forth all her senses. She asked for all the natural energy around her. She reached for the power of the wind, the storms, the earth, the flames, the sea. She reached for the forces that had guided her every blind step, and concentrated them within her and her carved staff.

Then she swung it at the nearest soldier. A resounding crack announced her accurate aim, and suddenly the camp was a seething mass of soldiers advancing upon her. As Xanthier fought Kurgan, Alannah and Claudius fought the mercenaries with the power of the elements surging through them.

Xanthier fell to his knees, his body weakened. He parried Kurgan's thrusts, but his strength was waning.

Halfway across the meadow, Brogan and Robbins flogged their galloping horses. They heard the screams, they heard the steel singing and they felt the ground vibrating with the fierceness of the battle. They saw the unfair fight and they both prayed they were not too late.

As they descended upon the scene, they each drew their swords and shouted fierce battle cries. Their presence shot hope and might into Xanthier's fighting arm, and he surged to his feet. He advanced, thrusting his sword at Kurgan with renewed speed. Kurgan stumbled, tripped, and rolled to the ground. He scrambled to regain his feet and was just able to avoid Xanthier's attack.

He backed up, fear filling his eyes as Xanthier continued to advance. Xanthier's gaze was cold, almost inhuman in its rage, and Kurgan began to tremble. He backed up again, then felt the brush of a horse's tail.

He lowered his guard for a split moment—and Xanthier plunged his blade home.

Kurgan's eyes widened and he stared up at his nemesis in shock.

Xanthier glared down at him, then twisted the blade. "You should not have threatened my family," he said softly.

A cry made Xanthier spin around, and he saw Istabelle step from her protected place behind Claudius. Alannah rode her stallion like an avenging angel upon a legendary Pegasus, her lithe body rippling with strength and her staff swinging with precise aim. Soldiers littered the ground around her, moaning in pain.

Nearby, Brogan and Captain Robbins flashed their swords, slicing their opponents with quick, decisive strokes. In moments, no mercenaries remained standing.

Then, suddenly, the glade was silent except for the crackling campfire and the heavily breathing horses. Claudius snorted, then whinnied stridently.

Xanthier stared across the fire at his twin brother, and Brogan gazed back. They smiled, then, taking several steps toward each other, they embraced in a tight, brotherly hold.

Epilogue

Alannah snuggled in Xanthier's arms and Istabelle leaned against them. The sails were full and they were sailing back to the island on the beautiful blue sea. Xanthier grimaced as his child accidentally poked his broken ribs, but he did not reprove her. The small pain was nothing compared to the joy that filled him.

"How did you convince the king to give back my island?" Alannah questioned.

Xanthier shook his head ruefully. "The queen convinced him. A woman is a powerful force when she gets an idea lodged in her head. And if you love that woman . . . well, the king didn't have a chance."

"Will you love me like that? Will you always want to please me?"

Xanthier kissed her hair, then buried his face in her neck. "I will always love you more than anyone could fathom. You are my soul. Without you, I was empty, but you have filled me with light. Your desires will guide my every waking moment. Whatever pleases you will make me happy, and"—he licked her ear—"I will endeavor to fill your days with all kinds of pleasure."

Istabelle scrambled to her feet and put her hands

on her hips. "You are forever kissing and holding hands. Some children would find that annoying!"

"Do you?" Alannah asked seriously.

Istabelle laughed. "No. I think it's sweet. Perhaps I will find a great love one day and act just like you."

Xanthier frowned. "No boys, Istabelle. You are not allowed any boys. They are a mischievous, devious, manipulating and ignorant lot, and you should do your best to avoid them completely."

Alannah giggled. "Just you wait, darling," she said. "If you think *I* gave you a wild time of it, wait until your daughter comes of age."

As the sails became smaller, Zarina watched from shore, just as she had done many years ago. Alannah's loving kiss good-bye still warmed her cheek. She had trusted in the fates that long-ago day, and the fates had saved her green-eyed baby, sending her to a magical island to grow up into a strong, lovely woman. It was more than she had ever dreamed possible for her child.

Now she watched once again as her darling sailed away. This time, the green-eyed woman had more than an amulet bag to protect her. She had a warrior who loved her as deeply as anyone possibly could. Her warrior was fierce, but his heart was tender. He would protect and honor her, love and cherish her.

Zarina sighed. Waves lapped the coast just as they had done before, and an offshore breeze raised goose bumps on her arms. The last time she had watched Alannah sail away, she had been terrified. She had ached with pain and throbbed with guilt. It had been an awful, horrendous day that had haunted her for almost two decades.

Today, she smiled. Today was glorious and fair.

She was beyond happy. She watched the sail get smaller and smaller as she stood on the coast with tear-filled eyes. She knew her daughter would be safe upon the Isle of Wild Horses. The love Alannah and Xanthier shared transcended all the past hurts and fears. It created a new world, a world of sensation and passion, a world far across the wild sea.

Don't miss the next book in
Sasha Lord's
exciting *Wild* series

Beyond the Wild Wind

Read on for an excerpt. . . .

Ruark swung off his mount and stripped his remaining clothing. He placed his boots carefully against a tree and draped his shirt and breeches over a branch. Then, with a small grin, he ran waist deep into the lake and dove under the water. The liquid against his sweaty body was incredibly relaxing, and he swam with long, smooth strokes until he was halfway across the lake.

There he stopped and treaded water. Glancing back, he saw movement at the shoreline. He shook his hair away from his eyes. *"What?"* he panted. He peered back toward shore where a woman was systematically rifling through his saddlebags.

"Stop!" he shouted.

The woman stepped away from his horse, holding his prized sword.

"You dare not!" he shouted as he started powering through the water toward her. The sword was his life, his occupation, his soul. "God help me, I will kill you!" he shouted as his strong strokes brought him rapidly to shore.

A falcon shrieked far above him.

The woman spun around and raced toward her horse. She quickly lashed the sword to her saddle and swung up, her skirts flying around her thighs.

"The unwary deserve to lose their belongings," she shouted back. "Feel lucky that I left you anything!" She kicked her mount over to his, then slapped his horse on the rump. It leapt forward and trotted angrily away as she laughed. "We shall see if you are an able climber," she called out as she tossed his breeches in the higher branches of a tree.

She laughed again. Her horse danced, its hooves flashing in the sunlight, and Ruark swept his gaze down her form, trying to imprint a memory of her face so that he could avenge himself, but she seemed to sparkle as if she were drenched in gold dust. Her hair was rich and vibrant, cascading down her back in shimmering loose, sable curls. Her shapely legs were strong and muscled and she sat on her mare as comfortably as any warrior he had ever seen, yet her thighs . . . her waist . . . her tightly encased breasts made him well aware that she was female.

Her horse spun as she stared back at him, and the glittering powder that covered her skin dazzled his eyes. *"What are you?"* he whispered.

Istabelle held her mare in check, feeling her anxious energy about to explode, but she couldn't tear her gaze from the warrior that was half immersed in the clear blue water. His long hair was slicked against his head, and his face was sculpted in harsh angles. The sun shone upon his shoulders and the bulge of his chest muscles glistened with moisture. Short, black curls dusted his chest, and she had a strange urge to find out what they felt like. She yanked on her mare's reins and the horse half reared in anger. Feeling more daring and alive than she had felt in months, she nudged her horse toward the lake.

"Can you catch me" she taunted.

Ruark's breath caught. *Did she really say that? Could she be daring him?* With sudden determination, he surged forward again. As his strong arms cleaved the water, he heard the pounding hooves of her horse racing away.

He burst out of the lake, water sluicing off his bare body, and whistled. His steed was well trained, and he had no doubt that it would come to his call. He strode to the tree where his breeches were dangling. Fury clouded his eyes as he saw how high they were.

"You will pay for this, little thief," he vowed as he jumped upwards and caught a sturdy branch. He pulled himself up, scraping his lower calf. "Augh," he grunted. He reached for a higher branch, tested its strength, then used it to stand up in the tree. His breeches were farther out, swinging on thinner limbs.

He looked around, seeking the woman's form from his vantage point. He could see her horse cantering through the woods to the west. *Good,* he thought. *I'll catch you and you will regret every second you cost me.*

He broke off a branch from above his head and used it to fish for his breeches. After several tries, he snagged the material and was able to drop it to the ground. With a growl of satisfaction, he saw his stallion standing nearby, his reins trailing on the ground.

He shifted, accidentally dragging his arms across the broken branch stub. Blood welled up and dripped from the injury, but Ruark ignored it. He climbed down to the lower branch, then jumped. Moving with increasing urgency, he yanked his breeches on then vaulted onto his horse. With a swift kick, he sent the stallion galloping after the thief.

Istabelle loped through the trees, feeling oddly guilty at her theft. True, the man had left his belongings unguarded, but she could have allowed him a peaceful swim. The water had looked incredibly inviting, and the sun was warm. In fact, if she had not come across him first, *she* would have been the one in the water and *he* would have found *her* clothes on a rock.

She glanced behind her, pleased to see that he was not following. She slowed her horse to a trot and motioned for the falcon to come down. The bird swooped low and perched on a stand mounted to her saddle. After praising the bird, Istabelle glanced at her own arm and rubbed the mica dust that covered her flesh. She really wanted to rinse off. She had spent the morning exploring the caves, and tiny particles of the sparkling material had clung to her sweaty body. She tried to pick a large flake off with her fingernails, but it stuck to her hand instead.

A sound behind her made her turn in the saddle and gasp. The warrior had found her! She saw his stallion thundering through the forest, his massive shoulders crashing through the underbrush with ease. A thrill raced through Istabelle, and she thrummed her mare's sides with her heels.

"Run!" she shouted. The falcon shrieked and rose back into the sky as Istabelle and the mare shot forward.

They whipped through the forest, their horses weaving in and out of the trees. Excitement raced through them, a mutual emotion of risk, danger and nameless need that drove them to win, to beat their opponent, to be acknowledged as the most skillful. For Ruark, the feeling bordered on a desire to prove to the world that he was the most powerful; for Istabelle, the feeling was an explosion against society's restraints. She bowed to no one. She was controlled by nothing. She lived to fling conventions to the wind and prove her independence.

She ducked her head under her arm to assess her pursuer, and was stunned to see he was much closer. She leaned to her right and she and the mare veered south where a series of stony crags dotted the landscape. Istabelle knew the terrain, had explored it often, and she figured she could confound the warrior by weaving among the obstacles.

Ruark saw her turn and he shifted quickly, closing the gap between them. The woman's luminescent skin beckoned him forward, and he forgot why he was pursing her, forgot why his blood was pumping. Suddenly, all that mattered was the chase. His heart thundered and he knew he wanted to catch her, to capture her and dominate her. He wanted to touch her glittering skin and feel its heat.

Rocks loomed ahead and Ruark was forced to slow. His war horse stumbled, his agility far less than the sleek mare ahead. As the stallion struggled to negotiate the stones, the mare slipped around a crag and was lost to sight.

Istabelle pulled her mare to a quick stop and searched the area. A cliff dropped off to her right, forming a wall of the lake, and a rock rose steeply in front of her. Behind her she could hear the blowing of the warrior's horse. Without further thought, she headed to her left toward a network of deer trails. Selecting one, she and the mare headed down hill.

Suddenly, the warrior burst onto her path, blocking her way.

She screamed in surprise and hauled on the mare's reins.

"You are very clever, little thief, but I have stayed alive by thinking ahead of people like you."

"How did you circle around me?" she demanded.

Not answering her, he moved his stallion closer. He saw the gleam of his broadsword tied to her saddle. "Drop the sword," he commanded. "I have killed for far less."

The woman raised arched eyebrows over silvery eyes. Her sable hair shimmered with golden streaks that bedeviled the eye. Ruark hesitated, at a loss before such an enchantress.

"I, too, have killed for far less," she said softly.

The velvet sweetness of her voice swept between them, seducing him. He jerked back.

The woman raised a thin sword and pointed it at his chest. "Do not come any closer," she threatened. "I will not hesitate to use my weapon against you."

"You cannot be serious. You are a small female and I am a seasoned warrior. I could smite you in less time than it would take to cough."

"I am deadly serious. And you forget, you were foolish enough to leave your sword unattended. I found it. It is now mine. What will you use to smite me?"

Casting around for something with which to arm himself, Ruark spotted a heavy branch nearby. Feigning acceptance, he shrugged. "I must admit defeat. I was unwary and you have bested me."

"I think you have not said that many times in your life, warrior." She deliberately stroked his naked chest with her gaze.

An uncomfortable stirring in his manhood made him narrow his gaze and clench his teeth. "No," he growled. "I have not."

"Perhaps you do not need the services of this blade, for you seem to have another just as strong." She smiled, her full lips curving into a delicious semi-circle.

Ruark hardened, despite his rising anger. "Silence," he snapped. "Remember what modesty a lady should possess."

"I am no lady."

"So I have determined." Ruark sent his stallion leaping forward, swiped up the branch and swung it at the woman's hands.

Don't miss
Sasha Lord's
steamy debut novel

Under a Wild Sky

0-451-21028-X

Ronin, a battered warrior, seeks refuge from his
enemies in a secluded wood, only to be attacked by
forest men. But when Ronin takes the men's leader
captive, he soon learns that this young man he's
holding prisoner is actually a beautiful woman whose
passion for life and love matches his own.

**"Stunningly imaginative and
compelling. Don't miss this first book."**
—*New York Times* bestselling author
Virginia Henley

Signet